TRUE
PLACES

ALSO BY SONJA YOERG

All the Best People
The Middle of Somewhere
House Broken

TRUE PLACES

a novel

SONJA YOERG

LAKE UNION
PUBLISHING

Published by Lake Union Publishing, Seattle

www.apub.com

Amazon, the Amazon logo, and Lake Union Publishing are trademarks of Amazon.com, Inc., or its affiliates.

ISBN-13: 9781503904781 (hardcover)
ISBN-10: 1503904784 (hardcover)
ISBN-13: 9781503904552 (paperback)
ISBN-10: 1503904555 (paperback)

Cover design by Caroline Teagle Johnson

Printed in the United States of America

First edition

*To the memory of my mother
and her garden*

"It is not down in any map; true places never are."

—*Herman Melville,* Moby-Dick

CHAPTER 1

The girl knew before she opened her eyes that Mama was gone. She always knew. The air inside the cabin cradled a hollow space, a missing shadow of warmth, an exhaled hum, the absent heartbeat. Early mornings were best for hunting, she accepted that, but loneliness was a heavy cloud to wake up in all the same.

She turned onto her back and listened to a squirrel hightail it across the roof. One beat of quiet; it had leaped. Her own limbs sensed the animal's limbs extending, forepaws reaching defiantly, no hint of hesitation, tail along for the ride. Gravity was a prop, a toy. Leaves rustled as the squirrel landed. The girl clenched her teeth, pulled in one side of her mouth, and sucked hard, letting loose a chatter. The squirrel answered.

The girl swung her feet to the floor, keeping the blanket around her shoulders. Pale, streaky sunlight filtered through chinks in the log walls. She tested the air with a breath. Not that cold. April was here, but winter crouched nearby, haunches twitching, ready to dump more snow, make sure they got down to the last of the deer jerky. Maybe they'd get lucky and outrun winter this time. Maybe today Mama would get a turkey.

She threw off the blanket, pulled on pants, and tucked in the shirt that fell to midthigh. Her father's leather belt was so long that after she cinched it she slid the dangling end nearly all the way around again. She crammed her feet into rubber boots, pushing her toes against the rags she'd stuffed into the ends to make them fit, and slipped her knife through a belt loop at her hip.

"Come on, Ash." She beckoned impatiently to the empty room, unlatched the door, and stepped outside onto the narrow porch.

Fog hung in the trees, a hush of silvery damp, but the girl could tell the sun would burn through before long and dry the grasses hunched under the weight of dew. The cabin stood in a small clearing, and the trees surrounding it had strained toward the heavens for a long time, long enough for the trunks to have become too thick for the girl to enclose them in the circle of her arms, long enough for anyone with decency to fall silent in reverence. The clearing was so circumscribed that if a bordering tree fell—and this she had imagined several times—the ones opposite would catch it in outstretched limbs before it crashed onto the cabin roof. Indeed, she had wished for this, to have a massive trunk leaning over them like the shaft of a giant arrow driven into the ground from above. It was unlikely. For all their mutability, trees stayed pretty much where they were.

A dove mourned from a stand of hickory to the east, and the rounded mauve notes soaked into her, mixing with the sleepiness hanging inside her like hundreds of cobwebs. She yawned and felt her stomach churn. She had to fight the urge to go inside and grab a piece of jerky. The longer she waited to eat, the less she needed. Besides, there might be a rabbit. Mama didn't mind if she cooked a rabbit for herself as long as she kept the fire small and well tended. And the girl always saved a piece to share later.

The clearing and the cabin it held were wedged in a crease between two steep ridges, hidden from sun, wind, eyes. She set off on a narrow track parallel to the east ridge and crossed the creek in two giant steps. The water music trailed after her as she wound south, stepping among knee-high arcs of Solomon's seal cast in uncertain light from the canopy above, sparse with new leaf and clouded in mist. As she walked, the slopes peeled away from each other, and soon the trees thinned.

Umbrellas of mayapples clustered at the bases of the trunks, tip to tip, then ceded to red trillium and foamflower, whose sprays of tiny blossoms reminded her not of foam but of stars.

Using a large black oak as a landmark, the girl found the first runway into the underbrush and checked the snare, adjusting the dangling wire loop. She inspected the other five she had set nearby, all empty. Tomorrow, maybe. Her stomach growled.

She continued through the woods, casting her eyes across the forest floor. Spotting a patch of wood sorrel, she plucked the stems near the ground and chewed the tender, sour leaves as she went. A group of tall, two-tiered plants caught her eye. Indian cucumber. She dug into the dirt at the base of a narrow stem and extracted a rhizome the shape and length of her finger. She wiped it on her shirt and ate it, relishing the crisp, cool taste.

A rifle shot rang out.

The girl paused, then smiled. Mama didn't waste bullets, as there were none to waste. Tonight they would have fresh meat. She knew she should wish for a deer, for its size.

"Let's hope it was a turkey, Ash. Turkey's our favorite."

~

The girl waited by the stream Mama would cross on her way home. Idle and hungry, she ate all the watercress she'd collected to have with the turkey; all that remained were a few ramps. Ash told her the story about the time he climbed a tree and came nose to nose with a porcupine. When he finished, she was restless. She drank from the stream and headed for the ridge in the direction of the rifle shot.

The fog had disappeared as surreptitiously as it had come. The sun was high and all the green in the world was rising toward it. She listened as she climbed, her skin and each of her senses bound together into solid awareness. Everything surrounding her, impinging on her, she felt and knew.

She did not call out. Mama was here in these woods, and the girl would find her, or Mama would find the girl, by and by.

～

Sunlight sliced through at an angle now, drawing a sharp breeze from below. The girl returned to the stream and to the cabin, but Mama was not there. She climbed the ridge again by a different route, always a different route so as not to leave a trail, and called out this time, her voice too high and bright. Worry tunneled like a mole through her belly.

She crossed to the north into a hemlock grove. The breeze swirled behind her—more wind than usual, a change in weather—and sent the tang of blood to the back of her throat. There, in the middle distance, a dark shape on the ground broke the pattern of the ferns. She approached and saw it was a turkey, one wing splayed across its body as if to cover itself in the shame of death.

The girl scanned around her, skin prickling, eyes narrowed, nostrils flared. "Mama!"

She listened through the wind sighing in the branches overhead, through the creaking of old wood, through the stirrings in the underbrush.

"Mama!"

A sound. An echo of something she hadn't heard. She moved toward it, around an outcropping, into denser wood for a short distance, then out into a glittering stand of saplings, tulip poplars, not what she would have expected here.

"Mama! Mama!"

She heard the muffled reply and stared at her feet, for the sound seemed to come from beneath her. She strode in a careful circle, ducking among the saplings, eyes upon the ground. She stepped over a deadfall and stopped short. A hole gaped directly before her, a void where the cloth of the earth had been ripped open. If she had not been scouting the ground, she might have fallen in. It was big enough to swallow her.

Her heart beat in her ears. She shook her head roughly and climbed back over the downed tree to the far side of the hole, giving it a wide berth. There, caught in a tangle of twigs, was the rifle with its familiar burnished walnut stock. She picked it up, checked the safety, and stood the rifle against a tree. Her stomach knotted. Mama would never abandon the rifle like that.

The girl approached the hole. Boulders big as children hunkered over the other side, with solid stone below lining the shaft as far down as she could see. On her side, freshly uprooted plants dangled into the void.

"Mama?"

A low moan rose from below.

"Mama!"

"I'm here." Mama's voice was a faint, wet echo. "Be careful."

The girl took a step back.

A gravelly scraping. Mama said, "My leg's broken."

Dropping onto her stomach, the girl crept to the edge, unsure of its stability. She grabbed a sturdy branch with one arm and shouted into the blackness. "How far is it? How far down are you?"

She thought she could hear Mama's ragged breathing, but it might have been the blood roaring in her ears, or the wind.

"Twenty feet." A long pause. A crow cawed high above. Another answered. "My ribs are broken."

The girl imagined her mother on cold wet stone, a hand on her rib cage, staring up at a brilliant, ragged circle. Twenty feet. Her mouth went dry. She pursed her lips. Study the problem. That's what Daddy always told her. Use all your resources.

"I'm going to get a rope, Mama. And some water and food." She waited, but there was no answer. "I'll be quick." She sprang to her feet and pushed her way through the brush at the end of the deadfall. She stopped abruptly and wagged her finger. "You stay here, Ash. You stay with Mama, okay? Do what I tell you for once."

She retrieved the turkey, not thinking of her hunger but only of what she was certain Mama would want her to do. The turkey had cost a bullet, and meat could never be wasted. At first she held the bird by the feet, but its head bounced on the ground, which seemed disrespectful, so she arranged its wings and tucked it under one arm, cradling its small, naked head, loose on its neck, in the palm of her hand.

~

By the time she returned, daylight was slipping away. She threw the backpack to the ground and knelt to unpack it. A blanket, a jacket, a nylon rope, a plastic jug of water, and two cloth bundles of jerky and the last of the hickory nuts. She fastened the rope to the handle of the water jug. Lying prone, she pushed the jug out in front of her and lowered it slowly.

"Water's coming!" She played out the rope until it went slack in her hands. "You got that now, Mama?"

"Yes." Her voice was throaty and seemed farther away than before.

The girl sat up and waited a few moments for Mama to untie the slipknot, then gathered the rope. "I'm throwing the food down." She tossed a bundle into the hole.

She moved a short distance away to where she'd left the pack and spoke in a low voice. "I don't think she can hold herself on a rope, Ash. Not with broken ribs." The girl coiled the rope in a loop, tied a bowline, and did the same with the next length. She worked for several minutes more, fingers deft and sure. Holding it aloft, she turned it from side to side and pulled on the knots to set them. "You know what it is. It's a harness. That's what I've figured out. Mama needs a harness so I can help her climb out. If she could slip her legs into it, that would be best, but if she can't manage that, then her arms will have to do."

She secured the end of the rope to the trunk of a maple and returned to the edge of the hole.

"Mama? Did you drink some water?"

Mama grunted.

"I'm gonna throw down the rope. I made a harness for your legs."

The silence from the hole was thick. The girl felt a shiver race down her arms. Since Daddy left, Mama hardly ever spoke, but this was a different species of silence.

"I can't climb," Mama said.

"I know you're hurt, and I can't just pull you out, but if you try climbing, I can take some of your weight. I can help you."

A breeze licked through the woods, and the sweat on her neck and back chilled. She was strung rigid and thin, like the wire of a snare, and exhaustion threatened to snap her, but her mind flew, sorting through possibilities, pushing aside the fear and hope battling for attention.

"Room," Mama said finally.

The girl's mind fell still, paralyzed. Her mother's voice was a frayed thread and yet full of the import and finality of her message. "It's a room." Her voice gave out.

The girl stared at the harness in her fists, her knuckles white beneath the dirt stains, then at the slick, gaping mouth of the cave. The meaning of her mother's words rose over her like a pall. She had assumed the hole was a shaft; the first few feet of the sides—what she could see—were vertical. But below that, she knew now, the walls spread wide, curved out, perhaps, to form a room. What shape and what size she did not know. It didn't matter. Mama could not have scaled the canted walls even if she had not been injured, and the girl was too slight to haul her out on her own. The girl knew the basics of mechanical advantage, levers and pulleys, but there was no horizontal branch of sufficient size to loop her rope over, and if there had been, she concluded in an instant, that, too, would not have been enough.

She tossed the rope to the side and retrieved the blanket.

"I'm throwing down a blanket."

"No!" It was a high bark, not like Mama at all. There was pain on all sides of it.

A feeling of dread entered the girl through every pore. She sat cross-legged beside the mouth of the cave, hugging the blanket that was too valuable to be sacrificed for brief comfort.

"I'm sorry, Mama. I'm really sorry."

Mama replied, "I know," or maybe it was only a muffled moan.

She imagined her mother's terror and pain expanding across the darkening floor of the cave, completely filling the stone-walled chamber. If only it had the power to lift Mama, carry her to the surface, harmed but close. But the girl believed in no magic and had been death's witness countless times so she could eat and live. Her mother was an animal, the same as she was, subject to the relentlessness of physical reality, and could not wheedle her way into some other realm of existence—the supernatural, the spiritual, or the transcendent— simply because she was in danger. Reality offered unvarnished truths, especially now, the two of them separated by an insurmountable yet perfectly ordinary arrangement of rock, and yet bound together still by a column of air and, for a short while longer, refracted sunlight. Her desire to be close to her mother kept her near the hole, and more than once she considered reattaching the rope to the tree and lowering herself into the shaft, for both their comfort. She might, not allowing for the unforeseen, shimmy up the rope again and rejoin the surface of the world. But those were only her thoughts, not her will. Mama was dying and there was no remedy for it.

Violet shadows hastened into the spaces between the trees. The air chilled. The girl put on her jacket and placed the rifle inside the backpack to protect it from the night's moisture. Wrapping the blanket around her legs, she assumed her vigil by the hole and, out of necessity, ate the jerky she had saved for herself. The food was dust in her mouth.

The light melted away, as the fog had that morning, leaving the sky pale and thin and touched with mallow pink, then retreated succinctly behind distant mountains. As the stars emerged at last, the girl sighed and spoke.

"I'm gonna sleep here tonight, and you should, too, Ash. She might not know we're here, but I don't want to leave yet."

She refolded the blanket and lay down, wiping her eyes with the back of her hand. The ache that had been accumulating in her bones was fierce now, and she gasped. She wanted her mama. A finger traced along her cheek would do, or the warm steady weight of Mama's body next to hers, by the stream or at the table. The girl tried, but it was impossible for her to imagine the magnitude of the loss of such things, having had them so recently and so often. It was like counting stars.

She lay still, the never-ending vault shimmering overhead, and gathered herself. "I'm gonna miss her," she whispered. She paused, nodded, rose on her elbow. "I know, Ash. I know you will, too. Come lie next to me. Try to sleep now."

Sleep came for her quickly, her body taking control. She woke before dawn, unfurled her limbs, and swept the dew from her face. Memories of yesterday replaced the vestiges of her dreams—the lingering sweetness of escape already lost to her—and sadness, thick and heavy as wet clay, fell onto her. She watched the night shapes around her resolve into familiar forms. When she was sure of where she was, she crept to the edge of the hole.

"Mama?"

Birds stirred in the branches around her but did not call.

Louder: "Mama?"

The girl listened, not only with her ears but with her entire being, melding the input from her senses, subtracting the background noise, pointing her full attention at the hole in the earth, at the stone vault.

Her mother's scent of loamy earth and sun-scorched grass lingered, faint, mixed with the bitter scent of fear, but that was all.

She listened a long while, until she was certain, then shrank back from the cave mouth and sat on her heels, rubbing a finger over a scab on her knee. Her stomach churned a slurry of acid and grief, her soul limp. Again she fought against the impulse to lower herself into the dark. That was based on a wish for something she couldn't have. Mama was not there, only a cold, broken body, heaped on stone, surrounded by seeping walls. Mama was gone.

The girl packed the blanket and the rope in with the rifle. She spun in a slow circle, memorizing the spot, hazy and green-smelling in the damp fresh of the morning.

"Come on, Ash." She shouldered the pack. "We've got that turkey to deal with."

CHAPTER 2

Suzanne lowered both front windows to combat the overbearing sweetness of the sixty hyacinths in the rear of the Navigator. She'd been delighted when the nursery offered potted plants as a donation for the Boosters auction, but she'd been told they would be tulips or daffodils. A single hyacinth in full bloom could send its scent to every corner of a moderate-size home; no one would be able to breathe, much less eat, with sixty blooming hyacinths in the Boar's Head ballroom. If the flowers could be wrapped in cellophane, it might be tolerable. She couldn't remember what they'd decided about packaging and presentation at the meeting last week. Fifty decisions at that meeting, plus a hundred more at two others—one for the faculty appreciation lunch and another for the food bank. Suzanne, as president of the Boosters, had put Greer Rensworth in charge of auction presentation. She remembered that much. Who else but a stay-at-home mom with degrees in interior design and marketing? At least that made sense, unlike the assumption that any plant-related task would be Suzanne's responsibility because she had majored in botany. In case the hyacinths needed emergency repotting on the trip home?

Her phone chimed—a text. She stopped behind the other cars at the intersection with Route 250 and picked up the phone from the console.

BRYNN: Forgot my English paper on my bed. Need it by 4th period.

She dropped the phone into the console and shook her head. Second time this week her daughter had left something at home. The car at the front of the line swung left and the others scooted forward. Suzanne followed suit.

Fourth period. Eleven sixteen. She glanced at the dashboard clock. Ten thirty-two.

She could make it home and then to the school with perhaps six minutes to spare. She didn't have to consult her phone to know there were countless other tasks waiting to occupy that time. That was, in fact, what time was: a narrow container for a relentless succession of tasks. The container could not be expanded, but the tasks could multiply exponentially. In fact, tasks were guaranteed to multiply. The law of entropy had undoubtedly been discovered by a mother with two teenagers.

The compressive nature of time was the most salient aspect of her existence. Time was a squeezing bitch. It never expanded, never gave up any slack, in a perverse reversal of the state of the universe itself. Her younger self would have been amused by this irony. Forty-two-year-old Suzanne had no time for irony, the snappy way it caught and twisted the truth, not even for irony about time itself.

Suzanne understood there were three options for dealing with time pressure. Option One: Perform tasks more efficiently. Move faster, triple-task, cut corners. Buy cookies instead of making them from scratch, and ignore the raised eyebrows or direct complaints from better, more efficient mothers. Drive faster and risk a speeding ticket with scheduling repercussions rippling for days afterward. Text at stoplights but not in front of the kids. Sleep less.

Option Two: Delegate more. Because she was in charge of so much (her mind flew too fast to bother to enumerate her responsibilities), she already delegated a great deal. Unfortunately, it was not as straightforward as it seemed. People were unreliable, especially the more competent ones, because of the inevitable burgeoning of their own to-do lists.

Option Three: Refuse to perform. This radical notion rarely surfaced, because Suzanne was so accustomed to being busy. Everyone she knew was busy; it was something they talked about as they caught up on emails at a swim meet or texted takeout orders to their husbands while waiting for prescriptions at CVS. Being busy was a by-product of the life she had chosen with her husband, Whit, although if she was perfectly honest, she wasn't sure the word *chosen* was accurate. Once their kids had started school, it was more like jumping into a fast-flowing river. You didn't choose. You swam to keep from drowning. Suzanne was an excellent swimmer.

In front of her Navigator, a pockmarked red pickup edged forward, engine gargling, the driver's elbow thrust out the window, sleeve rolled up.

Her phone chimed. Suzanne retrieved it from the seat and read the text.

WHIT: Meeting Robert at 5 so can't pick up Brynn from swim. Home by 8. Sorry!

With one hand she texted Ok, hit send, and tossed the phone onto the passenger seat. Another ripple shuddered across her schedule.

Suzanne flicked her turn signal, indicating right toward Charlottesville and home. Home, where that morning Brynn had leveled her with a look so contemptuous Suzanne had been certain her daughter was possessed. How could an expression that hateful, and directed at Suzanne, appear on the face of the child who had once—no, hundreds of times—looked upon her mother with love so pure it made her life, crystallized by that moment, almost too beautiful to bear? It simply wasn't possible. And yet Brynn's face had not lied. Suzanne's throat cinched shut.

The pickup turned right onto the main road. As Suzanne pulled up to follow it, her phone chimed. She snatched it off the seat.

BRYNN: ????

Suzanne dropped the phone in her lap. A gap in the traffic opened. She hovered, blinking back tears and staring at the brown, matted pasture beyond the road, bordered by a black triple-rail fence.

A honk from the car behind her.

Brynn at the breakfast bar hours earlier, her face, skin smooth as icing, framed by hair the color of champagne, one side grazing the brow of one eye, the other parted neatly over her shoulder, as if it were not hair but two sheets of silk. Her eyebrows neatly arched over her hazel eyes, the lashes coated with mascara. Her mouth pulled tight as if holding back the full measure of her disdain.

You are such a tool, Mom.

Suzanne slapped the turn signal all the way down, indicating left, crossed the intersection, and headed east, away from home. She pressed the accelerator and felt the weight and power of the car beneath her, heard the growl of the engine. In a few moments the fenced pasture gave way to woods, dark straight trunks and tangled bare branches separated from the roadside by a weedy verge. The foothills of the Blue Ridge Mountains rose before her, a nubbly carpet of muddy gray, running to olive in the sunlit patches. Suzanne gripped the steering wheel tight and drove faster, the wind whipping her hair from her face, then sending it back to sting her cheeks. The air was sharp in her lungs.

She could no longer smell the hyacinths.

$\sim$

The sign for the Blue Ridge Parkway entrance surprised her. She knew it was there but hadn't been paying attention, too occupied with controlling her emotions and the car, hurtling along at well over the posted limit of forty-five miles per hour. The sign for the parkway appeared, and, before the decision reached her awareness, Suzanne veered right onto the ramp and came to a jolting stop at the T intersection. The road was devoid of traffic. Turning south onto the parkway, she crossed an arched stone bridge.

She would drive until she felt like turning around, until she felt like going home. The idea of such a nebulous plan unsettled her; she didn't trust herself to know when she had gone far enough. Her day would be shot. If she reversed course this instant it would already be too late to drop off the flowers at the country club before her lunch meeting with Rory, the Boosters treasurer, and that didn't take Brynn's forgotten paper into account. Suzanne's thoughts tumbled along the falling dominoes of broken commitments. She spotted an overlook, pulled off the road, and came to a halt. Hers was the only car.

She would text everyone, cut some corners, turn around, and resume the necessary frantic progression of the day. She swiped to activate the screen and paused. No reception. Not one little bar. Texts might go through regardless, she knew that, but her finger balked.

Suzanne lifted her head. The foothills tumbled gently down to the valley floor, an undulating expanse, farmland and wood, hazy through lingering mist, still and mute. On the far side, mountains rose again, an ocean swell of dull ochre. The sky above the range was an indefinite shade at the horizon, grading to a somber blue overhead.

She was alone. Her chest constricted and her heart raced. She reached for the window controls, raised both front windows, set the door locks, and stabbed her finger at the radio button. A woman's voice, matter-of-fact and even toned, filled the car. Suzanne's breathing slowed. The car was safe. She was alone but not stranded. Her car had just been serviced; she brought it in every month religiously. She could head back right now to Charlottesville, to her appointments and obligations—the self-imposed chain that kept her linked with other people and immune to solitude, her enemy.

Placing her foot on the brake, she shifted into drive and thought again of her daughter's look of contempt, her dismissive, rude words. She thought of her husband's displeasure should the intricate clockwork of their lives fail to operate smoothly, and of the ease with which his responsibilities became hers. (She couldn't resent it, though, because he had work and she had only duties.) She thought of her son, who did not (would not?) fit in, which pained and frustrated her in equal measure.

She was alone in her car, but that had never been a problem. And today she would fail to text her absence. She would fail to rescue her daughter. She would allow the dominoes to fall without having a reason anyone would understand.

She would drive.

Suzanne rejoined the parkway and drove fast, neglecting to decelerate into the corners, jerking the steering wheel to feel the car hitch a little, like a prodded animal. She didn't cross the line to recklessness but did wish the road were twistier, her car more able to tuck nimbly into the turns. The Navigator had been Whit's idea, and she hadn't cared enough to disagree. She'd come to appreciate the very tanklike qualities she used to resent.

She switched off the radio as she passed the Wintergreen Resort and the turnoff for Love. A sign read: COME IN LOVE. STAY IN LOVE. LEAVE IN LOVE. She slowed. The road she was on snaked through dense woods, a circuitous track no animal would make. Perhaps it traced the contours or avoided rocky ledges. She couldn't know. All she could see was a tunnel of bare trunks and evergreen boughs surrounding her, open above, with reluctance, to the sky.

Her phone bleated periodically, like a fussy infant passenger. Suzanne ignored it and drove on, following the serpentine path through the maze of hills and out again onto the ridge, where the trees were pulled to the wings of the stage, where the valley to the east, or the one to the west, lay exposed, only to be veiled again seconds later.

As she passed a turnout on the right, she caught sight of something sizable lying between the gravel parking area and the forest. She checked her mirrors and came to a stop. There was nowhere to turn around, so she put on her blinkers and, keeping an eye on the rearview mirror, reversed up the road and swung into the turnout, backing past the trail entrance. Suzanne shifted the car into park and peered through the windshield.

The object, perhaps thirty feet away, was definitely a person, huddled in a squat and facing the other way. She scanned the grassy area that rimmed the turnout for a motorcycle, a bicycle, a backpack, but saw only a bear-proof trash can and a picnic table. The figure, clad in dark clothing, was motionless. Asleep? Injured? Dead?

Suzanne tapped her horn. The figure stirred. All at once she realized how small it was. Suzanne lowered the passenger window.

"Are you okay?"

The body gathered itself quickly onto all fours and lurched away, up a set of stone steps. It was slight, perhaps even a child. The hair was dark and straggly.

"Hey!" Suzanne turned off the engine, snatched the keys and her phone, and leaped from the vehicle.

The figure bounded away, agile but unsteady.

"Wait! I want to help you!"

Suzanne ran up the trail, negotiating the rough steps that ended at wooden railroad tracks running parallel to the road. The tracks, dappled with mute sunlight, bent in a graceful curve and disappeared around the hillside. Beside the tracks, sprawled across the ties, was the child—a girl, Suzanne guessed, but the child's face was so dirty and her features so thin and sharp Suzanne wasn't sure. The child propped herself up on one hand and twisted to stare at Suzanne with abject fear. The tension in her body signaled she would spring to her feet at any moment.

"Wait," said Suzanne calmly, keeping her distance. "I'm Suzanne. Let me help you."

The child let out a high squeal, muffling it with closed lips. The whites of her eyes were stark against her face. The clothes she wore were too large for her; her pants were rolled up and her long-sleeved shirt was frayed and torn at the neck as if it had been viciously chewed. The soles had begun to peel off her boots, which were secured around her ankles with nylon cord.

Suzanne took two steps closer, crouching a little and smiling. She was sure now the child was a girl. A terrified girl. "Where are your parents? Are they nearby?"

The girl trembled. Closer now, Suzanne could see the girl's cheeks were red beneath the grime. Her eyes were an unusual violet blue, the color of periwinkles.

"Are you hurt?" Suzanne reached out her hand, palm up, and inched closer. "Let me help you."

The terror fled from the girl's face. "Mama—" Her brow relaxed and she collapsed.

Suzanne rushed to her side and knelt. The girl's chest was rising and falling. Suzanne touched the back of her hand to the girl's forehead. She was on fire. Where was her family? She couldn't have been more than eleven, maybe twelve. Suzanne stared down the track in one direction, then the other. "Hello? Anyone there? Hello?"

A squirrel dashed across the tracks and leaped into the bushes.

"Hello?"

Suzanne's hands went cold and her pulse accelerated. She swallowed against the lump in her throat and reassured herself she was not truly alone. Sweat trickled down her spine. She turned to the girl. Not alone. Suzanne picked up the girl's hand, so small and bony it was barely human. And hot. The girl was feverish. Suzanne closed her eyes and pushed against the swell of panic rising from her diaphragm, spreading into her lungs. Not alone.

Marshaling her strength, Suzanne scooped the limp girl off the ground, shocked at how light she was. It was like picking up a log and discovering it was driftwood. She carried the girl down the steps and spotted a ratty backpack sticking partway out of a thicket. Suzanne continued to the car and, with effort, managed to hoist the girl into the passenger seat and strap her in. The girl's jaw was swollen and her exposed skin was marked with wounds and scars. Suzanne wondered if the girl had been attacked and abandoned but hoped the fact that she was fully clothed indicated otherwise.

Suzanne retrieved the backpack. The exterior pockets were rotted and torn and incapable of holding anything, and she didn't want to waste time rummaging through the main compartment, so she threw the pack onto the rear seat, climbed behind the wheel, and headed toward Charlottesville and the hospital as fast as she dared. Surprised and dismayed at how far she'd driven, she wished the miles would pass as quickly as they had earlier. The girl drifted in and out of consciousness, eyelids fluttering, cracked lips parting and closing, but she uttered only low moans.

Suzanne's phone continued to plead with her from the console. She considered pulling over briefly to call or text Whit and explain the situation, but dismissed it as pointless, as was the thought of calling 911 or the hospital. She was on the way.

On Highway 64 East, fifteen minutes outside of Charlottesville, the girl twitched and jerked awake. She screamed, eyes fixed dead ahead in terror, hands clutching the edge of the seat.

"What's wrong?" Suzanne reached across to calm her.

The girl whipped her head, following the path of one car, then another, again and again, then seemed to switch to tracking trees as they flew by. The sharp staccato movement alarmed Suzanne. The girl screamed again, a high keening, and scrabbled at the door and window, desperate for an exit.

"It's all right!" Suzanne checked that she'd locked the doors and windows and reminded herself to pay attention to the road.

The girl yanked at the seat belt, unreeling it, stretching it in front of her with both hands. She pulled her feet up, squatted on the seat, and slid out from under the belt. Before Suzanne could speak, the girl slipped over the console and tucked herself into a ball in the footwell behind the passenger seat.

"Okay, okay." Suzanne mustered her calmest voice, the one she'd used when her children were small and prone to tantrums, especially Brynn. "You can stay there. It's fine. We're almost there."

The girl whimpered and wedged her body more tightly into the space.

Suzanne focused on driving and monitored her speed, all the while thinking that the girl was behaving exactly as had their family cat, Rusty, the first time they had taken him to the vet, before they'd grasped the necessity of a carrier. Was the poor kid mentally disturbed? She didn't seem violent, just terrified. Terrified of Suzanne, the car, the world rushing past. Terrified of everything.

The girl lost consciousness again. At the University of Virginia emergency center, the staff transferred the girl's listless body to a cart, instructed Suzanne to move her car, and wheeled the cart through the double doors. Suzanne parked in the visitors' lot, grabbed her phone and the backpack, and entered the hospital. She spoke briefly to the attendant at the desk, then proceeded to the berth where the girl lay sweating on a bed. A nurse was taking her pulse. Under the lights and against the white linens, the girl's appearance was even more alarming. Her body was lost inside her clothing and her cheekbones seemed about to pierce her skin. But more than that, she did not appear to belong here. The girl was not simply ill or lost; she was otherworldly.

Suzanne stood to the side, the backpack at her feet. She'd been asked to wait for the police and had no idea how long they would be. She supposed she could wait in the lobby, but it seemed wrong to leave the girl's side.

A middle-aged woman came through the curtain—the doctor, Suzanne presumed. She had closely cropped pewter hair and wore scrubs and a look of habitual resignation. The nurse recited the girl's vitals. Nodding, the doctor snapped on gloves and began to examine the girl. As she palpated the swollen jaw, the girl's eyes flew open. Her gaze took in the doctor, the nurse, the lights, the equipment. She bolted upright and tried to jump off the bed.

The doctor caught her arm. "Hey, not so fast." She turned to bark at the nurse. "Give me a hand. She's incredibly strong."

The nurse placed a firm hand on the girl's shoulder. "What's your name, sweetheart?"

The girl pulled up her legs, cowering.

The doctor held up her gloved hands in innocence. "I just need to get a peek in your mouth."

Suzanne said, "Can't you give her something?"

"Not until I know what's going on with her, have a look at that jaw. She appears to be malnourished and is probably dehydrated, so I'd really like to get a line in."

Suzanne moved to the end of the bed and held the backpack aloft. "This is yours, right?" The girl stilled. "I haven't opened it." Suzanne placed it on the bed in front of the girl.

The doctor frowned. "We don't know what's in there—"

"Her stuff."

The girl dragged the pack closer. Suzanne came around the side of the bed and crouched beside it. "I know you're hurt. That's why I brought you here. This is where they heal people." The girl stared at Suzanne, her lips twitching. "Maybe you've been sick before. Everyone gets sick. I don't know where your family is, but maybe when you were sick before, your mother was there."

The girl sucked in air, hunched her shoulders, trembling, and peered at Suzanne. The girl's violet-blue eyes were awash in tears.

Suzanne reached for her hand.

"And now I'm here."

CHAPTER 3

Contents of the backpack, as logged by Officer Rodriguez, Charlottesville police. Stored in hospital locker, except as noted.

— Sleeping bag, synthetic
— Long-sleeved shirt (men's large)
— Knit cap in navy blue wool
— Gloves, fingertips cut off
— Down vest
— Canteen, army issue
— Comb
— Turquoise hair clasp
— Cook pot, fire blackened, no lid
— Plastic container, two quart, with lid
— Two empty tin cans
— Four small cloth pouches, hand sewn, containing:
    — needle and coarse thread
    — fish hooks and filament
    — ground substance (impounded, pending ID)
    — dried plants and roots (impounded, pending ID)
— Hunting knife, seven-inch blade (impounded)
— Pocket knife, folding, four-inch blade (impounded)

- Whetstone
- Fire starter, flint based
- Snare wire
- Nylon cord
- Nylon tarp, 8' x 10'
- Stuffed pink bear

CHAPTER 4

As Suzanne exited the hospital, her phone rang, a brassy rendition of "Battle Hymn of the Republic," the special tone she'd assigned to her mother, Tinsley Royce. It was simpler to answer Tinsley's calls and avoid the lengthy messages, escalating in urgency, and the reprisals that would inevitably follow a missed call.

Tinsley didn't pause for a greeting. "Are you all right?"

"Yes. Of course."

"Where in heaven's name have you been? I saw Rory in town on my way to my massage and she told me you missed lunch with her."

"Something came up. I texted her."

"She said you were vague."

Suzanne could picture them speculating but never veering into nosiness. Tinsley saved that for her daughter. Suzanne wove through the parking lot, keys in hand. Spotting the Navigator, she clicked it open.

Tinsley said, "Well, it's none of my business what you were doing."

If only the truth of that statement would be enough to hold Tinsley back from pursuing her questioning. "I found a girl on the parkway. She was all by herself and in pain, so I took her to the hospital."

"What were you doing on the parkway?"

Suzanne almost laughed. An abandoned, injured child was not nearly as intriguing as a woman with a full schedule taking a joyride on America's favorite highway. "Driving. I was driving."

"Well, I assumed—"

Suzanne opened the door and tossed her handbag onto the passenger seat. God, the hyacinths. She gagged at the smell. A quick calculation told her she had enough time to drop them off before picking up Brynn. "Mother, was there something you needed?"

"I know you're busy, dear."

"It's okay. What do you need?"

"The fund-raiser at the club is next month, and I'm supposed to be in charge of sponsors. Only I haven't a clue."

"Don't take this the wrong way, but why did you volunteer for it?"

"Your father insisted. He thinks that if everyone sees I'm being a good sport and playing the part, then everything is fine. Which from his perspective it is."

"You don't have to agree."

"You know your father."

Something in the way she said "your father" carried a whiff of disapproval, as if somehow Suzanne were responsible for Anson Royce because her existence had made him a father, and a poor one, thereby contributing to her mother's unhappiness, that massive, looming shadow. It was not logical but, then again, her mother's motivations never were. If Suzanne were to confront Tinsley, she would be devastated to hear that her daughter could think such things of her. And in the next breath Tinsley would bemoan another affair of Anson's, sprinkling the story of her humiliation (that was the very worst of it) with as many iterations of "your father" as syntax would allow.

"Whatever you need me to do, Mother. Let's talk about it tomorrow."

"If you have time. I don't want to be a bother."

"It's fine. I just need to catch up from today."

"You know, Suzanne, the police will take care of abandoned children."

"It was easier to take her myself." She thought of the girl's frantic behavior in the car. Perhaps she should have called for help. "You should've seen her, Mother. She was so thin and frail."

"Was she a meth head? I heard a report the other day on the news."

"No. Just a girl."

Tinsley paused. "Did you say why you were on the parkway?"

"Driving, Mother. Just driving."

~

Brynn stood among a flock of girls gathered in the Barrington School's front quad. All wore racing swimsuits under sweatpants that were rolled at the top and positioned below jutting hipbones. At five foot eleven, Brynn was the tallest, but not by much. Suzanne studied them. They were extraordinary creatures, like flamingos or giraffes, hybrid humans, or even further removed, a self-invented species. They behaved as a unit; when one reacted to a stimulus, or failed to react, the others did the same, like shorebirds switching direction along the tide line. Whatever it was—a boy passing by, a hilarious Snapchat, a comment from a despised teacher—a pointedly raised eyebrow was sufficient to secure instantaneous solidarity, especially if the eyebrow belonged to Brynn.

Suzanne came to a stop alongside the row of parked cars. Brynn ducked her head, the wet curtain of her hair closing the scene of her mother's arrival like the end of a dull play. The other girls refused to look at the car without seeming to do so. They continued chatting, tossing their hair, and running their thumbs over their devices until more than five minutes had passed. Finally Brynn shrugged, said, "See you guys," and left them, coincidentally in the direction of the car, thumbs flying across the glass surface of her phone with the grace of a skater executing her figures, until one hand reluctantly bowed out to open the car door.

"Where's Dad?"

"He had a meeting."

Brynn stuffed her bag under her feet and rested her hands, still manipulating the phone, on her knees.

Suzanne checked the side mirror and pulled out. "How was practice?"

"Long. Wet."

"And school?"

"Oh well, could've been better. For example, if I hadn't bombed on the English paper I spent the whole week writing."

Suzanne had forgotten about her daughter's text and felt a jab of guilt. Then again, Brynn had to suffer the consequences of her actions. Wasn't that how it was supposed to go? Don't bail out your kids. Let them understand firsthand the way behavior and results were linked. Learn the lesson. Do better next time. Suzanne knew Brynn would not listen to parental homilies. She also knew she couldn't stop herself from delivering one. Was she supposed to give up on being a parent?

"It's disappointing to get a poor grade, but the important thing is to try not to let it happen again."

Brynn's thumbs stopped. "Wait. That is so deep. Let me write that down."

"I know you want to blame me."

"Yup. Wasn't it only a couple days ago that you were late to my meet because Dad forgot his tennis bag and you had to run it up to the club for him?"

"That's different. Your father has a demanding job and I help him however I can."

"Right. And I'm just a lazy kid taking advanced classes and swimming varsity." She shifted her feet onto the dashboard, setting Suzanne's teeth on edge, and went back to her phone.

As Suzanne drove home, she considered where she had gone wrong with Brynn, not just today, but across a longer window of time. When had Brynn become so adversarial? When had Suzanne begun to fail to find a way to bridge the gap between them? She could not pinpoint the shift.

She could remember when a lollipop or a balloon was all it would take; it was that easy. The space between then and now was impossible for her to examine objectively. It pained her as much to recall the tender moments as the hostile ones, and the transition from mostly positive interactions to mostly awful ones had been insidious, like a spreading mold.

Suzanne pulled into the drive. Brynn got out and slammed the door shut without a word. Suzanne remained in her seat, in the quiet, searching her memory for how she had so monstrously failed Brynn and coming up with nothing more than a laundry list of shortcomings and oversights she doubted could account for the scope of Brynn's rage.

As Suzanne gathered her phone and her bag and left the car, her thoughts turned to her own adolescence. She was certain she had never been as openly hostile to Tinsley as Brynn was to her. She had not been an angelic teenager, but she was more circumspect in expressing her feelings toward Tinsley, to the extent that she expressed them at all.

Along the path to the front porch, snowdrops and crocuses bloomed at the base of a trio of Hana Jinam camellias that soon would be covered in huge white flowers edged with hot pink. When she and Whit had bought the house twelve years ago, Suzanne had replaced the tired foundation plantings with varieties guaranteed to celebrate spring. Now she bent to pull a few weeds from between the snowdrops and was reminded of her fourth-grade science poster, "Uses for Useless Weeds," and the reason she did not depend on her mother—or her father—to tend to her feelings.

Suzanne's excitement about her project—as she gathered plants from the backyard and roadsides, read library books about botany, and drew the poster itself, her lettering painstakingly even—had been quelled only by her mother's announcement that her father would attend in her stead. Tinsley played bunko the third Thursday of every month and wouldn't dream of missing it.

Suzanne remembered being anxious about this role switch but still eager to share her new knowledge with her father. He was a banker, and

Suzanne was determined to show him that weeds were as interesting as money and had many surprising uses. For instance, plantain, which grew in their yard, had medicine in its leaves that could heal cuts and stop bites from itching. Suzanne had tried it on her mosquito bites and reported her findings on the poster.

At the fair, her assigned spot was right across from the door of the gymnasium. Each time someone came in and it wasn't her father, she felt a pinch of worry. The evening dragged on, and kids started taking down their exhibits. Suzanne's father never appeared. Her teacher, Ms. Highcraft, offered Suzanne a ride home; in her disappointment, she'd forgotten she was stranded.

As Ms. Highcraft pulled up the long drive, Suzanne was surprised to see two cars parked in front of the house, including her father's black BMW. As Ms. Highcraft's headlights swung across it, a woman jumped out of the passenger side, scurried to the other car, and drove away, casting a red glow on her father as he got out of the car.

Her father thanked Ms. Highcraft, walked inside, and went straight to his study. Suzanne ate the dinner Marcia had left her, retreated to her room, and eventually fell asleep. Sometime later she woke to raised voices coming from her parents' bedroom down the hall. She went to her door, forcing herself awake.

Her mother's voice was high, like someone was grinding their heel into her foot. "Sarah saw you, Anson. She saw you leaving the Grille with that woman."

"Okay, so it was dinner."

"If I wake up Suzanne now, will she tell me you were at the science fair?"

"I lost track of time."

A loud crash made Suzanne jump.

Her father whisper-shouted, "For God's sake, Tinsley, get a hold of yourself."

Suzanne's stomach felt sour, and she could taste her dinner. The shouting went on, softer, louder. Her mother cried. Her father was silent. Then they began again. The stream washed over her, individual words catching at the edges of her consciousness now and again: *shame, whore, frigid, money.* Suzanne struggled to make sense of what the argument had to do with the woman who had driven away and with her father missing the science fair. Her mother was accusing him of doing something bad, that was obvious. He had caused "a disgrace," which Suzanne knew, even at ten years old, was the worst thing someone could do.

Suzanne returned to bed. Her gaze fell on her science poster leaning against the closet door. She read the definition she'd carefully written in Magic Marker: WEED: A PLANT THAT GROWS WHERE IT ISN'T WANTED.

She never forgot the lesson she had learned that night: she was not the most important person in her parents' lives. She was, in fact, less important than the woman who had driven away from the house, a woman Suzanne would never know. It was, without argument, a cruel lesson, but as Suzanne made a pile of the weeds she had pulled from the damp earth, she did not fall into the arms of self-pity. Instead she considered Brynn, who had always been at the center of her parents' universe, yet whose resentment of Suzanne was perhaps greater than any Suzanne had felt—or did feel—toward Tinsley. It was a conundrum, and one that mattered. Giving too little, giving too much. Subtracting from here, adding there. Caring for your marriage, your children, your parents, your reputation, your future, and, if you could manage it, your younger, more idealistic self. This complex calculus was based on theories of love and motherhood, and equations of duty and self-worth. But Suzanne could not work out the solution because the calculus was not predicated on her experience, on vows she had made or beliefs she had ascribed to, not anything she could rest her feet on or hold to her cheek. She wanted a balanced life but had only guesses, wishes, and fears when what she needed was answers.

CHAPTER 5

Night had fallen by the time Whit climbed the bluestone steps to the front patio. The sight of the white columns—eight of them—and the imposing door with the fox-head knocker never failed to give him a boost. The classic touches and impressive entrance were what had sold him on the place, that and the location, adjacent to the university. Demand would always be ferocious in this neighborhood. Whit found that reassuring because it meant he had chosen well. The equity in the house didn't hurt their financial standing either. He'd married a Royce, which meant they weren't likely to ever hurt for money, but he was proud of what he had contributed, in what he and Suzanne had achieved together.

He wiped his feet on the mat, stepped into the entry, and dropped his keys and briefcase on the side table next to the piano. His son, Reid, was descending the double staircase from the left, wearing, as usual, jeans and an Indian-style gauze shirt with a tab collar and flowing hem. The shirt was a solid, businessman blue, leaving an impression that was both too formal and too bohemian. As Whit had told his son too many times, fashion speaks volumes, and this fashion choice would prevent Reid from being taken seriously. At seventeen, it was something he needed to consider, pronto.

"Hey, Dad." Reid glanced from Whit's empty hands to the table behind him. "Did you get the pinkies?"

Baby mice for Reid's snake. A task he couldn't give Suzanne because her rodent allergy meant she couldn't tolerate the pet shop. "Oh, crap. Sorry, champ. I was slammed today."

Immediately he regretted the "champ," a tag he'd used years ago when Reid still admired him and took up whatever sport Whit selected. Now the word made Reid hang his head, either to control his resentment or to hide the shame of not being the right sort of son. The posture made the boy seem six years old again. Whit winced at the loss of that promise.

"Hi, Daddy!" Brynn shuffled across the entry from the living room in sweats and monkey slippers and threw her arms around him.

"How's my girl?"

She stepped back but held on to his hand, swinging it back and forth. "Great. Did you have a good day looking for money in the bushes?" It was their joke from when she was too little to understand what he did for a living. Fifteen years old and still just a big puppy.

"I did, actually."

Reid leaned against the wall and sighed. "Dad, the pinkies?"

Brynn tipped her head and scowled at her brother. "If that disgusting snake needs food, you should get it yourself. You've got a car."

Reid ignored her.

"Oh, that's right. You have a car, a brand-new Mustang, but it's against your religion to drive."

"It's not against my religion. It's a moral position independent of Buddhism." He turned to his father. "If you can't do it, I can get to the pet shop on the bus. It's just a pain."

Whit rejected Reid's views on the evil of cars, but Suzanne argued that having a strong moral position, no matter how inconvenient or ridiculous, was a sign of good character. Whit thought it was weird, and weird made life difficult for everyone. But he wasn't going to get into it, not now. "Putting it at the top of my agenda."

"Thanks." Reid made his way past his father en route to the kitchen and disappeared into the pantry. Always hungry. Reid called out, "Some dinner in here, Dad, if you want it."

"In a sec."

Brynn said, "Come hang out with me in the living room."

"Maybe later, sweetheart. Your mom upstairs?"

She shrugged. "I guess."

Whit found Suzanne stretched out on the chaise in their bedroom, laptop perched on her thighs. She had changed into her end-of-the-day outfit: yoga pants and one of his T-shirts, an ancient Bucknell one today. Whit, normally possessive, made an exception for her appropriation of his clothing; it was an intimacy that felt easy and right.

"Hi, Suze."

She smiled. The bedside lamp cast a soft light on her tawny hair and pale skin, freckles splashed across her cheekbones. His gorgeous wife.

"What're you working on?"

"The spreadsheet for the auction. Three days of emails." She closed the laptop. "How did the meeting with Robert go?"

Suzanne never lost track of his day's highlights. Considering what she had to juggle herself, it was remarkable. He sat on the bed, kicked off his shoes, and gave her a quick recap of the meeting, which, if all proceeded as planned, would result in the biggest residential development deal he had ever landed, big enough to virtually guarantee more, much more, would head his way. *More* was his favorite word.

"Sounds really promising, Whit."

His phone vibrated in his pocket. He retrieved it and checked the screen. "Robert," he said to Suzanne, and ducked into the dressing room, leaving the door ajar. Robert Shipstead filled him in on his post-meeting discussion with the head of his board, who'd happened to be arriving at the club for dinner as Whit and Robert had left. The tenor of their discussion about the development of Hampstead Farms was positive. Whit's mind buzzed at the possibilities. "Wonderful, Robert. That's wonderful. I'll be in touch about next steps."

Giddy, he rejoined Suzanne. "I'm starved. Have you eaten?"

"With the kids."

"Join me for some wine?"

She smiled and nodded. As she bent to stash her laptop and papers in the bag leaning against the chaise, Whit tapped his stockinged foot on the rug. The memory of an earlier phone call interrupted the bubbling thrill he was enjoying over the deal.

"Suze, so what's this I hear about you picking up a homeless person this morning?"

Suzanne straightened and stared at him, her expression quickly morphing from confused to incredulous. "My mother called you?"

His wife was always getting her back up about his positive relationship with her parents. It was irritating as hell. He happened to have a lot in common with his in-laws and thought Suzanne ought to let go of ancient history and move on. "Tinsley needed some info about the company acting as sponsors for her fund-raiser, and she mentioned you'd rescued someone on the parkway."

"She wasn't homeless."

"Okay . . ."

"You should've seen her, Whit. She was maybe twelve years old and couldn't have weighed more than sixty pounds."

"You carried her?"

"She collapsed. I couldn't leave her." Her voice dropped. "There was no one else around."

Oh, God. The panic thing. He crossed the room and took her hand. "You were alone. On the parkway. It's remote."

"Well, I wasn't really alone. And I didn't panic. I was fine, Whit."

He looked into her eyes, brown and honest as always. "Did you find out who she is?"

She shook her head. "At the hospital, she was too frightened to talk. The police came. They'll follow up with me as soon as they know anything."

"But she can talk, right?"

"Yes, she can talk."

Whit nodded. "Let's go downstairs and you can tell me the whole story." He led her into the hall and paused at the top of the stairs. "What were you doing on the parkway anyway?"

She shrugged. "Just driving."

He continued down the stairs, hunger pushing away any curiosity around his wife's motivations. He trusted her implicitly; it wasn't that. And digging around for deeper reasons had never been his strong suit.

Suzanne lagged behind, her voice floating down to him, but the words were not meant for him in particular.

"Don't you ever just want to drive?"

Nope.

CHAPTER 6

A cardinal whistled outside the window: *chew chew chew chew chew*. It was a good distance away, but the girl could picture it on a bare branch, throat puffed out, the whole of its body quivering with the effort of sounding purely itself. But she did not move. From her bed she could see the treetops and the blue mountains stretched flat against the sky. Structures poked out of the nearby forest—buildings, towers, she really didn't know—and she was higher than they were. This morning Nurse Amy had attached the bag filled with liquid to a pole and led her to the window. She'd looked straight down and her head spun. She lost her balance, landing sideways on a small low bed covered in green cloth. She had figured out the healing place was a tower, and she didn't trust it. There was little here she could trust, and without Ash beside her, she felt the undiluted misery of her situation. Like her mother, she'd fallen through the skin of the damp, sweet earth.

She startled when a man appeared in the doorway. He had thick black hair and glasses halfway between clear and dark. She wondered what they were for. He'd been here before, asking questions, but she didn't think she'd said anything to him. Since she had arrived here, her memories had been blurry and chopped up. His name was Officer, she remembered that much. A woman with short gray hair and a board with paper on it followed him in, and a nurse who wasn't Amy. The nurse handed her a glass filled with brown liquid. She sniffed it. Her mouth watered.

"Chocolate," the nurse said. "Thought you might like it."

She tasted it and gagged. Too sweet. She put it down on the little table attached to the bed.

Officer pulled up a chair for himself and another for the woman. "I'm Officer Rodriguez. You probably remember me from a couple days ago." He pointed to the woman. "This is Ms. Rappoport from Child Protective Services. We're both here to help you. I asked you a few things, but you weren't in much shape to answer. Feeling better now?"

She nodded warily.

"Mind telling us your name?"

"Iris."

"That's pretty," the nurse said, handing her the drink again.

Iris's stomach gurgled in hunger. She sipped the drink and tried not to taste it.

Officer said, "Last name?"

"Smith."

Officer and Rappoport exchanged a look like they didn't believe her.

"How old are you, Iris?"

"Sixteen last fall."

Officer's eyebrows shot up. He looked at the nurse, who nodded. As if she wouldn't know her own age.

"What day?"

"What do you mean?"

"Your birthday," Rappoport said, smiling.

"October usually. First day with good weather."

Officer, Rappoport, and the nurse all frowned.

Iris didn't see what was so hard to understand but decided to be helpful. "There's not much point in having your birthday on a day with bad weather."

Rappoport nodded. "But you know the real day, right?"

"No."

Officer sighed and went on. "Now, what about your parents? What are their names?"

"Mary and Jim."

"Okay. Your mother's maiden name?"

"I don't know what that is."

"Her name before she married your father."

"Oh. I don't know."

"Do you know where they are?"

"Mama's dead. She fell down a hole into a cave. I tried to get her out but I couldn't, so she died down there."

Officer straightened his back.

Rappoport said, "I'm so sorry, Iris. When did this happen?"

"Almost three years ago."

"And you've been living with your father since?"

"Oh, no. Daddy left a long time before that."

"How long?"

"I was ten."

"So who's been taking care of you, Iris?"

"No one. Because, like I said, Daddy's gone and Mama's dead."

Officer leaned forward, touching the tips of his fingers together. His eyes said he didn't believe her and it was making him a little angry. "Where was this, Iris? Where were you living before you ended up in the woods?"

"I've always lived in the woods."

The three of them all looked at each other, then stared at her. Iris closed her eyes to shut them out.

Finally Officer spoke. "You're saying you've been living in the woods by yourself for three years."

Iris thought to mention Ash but decided to keep him to herself. Ash had been with her, but she didn't feel like explaining how even if she could manage to find the words. She didn't trust these people, and it sure seemed like they didn't trust her. Annoyance prickled in her chest. "Yes, I have. And I want to go back. Mama and Daddy were right." She swept her arm wide. "Everything here is loud and crazy and corrupted. And it smells awful. I want to go back to my woods."

"Now, Iris." The nurse tried to pat her hand, but she pulled away. She'd had enough of all of them.

Officer and Rappoport asked her a few more questions, but she was tired and stopped answering. The nurse herded them out and brought Iris soup, which she ate without setting her spoon down.

"You sleep now." The nurse left but some lights were still on. How was she supposed to sleep?

Alone now, Iris thought about Ash, missing him more than ever, wondering where he had gone. She couldn't remember exactly the last time he'd been around. Not having Ash here made her frantic, like mice were running through her insides. She hadn't always had her parents; she had always had Ash. Daddy had gone, just left one day and never came back, she couldn't remember why. Something to do with Ash maybe, but that didn't make any sense. Daddy was gone, that was the meat of it. His laugh was the best sound in the world and Mama wasn't the same after he'd gone. She'd never been a talker and never surprised you with a hug the way Daddy did. That wasn't Mama. And then she'd fallen into the cave and there wasn't a thing Iris could do to help. Ash had been there. She'd helped him through it. Being a year and a half older wasn't much, but she took it seriously. She had to look out for Ash. For nearly three years, each other was all they'd had.

And now he was gone, too.

She couldn't work out where he might be, how he might find her or she him. The healing place was terrible. Sure, her jaw was better, and the dense fog of pain that had smothered her senses had lifted, leaving only a misty ache and a hole in her gum she could worry with her tongue. She had to be grateful for that. But she didn't understand this hard place. Too many people, too many names, too many noises and bright lights and grinding, whirring, shrieking, booming noises. She could not contemplate—that's what Daddy had called it—and she missed it as much as she missed Ash. Without the space and the quiet for contemplating, she could not know her own mind, trust her own perceptions, and she was lost.

~

Nurse Amy came at midday. She had a soft voice and only talked when she had something to say.

"If you want, I could help you take a shower." She pointed at the small room where the toilet and sink were. Iris had learned how those worked last night.

"A shower? Like rain?"

"Yes, or a bath." She thought a moment. "Like swimming."

Iris smiled. "Mama always wanted us to be clean. We washed in the river every single day." She saw the nurse glance at Iris's arm. Someone had cleaned a spot around where the needle went in, but the rest of her arm—her whole body—was filthy. Thinking of her mother, she felt ashamed. "I was sick. And hungry. Too hungry to bother—"

"It doesn't matter."

Nurse Amy fiddled with the tubes and bags and machines, then went into the small room and reached behind a white tarp hanging from a pole. Iris heard water falling. Where did it come from? How did it get up into the tower? She and Ash would divert the stream to irrigate something they were growing, or just for fun, but they never beat gravity.

Iris stood, the floor cold as stone. She felt weak and limp, and wondered if she'd ever get her strength back. Without it she'd have no hope of getting away from here, returning to the mountains.

She pulled off the dress they'd given her.

The nurse turned and saw her. "Oh. I'd have given you privacy."

"What's that?"

She smiled. "Never mind. Come on into the rain."

After Iris was clean, she dried herself with a towel that seemed like it had never been used. Nurse Amy was in the main room, changing the cloth on the bed. Iris put on the fresh dress Nurse Amy had left for her and noticed the rectangle above the sink. Last night when Nurse Amy showed her the small room, she had kept the lights low, the way Iris liked them. Iris had seen movement in the rectangle then, but thought it was some sort of machine. Now she wiped the mist from it with her towel. She twisted her head first one way then the other. She'd seen her reflection before in still pools of water, but never so clearly. She was filled with a drowning sadness because the girl she saw contained her family: her mother's small, straight nose and heart-shaped face, her father's eyes and eyebrows, though his irises were summer-sky blue, not leaning toward the color of violets, as he'd always said of hers. She had her father's square shoulders and straight hickory-brown hair, too. She could see that even though it was wet. Most of all, though, she could see Ash, because he'd borrowed pieces of their parents like she had, in different amounts, but it somehow made them more similar anyway.

Iris put her fingertips to her image.

"Ash? Are you there?"

~

She'd been in the healing place five days when another man, very tall and fat, came with more questions. He handed her a card that said "Detective DeCelle" and said he wanted to help her. First, he wanted to know where she'd lived. She said she didn't know, and he puffed out his cheeks.

"Mrs. Blakemore—Suzanne—found you at the Yankee Horse Ridge parking area. How far was that from where you lived?"

"Lived when?"

"With your mother. Before she died."

"A long way."

"Did you live in a house with her?"

"Yes."

"What town was that?"

"I don't know."

"You don't know the town? Was it in Virginia?"

"I think so."

"How about a street or a road?"

"There weren't any."

He tapped his pen on his chin. "Did you have electricity or running water?"

"Water ran in the stream."

"But no electricity?" He swept his hand at the ceiling and the walls, and she guessed he meant the lights and machines.

"No."

"Okay, so you lived there with your mother after your father left for how long?"

"About three years."

"Just you and your mother? No one else?"

"Yes."

"And how long did you stay in the house after your mother died?"

"A year and a bit."

He made some notes on a small pad. "I'm going to have an artist come in, someone who will draw your mother and father based on what you tell them."

Iris imagined someone who had never met her parents drawing their faces. She could barely remember Daddy's face. His hands she remembered clearly, thick fingered and broad as dinner plates. His hands could do anything: hang on to a swinging ax, tie knots in a fishing net, carve chunks of wood into legs for chairs and tables, and pluck her from the ground and into his arms as if she were a flower too pretty to leave behind.

Iris rubbed her nose and pulled the blanket up to her chin.

Detective looked up from his notes. "Why'd you leave the house, Iris?"

"People came."

"You were all alone, and when people showed up at the house, you took off into the woods."

"The house was already in the woods."

"Iris." He leaned back, the chair complaining under his weight. "Help me understand."

"Why? Why do I have to explain everything to you?"

"Because you're a minor. A child. And we have to know what happened—your mother's death, your father disappearing—and help you find some family."

"I don't know them."

"But they're still family." He paused, waiting for her to agree. Iris didn't see how it mattered. "Don't you want to help us find your father?"

She looked out at the mountains, purple in the long-shadowed afternoon. She knew Daddy was dead, because otherwise he'd have come back. But how could she explain that?

Detective said, "Why did you run away from the house, Iris?"

"People. People want to know things about you. People want you to follow rules. People put chemicals in the water, and ruin good food and hurt animals and waste things that are precious. People won't let you live a simple, good life." She faced him. "I don't need people, and I don't want them."

He was quiet for several moments. "Well, you're in with people now, and you're right about the rules. Maybe once you get used to it, you won't see things quite the same way." He reached inside his jacket, pulled out a folded map, and spread it on the foot of the bed. He said the green parts were public forest, where anyone could go. The lines were roads and the circles were towns. He pointed out the circle labeled CHARLOTTESVILLE, where they were now, and slid his finger along a gray line into a green space to where he said Suzanne had found her.

"Now, where do you think your house was?"

Iris studied the map. "Are there woods that aren't public forest?"

"Plenty."

"So there's more woods than what's green on here."

"That's right. Any of the towns sound familiar, say, from a sign you read?"

She shook her head. Her eyes scanned south. There was plenty of space with no roads and towns. She could've been anywhere. Her bearing had been northerly, pretty much, but it wasn't as though she'd been heading anywhere in particular. She'd followed her instincts about where the wildest parts lay, circling back to stay in them but never trying to go back home. Detective didn't need to know where the house was even if she could figure it out, and her parents wouldn't have wanted her to tell.

Iris pushed the map away. "I don't know where I was."

He folded the map and put it back in his jacket. "You were lucky Mrs. Blakemore found you. I reckon you wouldn't have survived much longer." He stood and adjusted his belt. His face went soft. "So maybe in the end it did matter where you were."

Her nose stung with tears. She turned to the window again, the mountains deep indigo against a rose sky.

Detective was right. She was here in this terrible place, and she didn't know what she should do or what she even wanted. She'd come out of the woods and left behind who she was.

CHAPTER 7

Suzanne racewalked across the polished floors of the hospital lobby toward the elevators and punched the up button. Several people were waiting, including two men in scrubs, but no one seemed as rushed as she was. Her life seemed ludicrous to her at times. She didn't dwell on it—it was futile—but she did occasionally entertain the notion that her activities and duties did not add up to a satisfying or even useful existence. Only the inescapable normality of her life stopped her from questioning it more often. Everyone was very busy.

She exhaled completely to relax herself, then checked her phone. Two missed calls and two texts during the last five minutes. Although she had planned her day carefully, she was running more than an hour behind. Brynn's orthodontist made them wait twenty minutes; then Brynn insisted on picking up a sushi lunch to take back with her to school, claiming Suzanne had agreed to the plan that morning. Suzanne had no recollection of the conversation, but it was infinitely easier to capitulate than to confront Brynn's inevitable disappointment and anger. What had the preschool teachers said to her and Whit about dealing with children with strong personalities? "Exercise their disappointment muscles." Brynn's had become decidedly flabby, but Suzanne did not have the emotional bandwidth to reinstate a regimen now. Like so many of her decisions, an artfully designed twenty-dollar lunch was just another stopgap.

The elevator doors opened. Suzanne pressed the sixth-floor button and stepped to the side as the others filed in. She checked the time on her phone, returned it to her bag, and stared at the closing doors, mentally reorganizing her remaining errands: order the gluten-free rolls and desserts the auction caterer would not provide; shop for the client dinner Whit had asked her to host tomorrow evening; buy green body paint, glitter, and shamrock decals for Brynn's Saint Patrick's Day swim team party (not at their house, thank God); and pick up Whit's restrung tennis racket. She'd already rescheduled her tennis lesson—without resentment. She kept up her game at Whit's behest because he liked teaming up with her for mixed doubles during the summer. Suzanne preferred to practice her strokes using the ball machine, which asked nothing of her whatsoever, not even a mild suggestion for more topspin on her backhand. But she and Whit had few shared activities, so she acquiesced to the lessons. In any case, the rescheduling had righted her day until she remembered she had to purchase Reid's SAT prep books so he could complete practice tests over the weekend. She stopped at Barnes & Noble after dropping Brynn at school, and it was there she had paused at a display of coloring books, enticed by the vibrant covers and intricate designs. When the children were small, she had laid huge sheets of newsprint on the floor, and the three of them had spent hours drawing designs with chunky crayons for the others to color in. Her confidence in how to be a mother had been absolute. She didn't know everything—she made mistakes—but she had the basics right and most of the details. Remembering herself as a confident mother evoked a feeling akin to grasping at the vestiges of a wonderful dream. The futility of the attempt only served to emphasize the magnitude of the loss.

Suzanne exited the elevator and checked in at the nurses' station. A nurse whose badge identified her as Lani entered Suzanne's name into the computer and pointed down the corridor.

"Fourth on the right."

"Is she doing okay?"

Lani rocked her hand back and forth. "Physically, she's improving. But the poor kid really doesn't want to be here."

Suzanne showed the nurse the tote bag she was carrying. "I brought her some things. Hope that's okay."

"As long as it's nothing dangerous, you're fine."

Suzanne made her way along the corridor, winding past wheelchairs, stretchers, and a crash cart. She'd been concerned about Iris since the police had called yesterday with an update. How could that tiny girl have survived for so long in the woods all by herself? And why would her parents have chosen to raise her without any contact with civilization? The detective had sounded skeptical, and Suzanne could see why. Then again, many parents had done stranger, more damaging things to their children, and at least Iris's parents seemed to have been adhering to some sort of philosophy. Suzanne was the first to admit she had no parenting philosophy she could articulate. There didn't seem to be time for top-down thinking; it was a minor miracle to arrive at the close of the day without significant mishap, take a deep breath, down a glass of wine, and get ready to do it all over again the next day. She had been disturbed to hear from the detective that Iris had tried to run out of the hospital. Suzanne had wanted to ask what would happen to Iris once she didn't need hospital care, but realized she knew the answer: either a family member would turn up, or the girl would go into foster care.

Iris was hunched in a ball on the bed with her arms around her shins and her cheek resting on a knee, facing the window.

"Iris." Suzanne spoke quietly. "It's me, Suzanne." She came to stand at the foot of the bed.

The girl's tidy appearance surprised Suzanne, although she should have expected it. With the dirt gone, the myriad scars and scratches on her limbs were obvious. A half-moon of white circled the lower edge of her left kneecap; another sliced across her right thumb, and the pinky toe on her right foot was gone. Her bones protruded everywhere, as if trying to escape the bonds of her skin. A wave of pity flowed through Suzanne.

"Do you mind if I stay a little while?"

Iris turned to her. Her eyes were beautiful but brimmed with sadness. "No. I don't mind."

Suzanne took a seat on the couch under the window and placed the bag at her feet. "You might not know this, but you're not the only one who doesn't like hospitals."

Iris blinked at her.

"Actually, most people can't stand them."

"Why?"

"Well, first of all, it's boring. Unless you love watching television, there's nothing to do."

Iris nodded.

Suzanne opened her tote. "I brought you these." She handed Iris a coloring book and a box of colored pencils. "Did you color when you were small?"

"A little."

"These are for adults. It's supposed to be relaxing."

Iris opened the coloring book and leafed through it, frowning. Maybe she didn't understand what it was for, or maybe it seemed pointless. Pointlessness was its attraction, but how could Suzanne explain that?

Iris closed the book and ran her finger across the half-colored-in cover. "Do you color?"

Suzanne laughed. "Me? God no. I haven't got time." She dug in her bag again. "The other problem with this place is it's never quiet, is it? Machines, people talking, doors closing . . ." She pulled a cell phone out of the bag and explained what it was.

Iris said, "Everyone seems to have one."

"Right. But you don't need to worry about everything it can do. I brought it so you could listen with these." She held up a set of noise-canceling headphones.

"Listen to what?"

"Whatever you want. There's music on here, all sorts. But I also loaded it with some nature sound clips, sounds from the woods."

Iris beckoned with her hand. "Show me."

Suzanne sat on the edge of the bed and demonstrated how to operate the phone. The girl was reluctant at first; perhaps she'd been told technology was evil. Suzanne helped her find the nature clips, then watched Iris's face as she listened. The girl closed her eyes and leaned against the pillow.

Suzanne returned to the couch and studied the girl. Iris was so strange, so dislocated from the world in which she now found herself. Suzanne was curious about what she was experiencing, what she knew and felt, and how she would adjust to the flood of information impinging on her. Clearly Iris was frightened and overwhelmed. Who wouldn't be? And she was alone. She was used to it, Suzanne reasoned, but being used to something is not the same as wanting it. A person can avoid something—in the case of Iris and her parents, the civilized world—and in doing so make it "other" and inherently terrifying. Suzanne understood this all too well. She could not be alone, had not been able to be alone since she was twenty-two, not without the risk of a panic attack. Avoidance reinforces itself.

Suzanne twisted to look across the treetops and roofs to the rolling hills and the mountains beyond. She imagined Iris wandering along the ridges, drinking from the streams, searching for food, sleeping on the forest floor, untethered and unaccountable to anyone but herself. Now Suzanne imagined not Iris but herself, alone in the woods. The thought made her heart beat faster, and for an instant she wasn't certain whether it was from fear or excitement.

~

Iris pressed the button to lower the volume. Water gurgled through a riverbed, a bright, clear sound. When she closed her eyes, she could see the water sliding over rocks and catching starbursts of sunlight as it fell. The water paused in small eddies and gathered quietly in the shallows where skimmers twitched on the surface and mayflies dipped and rose in undulating patterns. She lowered a bare foot into the flow, her toes grazing the slick surfaces of the stones. A jay called, brash and sure, and flew off, calling again, the sound trailing it like a wake. A towhee sang from a low branch, three husky notes, then *drink your teeeeee, drink your teeeeee.* The towhee sang for a long time, the stream flowing softly underneath the notes.

Iris let out a long breath. She felt someone come up beside her, familiar, like the stream.

Ash?

You remember pretending to be one, a towhee?

He came around in front of her, quick like always. He crouched a little, elbows pinned to his sides like wings, and jumped forward with both feet, barely touching down before leaping back low, scraping his feet along the ground, like the bird would do to scratch away the leaf cover. He grinned at her, eyes alive with river sparkle, and did it again.

Ash, where have you been?

He spread his arms. *Right here. Where else would I be?*

I thought I'd lost you.

He held out his hand. *Come on, let's see if that wood pigeon has laid her eggs.*

They picked their way along the stream's edge, feet light, legs strong, lungs full of morning's cool air.

The sound of the stream followed them. Sunlight glanced off their shoulders, and the woods rang with the call of the jay, the song of the towhee, and the hollow *rap rap rap* of a woodpecker hammering an old black oak.

Iris listened to the stream, the birds, the laughter of her brother. She listened, so fully entering the world made by the sounds that it seemed sound was all she needed and all there was. For a time she was there, and Ash was there, too, and she wanted nothing more than to feel those eggs in her hand, smooth and warm and white. Two eggs, one laid in the morning, one at night. One for her and one for Ash.

A touch on her hand. "Iris."

She opened her eyes, confused. A woman stood by the bed. She knew it was Suzanne, but for an instant she had mistaken her for her mother. They didn't resemble each other, except for hair the color of meadow grass in the fall. That and something in her expression.

Iris took off the headphones. Crestfallen at having to leave the woods and Ash, she felt herself spiraling down into a bottomless hole. She placed her palm flat on the bed to steady herself.

"I have to go now." Suzanne tucked her own phone into her bag. "But I can come back, if you'd like."

Iris pressed her lips together, holding back, holding herself in.

"I'll bring you something decent to eat."

Iris nodded.

Something decent. That was what her mother said to Ash and her when they'd gorged on berries. *You need to eat something decent.*

Suzanne was at the door when she stopped. "Tomorrow, Iris. I'll come by tomorrow."

"Okay."

The nurse came in, checked Iris's pulse and blood pressure, talking the whole time. As soon as she left, Iris put the headphones on and pressed play.

CHAPTER 8

Suzanne transferred the pan holding two roast chickens from the wall oven to the granite island and tented the chickens with foil.

Mia Stone slid onto a bar stool, propped her elbow on the counter, and took a long sip of red wine. "That's so like you. Why cook one chicken perfectly when you can cook two? In fact, why stop there?"

"Oven space. There's always room in my life for leftover chicken." She peeked at the fennel-and-potato gratin on the lower rack and closed the oven door. "I don't want guests disappointed when they can't get their first choice of cut."

"What are they going to do? Not leave a tip? Plus, two of those people are Malcolm and me." Mia refilled their wineglasses even though Suzanne had hardly touched hers. "I don't give a damn which parts I get. And we all know Malcolm is a breast man. I'm pretty sure he's breast certified." She tucked her chin to examine her modest chest. "More's the pity."

Suzanne laughed, but it was dutiful. Her friend's marriage problems were real—real enough for Mia to habitually employ humor as a cover. Suzanne had never understood how Mia and Malcolm Stone had stayed together as long as they had. They didn't seem to agree on anything, and both had personalities too forceful to put disagreements to the side.

Mia studied Suzanne over the top of her glass. "You really need to have a more complex relationship with Whit. What will you fight about when the kids are gone?"

"Nothing like thinking ahead." Suzanne glanced at the oven clock and picked up her glass. "Ten minutes until we sit down. Let's join the party."

Mia followed her, glass in hand. "Since when did six people eating chicken on a Saturday night constitute a party?"

"If you're here, Mia, it's a party." Suzanne meant it.

As they walked through the dining room, Suzanne reflexively checked the place settings. Everything looked fine; no surprise, considering Tinsley was responsible. Her mother had style and the nerve to impose it on her daughter without asking. The napkins were a case in point. Suzanne had always used a set of white jacquard ones someone had given her years ago, but three days after Tinsley saw her daughter had paired them with bone china and crystal, a package arrived containing rustic oatmeal-colored napkins. A note inside said: Mix casual with formal so it looks fresh. Love, M. *Fresh?* Suzanne thought. The napkins looked more like dishcloths. But these stylistic changes her mother wrought drew compliments, whether they were to table settings, throw pillows, or Suzanne's own wardrobe, and Suzanne was indifferent to all of it, so she let her mother have her way.

Suzanne and Mia entered the living room. Whit greeted them with that glorious smile of his, lavished equally on both women in acknowledgment of their friendship. Suzanne slipped into the space beside him on the couch. Mia took an armless chair, sitting sideways with her long legs crossed at the knee. Her husband, Malcolm, was deep in conversation with Chad Beecham. Malcolm's dark, wavy hair was swept back from his forehead, accentuating his angular features. His shirt was hand tailored, his shoes supple Italian leather, and his demeanor calm and confident. Suzanne had never felt comfortable around him and wasn't sure she liked him. It was easy to take Mia's side in their disputes. Chad

Beecham was a small, bald man with a hawklike beak and darting eyes. Suzanne found his appearance alarming, especially in contrast to that of his wife, Steena, a pastor's daughter true to type. The Beechams had recently moved to Charlottesville and had joined the country club to which the Blakemores and Stones belonged: Birdwood, part of the Boar's Head complex owned by the university. The dinner was ostensibly a welcoming gesture but had more to do with Chad Beecham's work as a hedge fund manager. Property development never happened without a great deal of money, and networking with potential investors was essential to Whit's job. Suzanne didn't enjoy schmoozing, so Mia's company served as compensation, giving Suzanne someone to talk to, at least in the kitchen. Malcolm helped grease the conversation. Because the Blakemores and the Stones were established friends, anyone invited into their company would be inclined to perceive the evening as less about business and more about friendship. Suzanne found such evenings tiresome but unavoidable and undemanding. All that was required of her was an hour of cooking and a few more of conversation, in which she took a back seat. Whit had insisted a cleaning service take care of the mess the next day, so Suzanne could hardly complain.

Mia leaned toward Steena Beecham. "Sorry if I missed this, but do you have children?"

Mia knew the Beechams had three, since she'd been discussing it with Suzanne earlier. Suzanne sipped her wine, noting that Mia's edges were serrated this evening; she might not behave herself. Oh well. Her friend wasn't under her control.

"Yes, three," Steena said. "Four, six, and eight years old."

"My, that's very organized of you," Mia said.

Steena was already into her next sentence. "Delightful ages, although we've never had a spot of trouble from any of them. Not once. Slept through the night by four months—all three!" She smiled and sat back, waiting for the praise due to her.

"You'll have to share your secret," Suzanne said.

Steena shook her head in humility.

Mia pounced. "Yes, do tell us how you do it. And once your kids discover hormones, drugs, and the opposite sex, come back and give us an update." She offered Steena a smile of such honesty and goodwill, the woman wasn't sure how to react. Mia was a successful lawyer and liked to practice on the unsuspecting. Suzanne found it both unsettling and amusing, but couldn't blame her friend for being a bit testy around smug parents, considering the difficulties Mia had with her three children. The youngest, thirteen-year-old Meryl, was sassy and boy crazy. Zane, the eldest, had been an obstreperous and intractable child who turned into an obstreperous and intractable adult; he'd dropped out of college and out of their lives, shouting expletives and pointing fingers as he went. Alex, the middle child and Reid's best friend, was a calm, sweet boy who had attempted suicide on New Year's Eve. Well, he may have. As Mia put it, Alex was a mess whether the incident was labeled a recreational overdose or the result of existential despair. The therapist would figure it out, and she and Malcolm, who were to blame one way or another, would try not to make anything worse.

Suzanne herded the group into the dining room and served the meal. She always chose dishes that were neither elegant nor fussy, believing people were more relaxed, and therefore happier, when their food didn't offer yet another challenge. Steena Beecham was hard to steer away from the topic of her children, but Suzanne discovered she enjoyed gardening as Suzanne did, or rather had, years ago, when she had time. Mia found common ground with Chad Beecham in discussing golf, the sport of power. She had a stealthy game equal to her legal one. Suzanne didn't know where her friend found the energy for so much competition and positioning. Perhaps work—real work—gave her purpose, providing the fuel for Mia's fire. Suzanne realized that she herself was more like Steena Beecham, dependent for her own growth on the light reflected from her children and their accomplishments. It should be enough; it was enough for many women. Then why did she increasingly feel like a spindly, yellowing houseplant leaning toward a distant window?

Whit caught her eye and nodded almost imperceptibly at his empty plate. Everyone had finished eating.

Suzanne pushed back her chair and placed her pointedly casual napkin beside her plate. "Let's have coffee and dessert in the living room."

CHAPTER 9

During dessert Whit watched Mia twiddle her fork with impatience as she chatted with the Beechams about weekend excursions from Charlottesville. He liked Mia, admired her intelligence and spunk, but he wouldn't want to be married to her. She didn't seem to take being married with children seriously enough, as if her own family's problems were a step removed from her. Mia called it living her life, but Whit found it subversive. Still, he couldn't blame Mia for being restless this evening. The Beechams were slow going once the topics of weather, children, and weekend activities had been exhausted.

He turned to Suzanne. A hint of a smile played on her lips, betraying nothing more than the satisfaction of delivering another competent meal to strangers and friends, and hiding all the boredom she probably felt. Boredom, hell, she was probably fantasizing about reading in bed. But business had its necessary evils and entertaining the Beechams was one of them. He cast about for something to talk about and remembered Suzanne's story from the other night. Now that was interesting.

"Suzanne, tell everyone about that girl you rescued."

Mia's eyebrows shot up. "You rescued someone? A runaway?"

Suzanne would've preferred telling Mia in private, but here they were. "Not a runaway exactly."

"How did I not know this? Never mind. If it was Meryl, I may or may not want her back."

Steena Beecham looked at the others, judging whether this was meant as a humorous remark. Whit smiled to reassure her.

"Her name is Iris." Suzanne placed her serving of pear crisp on the table and sat back in her chair. She related how she had encountered Iris and driven her to the hospital. "She'd never been in a car before. She jumped over the seat and cowered in the back." She went on to describe how terrified Iris had been of everyone and everything. "Imagine living by yourself in the woods for years, then being dropped in the middle of an emergency room." Her tone was not what Whit had expected. She sounded as if she were talking about someone she knew, not a stranger.

Chad said, "It's hard to believe she couldn't find her way out of the woods in all that time."

"She didn't want to."

"Why not?"

"It was all she knew. Plus, her parents taught her to mistrust people."

Whit said, "How do you know that?"

"The police told me."

He hadn't been aware the police had contacted his wife a second time. Why would they? Suzanne's involvement began and ended with bringing the girl to the hospital, or so he had thought.

Malcolm asked, "Are they preppers? Religious fanatics?"

"I don't think anyone knows," Suzanne said. "Her mother is dead and her father disappeared. They still haven't been able to locate any relatives or anyone who knew the family." She turned to Whit. "I haven't had a chance to tell you. I spoke with the police again today."

He was going to ask if she had been the one to make the call but didn't want to appear to be interrogating his wife. Suzanne was already stretched thin, and he worried about her.

Steena sipped her coffee. "Everyone has family. And one of the girl's relatives will be happy to take her in and give her a normal life."

"I don't know," Mia said. "I couldn't get my own mother to take my kids for the weekend."

Whit laughed with the others and tried to catch Suzanne's eye. It really was time to start nudging their guests toward the door. But she hadn't joined in the shared joke. She was concentrating on her hands folded neatly in her lap. He couldn't imagine what the problem was. It wasn't as if anything had happened. It wasn't as if the girl had anything to do with them.

After their guests left, Whit and Suzanne went upstairs and stuck their heads into Reid's room to say good night. He was reading, as always. Whit knew he should be thrilled, but he wasn't. What teenager hung out with a book on a Saturday night? Brynn had a swim meet early the next morning and was undoubtedly asleep.

Whit followed Suzanne into their room. "You seemed preoccupied tonight."

Suzanne sat on the chaise and unzipped her boots. "I was just thinking about how Steena said someone would be happy to give Iris a normal life."

"She's probably right. They'll find a relative somewhere."

"But that's the thing, Whit. I wonder what *normal* even means."

He had been unbuttoning his shirt and paused. He had a low tolerance for theory or philosophy or wherever Suzanne was going with this, especially as tired as he was. But Suzanne obviously wanted to talk it through. "You mean Iris might never be normal given how messed up her life has been?"

She frowned, the familiar crease over her left eye deepening. "Not really." She put her boots to the side. "Well, of course she's different and lacks all sorts of experience and knowledge compared to, say, our kids."

"I would expect she's pretty clueless."

She was silent for a long moment. "I've been to see her."

"Really?" First a police call she didn't tell him about and now visits to Iris. "Why'd you go?"

"She doesn't have anyone or anything, Whit."

He smiled at her. "You're a soft touch."

"I feel so sorry for her."

Whit pulled his pajama bottoms out of a dresser drawer. "They're taking care of her at the hospital, right?"

"She's still alone."

"And when she's better, Social Services will take it from there." He stripped off his shirt. "Our tax dollars at work, right?"

Suzanne pursed her lips. "Right." She picked up her boots and headed into the closet.

He shouldn't have said that, knowing how Suzanne felt the government should always do more. As a self-made man, Whit wasn't keen on unlimited handouts. He finished changing and climbed into bed.

Suzanne emerged from the closet, her expression showing she wasn't up for an argument about politics or anything else. "Anyway, like you said, Iris is definitely clueless about a lot of things, but she also has a lot of strength."

She walked over to her side of the bed wearing one of his T-shirts. It barely covered her rear end. He immediately felt less tired than he had a moment ago.

Suzanne said, "I'm wondering if a normal life is even right for her."

"She can't go back to living in the woods, can she?"

"Doesn't seem likely." Suzanne pulled the band from her hair and shook it loose.

"No, it doesn't. I can't imagine why she'd want to. But all that will be up to her family, once they turn up."

"Or her foster family."

"Or her foster family."

Suzanne pulled back the covers. Whit reached for her, and she slid into his arms, languid and warm. He breathed in the scent of her hair, which always smelled like something he'd like to have for dessert but had never tasted. He yawned again, desire succumbing to fatigue.

He kissed her. "Sweet dreams."

"Sweet dreams."

As tired as he was, his mind wouldn't clear. He couldn't help but think he'd missed something in the conversation about Iris, something more important than the fate of a strange girl from the woods. Whit was always on the lookout for signs that Suzanne was unhappy, but she wasn't easy to read. Maybe after all these years he still didn't know how to look, and he worried he might miss an underground tremor signaling something stronger, potentially devastating. He could trace the feeling back to when he'd fallen in love with Suzanne.

Mia and Malcolm's wedding reception had been winding down. The newlyweds had left two hours before, and the older guests had soon followed. The cover band had left the stage, the keyboard having been taken over by Malcolm's brother, who knocked out seventies hits. The small drunken crowd sang along, slurring the lyrics but holding on to the tune. A few couples swayed on the dance floor, energized into unsteady flailing by an up-tempo number. Almost everyone left was someone Whit knew from high school, although he'd seen only a few of them since graduation seven years before.

Whit and Suzanne sat on the floor at the back of the ballroom. They had been talking, dancing, and drinking as part of a larger circle the whole night. Whit had been surprised to learn that Suzanne had been living at home for eighteen months. Given the friends they had in common, it seemed odd they hadn't run into each other before now.

From his vantage point on the floor, Whit spied a champagne bottle under a nearby table and crawled over to retrieve it.

"Look at that. Half-full." He moved to fill her glass but she covered it with her hand. He filled his own.

"I see you're an optimist."

He smiled at her. He knew he was drunk but still could not get over how pretty Suzanne was. She had been two grades below him, so he didn't remember much about her from high school except she had seemed aloof, almost icy. Was she softer now, or was he just smashed?

"I am indeed. And I could use some air." He stood and extended his hand. "Care to stroll the fairways with me?"

"I've lost my shoes." Suzanne lifted her bare foot for his inspection.

He resisted the urge to take it in his hands and kiss her toes. "Does it matter?"

Outside the air was crisp for late May, and a damp mist stretched out before them, illuminated by pale light falling from the high ballroom windows. Whit whistled as they walked onto the fairway, picking up the chorus of "Maybe I'm Amazed" drifting from the ballroom. The fresh air felt great. He felt great with this beautiful girl by his side.

Suzanne rubbed her arms. She was barefoot in the wet grass and wore only a gauzy sleeveless dress. Whit realized he hadn't been very considerate and stopped, touching her arm.

"I left my jacket inside. Wait here and I'll run and get it for you."

"No, that's okay."

"I'll be right back." He sprinted off, enjoying the feel of working his legs.

Suzanne's cry—a yelp of pain and surprise—reached him as he set foot on the patio. He whirled around to see her collapse to the ground at the border of where the light fell. He sprinted back. She was clutching at her chest. He knelt at her side and saw her eyes were wide with fear.

"What is it? What's wrong?" His thoughts swirled. It didn't look like a seizure. He shouted for help but the music drowned out his cries.

Suzanne's breath came in gasps, and her features were twisted in agony. Whit scooped her off the grass, holding her to him. Her heartbeat was wild and her body tense. He came to his feet, clutching her firmly, afraid of dropping her or slipping. As he carried her toward the building, her breathing slowed and she relaxed a little.

"It's all right," she said, catching her breath. "You can put me down."

He lowered her but kept his hand on her back. "What happened?"

She looked away. "Please. I just want to go home."

"Are you sure? Not the hospital?"

She shook her head.

A taxi dropped them at the Royces' mansion south of town. Suzanne had told Whit she was staying with her parents until she figured out what to do next. Mia had told him Suzanne had been in Africa doing research, but when he'd asked Suzanne about it, she'd changed the subject. He didn't think anything of it. As for staying with her folks, who wouldn't want to live in this gorgeous place?

Suzanne had phoned ahead. Tinsley Royce answered the door and waved them inside. She looked Suzanne up and down, frowning. Suzanne was staring past her mother.

"Suzanne." Tinsley patted her daughter's arm. "Poor dear."

"This is Whit Blakemore, Mother. We went to high school together."

It was Whit's turn to be examined. Confused about what had happened to Suzanne and also by her mother's attitude, he fell back on his manners and smiled at her warmly. "Hello, Mrs. Royce. I was really worried about Suzanne."

She returned his smile and nodded. "She's had these unfortunate little episodes since returning from Africa. It's nothing, really." She gestured toward Suzanne, who was pale and unsteady. "You can see she's fine now."

Suzanne spoke in a low voice, her eyes not quite lifted to his. "Whit, thanks for bringing me home. I'll . . . I'll . . ."

Whit said, "No problem. As long as you're all right." He wanted to stay, do something for her. He felt responsible somehow and also protective of her, which was odd, considering that he remembered her as independent and self-contained.

Tinsley moved behind him and opened the door. "Thank you again, young man."

He said goodbye and got into the waiting taxi.

The next morning, Whit went for a long run to clear his alcohol-fogged head, then left a message at the Royces' saying he would stop by with the shoes and purse Suzanne had left at the club. The excuse was transparent, but he didn't care.

Anson Royce was putting his golf clubs in the trunk of his Jaguar when Whit drove up in his old BMW. He was proud of the car—a celebration of his first solo real estate deal a few months ago. Next to the Jag, it was nothing, but everyone had to start somewhere. Except the Royces. The Blakemores weren't hard up by any stretch; Whit's father was an aerospace engineer whose company won fat military contracts, and his mother taught economics and psychology at the high school. But even as a child Whit had wanted good things, expensive things, and had been eager to make a name for himself.

Whit approached and extended his hand. "Good morning, Mr. Royce. Whit Blakemore."

Anson Royce had a firm grip and squinted sternly at him. "Mr. Blakemore. I'm sorry your evening was spoiled."

"It wasn't. I hope Suzanne's better."

"Sure she is. She's just fine." He shut the trunk and jangled the keys in his hand. "There's nothing wrong with her except what's between her ears."

Whit winced inwardly at the remark.

Anson Royce gave Whit a knowing smile and shook his head. "Women." He clapped Whit on the shoulder and opened the driver's-side door. "Nice to meet you, son."

"You, too, Mr. Royce."

The cleaning lady showed Whit in and directed him to the den. Suzanne was curled in an overstuffed chair and put down her magazine when he entered. The shades had been lowered, and a hazy orange light spilled over her shoulder.

"Hey, Suzanne."

"Hi. You didn't have to bring that stuff."

"Well, it's not like it was out of my way."

They both laughed, because it was.

Suzanne offered to make him breakfast. Whit took a seat at the kitchen counter while she set to work cutting up fruit, scrambling eggs, toasting bagels, chatting about the wedding and the reception. When the food was ready she handed him a plate and hoisted herself onto the counter facing him.

"I sit up here whenever my mother is out because she hates it."

"She's a stickler, huh?"

"You could say that." She bit into her bagel and chewed thoughtfully. "I should explain about last night."

"You don't have to."

"Thanks, but I should." Suzanne put down her plate. "I get these attacks—panic attacks. Last night was number four. The first one was in Tanzania when I got lost in the bush."

"Sounds like the kind of thing that would make most people panic."

"Right. But this isn't just being scared." Her voice became thin. "It feels like I'm dying, like I'm dying of fear." Whit stopped eating. Suzanne stared at her plate. "I'm not used to talking about this. Mia knows, and my parents."

Her father had been dismissive, and her mother hadn't exactly been overflowing with sympathy. Whit wondered about Suzanne's relationship with her parents and realized that her aloofness as a teenager might have been something else altogether. Maybe she had been stressed. "Can you tell what triggers an attack?"

"I'm always alone outside."

"Like last night. I'm sorry I left you."

She shrugged. "No way you could've known." She slid off the counter, tossed the rest of the bagel in the trash, and put her dishes in the sink. He watched her move as if she were behind a plate of glass, on display. That's how she held herself, afraid to tip something over, break something. He swallowed hard. She was splintered, broken.

He pushed the stool back, placed one foot on the floor with the intention of going to her, putting his arms around her.

She spoke, her voice firm now, her huge brown eyes leveled at his. "I like you, Whit. But I've never been good at relationships, not even before this." She pinched her fingers at her temples, then flicked them open. "I've had boyfriends and slept with guys who weren't boyfriends, and whatever it was—good, bad, or indifferent—I dumped them all." She paused, staring out the window over the sink. "Not much of a résumé, huh?" She offered him a crooked smile.

"No, it isn't." He went to her and stood close. He lifted his hand as if to touch her face, but let it drop. "Guess you haven't found anyone you can trust."

Her eyes flashed. "Who says I'm looking?"

"You can find something without looking for it."

"And you can say things you can't deliver on."

"Ouch." He stepped back. "Does this mean you don't want to go see *Fargo* with me tonight?"

"No," she said. "I'll go."

He accepted her acquiescence. Her trust would take time, but he was prepared to be patient.

After two years, Whit asked Suzanne to marry him. She said yes. The joke between them, which they shared eagerly with family and friends, was that Whit had worn her down. The joke was permissible only because it wasn't true. They knew, and everyone around them also knew, that Suzanne had not been worn down but lifted up. Whit had pulled her up and out of the quicksand of mistrust, where it would've been so easy to stay. His business motto worked equally well in the interpersonal arena: No gain without risk. So the joke was that Whit had been persistent and patient, had lovingly cajoled Suzanne into accepting his love. Suzanne had seen Whit for the loyal and good person he was from the start, but had dragged her feet only because they were young, only twenty-three and twenty-five when they began dating, and had time.

As often as the joke was made, Whit never talked about the subtext with Suzanne, because it was a lie. The true subtext was that he really had worn Suzanne down, that his conviction had overcome her reluctance. Whit was proud of himself. But what he would not say aloud was that he knew he loved Suzanne more than she loved him. He had won her over, his dream girl. And he would do anything to make her happy, because he also knew Suzanne's role was more difficult than his. Suzanne's love for him, if that word applied, was an escape. If she had not gotten lost in Tanzania, they would not be together. She was pretending, in a sense. And he was doing everything in his power to ensure no one noticed, especially not Suzanne.

Nineteen years later, as he lay in bed with his wife asleep beside him, Whit realized that, at the time, he should have paid more attention to her acquiescence instead of focusing on the challenge of earning her trust. No one gives in without giving something up, and nothing is given up without cost.

CHAPTER 10

Suzanne guided the Navigator through the tight curves of the hospital parking garage, searching for a spot. Brynn sat beside her, hunched over her phone, feet on the dashboard, wet hair hiding her face.

"Are you happy with how you swam in the relay?"

"Yeah. I mean, it was my second-fastest leg ever, not that it helped. Hannah was napping on the block. She was so slow, Phelps couldn't have made up the time."

Suzanne pulled into a narrow space and put the car in park. "I'm sure she feels bad about it."

Brynn shrugged. She held her phone up, closed her eyes, and let her mouth go slack as if she were asleep, and took a photo.

"Brynn, that's really unkind."

"What?" she said, laughing. "It's not like she'll see it."

Suzanne knew better. Snapchat photos disappeared after ten seconds, but they could be captured in a screenshot and posted elsewhere. "Anyone can have a bad start. Try to be more generous."

"Speaking of starts, nice job missing the two hundred."

Suzanne sighed. "I'm sorry. I had so much to catch up on from the week."

Brynn cocked her head and looked at her mother. "You missed my best race. You know that's my best event. But I guess you were too caught up with, you know, the Stray."

"Don't be mean, Brynn." Suzanne slipped her phone into her purse. "Why don't you come in? Maybe if you met her, you'd have a little more empathy."

"No, thanks. I'll wait here." She fished earbuds from her pocket and inserted them.

Conversation over.

At the nurses' station, a nurse Suzanne had spoken with several times informed her that Iris had developed a serious staph infection and had been placed in isolation because her erratic behavior put other patients and staff at risk.

"I'm afraid you won't be able to see her until we get the infection under control."

"How long will that take?"

The nurse shook her head. "Hopefully not too long. But, as you know, she's very weak, so we're watching her closely."

Suzanne imagined Iris in her bed, staring out the window at the mountains, longing for something familiar. What did the girl have to hope for?

"Please tell her I came by."

"I will."

"And please tell her not to worry. We'll figure something out." It sounded pointlessly vague, even to her own ears. Suzanne knew she should go, but stalled at the counter, frustrated at not being able to see Iris and worried about the girl's health. "Have they located any family yet?"

"Not that I've heard." The nurse returned her attention to the computer. "Other than the social worker, all she's got is you."

Suzanne retraced her steps to the parking garage, realizing how much she had looked forward to seeing Iris. Was it simply because Iris was a curiosity, a wild creature abruptly caged on the sixth floor of a glass-and-steel building? Suzanne was reminded of a bird trapped in the house last week. It had pushed itself into a high corner, flapping uselessly at the glass, then slid down to the sill, clinging there, panting, unable to grasp the deception of glass. And yet, when she had cornered the bird, cupped it in her hands—so light, so alive—and released it onto the grass, the bird crouched for a moment, as if shaking off a bad dream, before flying off into a comprehensible world where solid things were never clear. Iris could not return to the woods; she would have to learn the nature of glass and steel. Her innocence had been shattered.

Brynn jumped up in alarm when Suzanne opened the door, not having expected her so soon. Suzanne explained Iris's condition.

"That sucks." Brynn sounded sincere.

"It does."

Brynn seemed to have abandoned her resentment over the failures of her teammate and her mother. Suzanne strove to reinforce this positive shift. "Anything special you'd like for dinner?"

"Not really. By the way, Grammy Tins is taking me to DC tomorrow to go shopping for prom."

Suzanne's voice caught in her throat. "I thought you and I were going to do that in town next weekend."

"DC kind of trumps Charlottesville, Mom."

"Well, if you really wanted to go to DC, you could've said."

"And you could've offered. But now you don't have to, because Grammy Tins did." She gathered her hair into a loose twist and snapped a hair band over it, letting it flop. "Besides, my style is closer to Grammy's anyway."

Suzanne squeezed the steering wheel. She half expected Brynn to add, "Not that you have a style." She had pointed it out before. Suzanne could hardly defend herself, because it was true. She didn't care that much, so for important events—or events that were deemed important—she let Tinsley choose for her. Her mother always chose well. That Brynn had uninvited her from what should have been a mother-daughter shopping trip left Suzanne feeling hollowed out and expendable. But practically speaking, Brynn was right; she and Suzanne would have ended up arguing over the dress (too tight, too short, too expensive) and the shoes (too high, far too high), so maybe it was for the best. She wouldn't say it, though, because if she happily abdicated everything to Tinsley or whomever else her daughter chose, she would cease to be Brynn's mother. She would never be necessary again. It might have already happened; the answers to most of life's pressing questions could simply be googled.

They drove the short distance home in silence. Suzanne parked in the drive, opened the hatch, and waited for Brynn to retrieve her bag. The front door of the house opened. A man about thirty years old strode down the front walk, a perturbed look on his face. He beeped open the car at the curb, slammed the door, and drove off.

Brynn closed the hatch. "Who was that?"

"No idea."

Suzanne went inside, Brynn at her heels, and followed Whit's raised voice into the living room, where Reid sat in the corner of the couch, feet flat on the floor, arms crossed, staring straight ahead, appearing almost bored. The only thing that gave away his strong emotion was his rapid blinking.

Whit, barely holding his temper, paced behind him.

"What's going on?" Suzanne said.

"Reid, please tell your mother what that gentleman wanted."

Reid spoke without turning to her. "To buy my car."

She approached him. "Your car? Why?"

"I don't use it, so I'm selling it."

Suzanne looked at her husband.

He nodded and spread his hands in frustration. "Unbelievable, right? On Craigslist."

Brynn laughed. "Nice."

Suzanne sank into a chair and regarded her son. "Reid. Talk to me."

"There's nothing to talk about. I didn't want a car in the first place. I told you guys that. So I decided to sell it."

Suzanne avoided eye contact with Whit. He'd been convinced that Reid would change his mind once he had a car of his own. Suzanne had bet he wouldn't. He was principled and idealistic and clear in his beliefs—traits Suzanne admired in him. Whit would have admired these traits, too, if they had not interfered with what he wanted for his son: to be more like other boys, to be athletic and popular, to have some swagger and be cool. Reid was not cool.

Whit glared at his son, incredulous. "You think you have the right to sell that car without asking?"

Reid swiveled to face him. "It's mine, isn't it? You gave it to me."

Brynn flopped down on the opposite end of the couch, grinning, thumbs moving over the screen of her phone.

Reid scowled at her. "More fodder for your coven?"

"Yup." She took his photo. He gave her the middle finger.

Suzanne said, "Stop it, both of you. Reid, did you have plans for the money?"

Whit interrupted. "It doesn't matter. He's not selling the car. He doesn't have our permission."

"I'd like to know." Her voice was quiet, calm. Inside, sadness and frustration soured her stomach.

"Donate it to charity." Reid and Brynn spoke at the same time.

"Oh, snap!" Brynn bounced in her seat. Suzanne hadn't seen her this animated in weeks.

Reid said, "I hadn't decided which one."

"Losers Anonymous?"

"Enough." Whit came to stand beside Suzanne's chair. "The title's not in your name, Reid. How were you planning to handle that?"

Reid looked at his mother. Suzanne knew the title was in her name; so did he. Did he really think she would let him sell it without discussion, without his father knowing? Reid was making a point, but she wasn't sure what it was. She leaned forward, as if by getting closer to him she might better see his motivation. "The title and ownership are not the most important thing here. When a gift is expensive, or holds special meaning, it's usually not right to sell it. Not without talking about it first."

The boy uncrossed his arms and swept his hair off his forehead. "Okay, I get it. I mistakenly assumed the car was actually mine because you gave it to me, handed me the keys on my birthday. But fine." He meant it. He always meant what he said; it could be unnerving. Lies, white lies and ones of darker shades, made it easier to get along. Those were facts of life Suzanne hoped her son would learn in time. For now, Reid's bald honesty, the purity of his beliefs, his recent attachment to Buddhism, and, above all, his renunciation of the automobile, symbolizing as it did the material success Whit prized, seemed designed to set him apart from his father. Suzanne knew there was no such design on Reid's part, but that didn't stop Whit from taking it personally. She'd spent long hours attempting to bridge the gap between them, find common ground, move one a step closer to the other. It was exhausting.

Reid turned to his father. "And since I never wanted the car, it couldn't possibly hold any special meaning, right?"

"Right," Whit said. "At least not for you."

～

Whit worked out his frustrations on the tennis court and returned home at dinnertime in an improved mood. Brynn had gone out for burritos and a movie with her circle of friends, and Reid was at Alex's. The boys, joined at the hip since the fifth grade, shared a love of reptiles, theology, and tuneless music. After the years the boys had spent together, Whit couldn't get over Alex taking a fistful of pills. He hadn't taken nearly enough to have put his life in danger, but everyone was referring to the incident as a suicide attempt, or a cry for help. The boy was in therapy, and Malcolm claimed his son was "rallying." Still, Alex had an aura around him that disturbed Whit. A kid of seventeen should not have a pall of death hanging over him. Whit worried it might be contagious. Reid was already too introverted and quirky, and Whit felt Alex might tip Reid in the wrong direction. Despite that, Whit was relieved the boys were at Alex's. He wasn't proud of himself for feeling that way, but it was the truth. And he was still angry with Reid about trying to sell the car.

Tonight, he and Suzanne would be alone. Whit hoped she didn't have a million phone calls to make or emails to answer or cupcakes to frost. He had stopped at Whole Foods and picked up an Argentinian malbec and a bunch of sunflowers, both her favorites, and when he stepped into the entry, the smell of rosemary and roasted meat greeted him. Had to be lamb, didn't it?

Suzanne was perched on a stool at the counter, a glass of water in hand. Her face lit up when she saw him. She rose, kissed him softly, and took the flowers from him. "How sweet." He watched her choose a vase from a high shelf—they'd never undone the childproofing and moved the breakable objects into more convenient cabinets—and noticed her movements were somewhat deliberate, as if she were underwater.

"Everything all right?"

"Sure." She filled the vase under the faucet and set it on the counter. "Sometimes it just seems impossible to have a conflict-free week. Or day."

"That was an obnoxious stunt for Reid to pull."

"He certainly made his point." She clipped the ends of the sunflower stalks with kitchen shears. "I wish the two of you could find a less combative way to communicate."

Whit retrieved a beer from the fridge. "I try, Suzanne. It may not seem like it, but I really do try." He searched the drawer where the opener was kept, pushing junk from one side to the other. What was all this crap doing in here? He found the opener and shut the drawer.

She arranged the stems without a word. Normally she would've just stuck them in the vase and called it good enough, but she was taking her time with it. Something on her mind, no doubt. He took a long sip from his beer.

"Hey, Suze. Let's not talk about the kids. If you don't need help with dinner, I'm going to grab a quick shower."

She looked up at him and smiled, her nose crinkling just a little, as it always did. "I'm all set. We can eat in fifteen."

"Have some wine, bae. BRB."

She laughed at his appropriation of teenspeak. "*Bae* is so 2015, Whit."

Halfway through dinner Whit poured the last of the wine into their glasses. Suzanne had been quiet, and Whit, softened by the malbec, was ready to hear why, even if it did mean talking about the kids.

"So you're pretty subdued."

She put down her silverware and dabbed her mouth with her napkin. "I'd been thinking of asking you to come see Iris, to meet her."

He frowned. Iris again. "Why?"

She met his gaze. "If you saw her, I think you'd understand."

"Understand what?"

"How vulnerable she is. And how special."

"Okay, but I don't see why it matters. They're still looking for her family, right?"

"I think so. Yes."

"And if they don't find anyone, then the system will take over."

She pulled back a little. "That's a terrible phrase and a frightening thought."

"We hear horror stories about foster parents because that's what makes news. I'll bet most of them do a really good job."

Suzanne sipped her wine, weighing his argument. "I can't see her slotting into just any family. Plus, she doesn't trust anyone."

"The social workers will bring her around. That's their job." He didn't like the direction the conversation was heading. Was she thinking they should foster this wild kid? Suzanne was worrying about something that had nothing to do with them.

His wife hung her head. Her shoulders trembled and she reached for the napkin in her lap.

"What is it? What's the matter?"

"She's really sick, Whit." Suzanne raised her head. Her eyes brimmed with tears. "I couldn't see her today. She's got a serious infection. I'm worried she might not make it."

Whit got up, squatted beside his wife, and stroked her head. "She'll be okay, sweetheart. You said she was strong, right?"

Suzanne wiped at her eyes. "If you could see her, Whit. She's so skinny and scared."

He took her in his arms and wondered how it was they had ended up talking about kids after all. A kid who wasn't even theirs. It pained him to see Suzanne so distraught.

"Okay, Suze, okay. I'll see where I've got an open slot in my schedule. I'll meet your little forest girl."

His wife nodded and began crying again. All he could do, all he knew to do, was hold her.

~

Three days later, Whit found himself standing at the foot of a hospital bed watching Iris sleep. One arm lay exposed on top of the covers, the IV needle taped to the back of her hand. Her wrist was no thicker than a broom handle, her fingers like twigs. So small. The bed, the equipment, he himself, seemed out of proportion and wrong somehow. Iris was asleep, but Whit got a hint of what Suzanne had described, that Iris was special. Suzanne had moved to the chair beside the bed. She smiled up at him but didn't say anything.

Iris stirred and opened her eyes. Whit was startled by their color. Iris studied him warily.

"Iris," Suzanne said.

The girl turned to Suzanne. Her face relaxed like a dose of morphine had just kicked in. Suzanne's smile was one Whit had not witnessed in a long while: open, loving, assured.

"It's wonderful to see you, Iris." Suzanne nodded toward Whit. "This is my husband, Whit."

"Hi, Iris. I'm glad you're feeling better. We sure were worried about you."

She gave him a small nod, less wary than before. And Suzanne turned her smile on him because he had used the word *we*. He hadn't meant to imply anything, but it didn't matter. When Iris tired, he and Suzanne would leave the hospital and talk about becoming foster parents for Iris. He knew exactly how the conversation would go. He would agree with her that Iris was in need. She would agree that it was only until Iris's family could be located, which might be soon and might be never. (Whit assumed it would be soon—everyone had family.) They both would predict that Reid would not object to having Iris live with them and that Brynn would. "Generosity and compassion are good lessons for her," Suzanne would point out, and Whit would have to agree with that, too. He knew they would fail to consider some things, that he would keep some of his reservations to himself, reservations that might grow into resentment. He knew all that.

Because the moment Suzanne smiled like that at Iris, Whit knew what their decision would be. He could not stand in Suzanne's way and break her heart.

CHAPTER 11

Suzanne was putting away groceries when she spotted her father's black Jaguar XJS pull into the drive, carrying both her parents, she assumed, since Anson never visited her on his own. Suzanne couldn't remember the last time she'd been alone with him for more than a few minutes. She didn't crave his full attention, not that their being alone together would secure it. Her father did not seek out her company, and she did not seek out his. If only she'd been a boy, although there were no certainties even when parents got the gender they wanted. Suzanne's constant management of Whit and Reid's relationship confirmed that.

Her parents swept into the house without knocking. Suzanne called out to them from the kitchen, although her first impulse had been to run out the back door and hide in the neighbor's yard.

"In here!"

Tinsley deposited her handbag on a counter stool, unwrapped the paisley scarf from around her neck, and laid it on top. She was dressed in indigo jeans tucked into boots with motorcycle details, artfully scuffed. On top she wore a white silk blouse and a pale-gray leather jacket. Her makeup was minimalist perfection, and her hairstyle managed to walk the line between classic and up to the minute. Suzanne was bewildered by her mother's abilities in this arena, how she could attain this appearance so precisely and yet be such a mess otherwise. Suzanne was the opposite and was certain Tinsley mused, as Suzanne herself often did, about the possibility that they were not in fact mother and daughter, or related at all. Their hair and their eyes linked them, however, and Tinsley bemoaned Suzanne's difficult birth in such detail it was unlikely she had not been present.

Judging by her father's clothing, Anson had been commandeered for this mission directly from his tradition of Sunday-morning golf followed by lunch at the club. "Hello, Suzanne."

"Hi. How was your game?" Suzanne avoided calling him by name. "Daddy" made her feel like a little girl, his little girl, and if he had ever inspired that feeling when she was small, he didn't now. "Anson" was out of the question. Far too forward and modern for him.

Tinsley cut in. "What's this I hear about you adopting this hillbilly girl?"

So Whit had told them. Suzanne was hardly surprised. "Would you both like some coffee?"

Tinsley pursed her lips as if this were a ploy. "If you have some, thank you."

Anson said, "Coke for me."

"Diet." Tinsley cast a glance at her husband's paunch, which was slight but nevertheless unacceptable.

Suzanne pressed buttons on the espresso machine and retrieved a can of Coke Zero and a bottle of milk from the refrigerator.

"Skim, please," Tinsley said.

"Of course."

Her father took a seat at the counter, accepted the soda from Suzanne, and filled her in on the details of his game. She listened in silence as she frothed the milk. The espresso finished sputtering. Suzanne made the latte, then passed the steaming mug to her mother.

"Lovely, dear. Thank you."

Suzanne nodded. "Now, about the girl. First, she's not a hillbilly."

Her mother waved a hand. "Well, you know what I mean."

"I do. Her name is Iris."

"Iris? How charming." She didn't sound sincere. "You haven't answered my calls or texts, so I was forced to speak with Whit about it. He said you had filled out paperwork."

Suzanne sighed and wiped the counter with a sponge. Why did Whit talk so freely with Tinsley? Her mother would forget half the facts and twist the meaning, and Suzanne would have to set her straight over something that was none of her business in the first place. Whit didn't see Tinsley as anything other than a slightly nosy old lady. Suzanne wished it were true. "The paperwork is an application to become foster parents, just in case Iris's family can't be found. The process takes time, so we decided to get the ball rolling." She didn't mention that the detective had offered to help expedite the background check and said that a judge could hasten the approval if necessary. "It doesn't necessarily mean anything."

Anson rolled his eyes.

Tinsley jumped up from her seat. "Of course it means something! Whit didn't sound that thrilled about it, reading between the lines. Just think, you might end up with her in your house!"

"I'm pretty sure that's the idea."

"Now, Suzanne," Anson scolded, "there is no call for sarcasm." His tone was mechanical, a ritualistic defense of his wife.

Tinsley waved her hands as if bats were swooping around her. "You don't know anything about this Iris. It's all a bit suspicious."

Anson said, "If the police can't find anything, it must be because she's on the lam."

Suzanne shook her head. "You both watch too much TV."

Her mother's eyes darkened. "And you have no right to endanger your family by bringing in an unknown element."

It was Suzanne's habit to absorb such pronouncements, to internally deflect them while not outwardly disagreeing with her mother. What difference did it make what opinions Tinsley held? Except in the end it did, because her mother wormed her way into every corner of Suzanne's life without, ironically, becoming invested in Suzanne in any way—not as a mother, not as a friend, not even as a pair of helping hands. The fact was that Tinsley had always depended on Suzanne. Tinsley's obsession with keeping the surface of her life as smooth as her flawless skin had meant her daughter was a receptacle for her many complaints about Anson. Tinsley was needy and could not lean on her husband, not when he was the problem, and airing her grievances outside the shadows of their family home was out of the question. Suzanne had learned to be a good listener and to keep her own counsel.

"I don't know, Mother. Seems to me that the moment a woman decides to have children, she is bringing an unknown element into her life, don't you think?"

Tinsley stiffened. "I don't know what you mean, Suzanne."

Anson spread his hands on the counter. "Now, I think we're getting a bit off track here—"

Suzanne ignored him. "I mean that motherhood is a crapshoot. You can try to do everything right, even think that you have, and still end up with a mess on your hands." She winced at her own unexpected burst of honesty. She turned her back on her parents and began transferring produce from the shopping bags into the refrigerator.

"Oh, Suzanne." Her mother's voice dropped a notch. "Reid's become something of an oddball, anyone can see that, but he'll probably grow out of it."

She closed the crisper a little harder than she meant to. Taking a deep breath, she shut the fridge door and faced Tinsley. "I wasn't referring to Reid, Mother."

"Is that boy still hanging around him?" her father asked. "You know the one. The pill popper." He jerked his chin upward to emphasize his distaste.

Suzanne glared at him. "Alex is Reid's best friend. And Reid would never let him down. Especially now."

Tinsley tittered. "You needn't be so defensive about Reid. And surely you didn't mean to say Brynn is a mess! She's so popular and doing well in school."

"That girl is a firecracker," Anson added. "She's going places." He smacked his hand on the counter for emphasis.

Suzanne looked from her mother to her father, gathering her patience. She could've countered that Reid was also doing well in school, at least in the classes that interested him, despite the fact that his best friend had attempted suicide. She could have added that being a firecracker at age fifteen wasn't necessarily a development worth celebrating. But she decided she had had enough of discussing her children with her parents. "I was speaking of parenting generally. But never mind. Whit and I will see what happens with Iris, and when we make a decision, if there's one to make, I'm sure you'll be the first to know."

After her parents left, Suzanne confronted the pile of unfolded clothes in the laundry. The kids were supposed to do their own laundry but usually only got as far as starting the washing machine. If they needed something, they just picked through the pile that Suzanne had run through the dryer. Suzanne didn't care about a pile of clean clothes behind a closed door, but Whit couldn't tolerate disorder. Fairness would dictate that he should therefore enforce the laundry rules, but he wasn't around to do it and not inclined to be the heavy. Suzanne had fifteen minutes, and there were worse jobs.

Partway through the pile, she came upon a T-shirt Reid had given Whit several years ago, picturing a pair of hiking boots and the words NOT ALL WHO WANDER ARE LOST. Whit had a fatal sense of direction; without GPS, he could get lost on the way home from the grocery store. When the children chided him for it, he would reply with the line from Tolkien. Suzanne smiled wistfully, remembering the laughter her son and husband had shared over the gift of the shirt. Reid was eleven at the time, gently testing out his hypotheses about what was good and bad about his expanding world, still trusting the frame of reference created by his parents. His world was theirs, so he and his father could laugh over each other's foibles. Nothing was threatened. Now any topic at all, however mundane, had the power to push them further apart.

She folded the shirt and added it to the growing stack. Her thoughts turned to Iris, alone in the forest for so long, neither wandering nor lost. Such freedom was foreign to Suzanne, and she wondered if her attachment to the girl was born of fascination with Iris's independence. Growing up, Suzanne had been at the mercy of the tangled misery of her parents' marriage; she'd had no agency and little love or attention as compensation. College was an escape route, and like a perennially captive animal, Suzanne had needed those years to begin to understand the mechanics of psychological freedom. Finally, believing in love at last, she'd allowed her heart to wander, and it was then that Suzanne had become truly lost.

CHAPTER 12

June 1995

The night noises of Dar es Salaam were versions of those of other cities—the car horns higher by a fifth, voices rising and falling in odd cadences, the air spiced with the smell of salt and fish, mixing with the acrid scent of fuel. Sheets thin as gauze. His lips, his skin, his breath, his muscles were versions of those of other men. *Here is another man who wants my body,* Suzanne thought, as she chose to give it to him. After, he dropped off to sleep while she listened to the city settling down, but not stilled, like a sick child succumbing to exhaustion and yet remaining awake.

The man was Dmitri Gregory, a postdoctoral student under Professor Reiner, who had been Suzanne's senior thesis adviser in botany. Suzanne had harbored a crush on Dmitri since starting work in the lab two years earlier. He was friendly enough but showed no indication of returning her interest until they found themselves traveling together here in Tanzania. Sitting next to him on the plane for fourteen hours, his elbow grazing hers on the armrest, had been exquisite torture. Dmitri had claimed the hotel looked too shady for her to stay in her own room. She didn't think he felt anything for her, but she wasn't about to turn down an invitation to share a room and a bed, as there was only one.

Suzanne had never been in love. She first understood what love was, and become aware of its tenuous relationship to sex, through the teachings of Tinsley, who shared the infidelities of her husband ("your father") with Suzanne as if Suzanne were not a child of thirteen, or fifteen or seventeen, but a close adult friend or marital therapist. Suzanne's father, Anson, did little to balance his growing daughter's views of men. Disappointed that Suzanne was born female, he neglected to spend time with her, and it never would have occurred to him to curtail his affairs because they might give his daughter the wrong impression of men. That chain of reasoning was too long for Anson, who believed people were born as they were and acted within their natures. If he was a man who enjoyed variety in women, that was that, and what Suzanne would be attracted to or tolerate in men had nothing to do with him. He asserted she had turned out just fine and felt thereby vindicated.

Suzanne's take, unchanged since her adolescence, was somewhat different. Men were unreliable, self-serving shits. That didn't mean she hadn't had lovers, or even a boyfriend or two, starting in her late teens, but her heart wasn't on the line—it wasn't anywhere anyone could damage it. Once she left home, she kept men away from her apartment and insisted on leaving theirs before morning. If a man wanted to get close, she'd make excuses to slow things down, or just break it off. Her friends shook their heads and said she acted just like all the douchebags they'd been jilted by. She shrugged and replied that she hadn't found the right guy yet and wasn't going to waste her time pretending. Only her very best friend, Mia, knew the real story.

A police siren wailed, becoming louder as it neared. Suzanne glanced at Dmitri. He did not stir. She couldn't put her finger on what was different about him. Maybe nothing. Maybe at twenty-one she had finally stopped seeing every man as a version of her father. Maybe it was being so far from home, in a land so strange the rules and ideologies she had come to accept as truth were no longer applicable. He was a wonderful lover, especially considering her body was foreign territory.

In retrospect, Suzanne would speculate that might have been the influence of Africa, too. It was a naked, sensual place.

In the morning, they searched out two herbalists recommended by an ethnobotanist Suzanne had contacted. Suzanne was looking for the pink root of *Hydnora abyssinica*, the focus of her research. Professor Reiner had brought her to Tanzania to assist with his work—the study of the effect of cattle grazing on plant diversity in the Ngorongoro Crater—but she had secured a small grant to explore the medicinal uses of the oddball plant *Hydnora*, whose roots were supposedly used to treat intestinal disorders and skin infections. If Suzanne could find it in the market, she might learn more about it from the herbalist. In the bush, she planned to search for the plant itself, a parasite with rhizomes belowground and no green parts at all. After a strong rain, a bizarre—some would say hideous—flower might erupt from the soil, thick walled and scaled on the outside. As it ripened, fleshy, muscled sections peeled back, revealing a pale pink interior like the mouth of a hippo. The flower was male to start with, giving off a putrid stench that attracted dung beetles. After a beetle crawled inside and became encased in a special chamber, the flower changed its sex to female and released the pollen-laden beetle to fertilize the plant on its way out. Suzanne readily admitted she was fascinated by *Hydnora*'s unique biology, but that didn't erase the argument for examining its potential medicinal uses.

They walked through the fish market en route to the first herbalist. Suzanne covered her mouth and nose with her hand to keep herself from gagging at the smell. The stall to which they were directed was empty. The elderly woman selling sundries next door told Dmitri in broken Swahili that the herbalist had gone to attend to a sickness plaguing his village to the north. Suzanne was only too happy to put distance between them and the fish market, so they hurried along to the second location, a small hut with a rust-riddled roof huddled beside a modern pharmacy. A middle-aged man squatted over a burlap mat. He wore a tall, straight-sided headpiece made of red felt and decorated with feathers. A string of small gourds hung from his neck. He was consulting with another man, who appeared very frail. The herbalist spoke rapidly while he packaged a ground concoction into folds of stiff paper. After the customer left, Dmitri described the *Hydnora* root as best he could. Suzanne scanned the rough shelves at the back of the stall for a tinge of pink.

Dmitri turned to her. "He knows it. Says it's very good medicine."

"But he doesn't have it?"

He shook his head. "Pretty much all he sells is what he gave that guy who just left."

"What was it?"

Dmitri shrugged. "It's for *ukimwi*."

One of the few dozen Swahili words she knew. "AIDS."

Dmitri did his best to question the herbalist about other sources of *Hydnora*, but soon a queue formed behind them, all wishing to obtain "the cure," as the man put it.

Suzanne touched Dmitri's elbow. "We should go."

The encounter had sobered them, and they returned to the hotel to gather their belongings. They boarded a twin prop to Arusha, where a driver met them on the landing strip. By late afternoon they arrived at the Serengeti Wildlife Research Centre, an array of low buildings slung against the base of a series of worn hills. Suzanne climbed out of the Land Rover and stood with her back to the hills. She stared out at the savanna stretching from her feet to a golden smudge of a horizon, the expanse broken only by sparse stands of fever trees, the sky old and pale. A breeze blew toward her, flattening her long skirt against her legs. She took a deep breath and shielded herself from the letdown she was sure was coming. It was over with Dmitri; she chose to end it in her mind before anything more could take root. Dmitri, with his dark, Mediterranean looks and slow, sensual smile, would distance himself from her, the new college grad. At the research center, others would intrigue him more, scientists from other disciplines, the staff. At the hotel in Dar, Dmitri had been chivalrous, then opportunistic. Here, where light ruled, and where they were not alone, he could shake himself off like a dog and pad away.

But he did not. The first night in the bush, he saved a seat for her at dinner, placed his hand on her knee while they ate, and made a point of including her in the conversation. There was nothing sexier than being taken seriously. Sleeping together wasn't straightforward in the dorm-style sleeping quarters, but Dmitri put his scientific ingenuity to good use, carving out slots in time and space for them to have sex. Suzanne responded to him as she had to no other man, and this confused her, since with each passing day, her flight response was dampened and she found herself thinking less and less about exit strategies. Dmitri was ardent but not overly serious, attentive but not clinging, and respectful of her intellect. And their intimacy had not diminished her attraction to him; she could see now that this had been a side effect of her skittishness and mistrust. If she could have faith in a man, her passion would not flag.

For six long weeks Suzanne allowed herself to slide, inch by inch, into love.

"You're beautiful," Dmitri said every time they made love.

Then, while watching her study a map or identify a plant before he could: "You're incredible. Do you know that?"

One night they sat shoulder to shoulder on the hood of a Land Rover drinking Tusker. In the middle distance, a herd of zebra bowed their heads to the ground and, nearer, a secretary bird stood frozen, then loped on, its head nodding to the slow rhythm of its legs. The sun hung low before falling precipitously to the earth like a meteor, sending up a splash of vermilion into the deepening blue. Suzanne felt wondrously alive in this moment, with the sun-warmed metal underneath her, the buzz from the beer, her skin taut from a day in the sun, her mind slaked by knowledge and possibilities, the wild beauty all around her, this man beside her. This man.

Dmitri touched her chin with two fingers, turning her face toward him. Her body hummed.

"You're perfect. Absolutely perfect."

She smiled and allowed the tears pooling in her eyes to fall.

"Especially like that."

"Crying?"

"No. Being honest."

He understood her. She hadn't had to tell him about her father, show him that rough scar. With him, in those moments, those boundless moments, her father didn't matter. Neither did her mother. The big, beautiful earth had spun away from her parents and their parody of love. Suzanne was far, far away in every sense. She at last was free, and that inspired confidence. She not only was worthy of love in the abstract but also could trust its sudden appearance in the palm of her hand, the instantiation of it. She had become someone entirely different from the girl at the science fair waiting for the father who never came, or the adolescent daughter of the mother whose confidences and complaints she had no choice but to bear.

When your childhood is taken from you, what takes its place? Suzanne had thought nothing would. Now she saw she could begin again. She could stand on the equator, where the days were equal to the nights, and find her own balance.

And as if that were not enough, she was doing the work she had always dreamed of, surrounded by intelligent, dedicated people with similar passion, seeking to unlock the impossibly complex design of nature, all her secrets, triumphs, and mistakes recorded in the life spread around them—animals, plants, fungi, microbes—flourishing and embattled. Biology was everywhere, of course, not just in Africa, but somehow it was more present here. Perhaps it was because humans had originated here, and her ancestral consciousness was being pinged by the sights, sounds, and smells. Suzanne didn't lean toward the meta-physical, but on the edge of the crater, a vast tureen frothing with life, or in the middle of the savanna, rolling to the horizon, stippled by wildebeests, her sense of wonder seemed too large for her. She was a child in this world, and its student. She was its caretaker and its disciple.

She was growing here in Tanzania, where the light was strong and pure.

She was not a weed.

~

As her departure for the States neared, Suzanne spent long hours driving to likely spots in search of *Hydnora*. Dmitri was occupied with an intense collection protocol for the grazing research and apologized for not being able to accompany her more often. He planned to stay in Tanzania two weeks longer than Suzanne, returning in time for the fall semester. As she scoured riverbeds and acacia stands for *Hydnora*, Suzanne imagined their reunion in the States and considered what shape their relationship might take back home. She didn't allow her thoughts to go too far; it was enough simply to relish the idea of doing ordinary things together—and not having to sneak off to have sex.

Five days before she was due to leave for home, Tennyson, one of the drivers, suggested to Suzanne they head south along the Kakesio, a seasonal river, toward Ololgumi, where a cluster of umbrella-shaped *Acacia gerrardii* grew. They bounced along a rutted track for forty minutes before crossing a dry riverbed. Tennyson pointed out the trees and circled them, scanning the branches. "You plant people forget to look up sometimes. See every blade of grass and miss a leopard."

The smell of decaying flesh wafted in. Tennyson frowned and leaned out the window. "Might be a kill."

Suzanne smiled. "Or something blooming."

She got out of the truck and searched the ground, marveling at how the small trees had escaped being hacked down for cattle feed. After a few minutes, she found the scaly tubes of *Hydnora* sticking out of the ground, a dozen or more. Some of the flowers had opened, the four petals hanging back from the center like thick, fetid tongues. She rushed back to the vehicle for her collection kit and a shovel. Tennyson helped her take root and flower samples from two specimens, noting the location, time, and position. Suzanne took photographs at each stage, shaking with excitement.

During the drive back to the research center, Suzanne formulated a plan for using Professor Reiner's industry contacts to obtain an analysis of the anti-inflammatory and antidiarrheal properties of the plant. Tennyson and Suzanne arrived as afternoon shadows were lengthening into dusk. Suzanne thanked Tennyson, dropped the collection kit at the botany lab, and headed for the dining hall. Distracted by her triumph, she barely noticed the couple leaving by the side door of the supply room adjacent to the lab. The center held forty people, not counting staff, and people came and went constantly. Many were strangers to her. But something in this couple's movement as they disappeared between the buildings snagged her attention. Suzanne veered off the dirt path and followed them.

She emerged from the alley and stopped. Dmitri was walking away from her, a few yards ahead, his hand on the lower back of the woman beside him. The tip of her blonde ponytail nearly touched his hand. The woman laughed, a tinkling sound, and she tilted her head to peer at Dmitri from beneath her bangs. It was Anneka, a research fellow from Austria who had arrived two weeks ago. Suzanne held her breath as Dmitri touched Anneka's neck just below her ear, and Suzanne knew he would now kiss her. Suzanne's stomach dropped. Dmitri bent his head, moving as if directed by Suzanne's thoughts, his lips an inch away from Anneka's. Suzanne turned away, horrified, and fled the way she had come.

She ran past the lab and into the parking area, darting between the vehicles. Someone called out to her but she paid no heed. She could not feel her legs, only the thudding in her temples. Bushes, trees rushed by in a blur. Her lungs ached but she kept running, the image of Dmitri's face as he bent to kiss Anneka hovering before her no matter how fast she ran. She stumbled on a branch, falling to her hands and knees, palms stinging. She clambered to her feet and took off again, the tall grasses whipping her legs. The brush thinned and she emerged onto the plain, panting, her mouth dry, her lungs in a vise grip.

A herd of gazelle scattered before her, quick shadows in the failing light. Suzanne slowed to a walk, gasping for air, coughing. Her nose was clogged with tears and her throat was raw. She wandered over a low rise, the vista bare except for a large, rocky outcropping—a kopje—to the west. Strips of magenta cloud paralleled the horizon; the sun had disappeared.

Suzanne stopped and stared at the outline of the kopje. Blocks of stone on the left and a large tree, perhaps a strange fig, on the right. It seemed distinctive, but she had no recollection of it. She turned around, expecting to see the lights of the research center, but there was only the vague outline of a distant slope. Her mouth felt filled with cotton. How far had she come? She hugged herself against the evening chill and spun in a slow circle, studying each feature she could discern, certain that she would recognize a landmark, shake her head at her own foolishness, and head back while there was still light.

But nothing looked familiar. She began to walk away from the sunset, down the slope she had climbed. She knew she had come through brush, but how long ago was that? The thought of entering a thicket in full darkness terrified her; she would surely become lost. A darker area about a half mile away might be the brush she had emerged from. But then why couldn't she see any lights? Her throat closed and her hands went cold. She was just as lost out in the open as she would be in the brush. In her despair, Suzanne lowered herself onto the ground and covered her head with her arms. She imagined Dmitri with his arms around Anneka in a quiet corner of a room, or in bed. Nausea rose from her stomach; she clenched her teeth to keep from vomiting.

She was so very stupid. Stupid enough to be taken in by his charms, to believe he was a good man who cared for her, would perhaps love her one day, one day soon. She was unbearably stupid.

A memory surfaced, unbidden. A week ago—not more than ten days, anyway—she'd had dinner with Dmitri, then lingered after he'd gone, talking to two women about their cheetah research. She eventually left and stopped by the lab, having forgotten her notebook there. Dmitri was at a computer and Anneka had one hip on the desk, her foot wedged in the rungs of Dmitri's chair, flip-flop lying on the floor. As Suzanne played the scene in her mind, Anneka had lowered her foot just then, had adjusted her posture at the sight of Suzanne, and yet Suzanne had not noticed at the time. She had not seen until now how Anneka's initial expression upon seeing Suzanne was cold and vanquishing before it shifted to a smile, how the reverse trajectory of Anneka's foot led to Dmitri's crotch. Suzanne had not seen this, or perhaps a million other things.

All summer her love for Dmitri had been like falling into an icy lake. The cold took her breath away—she gasped—but it was not truly cold at all. It was refreshing, awakening, cleansing. She'd never felt so alive, her blood buzzing with life. But what she had not paid attention to was the numbing of her toes and fingers, how the cold spread to her center, and to her brain, until she could not see what was in front of her. That's how frozen she had become. She should have known the truth all along. She thought that because she had finally fallen in love, Dmitri must love her, too. It had never occurred to her he might not.

A hyena whooped in the distance, sending a chill down her spine. Several more hyenas joined in, this group closer. Were they hunting? She tried to remember whether they called to each other before hunting, but her mind was scrambled by her anguish. If she had to wait until morning to find her way back, where was the best place to hide? Not the kopje, that was certain. Animals congregated there.

All at once, her heartbeat was thunderous in her ears and a searing pain drove into her chest. Sweat poured from her forehead, her underarms. She swayed and braced herself against the ground with her arms, too dizzy and weak to hold herself upright. She was having a heart attack. She would die right here, right now. Her heart beat like that of a hummingbird, and her entire body was awash with terror. She was dying. The pain in her chest engulfed her, and she squeezed her eyes shut.

Please stop. Let me die. Please stop. Please.

She curled into a ball, whining with fear, her throat closing around the sound. She could not feel her fingers or her toes. She was dying.

A chorus of hyena whoops and cackles. Insidious laughter.

Suzanne's heartbeat slowed, and her chest pain eased. She lifted her head. Pitch black except for a hint of blood red on the western horizon. No moon.

She sat up and hugged her knees. Her scalp and back were damp with sweat, and she shivered. Slowly her mind calmed, and her thoughts ordered themselves.

What had happened? A heart attack? It seemed so unlikely.

She revisited her decision not to try to find her way back and concluded that wandering around in the dark was more likely to compound her problems than solve them. She climbed the slope again; a higher position seemed better. She would sit tight, hope any predators nearby left her alone, and wait for morning. Maybe someone would notice her missing before then. Not Dmitri, perhaps, but someone. She was forlorn and exhausted, but the desperation she should have felt evaded her. The only thing she desired was never to feel the unfettered panic and sense of impending death she had just experienced.

The sky was clear, and stars shone like sun glinting off a lake of black water. She was small and alone and terrified that her heart would begin racing at any moment, as if it knew of danger greater than a ranging pack of hyenas or a stalking leopard, dangers deeper and wider than she could ever imagine.

She held herself very still, dismissing the idea of looking for a stick or stone with which to defend herself. She would trust in being inconspicuous, knowing full well that her scent was already in the nostrils of animals a mile away. There was nothing she could do.

On her right in the distance, a pair of lights bounced and wavered, partially blocked by vegetation. The sound of an engine rose above the rush of the breeze.

She stood, tears flooding her eyes at the possibility of rescue. She waved uselessly.

The vehicle was heading toward her, but obliquely. She started down the slope to intercept it, searching her memory for any information about the terrain. She started to run, but then slowed again, wary of alerting animals nearby. She listened hard for a telltale snort or footfall, and when she perceived the vague outline of a stand of brush, she veered away. Buffalo were more dangerous than hyenas or lions.

The lights were a hundred yards away. The vehicle had turned a few degrees toward her. She didn't shout; the engine noise would drown out her voice. Her foot slid into a hole and she fell sprawling. Her ankle had twisted. Choking back her cries, she got to her feet and limped toward the lights, which had swung toward her again.

Closer now, she shouted: "Hey! Hey!"

The vehicle was twenty yards away. The headlights illuminated the area separating them. Suzanne ran.

Someone inside shouted, "Watch out!" and blared the horn.

Movement in the shadows on her right. A pair of eyes shone white. Suzanne gasped and angled left, lunging for the passenger side of the vehicle. The door opened and Professor Reiner pulled her inside. Tennyson was behind the wheel holding a flashlight. He swept the beam to the side. A hyena faced them, ears forward, mouth open, eyes wide.

Tennyson sounded the horn again. The hyena loped off and cast a glance over its shoulder before dissolving into the dark.

Professor Reiner said, "Are you all right?"

Suzanne nodded and covered her face with her hands. Shame flooded her.

Tennyson shifted into drive and swung onto a faint track. "You are fine now, miss. You are truly fine."

She nodded again, for his kindness. But the utter panic she had felt would never leave her. Betrayal, solitude, and terror would be linked inside her forever.

CHAPTER 13

Rappoport, the social worker, came into the hospital room and took a seat on the couch under the window. Iris was coloring in the intricate outlines of a flower and didn't look up. She had gone through three books in two weeks and had decided that wherever she ended up, coloring books were a new survival necessity. She hated so many things about being in the hospital—being trapped, feeling weak, the horrible food, the stale air, the constant stream of people, the noise—but she could detach from it by coloring or listening to the iPhone, or both. She had discovered that the colors and patterns she chose depended on what she was listening to. This intrigued her. She'd never had a choice of what to listen to before except by moving closer or farther away from a bird, a stream, or a rustle in the undergrowth. Here it seemed people controlled not only sounds but images and smells and light, leaving Iris dizzy and confused. So much was possible with switches and swipes, but how was it better?

Her heartache had gotten worse because Ash had been scarce. She couldn't depend on him the way she had in the forest, and it saddened her to the point of suffocation. She couldn't talk to anyone about him; she didn't know where to begin. In the woods, Ash was obvious and everywhere, like the warmth of the sun. Not here. Ash didn't belong here, and this was the surest sign that she didn't either. She couldn't think and she couldn't be useful. Her senses didn't line up with the physical world the way they ought to, as if the light she needed was from a part of the spectrum that had been filtered out somehow, leaving her cold and in the dark.

Rappoport was talking, telling her how the information Iris had given them about her family had led to dead ends. Iris was about to ask what that meant, then figured it out on her own. Ends that were dead, like her mama and daddy. She didn't like to ask questions of Rappoport or anyone else unless she had to. The less she knew about this world, the better.

Rappoport sighed. "Because we can't find any of your relatives, we need a family to take care of you."

"I can take care of myself."

"I know you're independent, Iris, and I admire that. But we have to follow the laws. Until you're old enough, you'll need to live with someone." Rappoport leaned forward, her elbows on her knees. "You know you can't go back to living by yourself in the woods, don't you?"

Iris nodded. After she had tried to leave the hospital, Nurse Amy told her she couldn't disappear into the wilderness even if she could find her way there, which she wasn't sure she could, and even if she was strong enough, which she wasn't. People would look for her, bring her back. But this was the first Iris had heard about going somewhere else. For all she knew, she would just be moving from this bed to another one, trading one cage for the next. It was easy inside the cage; she was taken care of, fed, kept clean and warm, but all the comfort in the world couldn't blur her desire to return to the life she'd left behind. Frustration, longing, and despair gnawed at her insides, and she took refuge in the coloring book.

Iris could feel Rappoport's eyes on her. Iris continued coloring.

"Do you want to talk about how you feel about joining a family?"

Rappoport had asked her how she felt about things before. It sounded like an invitation to talk, but Rappoport was already straightening the papers on her lap, something she did as she got ready to leave.

She was always in a hurry. Iris thought there must be other children Rappoport needed to see in this hospital or maybe in a different one. But it wasn't just Rappoport. Everyone was in a hurry, which didn't make any sense, considering food was simple to get, no one had to make a fire to keep warm, and water flowed through the buildings, ready wherever you needed it. Iris could not figure out what people did all day, since they didn't have to hunt or collect food and firewood. She would've asked Rappoport or Nurse Amy or Suzanne about it, but they always seemed to be halfway out the door, in their minds anyway. Iris hadn't seen a single person completely absorbed in what they were doing.

She wondered if they slept or just kept on checking their phones all night. What exactly did they do on their phones? They weren't listening to the sounds of the forest, she was sure of that. She was anxious about what people were doing with their time, with their phones, in the cars, and under the rooftops she caught glimpses of out the window. She worried it was something bad, or evil. Her parents had hidden from other people, had kept Iris and Ash away, too, and Iris couldn't help but think they'd done the right thing. This was a very disturbing place. She wanted no part of it, despite the clean white sheets and warm running water. This built-up world was like honey, smooth and sweet on her tongue—until the bees attacked.

"Iris?" Rappoport leaned forward, impatient. "How do you feel about living with a family?"

If she didn't answer Rappoport, the woman would leave. She was, after all, extremely busy.

Iris exchanged a pencil the color of bluets for a deep-red one that reminded her of an orchard oriole. In a couple of months, the orioles would fly north and return to her woods. If she was there, she might spot one sneaking between branches, hop by hop, giving itself away by a tremor in the leaves and a flash of color more black than red.

She fought back tears, not wanting to cry in front of Rappoport, who would only ask more questions, want Iris to explain, all the while glancing at her watch. How could Rappoport understand? How could anyone? Iris focused on her coloring, making it neat, choosing colors she knew from her world, colors that spoke to her, colors that evoked sights and sounds and textures and emotion. The colors harmonized within her, melting together like the lazy babble of a stream, the flutter of the wind in the trees, and the excited warble of a bunting.

Iris soothed herself with these thoughts, lost in color and sound and joyful meaning. When she finally looked up, the seat under the window was empty.

CHAPTER 14

All Brynn wanted to do was grab something to eat and binge-watch *Scrubs*. But no, her parents practically arrested her when she came in the door after swim practice.

"Family meeting at five, remember?" Her mom used the voice that sounded exactly like the reminder calls from the orthodontist's office. It pissed Brynn off even more than usual because yesterday her mom had missed the swim awards ceremony. Totally blown it off. Most Improved didn't rate, apparently.

Her father was holding a glass of wine and a huge plate of cheese and crackers, plus olives and artichoke dip. Bribery, mom-style.

Brynn snagged two crinkly black olives. "Just text me the minutes when it's over, okay, Daddy?"

He smiled at her. "Sorry, pumpkin. Attendance is mandatory."

She swung her backpack off her shoulder and let it drop with a thud.

Her mother pretended not to notice. "I did mention it this morning."

Brynn cut past her into the living room. "Let's get this over with. I'm wiped out."

Reid was lounging on the good couch, the comfortable one, taking up all of it with his giraffe legs. He didn't look up from his book but moved his legs to give her space.

"Thanks." Family meetings didn't happen often, but it was usually kids versus parents, despite all the talk of "the family unit" and "pulling together" or some other such crap. If she couldn't get her way by twisting her father's will, Reid was likely to be her only ally.

Brynn pulled out her phone from the pocket of her sweatshirt and texted her friend Lisa.

BRYNN: Family meeting. Call SWAT team if I go dark.

LISA: Your mom made snacks, right?

BRYNN: Yup. She's so extra.

LISA (via Snapchat; Lisa wearing a short skirt, patterned tights, combat boots, and a tiny cornflower-blue tank, her long dark hair pulled into a messy bun on the top of her head): For tonight?

Brynn arranged a look of exaggerated lascivious delight on her face, took a photo, and sent it to Lisa on Snapchat.

"Brynn, can you put away your phone, please?" Had her mother always had that voice? If so, that would account for why Brynn was constantly stressed. Listening to that for fifteen years would be like being stuck in a room with chalkboard walls and fifty-seven psychotic cats.

BRYNN (via text): No one gets out alive. (Munch's *The Scream* emoji)

Her father put the cheese plate on the coffee table. Brynn put a pile of cheese and olives on a napkin, crossed her legs underneath her, and settled in.

Reid turned his book upside down on the arm of the couch. Their father flinched. He was OCD—not officially, but close enough—which was okay with Brynn, since she appreciated things done the right way, too. The fact that their father failed to call Reid on the book abuse violation meant the topic of Sharing Time had to be serious. As if she didn't have enough to deal with.

Her phone vibrated. She inched it out to peek at the screen. Ophelia. Blindly and with one hand, she texted, Later, bb, and slid the phone back into her pocket.

Her mother clapped her hands together, rested them on her knees, and leaned forward. Like a kindergarten teacher. "We have important news. Both of you know about the girl who was living alone in the woods."

"We know all about Iris, Mom," Reid said.

"Well." She glanced at their father before spitting it out, and in that one look Brynn understood he was not totally on board with whatever this was. That meant it was going to suck worse than she thought.

Her mother went on. "The police haven't been able to find any of her relatives, and now that she's ready to leave the hospital, she needs a family to live with."

Brynn shook her head. "No, no, no, no, no, no—"

"Hear your mother out." Her dad gave her a look.

"She has unusual needs, so finding the right family isn't straightforward. Plus, Iris knows me already." Her mother hesitated. "She doesn't really trust anyone. She's been taught not to. But she seems to trust me."

Reid said, "Don't you have enough to do, Mom? You haven't exactly got a lot of free time."

"For awards ceremonies, for instance," Brynn said.

Her dad nodded. "Your mother said she could make it work. We'll all have to adjust a little."

Brynn groaned and pulled her knees up so her parents couldn't see her texting Lisa in her pocket.

BRYNN: Wild child is moving in. FML

LISA: !!!

BRYNN: Your couch is comfy . . .

Her mother looked nervous. She knew this was a ridiculous idea. Brynn had never known anyone who had a foster kid living with them. It was the kind of thing people did because they were too religious and wanted to save the world, or because they needed the money. It wasn't something people who already had money did. People with money who gave a shit about this sort of thing raised money, not sketchy kids.

Brynn said, "Why are you doing this to us?"

Her mother sighed like she hated air. "Because Iris needs somewhere to live. She's only sixteen."

"But it's not your problem."

"You're right. I could turn my back on her and let her go to strangers." She stared at Brynn, waiting for it to sink in, as if she'd said something monumental. "But that seemed wrong. And your father agrees."

Brynn said, "Do you, Dad? Because you're pretty quiet over something that's about to ruin our lives."

Her dad shrugged. "I'm not going to pretend I don't have reservations. But she's a terrified kid who needs help. And she has a lot to learn about modern life." He spread some dip on a cracker and gestured with it. "Think of her as an exchange student."

"Seriously?" Brynn sank farther down into the cushions. "This is a disaster. I'll never be able to have anyone over here again. You guys won't be seeing much of me, you know that, right?"

"Brynn . . ." Her mother shook her head.

Her mother wasn't taking her seriously. What else was new? It made Brynn furious. Her mother talked about respect all the time, how she wanted more of it, but she didn't show her own daughter much. Her mother always knew better, always made the right call, and Brynn was just some dumbass kid. "Maybe that's what you want, Mom. You don't like the kids you have, so you thought you'd get another one."

"Brynn, that's absurd."

"Is it? You're always trying to control me, make me someone I'm not." Brynn pointed at her brother. "And you do the same thing to Reid."

Reid sat up straighter, but his voice was dead calm. "Defending me. That's a new twist."

Brynn said, "Well, you need help, that's for sure. Freak."

"Stop it, Brynn!" Her mother was halfway out of her chair. Brynn covered her head with her arms as if her mother were going to hit her, which she had never done. Whenever Brynn stood up for herself, whenever she was honest, she sensed her mother's rage snaking under the surface, about to leap out, so Brynn instinctively defended herself. There didn't have to be actual violence for her to feel like it was present and real. Brynn wanted to smack her mother or pull her hair practically every day and assumed her mother must feel the same, at least occasionally. One thing she'd learned pretty quickly once she became a teenager: adults aren't all that adult.

Her father put his hand on her mother's shoulder and stuck her back in her seat. "For God's sake, calm down. All of you."

Reid was just sitting there, calm as could be, probably meditating in secret. It was so rude. Her dad was awesome and put up with more than he should from her mother and Reid. Her father's disappointment in Reid was something Brynn had sensed long before she had understood it. A couple of years ago, she'd heard her father talking to another dad after she'd won a big race. "I'm so proud of her," he'd said. "Daughters are the new sons." She knew then that her role was to be her father's joy, his favorite, and anything her mother or Reid did to interfere with that was unacceptable. Her dad hadn't blown off the awards ceremony. He always showed up when he could shake free from work. And whether he actually showed up or not, he treated her like an adult, unlike her mom, who acted like Brynn was still a baby. Either that or on the verge of becoming a delinquent. Her mom didn't trust Brynn to be in charge of her own life. It was insulting. But her dad appreciated her maturity and didn't constantly judge. He was the best and deserved the son he dreamed of having, even if it happened to be a daughter.

Her father sighed and finished his wine. "Maybe another teenager is not exactly what we need."

Her mother's voice was low and steady, but the way she strung out her words meant she was furious, as if the sentence were a ticking bomb that she had to figure out how to disarm before she got to the end. "Aside from the fact that we'd already come to a decision, Whit, the truth is Iris needs help and we are more than able to help her, so we should stop and think about her, the situation she is in, instead of ourselves."

Brynn looked pleadingly at her father. "Daddy . . ."

He lifted his hands and turned to her mother. "You're right. I'm sorry. We have decided. Assuming we get the official approval, Iris is coming to live with us. I know how strongly you feel about her and, given everything you do for all of us every day, we should have your back."

Her mother smiled and reached for his hand. "Thanks, Whit."

Brynn turned away in contempt. Her mother didn't even have a real job. Sure, she ran around all day, but it wasn't as if she had to. Other moms worked. Her mom kept herself busy, and now she wanted to take on a random stranger as a side project. Her dad was letting her mother have her way because he couldn't say no to her. He was too nice.

Reid picked up his book. "Personally, I think Iris sounds intriguing. Is she going to go to school with us?"

Brynn hadn't thought of this. Her brain lit up in flames. School was the one place where she had control over her life. "Not happening."

Her mother said, "Not for a while. She has a lot of adjusting to do."

Brynn stood up. "I'm done. This whole thing sucks." She stormed out before her mother could say another word.

Upstairs, Brynn showered, wrapped her hair in one towel and her body in another, and retreated to her room, door closed. She pulled a half dozen outfits from her closet and laid them neatly on the bed, matching shoes and boots to each one. The process calmed her. Colors, textures, styles, levels of provocativeness all had to be meticulously balanced. It might only be a lacrosse game, but presentation was everything. She tried on the first outfit: her favorite skinny jeans (why had any other kind ever been invented?), gray suede booties, and a fluffy white sweater with a wide, low neckline. She stood in front of the full-length mirror on her closet door and turned first one way then the other, considering. Her legs were too long. With the white sweater, she resembled a Q-tip. She tore off the sweater, tossed it on the floor (so unlike her except when angry) and put on a pale-blue J.Crew button-down shirt she'd worn just once, leaving the top buttons undone so the lace edge of her push-up bra was just visible. Better. She texted Lisa a photo of her reflection.

LISA: Keep it.

BRYNN: Thanks, bb.

She stared at her reflection, forgetting for a moment about the clothes. Her face was the real problem. Tears stung her nose. Why did she have to have her father's long, horsey face? It looked fine on him, sophisticated and strong, but on her those features were a huge liability. Her eyes were all right—blue and not puny—and her mouth was, well, a mouth. But her nose was a full inch longer than it needed to be. It was so unfair. Her mother was beautiful. She had big brown eyes, high cheekbones, and full lips. And her nose wasn't anything you'd notice, which was exactly the point. Everyone said her mother looked like Julianna Margulies, except Brynn's friends, who knew Brynn would go ballistic at the mention of it. In Brynn's opinion, her mother was prettier than Julianna Margulies, because Suzanne had thick, honey-colored hair that contrasted with her brown eyes. And the worst part was her mother didn't play up her looks at all, just pulled her hair into a ponytail, put on some lip gloss, and wore the clothes Grammy Tinsley bought for her, but never in the right combinations. Her mother was gorgeous without any effort. How unfair was that?

Of course, her mother always told Brynn she was a pretty girl, pointing out her fine blonde hair or her eyes, but Brynn had known the truth for a long time. As early as third grade, boys had started whinnying whenever she went past. Until then, she had been proud to have a beautiful mother. Slowly it dawned on Brynn that her mother wasn't something she owned, and her beauty wasn't shared. Worse, her mother could never understand how Brynn suffered because she was an ugly duckling. Beautiful people were totally blind to how much looks mattered. They automatically got all the attention—not just from boys but from other girls, too. Maybe when her mother was younger it didn't matter as much, but now when photos were everything, and people spent all their time stalking each other, stalking themselves to see what everyone else saw, having a horsey face wasn't just a little unfortunate. It was a catastrophe.

Brynn double-checked her outfit in the mirror, inspecting her butt, which she already knew looked awesome in the jeans.

Thank God she was tall and had money for the right clothes. Otherwise she'd be invisible, a nobody.

CHAPTER 15

Nurse Amy stepped onto the car door ledge to show Iris how to buckle the seat belt, then squeezed the girl's hand. "See you for your checkup in a few days."

"Thanks."

Suzanne climbed in through the other door. "It's not far at all." She smiled and turned the key that started the motor. "I'll go slow."

Iris faced front and avoided looking out the side windows like Suzanne said. The movement of the car made her stomach queasy. She could run almost as fast as this, so it had to be because she was being moved instead of moving herself. Carried along from one cage to another.

The buildings were crammed along the road. One after another after another with little or no space in between. All the surfaces were hard except where trees grew out of square holes: maple and beech and other types she didn't recognize. Suzanne turned the car onto another road and again onto another. The turns sloshed Iris's insides, and she grabbed the side of the seat. There were more trees now, bigger ones, and the buildings had no signs, just numbers. Small patches of very short grass grew in front of each building.

"What are these?"

"Houses. Each one is for a family, like your house in the woods."

Iris examined Suzanne's profile for signs she was joking, although Iris couldn't remember Suzanne ever making a joke. If she was serious, it meant the families were very large. She wondered if this was part of the overpopulation and damage to the earth her parents had warned her about. Iris understood exponential growth and limited resources. She understood the earth was a beautiful, precious, finite space. She understood she was part of a deeply interdependent natural system that could be thrown out of balance or destroyed entirely by greed and carelessness. Iris hadn't thought about this in a long time because she had been too occupied with surviving on her own, but her comprehension of the world as a whole and her responsibility to it was a given, like gravity, or the seasons. Now she absorbed what she was seeing in light of what she knew. Curiously, there was little sign of overpopulation, or any population at all. A man was getting into a car. A woman walked beside the road holding the hand of a small boy. When her mother talked about overpopulation, Iris had imagined people shoulder to shoulder with barely enough room to turn around, like a brood of nestlings tucked into a nest.

"Where is everyone?" In her confusion, Iris hadn't realized she had spoken her thoughts.

"What do you mean?"

Iris didn't answer.

After a few more houses, Suzanne turned into a tiny road ending at a white house with two layers of windows and a porch as wide as the main road.

"Here we are." Suzanne stopped the car and pushed on the red part of the seat belt latch. Iris did the same. Suzanne smiled and seemed about to say something but decided against it. Iris was glad. Leaving the hospital, the car ride, the huge houses, the strange trees, and the hard gray surfaces overwhelmed her senses and her thoughts. She wanted all of this noise and confusion to stop.

Suzanne pulled a handle on the car door, leaning back so Iris could see. Iris imitated her and climbed down. Huge pink, lavender, and blue flowers she'd never seen before lined the tiny road, and in front of the porch were bushes with long pale-purple blossoms and a sweet smell. Beside the bushes stood a redbud, its branches heavy with clusters of tiny magenta flowers. She went to it and reached to touch the familiar blossoms, her eyes filling with tears. She turned her face to the sun.

"Iris?"

Suzanne waited on the steps to the porch. Iris exhaled in resignation and crossed the short grass meadow to join Suzanne. Bordering the steps were several dandelions; she stooped to pick the leaves.

"Oh, you don't have to do that," Suzanne said.

A girl appeared at Suzanne's side, the tallest girl Iris had ever seen, and nearly naked, wearing only tiny black shorts and a top made of two triangles and some string. It was a warm day, especially for April, and Iris could see why the girl wouldn't want to wear a lot of clothes. But Nurse Amy had explained to her about modesty—rules about what to show when. Iris must have misunderstood. The girl's body was strong and didn't have a scar or bruise that Iris could see. She seemed to have been created just this morning.

"Brynn," Suzanne said, "This is Iris."

"Hi." Brynn didn't smile. Her eyes went to the leaves in Iris's hand, and she made the same face Ash used to make when he ate an unripe blackberry. Brynn turned to Suzanne. "Is she weeding? Because I'm pretty sure you're not supposed to make slaves out of foster kids before they even step foot in the house."

Iris didn't understand. What was "weeding"? Brynn also appeared angry, which confused Iris.

Suzanne frowned and looked uncomfortable. "Iris, were you collecting those?"

"Yes. I can find more and we can share."

"Seriously?" Brynn said, laughing without happiness. She seemed to have expressions and emotions in strange combinations. It was like trying to decode all the different calls and postures of crows. They were impossible to decipher.

Suzanne said, "Brynn, did you know they sell dandelion greens at Whole Foods?"

"Good to know, Mom. Iris, welcome to civilization." She went inside.

Suzanne stared at the spot her daughter had occupied a minute ago, a sad look on her face.

Iris laid the dandelion leaves on the ground. She had so many questions but couldn't decide what was important to know. She felt tired and wanted to be somewhere quiet by herself.

Suzanne opened the door. "Let's have some lunch; then you can rest in your room."

Iris nodded and followed Suzanne inside. She couldn't absorb everything she was seeing and had to remind herself to pay attention to what Suzanne was showing her and saying. They went through some rooms with chairs and couches and into what Suzanne said was the kitchen.

Brynn stood in the middle of the room with her arms crossed. "There's nothing to eat."

Suzanne walked past Brynn and pointed to some tall chairs. "Iris, you can sit there, okay? How about a turkey sandwich?"

"I hate turkey," Brynn said.

"You can have whatever you want, Brynn. I'm just going to make something for Iris."

"Awesome. But like I said, there's nothing to eat."

Iris climbed into a chair. Suzanne opened a large metal cabinet with lights inside. It was full of food. Iris glanced at Brynn to see if she noticed how much food there was, but she still looked angry. Iris pulled her heels onto the seat, hugged her knees to her chest, and tucked her head between her arms. She almost wished she could go back to the hospital. At least she knew what to expect there.

Suzanne put the sandwich in front her. Iris's mouth watered and she took a bite. It was one of the best things she'd ever eaten. Iris ate quickly, concentrating on the delicious sensations in her mouth and trying to block out the sharp words between Suzanne and Brynn.

When she finished eating, Suzanne took her plate. "I'll give you a quick tour, just so you know where things are."

A door in the kitchen led outside to more chairs and tables on an area covered in flat stone. Beyond that were short grass, flowers, and trees. She could see parts of other houses, each with its own patch of short grass, divided from the others by fences or plants.

"This is our backyard."

"I like this part."

"I thought you might."

Suzanne walked her through the rest of the house. Iris was again puzzled by the absence of people and began to realize that only Suzanne, Whit (whom she'd met at the hospital), and their two children lived here. And now her.

The second layer of the house Suzanne called the "upstairs," one of the first things she'd said that made sense. "We're almost done."

Iris stopped, sniffing the air. "What kind of snake lives here?"

Suzanne seemed surprised. "You can smell it? It's a black snake. A pet." She knocked on one of the many doors. "Reid?"

A voice from inside. "Coming."

The door opened and a boy stood before her, also very tall. He had Suzanne's eyes. "Hi. I'm Reid. But you probably guessed that." He smiled and squirmed a little, as if his skin didn't fit him right. He looked down at his feet. Iris looked at them, too, and wondered what was so interesting about them.

"I'm Iris."

Reid nodded and glanced at her, longer this time. "Well, if you need anything, I'm right here. Except when I'm not."

Suzanne said, "School, you mean."

"Yeah, school."

"Thanks, Reid."

Iris's room was next to Reid's, opposite a bathroom. Brynn's room was at the end of the hall, but Suzanne didn't take her there. Instead she settled Iris in her new room and left, saying she would come back later. Iris gazed around the room in wonder, unable to digest that this entire space was hers. At the hospital, she'd reasoned, she had her own room because she was ill. Suzanne had said the clothes in the closet and drawers were hers to use, but she decided to look through them later. She lay on the bed and stared out the window, thinking she would never be able to sleep in this strange place. The window was open, and the warm breeze reached her. Birds sang, a pair of wrens dueting and a mockingbird running through its repertoire, three times for each call. She closed her eyes and listened to the birds, and before she could worry about anything else, she fell asleep.

When she awoke, it took Iris a moment to realize she was no longer at the hospital. Suzanne was in the doorway, silhouetted by light behind her.

"Dinner's ready, if you're hungry."

"Okay."

Iris was hungry, even though she'd had lunch. It was as if eating made her hungrier. She would have liked to eat in her room, but Suzanne didn't offer that.

Suzanne's family was waiting at the table. Brynn was talking to Whit and seemed happier than before. Suzanne talked to Reid, but he didn't say much. Iris didn't want to talk. She wanted to eat, so she took her plate to the kitchen, where she had eaten before. She pretended she couldn't hear the voices in the next room and finished her food without tasting it. As she passed through the room where the others were, she told Suzanne she was tired and went upstairs. All that food and all that commotion exhausted her, and as she lay on the bed staring out the window and worrying about what would happen to her, she fell asleep.

She awoke sometime later, confused again about where she was. A small light glowed a few inches above the floor near the door. Suzanne's house, she remembered. It felt like the middle of the night even though it wasn't fully dark outside. She went to the window overlooking the backyard. Most of the yard was in deep shadow; the light came from the front of the house. Filled with a sudden longing, Iris pulled the blanket from the bed and left the room. She paused in the hallway and listened. No one was moving around. She crept to the stairs and down to the kitchen. She turned the knob of the outside door but it would not open. Her fingers found a latch above the knob, which she twisted slowly until it clicked.

Outside. Alone. How long had it been? She had lost track of the weeks since Suzanne had found her. Iris breathed in the cool night air, the scent of blooms lingering, and crossed the cold, flat stones onto the short grass and then to the far corner, where the shadows were impenetrable. She wrapped the blanket around her and lay down facing away from the house and the light in the road. A car drove by somewhere in the distance. A dog barked several houses away. A door opened and closed. Finally it was quiet. Not woods quiet, but better.

Ash? Are you there?

A feeling, like honey slipping down her throat.

Yeah, I'm here. Where else would I be, chipmunk?

Iris put her hand over her mouth to stop from laughing. He called her that because she never could stay still. *I thought you got lost?*

Not me. There was a pause. *You maybe.* His voice trailed into a pool of thick sadness.

Iris's throat closed. *I'm sorry.*

What are you going to do?

I wish I knew. She reached her hand out into the darkness to be closer to him. She wished with her whole heart she could have him back, be in the woods with him again, kicking through the stream together, hunting rabbits and squirrels, lying on their backs outside at night watching the stars blinking down at them. Curled in her blanket, arm outstretched, Iris thought she felt a slight thickening of the air between her fingers.

Don't go, Ash. Don't leave me.

The night fell into a thorough silence. Iris tucked her hand into the blanket, closed her eyes, and pulled the silence inside herself. Around the small yard in which she lay huddled, a wood emerged, hundreds of trees pushing up from the earth in all directions, straining for the stars, stretching their limbs wide: hickory and bull pine, sycamore and black cherry, sassafras and hornbeam, sumac and ash.

CHAPTER 16

Brynn groped for her phone on the nightstand and shut off the alarm. No way it was time to get up already. She pulled the covers over her head. Her legs felt like tree trunks after the huge set of kickboarding at last night's practice. It was all good, though. She was getting stronger and faster. No pain, no glory. And if she didn't get her ass out of bed, no breakfast.

She slipped a sweatshirt over her cami, grabbed her phone, made a pit stop in the bathroom, and headed downstairs. Her mom blazed by Brynn on the staircase and nearly wiped out on the way to the kitchen.

"What's going on?" Brynn followed her, since that's where she was going anyway.

Her mother screeched to a halt by the fridge. Reid was coming in from the yard. Brynn was not awake enough for whatever happy hell this was.

"You found her!" Her mother rushed toward the door. Brynn saw the Stray behind him, wrapped in a blanket like a homeless person, which, now that Brynn thought about it, wasn't far off the truth.

Reid grabbed a paper towel off the counter and wiped his bare feet, soaking wet and covered in grass. His hair was a mess and his clothes looked slept in; in other words, same as ever. "Yeah. She was asleep way in the back, practically under the hedge."

Brynn took out her phone. Iris came through the door and Brynn snapped a photo. The girl literally had sticks in her hair, and those weird eyes of hers were even bigger than usual, if that was possible.

Her mother spun toward her. "Brynn!"

BRYNN to Lisa (via Snapchat): #campingfail

Brynn said, "Can I have my breakfast now? I'm starving."

Her mother was struggling to control herself, like her mom-self was John Hurt in *Alien* and her true feelings were the thing about to explode out of her chest. "You know where everything is." She went over to the Stray. "We were really worried about you."

"Why?"

Brynn dumped granola into a bowl. "Yeah, Mom, why?"

Reid was pouring a giant glass of milk. "Lay off, Brynn."

Her mother ignored her and spoke to Iris. "Because we expect you to sleep in your bed, or at least stay in the house."

"Why?"

"Because now that you live here, we're responsible for you, and part of that is knowing where you are."

Brynn thought, *Or at least telling herself she knows where her kids are.* "Maybe you could leave a note. 'Sleeping in the neighbor's compost tonight.'"

Her mother sent her an evil look.

Brynn shrugged. "I was going to suggest an invisible fence but thought that might be mean."

Iris was hanging on to one side of the doorframe with both hands, looking totally confused. Brynn did feel sorry for her, just a little. It was impossible not to. For one thing, she was tiny and emaciated. She was less than five feet tall and probably didn't weigh seventy pounds. And clueless didn't begin to cover it. But Iris didn't seem stupid, so she'd catch on soon enough. Her mom was the stupid one, acting like she was gunning for an A in Foster Parenting. It wasn't like Iris was difficult. She wasn't drug addicted. She didn't smoke or even swear. She hadn't had the crap beaten out of her, at least not that anyone had mentioned, and even though she was covered in scars, there was a good chance they were from living a little too close to nature. No, Iris wasn't damaged goods, which made her mother's hovering and intense concern really annoying. Iris was just another project for Supermom, to take her mind off the fact that she didn't have a life.

Reid was chewing a bagel and reading the newspaper their dad had left on the counter before he'd gone to work. Her mother faced away, at the stove, cooking eggs for Iris, who was still standing there in her blanket.

Brynn checked the time on her phone, slid off the stool, and put her bowl in the dishwasher. "I'll be ready in twenty, Mom. Oh, and you might want to wash that blanket. It's got slugs on it."

In her room, Brynn changed into the clothes she'd selected the night before and put on her makeup at her desk, where the lighting was better than in the bathroom. Her phone vibrated.

SAM (selfie of him grinning via Snapchat): Hey, getting dressed? Flash me?

Sam was a junior on the swim team. All her friends had been shipping Sam and her for weeks. She liked him okay and she had to agree they would look good together. But he needed playing.

BRYNN (photo of her feet in sock monkey slippers): Can you handle it?

She applied the first coat of mascara. God, boys were slow. Finally her phone buzzed.

SAM (selfie of him winking): Monkey see monkey do

Points for humor. She applied a blush, another coat of mascara, and lip gloss in Jammy. Her phone vibrated again. She smiled. Couldn't stay away, huh?

LISA: Trevor invited us to the party at the club. Alibi time?

BRYNN (smiley face with shades): Think Sam will be there?

LISA: Yup. Asking for a friend?

BRYNN: Yeah, a hot one. Later, bb.

~

Thursday rolled around again, and Brynn met her friends at the lacrosse game because nothing else was going on. The game was a total bust. The opposing team was crushing them and it was too sad, not that Brynn and her friends were actually watching the action. Also, Sam and the other boys they'd thought would be there hadn't shown up, so the girls walked to Lisa's house because it was closest. Brynn texted her parents to let them know where she was going. It was lame—she could be anywhere—but easier in this case just to do it. Kendall pulled out a joint and they passed it around among the five of them as they walked. When they got to Lisa's, her mom was on the phone and pretty much ignored them as they raided the fridge and ducked into Lisa's room. They all agreed she had the best bedroom, not counting Brynn's.

Lisa threw pillows on the floor for them to sit on. "Brynn, when are you gonna have us over so we can meet her?"

"By 'her' I assume you mean the Stray." Brynn sighed. "The answer is never."

"Oh, come on," they chorused.

"No, really. The zoo is closed." She pulled out her phone, anxious to change the subject. "Tinder roulette, anyone?"

"Hell yeah." Kendall put down her Vitaminwater and clicked open the app.

Lisa volunteered to call time for the first round. "Ready, sistahs?" Brynn and the others poised their thumbs over their screens. "Okay, go."

The four girls swiped left across profiles, saying no to guy after guy. The rules were they had to swipe left until the timekeeper called time. The guy who was on the screen when they stopped was the one they had to swipe right for. They had to keep up a steady pace; no hovering over a hot guy hoping time would be called, making a right swipe mandatory.

"Tick-tock," Lisa said.

"Come on. Say it." Steph was the shyest of them all and hated this game. She felt guilty about swiping left past so many people who didn't deserve it.

"Bye-bye, hunky boy." Kendall sniffed.

"So many hunky boys . . ." Ophelia had a boyfriend, a senior named Andrew, but was all about Tinder. Andrew might or might not know how much time she spent on it. Brynn knew Ophelia had hooked up with at least two guys from it. Ophelia didn't care. "Judge me," she'd said. "Then fuck off."

"Stop!" Lisa held up her hand. "Like him. In fact, I dare you to super like him."

"Not doing it." Kendall held up her phone, which showed a balding man with moobs drinking Coors in a bubble bath.

They all laughed.

Brynn glared at Kendall. "You have to. Rules." She turned to Lisa. "I accept your dare with pleasure." She let them see Robby, a tall, athletic guy in a wrinkled white button-down, the UVA stadium scoreboard in the background. "Holding. A. Pug." She swiped up with dramatic flourish.

"He's gorgeous," Ophelia said. "I'd do him."

"Of course you would." Brynn smiled at her, to let her know it was a joke. Ophelia was a lot of talk, despite the hookups, and claimed to have been a virgin until her current boyfriend. They were all virgins, as far as Brynn knew. Blowing guys didn't count. They all did that.

Kendall called for another round of roulette. All the hits were lame. They hung out until Lisa's mom broke it up around ten. Brynn texted her parents that she was getting a ride with Kendall's dad. On the way home, her phone blinked with a notification from Tinder. Robby had liked her and sent her a message.

ROBBY: Look at you, pretty girl.

BRYNN: Your pug is adorbs.

ROBBY: Jason gets all the super likes. I'm his agent.

BRYNN: Lol

ROBBY: What are you up to?

BRYNN: In transit. Tell Jason I'll catch him later.

ROBBY: Don't keep him waiting. He's drooling.

Brynn stashed her phone in her jacket pocket. Trevor's party, such a coup only hours before, now seemed like a monumental waste of time. Campus parties were everything. She'd been to a couple before with her friends, but they had totally crashed them. They had been nobodies, high school nobodies—in other words, fresh meat. But going with someone like Robby, now that was different. That was goals AF.

CHAPTER 17

Reid sat with Iris at the counter while she scarfed down vast quantities of scrambled eggs, sausage, and toast. Whatever else she might have trouble with, eating was not on the list. She used her hands to eat almost everything, and when she did use a fork, she held it in her fist like a toddler. He was fascinated with what the Venn diagram of her knowledge and his might look like: what he knew and she didn't, what they both knew, and what she knew and he did not. He guessed that, despite her ignorance of technology and modern stuff, Iris knew a lot about the world. It might not have been her choice, but she had pretty much renounced materialism, too, which was cool. Reid realized this didn't mean Iris was made of starlight or even had deep thoughts, but he was curious about her. He wanted to ask her lots of questions but worried about spooking her.

His mother was on her phone, texting at near-Brynn speed. Incoming calls made soft dinging sounds every few seconds. Only seven fifteen and the world of Moms on a Mission was wide awake. His mom sighed and put the phone on the counter.

"Reid, remember Trevor's party is tomorrow night."

"I don't think I'm going."

"Not even for a little while?"

Reid stared at his empty plate. This wasn't about Trevor Gillings. This was about Trevor's father, who ran the bank where Reid's father got funding for a lot of his deals.

His mother kept at it. "He's been your friend since fourth grade."

"Correction. He was my friend in fourth grade. He's changed a lot, Mom. Not for the better." Trevor was a classic lax bro: a partier and a slick guy with the girls.

Reid could see his mother struggling, pulled in one direction by Reid's father's insistence that his real estate deals were family business, and in the other by her view that Reid should be free to choose his own friends and spend his time how he wanted, within reason. His mother agreed with Reid in principle—she admitted it—but in practice it was murkier, because she had to go up against Reid's father over it. Sometimes, like now, Reid got the impression she wished he'd toe the line just because it made things easier for her. He'd done that occasionally. But now he realized that his mother was perfectly capable of getting her way with Reid's dad when it mattered enough. Over Iris, for example. It frustrated and annoyed him, not because he didn't want Iris around, but because his mother's loyalty had always been a rock-solid given. He'd always assumed she was in his corner because she believed in him, cared about him enough to defend him. Now he wasn't sure.

She was looking out the window, at the weather maybe, or nothing.

"Mom? Trevor isn't going to care whether I show up."

She nodded. Reid waited for her to say he was right, he should be able to choose his own friends, but she kept staring out the window. She wasn't backing him; she was bailing.

Iris spoke over a mouthful of food. "Does he have other friends?"

"Yes, lots."

"And they're not your friends?"

"No."

Iris thought this over. "How many people do you know?"

"You mean about my age? A couple hundred or so at school. Plus kids from other schools."

Her eyes widened. "That's too many. How many friends do you need?"

Reid glanced at his mom, who had turned from the window. Her eyes were almost as wide as Iris's. Reid got the idea Iris didn't usually talk this much.

"If it's the right friend, just one."

~

After school, Reid went to Alex's. They ate Chinese takeout that Alex hoped wasn't meant for dinner, then went outside to play horse. Reid didn't like basketball as a team game, but horse was different, especially with Alex. He cared enough to try hard but not enough to remember who had won two minutes later.

Reid dribbled the ball a couple of times before launching his shot. It caught the inside of the rim and fell through the net.

Alex grabbed the rebound. "Lucky shit."

They hadn't played horse much lately, and Reid thought maybe they'd been hanging out less overall since the Incident. That's how they referred to Alex's overdose on the rare occasion it came up. Mostly they kept the topic and everything related to it, like Alex's therapy, at a distance, as if it had happened to someone else, someone they knew pretty well but didn't care that much about. As Reid waited for Alex to take his shot, he realized that not talking about the Incident was bogus.

Alex set up where Reid had shot from, took the shot, and missed. "Shit. H," he said.

Reid scooped up the ball and cradled it with his elbow. "So I want to ask you something."

"You want me to explain girls again?"

Reid smiled. "Seriously. Is this a chill time to talk about death?"

Alex stuck his hands in his pockets. "The Incident."

"Yeah, the Incident." Reid bounced the ball to his friend. "What happened?"

"You know what happened. I took a shitload of pills." He side-armed the ball to Reid.

Reid caught it, slid it to the ground, and trapped it under his foot. "Walk me through it."

Alex looked at him sideways, shoved his hands deeper into his pockets. "I told my parents. I told the shrink. I said I was honestly glad I didn't off myself. I think I told you that, too."

"You did. But walk me through it."

Alex blinked at him.

"I want to know."

His friend nodded. "Okay. Give me the ball." Reid tossed it to him, and Alex wandered the driveway, dribbling. "New Year's Eve and I was bored out of my skull. You had the nerve to back out of our plans because of a cold."

"The flu."

"Okay, man-flu. I forgive you." He spun on his heel, changing direction. "My parents were out, I was bored, so I had a cocktail. Rum and Mountain Dew."

"Classy."

"Right? So good I had another one. Still bored, so one more. Nothing but crap on TV, but I figured getting high would improve my attitude, so I smoked a joint. TV still sucked. Now it's almost midnight and I'm rummaging in my parents' bathroom and I find a stash of pills I'd never seen before." He came to a halt in front of Reid. "Secret stash." Before Reid could say anything, Alex walked away, bouncing the ball. "So I take a couple Xanax and wait for it to kick in. I'm just messing around, seeing what happens. And what happens is that I'm feeling different. One drink is different than none, two is different than one, three is even more different, especially if you add weed." He stopped, took a shot. All net.

"Your go," he said, but kept the dribbling the ball. "That's what no one gets, not that I've tried that hard to make my point."

"What? What doesn't anyone get?"

Alex held the ball in front like he was resting his hands on a beer gut. "Everyone talks about depression, about pain. It wasn't about pain. I wasn't in pain. I just wanted to feel different. Every time I took something I felt different. Inside each pill was a door and I wanted to keep opening them, see what was there. Sure, I lost my judgment—that was the dumb part, opening too many doors—but that wasn't the goal, if we can talk about Mountain Dew cocktails in the same breath as goal setting."

Alex stared at Reid expectantly. Reid nodded, though he wasn't sure he understood.

Alex went on. "If you feel different enough, you don't care what happens to you because it's not really you anymore. That's my point. But it's not the same as wanting to die. Not that I know. I'm just guessing. My best guess is it's not even close."

"I get it."

"Here's the other thing, though. The really fucked-up thing." He swiped the back of his hand across his mouth. "The shrink put me on Zoloft. Guess what? It makes me feel different." He laughed. "Joke's on them." He handed the ball to Reid. "That's all I've got."

"I get it." Reid bounced the ball a few times as if deciding when to take his shot but actually thinking that Alex was exactly right. Reid had the sense that his self—who he was—wasn't a fixed point somewhere inside of him. His self seemed more like a moving target, or like an amorphous blob that ought to be in a container with a label but wasn't. Maybe that's why he resented his father so much. His father acted like he knew who Reid ought to be and got pissed off when Reid couldn't come up with an alternative. He didn't have an alternative and wasn't going to pretend he did. It was hard, trying to figure yourself out, because it meant you didn't belong. All the kids he knew except for Alex stuffed themselves inside boxes to avoid the fear of not belonging.

Reid looked his friend in the eye. "I get it. I really do."

Alex clapped him on the shoulder. "No one does different like you. Now shoot, you pussy."

CHAPTER 18

Suzanne came down the stairs carrying a bundle of sheets long overdue for washing. She had underestimated how much time Iris would take from her day. Less than two weeks had passed since Iris had left the hospital, and Suzanne didn't yet feel comfortable leaving her at home alone. Suzanne and Whit had attempted to impress upon her the importance of staying in contact, but sixteen years of free ranging was hard to overcome. When Iris first arrived, she slept a lot; the doctors had said she would do so until she fully recovered from the infection and gained sufficient weight. Suzanne had been able to accomplish most of her duties then, but now Iris had more energy. Yesterday, while Suzanne had been on the phone taking care of Booster business, Iris had climbed to the top of the fifty-foot maple in their neighbor's backyard. At times Suzanne felt she'd taken on the responsibility of caring for a large, intelligent cat.

Iris was perched at the kitchen counter with her feet on the seat, leafing through *The Sibley Guide to Trees*. Suzanne went through to the laundry room and stuffed the sheets in the washer. It occurred to her that Iris's knowledge of trees was probably vast, even if she didn't necessarily know their scientific names or geographical distribution. Suzanne hadn't thought of asking Iris what she knew; she had been too busy teaching Iris about the world she lived in now. Suzanne filled the detergent dispenser, started the washer, and returned to the kitchen.

"Do you like that book?"

"Yes."

"Why?"

"I didn't know there were so many trees, different trees, in other places."

Suzanne nodded. "What about the trees you know already? Did you learn anything new?"

"No. But I don't know a lot of the words."

"I've got some other books. Hang on."

In a box in the attic she found her college botany textbooks. Why she had held on to them for all these years was anyone's guess. Many of them were too technical, such as *Introduction to Ecological Biochemistry*, but Suzanne thought some others might spark Iris's interest and perhaps give the two of them common ground.

Suzanne carried the books down the narrow ladder, folded it into the ceiling, and brought the stack into the kitchen.

"These were my books in college." She spread them on the counter: Stern's *Introduction to Plant Biology*, Herrick and Snow's *Iroquois Medical Botany*, and Balick and Cox's *Plants, People, and Culture: The Science of Ethnobotany*.

Iris scanned the titles. "What's an Iroquois?"

"A Native American." The girl stared at her. "An Indian, the people who lived in America before the Europeans arrived."

She picked up the book, opened it carefully, and turned a few pages. "My mother had a book like this but with more drawings."

"She did?" Suzanne had not thought to ask what books Iris's family might have had. She made a point of not prying, respecting Iris's connection to her home, the woods, her past. Whit and the police had a different view, claiming they had a right to know. Suzanne agreed that finding Iris's family was important but didn't see the rush. Iris was recovering from one ordeal while coping with another. More, Suzanne could tell Iris's memories were sacred to her. They were all she had left.

Iris studied the drawings closely, running her fingers along the outlines of the leaves and flowers as if touching the plants themselves.

"Did your mother teach you from the book?"

Iris looked up from the pages, her violet-blue eyes less guarded than usual. "Yes. We had to know the plants. For food, for medicine." She lowered her head and became very still.

Suzanne suspected for the first time that Iris was holding on to more than memories. The girl had secrets, too. But pushing her now would only drive her further into herself. Instead Suzanne reached for the ethnobotany text, held it in her hands for a moment, feeling its weight, then turned to a random page and began to read. How had she forgotten how fascinated she had been with the intersection of people and plants? Each culture across the world, no matter the habitat, had discovered the utility of plants not only for food but also for medicine and in religious practices. Often all these uses were linked: sustenance, wellness, and spirituality were bound together, the way a plant is rooted in the earth while reaching for the sun. And despite the advances in modern medicine—and they were considerable—powerful natural sources of healing were being discovered, or rediscovered, all the time. Everyone knew about penicillin, aspirin, and digitalis, but hundreds of other, lesser-known medicines had been derived from plants. An extract from yew trees was one of the most potent drugs available against breast cancer, and the rosy periwinkle was used to treat childhood leukemia. Who knew how many more were yet to be uncovered? Plant compounds held so many answers, if we only knew the right questions. Suzanne lost herself to the ideas and possibilities.

The next time she looked up, the oven clock said 4:40. Iris was slumped over, dozing on the open book.

"Crap," Suzanne whispered. She slipped off the stool and rummaged through the freezer for something to cobble together for dinner. Whit and Brynn had complained about the family's recent overreliance on takeout meals, but Suzanne hadn't had a chance to go to the store this week. Iris panicked when faced with crowds—anything more than a couple of people—and Suzanne had been too tired to grocery shop during an evening when Whit was home.

The doorbell rang. Suzanne set a package of Italian sausages and a container of marinara sauce on the counter and peered out the window. A white car she didn't recognize stood in the drive. Suzanne wiped her hands and went to the door. A woman about Suzanne's age greeted her with a sharp nod. She fished in the pocket of her sagging tan blazer, extracted a card, and handed it to Suzanne.

"Elizabeth Granger from Social Services, filling in for Ms. Rappoport."

"Oh, I hope she's all right."

"I really can't say."

Visits from Social Services were not announced—Ms. Rappoport had come the day after Iris moved in—but this stranger's stern manner ruffled Suzanne.

"Please come in. Iris is in the kitchen." She closed the door behind Ms. Granger and led the way, resisting the urge to look around for anything untoward. What could there be? And yet the presence of the social worker, an inspector, made her suspicious of her own suitability as a parent. Had she left an open bottle of wine on the counter? Were the bathrooms a mess? It was ridiculous that her mind went to these irrelevant details, but she couldn't help it.

Iris lifted her head and swiveled her stool to face them. Suzanne gave her a reassuring smile, and it was genuine, because Iris looked nothing like the girl who had been near death six weeks ago. She had a touch of color in her cheeks, which were no longer gaunt, and the circles under her eyes, dark as bruises for so long, had begun to fade. During the two weeks Iris had been at home with them, Suzanne had introduced her to basic grooming—using clippers for her nails, for instance, instead of a knife or her teeth—but Suzanne wasn't sure how far to go. People stared at Iris during excursions to the doctor and dentist because she was frail and unkempt. She didn't care how she looked, an attitude that drew attention in a town replete with the healthy and self-conscious. Just yesterday, Suzanne's hairdresser, Rae, a quiet woman not prone to gossip, had come to the house and cut Iris's hair. Iris had no opinion about styles, so Rae chose a shoulder-length layered cut with bangs. "You won't have to do a thing, Iris. Just comb it through and that's it." The cut was perfect, fresh and tidy, and accentuated Iris's beautiful eyes. In the doorway to the kitchen, with Ms. Granger behind her, Suzanne felt proud for the first time of the positive changes in the girl.

Suzanne introduced Ms. Granger to Iris and offered the woman something to drink.

"No, thank you." She moved to the far end of the counter, removed a sheaf of papers from her case, consulted them, and spoke without looking up. "Iris, is it? Sixteen years old." She regarded Iris, frowned at the unlikely veracity of this figure, and returned to the paperwork. "And no known family."

Suzanne came around the counter and stood at the kitchen sink, as near as she could get to standing between them. Ms. Granger ignored her and began asking Iris a series of questions about what she had been doing since the last visit. Iris replied succinctly.

Voices floated in from the entry. Suzanne glanced at the clock. It would be Tinsley dropping off Brynn from an after-school project. Suzanne's stomach knotted.

"Oh, here you are." Tinsley's tone suggested Suzanne had been evading her, which was not far from the truth. Brynn followed her in and went straight to the fridge, her gaze lingering on the caseworker. Tinsley gave the woman a quick up-and-down and swooped in on Iris. "So this is Iris! How lovely to meet you, dear, at long last!"

Iris pulled back as she studied Tinsley's face.

Suzanne said, "Iris, this is my mother, Mrs. Royce." She introduced Ms. Granger to her mother and daughter and turned her attention to

Iris, who had clamped her hands over her ears. Too many people. Too much talking.

Ms. Granger made a notation on her sheet. "This is the first time your mother has met Iris? Is she visiting from out of town?"

"Oh, no!" Tinsley interjected. "My husband and I aren't far at all. I don't quite know why we haven't been invited."

"Iris is recuperating, Mother. As you know."

Ms. Granger said, "We prefer the foster child to be integrated into all the normal family activities."

"Good luck with that," Brynn said as she ate from a pint of mango gelato. "Especially the 'normal' part."

Ms. Granger consulted her watch. "Iris." When the girl did not respond, the caseworker shouted her name. The girl slid her hands from her ears. "Please show me your bedroom."

Iris looked at Suzanne, who nodded.

As Iris crossed the kitchen on the way to the stairs, Brynn said, "She wants to see where you sleep, Iris, so you really ought to show her the hammock." Brynn pointed at the back door with her spoon.

"Really, Brynn." Suzanne understood her daughter had become increasingly jealous of the attention Iris was absorbing, but this was too much.

Ms. Granger went to the window and peered into the yard. "Mrs. Blakemore, is Iris sleeping outside?"

"Sometimes, yes. When the weather is nice. It relaxes her."

"Is that right? I'm surprised you didn't construct a kennel for her." She frowned as she scribbled on her pad.

Brynn stifled a laugh and Suzanne shot her a look.

Tinsley sighed and adjusted her handbag on her arm. "I'm sure my daughter and her husband are doing everything they can to help this unfortunate girl." She blinked in Iris's direction.

"Thanks, Mother," Suzanne said.

Tinsley wasn't finished. "But clearly a child that tumbles out of the woods is simply too wild to be inserted into a civilized situation such as this." She swept her hand to include everything around them. But what bespoke their civilization? The stainless-steel appliances? The Brazilian granite? Certainly not her mother's manners, referring to Iris as if she weren't there.

Ms. Granger appeared annoyed. "I'm not here to discuss theory. I'm here to see that Iris is safe and cared for."

Tinsley ignored her and continued in the same vein, talking in a loud voice about what was proper and right. Suzanne wanted to silence her mother, whose opinions on this matter were irrelevant, but didn't know how without appearing rude or overly defensive.

Iris had been standing in the doorway to the dining room, following the volley of conversation. "I am." Her voice was a whisper.

Suzanne put her hand on her mother's arm to quiet her. "Iris, what did you say?"

She lifted her gaze from the floor and spoke directly to Suzanne. "I am safe and cared for."

The room was quiet for one beat. Two.

Brynn tossed her spoon in the sink, letting it rattle. "Before we get too deep into this Lifetime movie, did anyone mention the squirrel Iris skinned and stashed in the fridge?"

Suzanne bore the astonished glares she received from both her mother and Ms. Granger and decided it wasn't worth mentioning that the squirrel had been roadkill.

A half hour later, the kitchen was empty. Brynn was doing homework in her room, and Iris was napping, or perhaps coloring. Suzanne was simultaneously cleaning the kitchen and making dinner. While the sausage defrosted in the microwave, she opened the dishwasher to load it and found the dishes inside were clean. Reid had been charged with emptying it before school that morning. Suzanne sighed and began putting the dishes away. Before Iris, the house had been tidy, obsessively so.

It didn't bother Suzanne to know four loads of laundry were waiting, the stack of mail on the entry table threatened to slide to the floor, and the dining table was covered with art supplies and paper from Spanish fiesta posters she'd helped Brynn with last night. It didn't bother her in the least, but it would irritate the hell out of Whit. The cleaning people were due in the morning—today was Tuesday, wasn't it?—which meant Suzanne had tonight to organize it all. She'd just have to move a little faster.

As she executed the mindless subroutines (rinse, wipe, chop, stir, rinse, wipe), she replayed the visit from the caseworker, wincing at her mother's comments, though they were hardly unexpected. And Brynn. Brynn was angry, angrier than usual, and Suzanne felt responsible. She would find a way to spend time with her daughter, perhaps take her out to dinner this weekend, just the two of them. Yet the idea made her uneasy; they were likely to sit in strained silence or stumble over conversations that meant nothing, or everything. But she had to try. She had sought to make Brynn understand why helping Iris was the right thing to do, why she felt an obligation because she had found the girl, but realized now this was the wrong tack. Long before Iris had come into their lives, Brynn had pushed Suzanne away. Her daughter still needed her—to do things, to play the role of mom for others, and, occasionally, to hold her as only a mother could. Mostly, though, Brynn was contemptuous and dismissive. Suzanne had to get past the pain of that and find a way to reach her daughter. She wasn't certain she had the will to give more, to risk more; she'd already spent fifteen years giving to Brynn. Hadn't she earned a spoonful of compassion, a hint of friendship? Instead the scales tipped toward Brynn's side more than ever. Brynn seemed impervious to Suzanne's best efforts, and Whit was no help. Suzanne had asked him to step in, to address Brynn's anger and manipulation, but since he saw a different Brynn, Suzanne's data were suspect.

Mothers and daughters. Could Suzanne reasonably expect a better relationship than the one she had with Tinsley?

Suzanne set the water to boil for the pasta and began chopping onions for the sauce, keeping faith with the idea that a home-cooked meal was a building block for a stronger family. It almost made her laugh. She did, however, hold on to the thin hope that having brought Iris home would help their family, not through a common bond—they were not aligned over Iris—but through a revival of her own enthusiasm for parenting. It did, in the end, fall on her. She'd done everything she could for Brynn and Reid—at least she thought she had—and it clearly had not been enough. They did not, the four of them, share a life. They shared a home, money, the TV remote, but Suzanne couldn't identify what held them together, other than the fact of being family. She worried that this, too, was a failure in parenting, for she was certain other families had more cohesion. If they didn't, why didn't it bother anyone except her? Maybe it did. Maybe mothers everywhere, and fathers, too, in smaller numbers, questioned what they had done, what they had accomplished in having children, raising them, in giving up and giving in, in giving, giving, giving.

Suzanne would give to Iris. And because the girl was so different, perhaps Suzanne could discover where she had gone wrong, discover how her family, which was once imbued with more promise than she could have imagined, seemed to be held together by the fact of their relationships and by the force of her will rather than by shared goals and mutual respect.

She would give to Iris and hope for the gift of insight in return.

CHAPTER 19

Whit ran up the front stairs, exhilarated by the success of his afternoon. The enormous tract of land he'd been vying for—over a hundred acres right outside of town—was nearly his. Last week the deal had looked shaky; the landowner, a farmer whose family had worked the land for generations, had gotten cold feet, and had begun fantasizing that his sons would change their minds about their white-collar jobs in Richmond and Annapolis and take up farming, as he'd always hoped they would. The only answer to equivocation, especially this late in the acquisition process, was more money. Whit was confident the package would hold together. Hell, they were going to walk away with more than any other residential deal in the area's history—but no one wanted to dip deeper into their pockets, even if all it required was a bit more leveraging. But he had calmed everyone down and gotten the key player on board: his new buddy Robert Shipstead. The rest had followed as he'd known they would. Business was relationships. It had never been clearer.

He went inside and dropped his briefcase at the foot of the entry table, steadying the sloping mountain of mail on its surface. He felt a pinch of exasperation but pushed it aside and strode through the dining room, where the mess from some school project still hadn't been cleaned up after two days. Thank God they were going out.

"Hey, sweetheart." He winced at the state of the kitchen and, worse, the state of his wife. She held a mixing bowl in the crook of her arm and scooped the contents into a pan. Her hair had fallen out of the clip, and she puffed it away from her face. Her shirt was splattered with tomato sauce.

"Hi. How did your day go?"

"Fantastic. But we have dinner with Robert and Juliette. And Malcolm and Mia, remember?" Whit kept his tone light.

She froze, spatula held aloft. "Oh, crap. The social worker came by and I got behind. How much time do I have?"

"Ten minutes to be on time."

"I can do it." She dumped the rest of the pasta in the pan, set the bowl in the sink, grabbed the container of shaved Parmesan, and tossed a handful on top. She punched the controls on the wall oven and slid the pan in, then punched some more to set the timer. As she returned the perishables to the fridge, she said, "Whit, please let Reid know he needs to look out for Iris. And tell Brynn the pasta will be ready in thirty minutes." She glanced around her. "And the kitchen needs to be cleaned up before we get back."

"Brynn has to clean up?"

"No, the three of them should work it out." She was already on her way upstairs.

Whit followed. "What's the bribe?"

Suzanne laughed and shook her head. "I've got nothing. Appeal to their sense of fairness and duty."

"I'll put three tens on the counter."

"Two. We haven't made Iris into a capitalist yet."

They arrived at Triomphe only five minutes late and, critically, before Robert and Juliette arrived. The ink wouldn't be dry on the deal for another month, so every meeting was a presentation, an opportunity to shore up the deal. Usually this felt like pressure, but tonight it could not have been easier. Whit was on the cusp of becoming the person he'd always dreamed he might be. He could never quite relax when the kids were small, leaving the whole family vulnerable. One bad stomach bug could upend a week's worth of plans. Maybe they weren't out of the woods yet, but Whit could see the light coming in from the clearing. Brynn was learning to drive. The milestones were spreading out, and his career was gaining momentum at just the right time. It was a great feeling.

The three couples sat at a round table, away from the noise of the bar. Malcolm and Mia were in top form, meaning Mia was on the charming side of outspoken and Malcolm did nothing to provoke her. The food, as always, was superb, and the wines—Whit deferred to Robert on this—were delicious. And Suzanne? Well, no woman in the world could look so beautiful with only ten minutes' prep time. She wore a simple orange silk dress and the silver hoop earrings and bangles he'd given her last Christmas. She had piled her hair on top of her head and allowed a small wave to fall from each temple. Her eyes, those gorgeous brown eyes, caught the light whenever she looked his way.

Mia, on his left, touched his elbow and leaned in a little, confiding. "She's exhausted, you know."

"She looks fantastic."

"Well, yes. It's Suzanne. But believe me, she's exhausted."

"We all are. Isn't that a badge of honor these days?"

She rolled her eyes. "Even you probably noticed there are three kids in your house now."

"Even me?"

Mia sped right by. "What do you think of her?"

"Iris? She's quiet. Sleeps a lot. Her manners are worse than mine."

She nodded. "She's like an extremely fast toddler."

"Suzanne must've told you that I wasn't crazy about the whole Iris deal."

She laughed a little and sipped her wine. "'The Iris deal.' I like that."

"She didn't have to do it."

Her face became serious, her blue eyes shading to navy. "She absolutely did."

"Why?"

"Damned if I know." She picked up her fork and stared at her plate as if seeing it for the first time. Typical Mia, she'd eaten the shrimp off the risotto and left the rest. "I'm not sure she knows."

The conversation seemed like a riddle. He was becoming impatient. "I don't get it. I don't. Suzanne has so much going on already."

"Don't we all? That's the point, Whit." She stabbed the air with her fork. "It's not a whim. It's not a fluke. I don't know what's up with Suzanne and Iris, but it's something."

"Something?"

"Yes, something. And God knows we all need something."

Whit looked across the table at Suzanne. She was listening to Robert describe a recent vacation in the Maldives. She wasn't a fan of beaches, but you wouldn't know that from her expression. He was struck by how skilled she was at not appearing exhausted, at not giving away that she'd thrown herself together in ten minutes and was probably bored out of her mind by this guy she had to pretend interested her. Maybe he did interest her; Robert was all right. That was the thing. It was so hard to tell with Suzanne, even if he asked. His wife accommodated everyone—the kids, him, her parents—keeping them together, keeping things running. Duty. Suzanne wore it like a cloak.

Suzanne caught his eye and her smile sent an uneasy ripple through his stomach, the tail flip of a fish. "We all need something," Mia had said. Whit had tried to give Suzanne everything, to prove himself, and tonight, before Mia spoke, he'd felt he had succeeded. He was worthy.

But now, as he returned his wife's smile, doubt settled on him like a fine mist. What if what Suzanne needed wasn't something he could give?

CHAPTER 20

Reid was relieved the three of them had managed to clean the kitchen without fighting or, rather, without Brynn picking a fight. It helped that Iris loved washing dishes. "It's the warm water," she said.

He had retreated to his room to finish his calculus homework, saving his reading for AP English until after he had meditated. It was only nine o'clock, so he texted Alex to see if he wanted to come over, but Alex had blown off his work for days and was in catch-up mode. Reid couldn't understand why Alex created stress for himself, especially now, with all the teachers cutting him slack, telling him not to worry about deadlines too much. As if what had happened on New Year's Eve had anything to do with schoolwork. Adults assumed a kid who did that was depressed, but the truth was kids—even smart kids, especially smart kids—did stupid shit all the time for no other reason than to experiment, to see how it felt, as Alex had said. For some kids it was cutting. For other kids it was bashing the shit out of someone on the field, or being an asshole on social media. It was all the same. Everyone felt too much and not enough at the same time. Reid did, too, which was why he meditated. It flattened things out, if only for a while. Getting balanced was impossible. High school was a wild ride, and sometimes the sane response was to jump off, even if it meant getting hurt.

If only Alex would meditate. He would argue the fine points of religious theory for hours, but he wouldn't sit still with himself. Reid didn't press him, though. He respected Alex too much.

Reid closed his book, left his room, and went to Iris's door, which was partly open. She was talking softly. He couldn't make out the words, but the rhythm of her speech sounded like a conversation. Confusing, because the phone she used to listen to music wasn't activated for calls, messaging, or browsing. His mom didn't want Iris exposed to too much at once. Reid felt awkward about interrupting, even though he knew she couldn't really be talking to anyone. He had turned away to go back to his room when Iris spoke clearly.

"Someone there?"

He stuck his head inside. She was sitting on the floor in profile to him, her back against the bed, facing the window. She faced a window whenever possible. As she turned toward him, she pushed something under the bed, but it was hard to see what since only the bedside lamp was on. "Sorry," he said. "Didn't mean to interrupt."

"It's okay."

Out of the corner of his eye, he saw something scuttle along the darkened baseboard. "Did you see that?"

"A mouse."

"Oh." There were mice in the basement—everyone had mice in the basement—and once in a while, one would turn up in the kitchen. "Do you have food up here? Maybe my mom didn't tell you about not bringing food upstairs."

She dipped her chin. "She told me. But I . . ."

She motioned for him to come closer and lifted the bed skirt. He bent down. It took a moment for his eyes to adapt. Boxes of crackers and cookies, a pile of energy bars, a few apples, a bag of something, nuts maybe. A lot of food.

"Why?"

She shrugged. He noticed it was a habit she'd adopted in the last week or so, no doubt copied from Brynn—or maybe him.

"Are you planning to run away?"

She shrugged again.

Reid let it drop. At least she was trusting him enough to show him the food stash. He stood up. "Well, the mouse is a problem."

Iris nodded. "Sit on the bed and don't move."

"We can set a trap."

"What about Vishnu?"

His snake would only accept live prey, but Reid had never given him anything more challenging than a wriggling pinkie. "He does need to eat, but we get baby mice for him."

She shook her head hard, squeezing her eyes tight. "There's a mouse *here*."

Iris's circumstances in this house, with his family, confounded her to the brink of madness. Her logic was inescapable, and Reid felt for her.

He climbed on the bed and crossed his legs, curious about how she'd go about luring the mouse and catching it. He settled himself. It could be a while.

Iris crouched low and moved noiselessly to the far wall under the window. Half the room was in total darkness, including the area near the door where he had seen the mouse. Iris was completely still and, although half in shadow, nearly invisible. Her head was cocked, and the tips of her fingers grazed the wood floor. She slid forward so slowly he was not sure she had moved at all; only the pattern of shadow on her back gave her away. She was not simply predatory. She was not of this world, at least the world he knew. The air in the room seemed to have become denser from her concentration and the disguise of it. Reid held his breath.

A shadow flickered and snapped. Iris sprang to her feet and took a step toward the bed. Dangling between her thumb and index finger was the mouse, immobilized by the pinch at the scruff of its neck.

Reid jumped off the bed. "Whoa! That was awesome!"

For the first time since he'd met her, Iris grinned so wide her eyes crinkled at the corners.

She followed Reid into his room. He lifted the lid off the cage—an extra-large terrarium with a mesh top—and Iris dropped the mouse in. It froze on the shaving-covered floor, either because it was stunned from being handled or because it had detected the snake. The snake was sprawled along one side of the cage, half-uncoiled. It lifted its head, testing the air with its tongue again and again. The mouse shook itself and circled its head, sniffing and searching, one circle, two, three. It took a few tentative steps. The snake stiffened. It had spotted the mouse. Reid was reminded of Iris only moments before; the intense concentration and something else as well, the cold confidence of a machine, a laser-guided missile.

The mouse turned and scrabbled at the glass wall, rising up on its hind legs. Uncoiling completely, the snake approached, sliding silently, its head tracking the mouse's uncertain movements until the snake's nose was inches from the mouse, now backed into a corner.

The snake struck and tucked the mouse into a coil, one loop, two. The mouse was locked in a noose from which it couldn't possibly escape. It happened so fast, like a magic trick that succeeds even when you are paying close attention. When Reid fed pinkies to Vishnu, the snake didn't give them the big squeeze. He just swallowed them.

Iris watched without emotion. Reid figured she'd seen a lot of animals die, and had killed some of them herself. After a few moments, she went to sit in the chair by the window. "Why do you have this snake?"

"A couple years ago I was mowing the lawn."

Iris shook her head in a way he'd learned meant she didn't understand.

"The short grass around the house? When the weather gets warmer, it has to be cut once a week."

"Why?"

"Why? Oh, you mean why do we bother?"

She nodded.

"So people can walk across it, play on it, I guess."

"I've never seen anyone do that."

"Maybe more when we were little."

She nodded, unconvinced.

"Anyway, I was mowing the grass, with a machine. Normally we pay someone to do it, but they hadn't come for some reason. Mom was having people over and wanted it cut, so she asked me."

"The people were going to play on the lawn?"

"No. They were going to be near the lawn, so she wanted it to look nice."

Iris didn't even nod. She was right. It was stupid.

Reid sighed. "So the lawn mower, the machine, hits this snake. Just the tip of its tail got chopped off. He was only a foot long then." He expected Iris to nod but she didn't. "What?"

"The snake would have healed if it was just the end of the tail."

"Well, I didn't know that. I wanted to help it."

She smiled, just a little.

Reid felt foolish. He gestured toward the cage. Vishnu was working on swallowing the mouse; it was halfway down, more actually, because getting past the mouse's shoulders was the hard part. "He's been here since. My dad was against it, didn't want him in the house. He said a snake wasn't worth getting upset about."

"Suzanne disagreed?"

"Well, I don't think she wanted it either, but she could see it mattered to me."

Reid paused, feeling he'd gotten to the important point of the story, the message he wanted to relate to Iris. His mother had backed him up. The snake was a reminder of that. His father always seemed to win. He was a winner! Brynn, too. Keeping the snake, with its strange odors, its sinister blackness, its appetite for live meals, was proof that sometimes the messy, the ugly, the imperfect could win. His father had offered to get him a snake from a pet store, one that didn't smell and would accept dead prey, or frozen ones they could keep on hand, like those tamales from Whole Foods he loved. But Reid wouldn't budge. He didn't see why he should.

Reid's relationship with his father hadn't deteriorated gradually. Reid could remember the exact day. He had been twelve, and his father had enrolled him in a summer tennis program at the club. Reid protested. He preferred baseball and reading. Tennis was nerve-racking. He held his breath the entire time the racket was in his hand, terrified the ball would go out or into the net, which it always did eventually. He couldn't get over the inescapable fact that he could hit a dozen or more great shots in a single rally and still lose the point. And after that point was another. On and on and on.

But his father was adamant. "Your forehand will be so strong from baseball. You'll see."

Reid had no choice but to give in. And he did try—he wasn't a quitter—but that didn't add up to much. Many of the boys played year-round, and some who didn't were more talented and motivated than he was. Reid performed well in the drills. His father was right about his forehand, and Reid had a long reach at the net. But when it came to playing for points, the weight of the matches bore down on him. He concentrated on not losing badly, which wasn't the same as trying to win. His father monitored his performance, stopping by to chat with the coaches and showing up at random times. Reid became irritated. He felt he'd done what his father wanted. He was wasting twelve hours a week at tennis camp, but for his father, it wasn't enough.

Reid sat out the midsummer tournament, feigning illness, but found no way to avoid the competition at the summer's end. It was single-elimination format. He'd won his first match, beating a kid who wanted to be there less than he did. His father was so overjoyed it made Reid want to drill a forehand into his father's stomach. Reid's opponent for the second match that afternoon was a boy Reid knew he could beat if he tried. But something in him turned sour. His father stayed to watch, even though it was midweek and he should have been at work. That caused the sourness inside Reid to harden into a rank mass, the way a dead animal becomes a vile piece of flattened leather. He threw the match but he did it slowly, playing well at first, then losing his edge, finally faltering completely. He ended the match on his service game with four double faults, then shook his opponent's hand and walked off the court.

His father practically assaulted him. "What the hell happened?"

"I didn't need to win."

"What do you mean? You had that match."

Reid shrugged. "What difference does it make?"

Blood rushed to his father's face, and it frightened Reid. His father was pretty even tempered. "What difference? You have everything. You have every privilege imaginable. You don't have the right to throw things away, to be mediocre."

Reid felt his own cheeks redden. He raised his arm to wipe his forehead on the sleeve of his polo shirt.

His father snatched his arm out of the air.

Reid yanked his arm back. "What? It's just tennis." But even as he said it, he knew it was a weak defense, although he wasn't sure why.

"'Just tennis.' You won't get anywhere with that sort of thinking."

"Maybe I don't want to get anywhere."

His father laughed and shook his head. "You don't know it yet, but you'll find out. If you don't have ambition, Reid, you're not a man. You're not anything."

Reid glared at his father. Irritation and confusion and pure emotion he didn't know how to define roiled inside him. He walked away, dropping his tennis bag at his father's feet. Later, in his room, he scratched through his father's words, pulling at them like rubber bands binding him. And much later, when his anger subsided, he explored the idea that his father was wrong, that it was possible to be a man, a good man, perhaps better than his father, with no ambition at all.

Now, in his room, Reid returned his attention to the snake, and to Iris, who was looking out the window and frowning.

"What?" Reid said, curious as much as frustrated.

"Why is Vishnu still here? He healed a long time ago."

Reid opened his mouth to explain, but what could he say? That having a snake was cool? That he got perverse enjoyment from knowing his father didn't want it here?

"Tell you what, Iris." He crossed to his desk and picked up his laptop. "Let's go downstairs where the Wi-Fi is stronger, and maybe we can look for a good place to set Vishnu free."

~

Brynn came downstairs on the hunt for ice cream. On her way through the living room, she spotted Reid's head sticking out over the back of the couch. It had been forever since they'd hung out, just the two of them. Either she or Reid—or both—were too busy nursing a wound from a run-in or a slight, or just feeling that their mom or dad had favored the other. Maybe their parents should've had three kids so it'd be harder to feel singled out, or alone.

She decided she'd test the waters, see if Reid could manage not to be a self-righteous jerk for a change.

"Hey, you want some ice cream?" Brynn came around the couch. Shit. The Stray was curled up in the corner of the couch. She was such a runt, Brynn hadn't seen her. Reid was scrolling around a map on his laptop. Iris closed her eyes when the image moved. Unbelievable.

"Sounds good." Reid gave a guarded look and said to Iris, "Want some?"

Iris untangled herself. She had this creepy way of tucking her arms and legs around her body, all elbows and head, like a chick stuffed inside a shell, big eyed and wet. "Okay."

Brynn clenched her teeth. All she'd wanted was to chill with her brother for a while, and now she was the ice cream waitress. She stomped off to the kitchen before her anger flew out of her. She didn't like to lose control; it frightened her. But so many things pissed her off, especially since Iris had arrived. Their family was kind of messed up—whose wasn't?—but Iris somehow made it all too obvious, at least to Brynn. She could see how her mother was hungry to pour her time and energy into another project, in this case a random kid somehow more worthwhile than her own daughter. Not exactly an ego boost. She could see how her dad, strong in every other way, didn't have the balls to stand up to her mother and keep this misfit from ruining their lives. And right now, Brynn could see all too clearly how her brother, who once upon a time was a cute, lovable kid, had become such an absolute loser that he would actually choose an anorexic hillbilly half mute over her.

She yanked open the freezer compartment and pulled out the ice cream containers: a new pint of Chunky Monkey (her brother's favorite), a half-pint of Cherry Garcia (her dad's), and a near-empty chocolate gelato. The quart of vanilla her mother always kept on hand didn't count. It was so fucking symbolic that Brynn's favorite dessert was the one they were out of. How hard was it to go shopping?

Her phone vibrated in her pocket. She checked the screen: a text from Robby. They'd been exchanging texts and Snapchats practically every day since she'd found him on Tinder roulette two weeks ago, and they'd had one extremely memorable Skype session at the end of which he'd asked her to take off her shirt. She'd given him a flash—some boob—then said she had to go, which was sort of true since she could hear her parents coming upstairs. She hadn't heard from him since.

ROBBY: Want to meet up sometime? Daytime's fine if you're scared of the dark. (smiley face)

BRYNN: Sounds dope! Maybe I'll let you know, ok?

Meeting a college boy for who knows what. Her parents would die, but only if they knew.

Brynn got three spoons from a drawer and opened the gelato. "Ice cream's in here!" She wasn't about to take orders.

As Iris walked in, followed by Reid, a thought crossed Brynn's mind. Being pissed off at Iris wasn't going to do anything. Neither was blaming her parents or Reid. If Brynn wanted to get rid of Iris, she had to make everyone see how a kid like that was never going to fit in here. The social worker could find a different family, or Iris could just take her backpack and slink back into the woods. It didn't matter to Brynn. What mattered was getting her life back, the one she had a right to. And it might be that the best way to accomplish that would be to make friends with Iris, or at least pretend.

"Iris," Brynn said sweetly. "Which one of these do you like best?"

The girl gave her a look like she expected to get poisoned. Brynn couldn't blame her but kept on smiling just the same.

CHAPTER 21

Morning sun angled through the kitchen window as Suzanne made phone calls and wrote emails at the counter. She was not keeping up and spent much of her time apologizing to the other members of the Boosters committee, the carpool moms, school personnel—everyone who had depended on her. No one felt more neglected nor voiced her disapproval more vocally than her mother—with the possible exception of Brynn. Suzanne rued the day she had promised Tinsley help with her charity fund-raiser, for which Suzanne had neither the energy nor the will. How was it that she had never considered refusing her mother or, indeed, the other requests? How automated she had become. She performed duties because she had been asked, or because it seemed to be required of her, a justification of her own relevance necessitated by the privilege she had been born into, a special shiny coating she had never thrown off. Tinsley didn't seem to suffer from it, and Suzanne envied her that.

She closed her laptop. A wave of despondency and self-pity flowed through her, both unfamiliar emotions. Her hectic schedule had prevented the reflection necessary to breed such feelings, and that was a good thing. Now Suzanne had to be home almost all the time, tutoring and supervising Iris. There were few meetings and no lunches, no one-on-ones over coffee. Suzanne was as busy as before but nevertheless now found time to enter rabbit holes of self-examination and worry. Perhaps it wasn't time, per se, but being forced to evaluate her life in order to explain it, justify it to Iris.

Suzanne rose, dismissing self-reflection in favor of action. She placed her coffee cup in the dishwasher and went upstairs to Iris's room. The girl lay on the floor, gazing out the window at the sky. The healthier Iris became, the sadder she seemed. Weren't the strongest animals at the zoo the ones that seemed to suffer the most? Suzanne had been trying to acclimate Iris to people, traffic, machinery, but progress had been slow, and it was easier most days simply not to bother. Even a walk down their street had the potential to traumatize the girl. A few days ago, a police car had suddenly appeared, lights flashing, siren wailing, and Iris had collapsed into a ball on the sidewalk, where she stayed for half an hour. Still, Suzanne couldn't give up. They both needed to get out.

"Let's go for a walk, okay?"

Iris didn't move. "Walk to where?"

"I thought we'd take a short drive to a park."

"A park?"

"A place with grass and trees, and no houses."

"Are there people?"

"Maybe a few. Maybe none."

Iris shrugged. "If it's not far."

The girl's grudging consent reminded Suzanne of Brynn. How had that happened? She pushed the comparison out of her mind. Iris was insecure and afraid. Brynn, on the other hand, was truly indifferent, except when she was adamant.

They were ready five minutes later and rode in silence during the short drive to Pen Park. Several golfers dotted the fairways and greens visible from the road. Suzanne turned left past the tennis courts, most of which were in use. Farther on, at the parking lot for the trail, there was only one other car, and the adjacent baseball diamond stood empty. Suzanne breathed a sigh of relief.

She stashed her handbag under the seat, grabbed a water bottle from the console, locked the car, and slipped the keys into the pocket of her jean jacket. Had she been with anyone else, she would have commented on the perfect day: fresh April air, leaves beginning to unfurl on the early-blooming trees, the scent of grassy warmth in the air. But Iris preferred silence and Suzanne respected her wishes. Small talk was just that, after all.

Somewhere in the nearby trees, a pileated woodpecker sang out its stuttering laugh of a call. Suzanne glanced over the hood of the Navigator to where Iris was waiting. The girl was listening for the call to repeat, and when it did, she smiled.

The beginning of the trail was a fitness course. The trail was paved and offered exercise stations every few hundred yards. If Iris was curious about these, she didn't let on. She peered intently into the surrounding woods and strayed off the pavement onto the grass verge peppered with violets. Suzanne thought to direct her back to the trail but didn't have the heart to break the silence for yet another rule about life in civilization. Stepping on a few violets didn't seem so egregious. In any case, Iris seemed to instinctively avoid treading on the flowers. Her small feet hardly made an impression at all.

After a quarter of a mile, Suzanne pointed left to a dirt path. "This way, Iris." The nature trail ran for a mile and a half through a swath of woods between the Rivanna River and the golf course.

Suzanne had supposed Iris would walk beside her now that the trail was not paved, but she continued on the verge, staying slightly ahead of Suzanne, and allowing her hand to brush across the understory plants. Suzanne was about to remind Iris to be cognizant of poison ivy, but Iris undoubtedly knew more about plants than she did. Suzanne resolved to stop worrying about Iris and enjoy the walk, a rare unscheduled slice of freedom in her day. She half closed her eyes, feeling the sun on her face and relishing the quiet.

A rustling noise startled her. She caught a glimpse of Iris's white shirt disappearing into the shrubby edge of the woods and bounded after her.

"Iris!"

The girl was moving so fast Suzanne thought she was hallucinating. The white shirt darted between trees, the low branches seeming to part for her.

"Iris! Wait!"

Suzanne pushed her way through clumps of dense bushes, stepping over downed logs and casting off thorny brambles that caught her clothing. Iris had disappeared, but Suzanne could hear her ahead and pressed on. What was the girl doing? Running away? She could've done that from home.

Suzanne ran, panting and winded from the effort of squeezing through narrow gaps between trees and disentangling herself from the clinging, strangling growth. She called for Iris again and again. She stopped to catch her breath and listen. A squirrel scurried across branches above her head. A mourning dove cooed.

She turned around, half expecting Iris to materialize behind her, instead of in front, the way she'd gone, but there was nothing but woods, thick and green and moist. Suzanne spun slowly in a circle, once around, twice, three times, searching, listening, hoping. With each turn, her breath quickened. During the third turn, all she could hear was her heart thundering in her chest. Sweat trickled down her back. Her hands were ice cold.

"Iris!"

Suzanne fell to the ground, clutching her heart, the pain in her chest exploding. Fear dove through her like a stooping hawk, talons piercing her skin.

~

The path confounded Iris. The hard surface was an affront to the woods crouching on either side, almost as wrong as the trees in town given only a small square of earth to grow out of, roots pushing up from below, cracking and buckling the sidewalk, teaching a lesson no one seemed to hear. The dirt path was better, but Iris couldn't be adjacent to the woods, running her hand along the supple leaves and spiky stems. It wasn't enough. She had to go inside.

As soon as she did, Ash called to her. *Hurry up, you slowpoke!*

So she ran after him, her legs springing with pent-up energy, her lungs sucking in air that smelled of violets and beginnings. As she bounded through the woods, among the trees, with the trees, the quiet power of the seasons, all four, but especially spring, was inside her again. She couldn't feel it staring out a window, or reading about birds in a book, or even climbing a tall maple. She had to be enveloped in green to feel the buzz of her own life.

Hurry up, Iris!

Ash was here. Everything was all right now. She ran headlong into the wide joy of it. Running, running, running.

She came to a stop beside a walnut tree. Her scalp tingled and her muscles hummed. She wiped the sweat from her forehead with the back of her hand, feeling alive for the first time since she'd left the woods. But this was only a park, and she didn't know exactly what that meant.

She asked Ash, *How big are these woods anyway?*

Instead of Ash's voice, which was completely different from any voice or any sound, Iris heard her name, a shout coming from behind her, far behind. She held her breath and listened.

Again, her name. It was Suzanne. And there was terror in the sound.

Dread descended on her like a sudden downpour. She put a finger to her mouth and bit the nail.

Ash! I don't want to go.

He didn't answer.

Ash!

All the joy she had felt leaked out of her, and she banged her fists on her thighs in frustration. Her eyes welled with tears. "I don't want to go," she said out loud, and laid her cheek against the rough bark of the tree.

She stood there a moment more, then ran back the way she had come, feeling the weight in her legs and the pull in her heart with each stride. What had been untethered flight became effort, tied to the earth. She heard Suzanne whimpering. Iris pushed aside the branches of a small sumac and saw Suzanne, crouched, her jaw muscles tensed, her hands gripping her knees, white knuckled.

Iris squatted beside her. "What's wrong?"

Suzanne's shoulders trembled like the haunches of a rabbit caught in the open. Iris thought to lay a hand on her back, but she had never touched Suzanne and didn't know if it was the right thing to do, considering her state. Suzanne lifted her head. Her face was gray. She pitched forward onto her hands and vomited. Suzanne retched again and again until there was nothing left. Iris breathed more easily; in her experience, vomiting was restorative. If only she had some mountain mint to give Suzanne. She would feel better right away.

Suzanne wiped her mouth on her sleeve and pushed herself to her feet.

"What's wrong?" Iris said.

Suzanne's eyes were wet and red. "It's just something that happens. Not often."

Iris nodded but didn't understand at all.

Suzanne smoothed her hair, licked her lips, and adjusted her jacket. She was pulling herself together now. Her body and her mind were sewing up the hole that had been ripped open. She spoke softly. "Please don't tell anyone."

"Okay."

"Not even Whit."

"Okay."

"I'm not asking you to lie."

Iris nodded, unsure what sort of lie the not telling might become. It was one of the most confusing things about living with the Blakemores, all the things people didn't say or only half said. She tried to remember if her family had been like that, when they were all together. It was so long ago, she wasn't sure, but she couldn't think of anything they would have to lie about. She and Ash would try to duck out of chores now and again, say they'd checked a trapline or a nest when they hadn't, but they didn't do it often. If they did, they all might starve.

Suzanne said, "Let's go back," and started off.

"It's this way." Iris pointed northeast.

Suzanne fell in behind Iris, who made sure to go slowly until they emerged from the woods and rejoined the trail.

The air around Suzanne was heavy with thoughts. Finally, she said, "You ran off."

It was a statement, a question, and a complaint.

Iris shrugged. It was the easiest thing to do when she had done something wrong or wasn't sure.

"I came back."

They returned along the trail to the car without talking. As they drove out of the park, back into the noisy, busy world, Suzanne said, "What was it like being alone all that time?"

"What do you mean?" Iris was stalling, not sure if Ash counted. He counted to Iris, more than anything, but if she was learning anything in living with the Blakemores, it was that the things that mattered to Iris didn't matter to them.

"Were you lonely?"

"Sometimes. I got used to it."

"That makes sense. People can get used to just about anything."

Iris doubted that was true. People put up with things, but that wasn't the same as being used to them. Maybe Suzanne was talking about herself.

Suzanne said, "When you were lonely, did you ever think about leaving the woods?"

"Not really."

"Not even when you were cold and hungry?"

"When I was cold and hungry, I wanted to be warm and full. That's different."

Suzanne was quiet a moment. "I've never been hungry. Not the way you were."

"How would you know?"

She sighed. "I guess I wouldn't. Just like I don't know what it's like to be alone. Not really."

Iris turned to look out the window. They were on the street where the Blakemores lived, just like that. One minute she was running through the woods with Ash, her hopeful mind convincing her she was free somehow, and the next she was being locked back in her cage.

What Suzanne didn't understand and what Iris didn't think she could explain was that being alone was different for her. She hadn't wanted to be found, not that anyone had been looking for her. No one knew she existed, not one single person in the whole world except her and Ash. She wasn't alone. She was free.

CHAPTER 22

Whit came through the door at six thirty and found Suzanne bustling around the kitchen at a frenetic pace, collecting dishes from various surfaces and ferrying them to the dishwasher. She answered his greeting with a quick "Hi!" and grazed his cheek with a kiss on her way back from the pantry. She paused to gather papers from the counter and straighten them.

"Sorry. I meant to do this earlier. The day got away from me."

He exhaled and went to the wine fridge. "Well, I had a tough day, too."

Suzanne was stuffing the papers into her laptop case. Her hands stilled, and Whit thought she must have something important on her mind. Well, she'd tell him when she was ready. First things first. He bent over the door of the wine fridge and selected a bottle of Viognier. Something crisp. And with a screw cap. What a marvelous invention that was.

He reached into a cupboard for a glass. "You want some?"

"Sure. Good idea."

Whit poured two glasses, handed his wife hers, and glanced over her shoulder at the oven. The digital display showed only the time.

Suzanne followed his gaze. "I didn't have a moment. Plus, Brynn is at Kendall's and Reid is at Alex's. I thought I'd make a salad for us."

"What about Iris?"

"She said she'll have something later. She had some exercise today." Her eyes skated to the side. "Won't take ten minutes."

He really didn't want to be that husband, the Ozzie to her Harriet. He knew it was neither fair of him nor good for their marriage. He kept up his end of the bargain better than most men he knew, who complained about aspects of family life he took in stride: exorbitant expenditures, no downtime, frequent and interminable school and sporting events, most of which interested him not at all. Whit cheerfully accepted most of it, but disorder and uncertainty were like slivers under his skin; he could not relax. As much as Suzanne denied it, Iris was the agent of this mess.

Suzanne touched her wineglass to his. "Cheers."

"Cheers."

Whit took a long drink, nearly draining it. "Back in a flash." He went upstairs and changed into sweats and a T-shirt, doing his best to ignore the overflowing laundry basket in the closet and the image of the utter disaster he knew lay beyond the closed door of his son's room. On his way down the hall, he considered sticking his head into Iris's room but could not think of what he would say to her. After two weeks he was not comfortable around her. Her manner was too odd and she was far too quiet, leaving him to ramble on to fill in the gaps.

Suzanne had set two places in the dining room. He refilled the glasses while Suzanne composed the salads—an artful arrangement of tomatoes, marinated artichokes, goat cheese, and cold salmon over arugula.

"Looks beautiful, darling."

She smiled and his heart warmed.

As they ate, he related the broad strokes of his day—a series of hitches in the major deal he was putting together. She listened with her usual attention, but Whit couldn't help but feel she was making an effort in doing so. Her face looked drawn.

"Is anything wrong, Suzanne?"

"What? No." She stabbed a piece of salmon. "I'm fine."

He studied her a moment longer. What more could he do than ask? He had been married long enough to know she would tell him what was on her mind eventually—if he needed to know. He had never expected full disclosure. There wasn't time for that. They both had to curate their confidences. There was, however, something he was compelled to disclose.

"By the way, Detective DeCelle wants to stop by to talk to Iris tomorrow evening."

Suzanne put down her fork. "Why?"

"I called him this morning, just to see if they had any news, and he thought it was time to follow up with her, now that's she's better."

"You called him?"

"Yeah."

"Why?"

"I think I just said."

"If they had news, they would let us know."

Whit took a bite of tomato. "Maybe. They're busy. Doesn't hurt to follow up. It's best for Iris to be with family if they can find them. We're together on that, right?"

Suzanne blinked at him.

He couldn't tell what she was thinking. It was possible she was angry—she wasn't transparent. "It's just a conversation, Suzanne. She might remember something."

"She might."

"Don't you think it's odd that she doesn't seem interested in locating her father?"

"He disappeared six years ago."

"Still." He studied Suzanne as she ate; she was taking very small bites, pushing her food around. "Aren't you curious?"

"About what?"

"Her father. Her family."

"Sure. But forcing the issue isn't necessarily the way to get answers." Her fork clattered onto her plate. She picked it up and looked at him. "She's fragile, you know." She was making it sound as if he were suggesting waterboarding.

"I know." In truth, other than being skinny, Iris didn't seem fragile to him. Weird. Dissociated. But not fragile. Whit didn't wish to argue, however, so he attempted to be conciliatory. "The detective said he was planning to follow up anyway. It was on his calendar."

Not exactly the truth, but near enough.

~

The next evening, after an early dinner, Brynn slipped into Iris's room.

Reid's door opened across the hall, and he followed her in. "What're you doing in here?"

Like he was Iris's security detail. "Don't rat me out. I only want to listen to the cop grill Iris."

Reid twisted his mouth, considering.

Brynn thought of all the times she and Reid had sneaked into this room to spy on their parents' conversations.

"Join me, bro. Just like old times."

Her mother had nixed her request to be there while the detective questioned Iris, but that didn't mean she and Reid had to miss out. She smiled her most innocent smile. Reid rolled his eyes and she knew he was giving in, probably just as curious as she was about Iris. He went out to close his door, then shut Iris's door behind him. Together they lifted the easy chair out of the corner to expose the heating vent connected to one in the living room ceiling. Brynn slid the lever on the vent, opening the louver all the way. They lay on their stomachs with their heads inches from the vent. Voices rose from below. The detective started with straightforward questions about how Iris was feeling and whether she was settling in. Iris gave one-word answers, as usual.

"Do you have anything more to tell us about where your house is?"

"No."

"What sort of a house was it?"

"Wood. One room." A pause. "About the size of this one."

"And the roof?"

"Wood and metal."

"How did you heat it in the winter?"

"Wood." Iris sounded exasperated, like no one in the world just cranked up a thermostat when they were cold. "We had a wood stove. We cooked on that. Or outside."

"Okay. And there were no roads, you said before. What about trails?"

"We tried not to make trails. We went different ways, especially below the house."

"Why below?"

"Because that's where a stranger would probably come from."

Brynn whispered to Reid. "Stranger danger." He elbowed her.

In the living room, the sound of paper being shuffled.

"So, Iris. I know your family hunted and trapped for food, but didn't you need supplies sometimes?"

A long pause. "Daddy went down three times a year."

Their father said, "You never mentioned that."

"You never asked me."

The detective spoke. "How long was he gone on these trips?"

"Three or four days."

"And he walked to a store and carried it all back?"

"No. A friend helped him. His friend had a truck."

Brynn glanced at Reid and raised her eyebrows. Reid whispered, "They had to get stuff somehow."

The detective said, "You don't happen to know the name of this fellow?"

"Buck."

"Buck. Just Buck?"

"Yes."

"Buck with a truck." He didn't sound amused.

Brynn bit her lip to stop from laughing.

"Yes." Iris drew it out, like she was talking to an idiot.

"Now, Iris. How did your father pay for these supplies? Did he have a pile of cash in the house?"

"I don't know. I don't think so."

Their father said, "Maybe he went to a bank? Had an account to draw from?"

"If he didn't want to draw attention to himself," the detective said, "it's more likely he picked up a check from a post office box and cashed it."

Their mother spoke for the first time. "Like a disability check?"

"What's disability?" Iris asked.

"When someone has an injury or a medical problem of some kind." Their mom loved to tell Iris about everything, like she was Siri.

"There was nothing wrong with my father."

Defensive much?

"And one day," the detective said, "he just left and never came back. Why would he do that, Iris?"

Silence. Brynn swallowed.

The detective's voice was casual. "I'm wondering if maybe he was a veteran." Obviously Iris had no clue what that was either. "Did your father fight in a war?"

"I don't know."

"I find that hard to believe. Most kids know the basics of their parents' lives."

Iris was getting pissed off. "My parents didn't talk about the past. They said it was pointless. They were right. My father left six years ago. If he was alive, he would've come home. So he's dead. What's the point of talking about him?"

Their mother said, "You can't know for sure that he isn't alive, Iris. Even if you think he isn't, don't you want to find out for sure?"

"I do know!"

Brynn and Reid looked at each other, as shocked by Iris's outburst as if Vishnu had spoken.

"Iris." The detective dropped his voice. Brynn could only just make out the words. "Was there a problem in your house?"

"What do you mean?"

"Did your mother make your father leave?"

"No!"

Scuffling sounds. Brynn imagined Iris getting up and pacing, maybe scrabbling at the walls like a hamster in a cage. Brynn wasn't being mean. She liked hamsters.

"Please calm down, Iris." Their mother was trying to smooth things over.

"Leave me alone!"

Boy, Brynn thought. *Can I ever relate.*

The detective said, "I think that's enough for now. But, Iris, just so we're clear. The police have an obligation to try to find your father. We don't need anyone's permission." A long silence. "And that goes for your mother, too. Because unless and until we find her body where you say it is, we can't really be sure what happened to anyone."

Iris screamed, "She fell! I tried to get her out! I tried!"

Brynn bit her lip. Iris's quick steps receded from the living room.

"She's coming upstairs."

Brynn and Reid jumped to their feet, shoved the chair back in place, and ducked into the hall. Iris, her face red and scrunched in pain and anger, was rushing toward them, heading for her room.

Brynn moved in front of Reid and positioned herself by Iris's door while not exactly blocking it. "Oh, Iris."

Iris slowed and looked up at her with those anime eyes, welling with tears but also wary. Fair enough.

Reid said, "It's gonna be okay." He lifted his hand to touch her shoulder, then stuck his hand in his pocket instead.

Their mother appeared at the top of the stairs. Iris spun to face her. Iris's eyes had darkened to deep violet and her jaw was set.

"I don't want to talk to you."

Her mother inhaled sharply.

Brynn stepped closer and put an arm around Iris's shoulder. The top of the girl's head didn't even reach Brynn's chin. "I don't blame you," Brynn whispered. "Come with me." Iris hesitated for one second before letting Brynn steer her away. When Brynn reached the door to her room, she turned to look over her shoulder.

"Brynn." Her mother's tone was stuffed with warning and mistrust.

"Mom." Brynn coated her voice in chocolate. "I got this."

"Brynn!"

Brynn pulled Iris into her room and shut the door before her mother lost it.

"Sit anywhere." Brynn hoped Iris wouldn't choose her bed. She was particular about her bed.

Iris went to the window seat. Where else?

Brynn picked up a nearly full Honest Tea—Moroccan mint green tea, her favorite—and handed it to Iris. "Here." The Stray looked at it like it might explode. "You should always hydrate after crying."

Iris wiped her eyes with the hem of her shirt. Brynn caught a glimpse of her belly, what there was of it. God, she was scrawny. Iris sipped the drink tentatively and handed it back to Brynn.

"Keep it."

Brynn cast about her room for something of interest to Iris, something to calm her down. Unfortunately, nature was little in evidence. But maybe that was the wrong approach. Maybe Iris needed to see how fun it could be to not run around in the woods and eat rabbits. Brynn's mom had been trying to teach Iris all sorts of things, very gradually—too gradually if you asked Brynn, which no one did—but none of Iris's lessons could remotely be considered fun, except eating normal food, and Iris had the hang of that. No, if Brynn was going to get this weirdo out of her house and get her life back to normal, she'd have to do it her way.

Brynn carried a spare chair to her desk and waved Iris over. Iris perched on the edge of the chair. Brynn woke her laptop and clicked to a Facebook page. "Check this out. Prom is soon. That's a dance where everyone gets super dressed up. No one cares about the dancing. It's all about the dresses, the shoes, and all the rest. Want to see?"

Iris nodded carefully, as if she were an anthropologist being invited to dinner by cannibals.

Brynn scrolled through some photos, all of girls in formal dresses. "So these are my classmates. Not necessarily my friends. Everyone posts their dresses here. Tell me which ones you like, okay?"

"Okay."

Brynn stopped on one of a girl in a hot-pink strapless sheath, very tight and skanky short. "Well?"

Iris said, "Is she your friend?"

"As if. I mean, no."

"I don't like the dress."

"Why not?"

Iris considered. "Mostly the color."

Brynn nodded. "Good call."

They reviewed several more dresses together. Iris preferred simple designs and natural colors. What a shock.

"Tell you what," Brynn said. "If you want, we can take some photos together before prom."

"Why?"

Brynn ignored this. Where would she start? "You'd have to dress up."

Iris frowned. "I don't understand why you do this. Not just for this prom, but every day."

"It's fun. It's decorating yourself, making yourself look good."

"So people will like your photo on the computer?"

Maybe she wasn't so dense. "Yes. So people, the right people, pay attention to you."

Iris blushed. "I don't think I want that."

"Oh, I think you do." Brynn picked up her phone from the desk and swiped a few times until she found Sam's profile pic and showed it to Iris. "Well?"

"This boy is your friend?"

"Yup."

Iris thought for a moment. "And he likes you because a lot of people pay attention to how you look in your photos?"

"Right." Not that she would ever put it that way. She pointed at Sam's photo. "Plus, he's hot."

"Hot?"

"Oh boy." Brynn got up, flopped onto the bed with her arms splayed, and spoke to the ceiling. "We have so much work to do, Iris. So much work."

CHAPTER 23

All five of them climbed into the Navigator. Iris was in the middle seat in the back and Whit drove. Suzanne was unused to being a passenger in her own vehicle and fiddled with the seat controls. Whit turned on the radio, clicking through her presets twice before settling on a station.

She was skeptical of the wisdom of the entire family, including Iris, having dinner at her parents' house, and had said as much to Tinsley and Anson, and to Whit. In fact, she was more than skeptical; she knew it was a terrible idea, especially since only two days had passed since Iris's interrogation by the detective, two days during which Iris had been quiet and withdrawn, even for her. Perhaps Iris had assumed the reappearance of the detective was Suzanne's idea, or that she had at least been complicit. Either way, Suzanne wouldn't point a finger at Whit even though she was disappointed in him. Parents should present a united front even when it turned out they weren't as united as they ought to be.

Instead Whit had minimized the aftermath of the interrogation and used the incident as evidence that Suzanne was coddling the girl. Iris needed to be challenged; otherwise, how would she ever adapt to the real world, as he put it? He had a point, but it wasn't as if Suzanne had not been encouraging Iris to gradually try, if not embrace, the trappings of modern life. Iris had mastered several apps on her phone, although she failed to see the point of them, and could tolerate longer rides in the car and more people in stores and public places for short periods. She enjoyed the occasional television show if the topic was nature, geography, or science. Whit had suggested she try cartoons, but they did not hold Iris's attention. She said nothing looked real and objected to animals acting like people.

"She's not a little girl," Suzanne had reminded him. And yet in many ways Iris was a little girl. There was so much she didn't understand. But the longer Suzanne spent teaching her those things, the less important the lessons seemed. What happiness or insight into her own existence would Iris gain from navigating the aisles of a supermarket, mastering the controls of the microwave, or learning what an extended-care facility was? Iris, it seemed possible now, was hardly naive at all.

Suzanne worried about her anyway. Brynn, for reasons opaque to Suzanne, had suddenly softened to Iris. Suzanne hated herself for being suspicious and avoided being caught checking up on them. Reid had spent most of the last two days with Alex, which Suzanne couldn't help but interpret as relinquishing Iris to Brynn, or even as a commentary on the whole family. They didn't seem capable of being happy at the same time; that was the crux of it. Suzanne, the puppet master, was weary of untangling the strings and wondered if she'd done Iris any favors bringing her into the Blakemore puppet theater.

They had left Charlottesville behind. The landscape opened, revealing pastures, patches of woods, and farms with their backs to the hills. The setting sun shot rays of light between the trees. Suzanne shielded her eyes.

In truth, she didn't feel much like a puppet master. She wasn't in control, not anymore, not for a long time. Maybe the theater was in her believing she "ran" her family. She did things for her children, for their school, for their sports and activities, for the community, for Whit, for his business associates, for her mother and, indirectly, for her father, giving the illusion that she was the hub. Iris was one more spoke on the wheel. But the hub does not turn the wheel. The hub is the small, hard knot in the center, a place of convergence. The spokes were vectors, directed outward. She was in the middle, immobile, bearing the centripetal force.

No wonder she was exhausted. And frustrated.

Suzanne twisted in her seat to speak to Iris. "Are you feeling all right?"

The girl nodded. Brynn rolled her eyes without looking away from her phone.

They entered the paved drive through an ornate iron gate bordered by forsythia whose arching branches were heavy with blooms. A springhouse straddled a narrow creek choked with watercress. Hickory Hill stood above them, its Georgian stateliness commanding the broad hilltop. Two sets of dual fireplaces and windows oversize for the period spoke of a long history of deep pockets. A carriage house flanked the right side and an elegant red barn the left, both separated from the house by a wide lawn. Shade trees—two-hundred-year-old walnut and black oak—confirmed the estate's longevity. It was beautiful, she had to admit.

"Suzanne's childhood home, Iris." Whit's tone was reverent.

Iris did not respond. Suzanne could guess at her reaction and had no desire to see it. She was always embarrassed to bring people here but never more than today.

Anson greeted them at the door, gin in hand.

"Welcome! Find the place all right, did you?"

A dig about not visiting more often. Suzanne introduced Iris, then walked past him with the peonies she was carrying. "I'll just bring these to Mother."

Suzanne found Tinsley in the dining room arranging platters on the sideboard. She wore a full skirt covered in blue flowers and a crisp white shirt. Suzanne felt underdressed in jeans and her favorite black T-shirt, but that was nothing new.

"Suzanne." Tinsley gave her a once-over.

"Hi, Mother. Everything looks delicious." She noticed the table was set. "I'm surprised we're not eating on the patio. It's lovely out."

"I was worried about Iris running away!"

"We could tether her to a chair."

Her mother's eyes widened as if she were considering this proposal, then registered Suzanne's sarcasm. "I was only thinking of the girl."

"I know. Sorry." And she was. After all, hadn't Iris run away into the woods a few days ago? "I haven't been sleeping."

"I did say this would be too much of a burden on you."

Tinsley's tone was scolding but nevertheless contained a measure of true concern. Suzanne wondered what it would be like to experience a pure positive emotion from her mother, then dismissed the idea as too improbable to dwell upon. Suzanne had tried to be openly loving with her children and had been careful not to take away with one hand what she gave with the other. Had she succeeded? Five years earlier she would've been certain she had.

Suzanne showed her mother the flowers. "I can put these in water for you."

"They're gorgeous. Thank you."

Anson fixed drinks for everyone, and they helped themselves to fried chicken, sweet potato biscuits, and an array of salads. Tinsley, who didn't enjoy cooking and therefore did not cook, had acquired everything from Whole Foods and a small grocer in town. When Suzanne lived at home, they had had both a maid and a cook. Now Tinsley managed with a cleaner who came three times a week and a professional chef ("Maurice is a dream!") who took care of dinner parties and evenings alone with Anson when it was simply too much trouble for Tinsley to procure dinner herself. Tinsley had almost canceled the family dinner when she'd learned Maurice was out of town, but her curiosity about Iris had won out.

Anson took his seat at the head of the table and glowered at his plate. "Looks almost as good as the fried chicken at the club." He turned over a leg, eyeing it with suspicion. "Almost."

"Let me refresh your drink, Anson." Tinsley's answer to everything. Anson swatted the air, dismissing her as bartender. Tinsley turned to Reid. "It really is very good chicken."

"I'm a vegetarian, Grammy. As you know."

She sighed as if it pained her to be reminded. "It just seems so . . . unnecessary."

"I'm thinking of going vegan. I practically am already."

Whit shook his head. Brynn groaned.

Suzanne was simultaneously proud of Reid for holding his ground and annoyed with him for making a target of himself. She drank from her gin and tonic, savoring the caustic bite of the gin.

Anson thrust a chicken leg at Whit. "You need to get on top of this vegan thing, son."

"Suzanne does the meal planning. The rest of us can still eat meat."

"In a family, everyone should eat the same thing."

"That's why we go out," Tinsley said. "Reid, what's wrong with an egg?"

Reid pursed his lips.

Iris, seated beside Reid, had been concentrating on her dinner, hunched over her plate. At least Suzanne had been able to break her of the habit of shoveling food with both hands. She noticed Iris's fingernails had been painted dark blue. Brynn, obviously, but when? Painted nails seemed wrong on Iris, like pierced ears on a baby.

Iris, her mouth full, turned to Reid. "Are eggs wrong?"

Reid looked around the table as if deciding whether to waste his breath. "We can talk about it later, Iris."

Brynn laughed. "Yeah, the Real Meaning of Free Range lecture is dope."

"Is someone smoking marijuana?" Anson stared at the children, his gaze lingering on Reid.

Whit said, "No, Anson. It's an expression."

Suzanne thought she detected a slight smile on Brynn's lips. She took a long sip of her gin and tonic and immediately felt woozy. She normally had only a glass of wine and had forgotten about her father's heavy hand.

Tinsley changed the subject. "Any news on finding Iris's family?"

"Mother, I don't think—"

Anson cut in. "If you ask me, the whole situation strikes me as unlikely."

Tinsley was miffed at being interrupted. "I don't recall anyone asking you."

Anson turned away and addressed Whit and Suzanne. "Tell me, how could they survive for so long with nothing? Even in the winter? I don't buy it."

"Without Whole Foods, you mean?" Reid said with mock innocence.

Whit gave him a look. "I'm skeptical, too, Anson, but there was a case when I was in high school, I think. Remember that guy who bombed all those abortion clinics? Two people died. His name was Rudolph, maybe? Anyway, he disappeared into the North Carolina woods. The FBI hunted for him for five years."

Anson nodded. "Good example, son. So any news?"

Whit helped himself to another piece of chicken. "The detective stopped by the other day. They seem to think her father might be a veteran."

Suzanne had been listening to this exchange, incredulous. "Why is everyone talking about Iris as if she isn't here?"

Whit gestured toward the girl. "She's welcome to chime in anytime."

The way he said it, it sounded as though Iris were a hostile witness. Suzanne shot a questioning but stern look at him. *Whatever it is you're doing, back off.*

"Another vet, huh?" When Anson's deferments during the Vietnam draft had run out, his family finagled a desk job for him. He loved to refer to himself as a vet. "What war would that have been?"

Brynn was quick to show her knowledge of history. "Probably the Gulf War, Grandpa."

Anson nodded. "He's got the syndrome then, Iris?"

Iris had stopped eating during this exchange, although she hadn't looked up from her plate. Now she turned to Suzanne's father, her gaze steady. "My father is dead."

"Then why are they looking for him?" Anson's tone was affable, as if he was hoping she could clear things up for him.

"Iris," Suzanne said, "you don't have to say anything."

"Why shouldn't she?" Reid said.

"Well, even if Iris is right," Whit said calmly, "there should be relatives."

Why couldn't he leave it alone? This was a family dinner, after all, not a debrief. Suzanne caught her mother's eye.

Tinsley nodded. "I shouldn't have brought it up." She tore a biscuit in half and pulled off a small corner, considered it closely, and spoke across the table to Reid. "Now, Reid. I promised Queenie Bourne you'd help out at the golf scramble fund-raiser. It's a tradition, and your grandfather and I are counting on you."

Reid's gaze was fixed on the wall over Tinsley's shoulder. He did not move or speak.

Suzanne picked up her glass and drained it, gripping the empty glass to resist the urge to throw it. The problem was she had only the one glass, which would force her to choose among her mother, her father, and Whit.

Whit leaned forward to intercept Reid's gaze. "Your grandmother asked you a question."

"It wasn't a question."

"But when your grandmother speaks to you, you should respond."

Anson nodded gravely. "Basic respect, son."

Tinsley shot him a look that Suzanne understood immediately: *Says the philanderer.*

Suzanne looked around the table. This was her family. These were her loved ones. These were her parents, her husband, her children. She did not feel love for them. She did not feel love between them. She knew it must be there, had been there, this love: filial, romantic, maternal. It couldn't just evaporate, could it? Except maybe it had, because the people around this table were not a family. They were not a loving unit. Suzanne didn't know what they were.

Her mother was filling her glass with white wine. Suzanne put two fingers on the base of her own wineglass and slid it toward her mother. Tinsley filled the glass and caught her daughter's eye. A thin smile spread across Tinsley's face, knowing, confiding.

You see how it is. This is my life.

And it's yours.

CHAPTER 24

After they finished eating, Grammy Tinsley told them to leave everything where it was. "The elves will be in first thing tomorrow."

Brynn loved this about Grammy. How wrong would it be to ask if she could move in? Grandpa was a zero but easy enough to ignore. Plus he adored Brynn and therefore would be blind to anything she did, not unlike her father.

Grandpa herded them into the living room, looping his arm across Whit's shoulders and directing the favored son to the seat next to Grandpa's black leather easy chair—his throne, as he put it.

Chocolate-chip cookies, brownies, and lemon squares waited on the coffee table. Brynn snagged a brownie and the corner seat on the comfiest couch. Reid loped over and sat on the opposite end. He looked like he'd been smacked for peeing on the floor.

Grammy headed straight for the bar in the corner. "I'm having more wine, but if anyone wants coffee, I suppose I could manage it."

Brynn vowed that her first house would have a bar just like Grammy and Grandpa's, all dark wood and soft lights and sparkling glasses. Grandpa joined Grammy at the bar and poured whiskey into cut-glass tumblers for Brynn's father and himself. Brynn's mother helped herself to another glass of wine. Was that her third? So much for the designated drivers. Oh well, either Reid would step up or they could call a cab. Or maybe Brynn would stay right here and never leave. Squatter's rights.

"Brynn," Grammy said, "I nearly forgot. The seamstress dropped off your dress. Try it on if you wish. It's on the bed in your mother's old room."

Brynn jumped up from the couch and threw her arms around her grandmother. "Thank you!" She rushed over to Iris, who crouched near the doorway, as far away from everyone else as possible. "Come with me!" Hanging with Iris was always good for a laugh and had the added advantage of irritating the shit out of her mom.

Iris hesitated. She was terrified of everything, except natural, dirty things, and was probably calculating whether being dragged into the far reaches of an unfamiliar house was preferable to hanging out with the rest of the family. Brynn made the decision for Iris, taking her by the arm and pulling her to her feet. They disappeared into the hall and up the stairs.

Grammy Tinsley had redecorated Suzanne's room a few years ago; she wasn't one of those sentimental moms who turned their kid's room into a shrine. The color scheme was shades of gray with red accents. Brynn adored the look, especially the little touches that made it all work, like the thick charcoal cashmere blanket on the end of the bed, and the throw pillows, each featuring a prancing red horse with a long black tail, stenciled with flowers. Maybe when she went to college, Grammy could design her room.

The dress lay on the white spread. It was more beautiful than she remembered: a short black cocktail dress with a jewel neckline made of embroidered silk and wool tulle. The lace bodice was embellished on the front and back with jewels and embroidered with flowers and pink hummingbirds. It was to die for.

Brynn held it against her and spun to show Iris. "What do you think?"

Iris shrugged, then Brynn's expectant look registered. "Maybe if you put it on."

"Just what I was thinking."

Brynn shut the door of the room and stripped down to her bra and panties. Iris turned away.

"It's okay when it's just girls."

Brynn's phone buzzed somewhere in the crumple of clothes on the floor. She retrieved it.

ROBBY (via text): Thinking about you all the time. When can I see you?

BRYNN: In a flash. (winking emoji)

"Iris. Take a photo, okay?" She showed her how to frame it and what button to push, then climbed onto the bed. She leaned back on her elbows and crossed her legs at the ankle. Demure but not too demure. She glanced at her boobs. Why was she so flat? She adjusted her pose so her forearms pushed in against her boobs, giving her maximum but still pathetic cleavage, and tossed her head, spilling her hair over one shoulder.

Iris stared with her mouth open.

"Take the photo, Iris."

She held the phone awkwardly, like it was about to detonate.

"Just push the button already."

Iris complied. Brynn took the phone from her and reviewed the photo, evaluating her body, the pose, her underwear. Stalking herself. "Not bad. You show promise." She cropped it so her face wouldn't show.

BRYNN (via Snapchat): Testing, testing . . . 1, 2, 3 . . .

Iris was looking over her shoulder. "I don't understand."

"You will. Eventually."

"Who's Robby?"

"Never mind."

"Is he your boyfriend?"

Brynn smiled.

"Aren't you going to the dance with Sam?"

"Sam's just a friend."

Iris thought about that. "You said he was hot."

"I did. He is."

"That means you want to have sex with him."

"Whoa . . . who told you that?"

"I figured it out." She looked at her feet. "I watch TV sometimes. Nature programs, mostly. But some other ones. People our age are very interested in sex."

Brynn laughed. "No kidding." She considered Iris in a new light. "You remembered Sam." Iris's cheeks turned red. "Iris! You kill me!" Brynn wanted to explore this further, especially the nature programs, but had other things on her mind at the moment. "You can't tell."

"Tell what?"

"About the photo. It's private."

"Okay."

"Private means you can't tell." Brynn tossed the phone on the bed, picked up the dress, and slipped it on. "Zip me, Iris, okay?" Iris obeyed. Brynn did a quick 360 in front of the floor mirror beside the wardrobe; even without heels and an updo, she looked seriously hot. Her phone buzzed again.

ROBBY: Niiiice. Who's there with you?

Brynn laughed. "Your chance, Iris."

"My chance?"

"Hang on." Brynn flung open the wardrobe doors, remembering from playing hide-and-seek as a kid that Grammy stored her off-season clothes here. Sure enough, front and center was the absolutely perfect thing: a short fur coat.

She showed it to Iris. "Put this on. And take off your jeans."

Iris's eyes were wide. "What animal is that?"

"I'm guessing mink, but this isn't a biology lesson. Well, not precisely." She smiled at her joke. "Quick now. Off with the jeans. Don't worry, you're so short, the coat will totally cover your butt."

Iris slowly removed her jeans. God, the girl was skinny. Her calves were no bigger than Brynn's biceps. Brynn helped her into the coat. It did cover her butt—barely.

Brynn had an idea.

"Wait here, Iris. We're going to have some fun, okay?"

Brynn stole into her grandmother's bathroom and returned with black eyeliner, a comb, and some hair ties. Iris was sitting on the floor in the mink coat, her bare legs tucked underneath her. She looked like a woolly caterpillar.

"I'm just going to color on your face a little and put up your hair, okay?"

"Why?"

"Why not, Iris? Don't you see that most girls wear makeup? It's not evil. It's not wrong. Right now this is just for fun. Don't you want to have fun with me?"

She shrugged. "Okay."

Brynn knelt in front of Iris and instructed her to close her eyes. She applied a thick circle of eyeliner along Iris's lower and upper lashes and made her eyebrows, which were naturally thin and pale, into swatches that would do Jake Gyllenhaal proud. She didn't go full unibrow, though. She wasn't mean. Satisfied with Iris's face, Brynn tied a ponytail on the top of Iris's head, allowing the hair to fall in all directions. Iris pushed the strands from her face.

"Perfect! Let's snap it!" Brynn took a photo before Iris could protest, or see herself in the mirror, and posted it on Snapchat.

BRYNN to LISA, KENDALL, OPHELIA: #posterchild #foster-fail #gotpants?

BRYNN to SAM: Check this out

Grammy Tinsley called from the hallway. "Brynn, dear, why don't you come show everyone?"

What a fabulous idea. She ran to lock the door in case Tinsley was thinking about coming in. "Be down in a sec!" She went to Iris and gave her an irresistible smile. "Grammy wants us to show our outfits."

Iris felt around the top of her head and frowned.

"It's just a game. It'll make everyone happy."

Iris picked up her jeans and started putting them on.

"Right. Pants," Brynn said. "Good call."

Brynn led Iris downstairs. Just outside the living room, she smoothed her hair and arranged her dress. She took Iris's hand and strode into the middle of the room.

"Here we are—" Brynn struck a pose, hand on her hip, casting a sultry look over her shoulder. "Beauty and the Beast!"

For a couple of seconds, everyone was frozen, taking it in.

Too much? A warm flush crept up Brynn's neck.

Grandpa Anson's eyes widened and a smile spread across his face. He slapped his knee and let out a big, booming laugh. Brynn shot him a smile.

Grammy Tinsley joined in, laughing and covering her mouth with her hand to show she wasn't laughing *at* anyone. "You look absolutely gorgeous, Brynn. And Iris, well, that look is just too funny for words."

Brynn glanced at Iris and followed her gaze to Brynn's mother. That saying, if looks could kill? Right there.

"Funny, Mother?" Suzanne spit out the words. She sprang up from her seat. "This is funny?"

Brynn's dad was gauging responses, but Brynn could tell he thought it was a pretty good joke, too, especially after a few drinks. "Now, Suzanne, calm down. I don't think Brynn meant anything by it."

Brynn's mom spun toward him. She seemed a little unsteady, drunk maybe. "She dresses Iris up like that and it's okay with you?"

"I didn't say that."

Reid said, "Actually, Dad, you pretty much did."

"I don't need you to weigh in, Reid."

"Just keeping it real, Dad." His voice was slick with scorn. He really was a dick.

Brynn stepped closer to her mother. "Don't you like the dress?"

"I was focusing on Iris."

"What else is new."

Anson had recovered from his bout of laughter. "Well, I love it. You look stunning."

"Thanks, Grandpa. It's Valentino."

"Valentino?" Brynn's mother examined the dress, taking in the embroidery, the crystals, the detailing. The cords in her neck were sticking out and her eyes were hard, dark marbles. "For a high school prom? Mother, are you out of your mind?"

"It was what Brynn wanted. Her heart was set on it."

"Her heart? Are you serious, Mother? What did that dress cost? A couple thousand?"

Brynn shot a look at Grammy, hoping she wouldn't actually say and send Brynn's mother off the deep end. Grammy, true to form, just raised an eyebrow that said *Discussing price is crass.*

"What is wrong with all of you?" her mother shouted, waving her arms like a crazy person. "What the hell is wrong? It's like you're all infected with the same disease!"

Her father stood, looking like he was going to grab hold of her mother, then thought better of it. "Suzanne, Brynn didn't mean to hurt anyone." He turned to Brynn. "Tell her."

"It's true, Mom. I told Iris it was a game."

Grammy straightened the watch on her wrist. "And it's just a dress."

Her mother stared at Grammy as if she didn't know her. She held her arms rigidly at her sides and tilted forward at the waist, like she was about to be shot out of a cannon. A cold feeling entered Brynn and she hugged herself.

Her mother lowered her voice, speaking from the soles of her feet. She nodded again and again. "Just a dress. Just a couple thousand dollars. Just a little game." She sat heavily on the couch and clutched her head with both hands. "Just a dress. Just our whole damn life."

~

Iris sat on the closed toilet lid upstairs in Suzanne's mother's bathroom, feeling a little sick. Brynn shook liquid from a small bottle onto a white circle of fuzzy cloth. She told Iris to close her eyes and cleaned off the black makeup.

When Brynn stopped wiping, Iris opened her eyes. "Suzanne was really upset."

"Did you notice how everyone else thought it was funny?"

Iris nodded even though Reid hadn't laughed either.

"My mother just gets upset about silly things. It was fun, right?" She picked up a brush. "You want me to do it?"

"Sure." Iris didn't know why she agreed. She liked doing things herself. But something about being with Brynn made it easy to go along, like walking downhill instead of climbing up. Brynn made you want to be with her even if you weren't sure you liked where she was going.

Brynn came around to brush the back of Iris's hair. She did it gently. "That's why we're not telling my mother about the photos. She doesn't understand."

"Why not?"

Brynn let out an enormous sigh. "Because she's forgotten how to have fun, the kind of fun that young people have." She paused with her hand on the back of Iris's neck. It felt nice. "But just because she's forgotten doesn't mean we can't have fun, right?"

"What sort of fun do you mean?"

Brynn peeked over Iris's shoulder and looked at her reflection. "Well, on prom night, when my friends come to take photos? You can wear one of my dresses and we'll do your makeup and hair." She gathered Iris's hair and twisted it into a bundle at the back of her head. "You could be really pretty, you know."

Iris's cheeks went red.

Brynn leaned close. Iris could feel her breath on her cheek. "It's exciting, isn't it? The idea of *fun*? A little *secret fun*?"

Iris's cheeks were really hot now. Brynn was right. It *was* exciting.

~

Reid drove them home. Suzanne was amazed he didn't utter a single word of protest when Whit asked him. The ride home was silent—and sobering. Suzanne berated herself for having had too much to drink but suspected she would've reacted strongly to Brynn's stunt even if she had been stone-cold sober.

When they got home, the kids absconded to their rooms. Tomorrow was a school day, and they undoubtedly sensed the evening was not quite finished for their parents and were only too glad to get away.

Suzanne went to the kitchen and poured herself a large glass of water.

Whit appeared, took off his jacket, and ran a hand through his hair. "You okay?"

"You mean aside from Brynn's humiliation of Iris?"

"Was Iris humiliated? I didn't see it."

Suzanne shook her head in dismay. "She's not socially sophisticated enough to know she was being made fun of, but that doesn't make it right."

"Okay, fair point. Or you could look at it another way: no harm, no foul."

"Really, Whit? That's the way we are raising our kids?"

He paced in front of the counter with his hands in his pockets. Suzanne knew he hated generalized discussions of parenting strategy.

He preferred to solve problems on a case-by-case basis. Or pretend they didn't exist.

He stopped and shrugged. "Look. Brynn was being playful. Iris wasn't mad at her afterward, not even after you flipped out. They were all chummy. So what really went wrong?"

Suzanne held on to the edge of the counter. "Whit, I can't believe you don't get this."

"I do get it. I just disagree with you."

"A Valentino dress for prom is fine, is it?"

"Why not? Who's going to know how much it cost? And even if they do, it's not as if everyone doesn't know your folks have the money."

"I can't believe I have to walk you through how wrong it is. The dress and so much else."

"You don't, Suzanne. I know the argument. I hear it all the time from Reid. I just don't buy it." He stared at her, letting his dismissal sink in. "Anyway, the dress isn't the issue. The issue—your issue—is that your mother went shopping with Brynn. And maybe it's also that Iris is choosing to hang out with Brynn."

Instead of you. His words were cotton wool stuffed into her mouth, suffocating her. She spoke from the white-hot ball of anger in her stomach. "Jealousy. That's your take on my reaction, despite what I've just said."

He lifted his hands in defense. "Hey, it's pretty normal, Suzanne." His tone softened. "Teens break away. It hurts."

Suzanne turned from him, praying he would not utter another word.

Breaking away.

Or driving off. The wheel in her hands, and the road before her.

She could picture it winding, empty, endless.

The whine of the tires, the breeze from the open window.

The faint scent of hyacinths.

CHAPTER 25

Whit beckoned Iris to follow him to the car. She hesitated in the door-way, waiting for Suzanne's blessing.

"You don't have to go if you don't want to," Suzanne said.

Whit sighed. "I'm trying to help here. You could use a break, a nap. I know you didn't sleep well." *Because you were furious with me.* Whit acknowledged he was escaping more talk about last night's debacle at her parents' house and focusing instead on making what amends he could. He'd promised to talk to Brynn after her swim meet, and now he was offering to spend a little quality time with Iris—and Suzanne was balking.

Whit and Suzanne waited for Iris to respond. She seemed bored by the discussion, as if it had nothing to do with her. Maybe she was right.

"Iris." Suzanne placed her hand on the girl's arm. "Are you sure you're okay to go?"

She shrugged. "Sure."

"Okay, then!" Whit bounded down the porch steps.

Iris followed, catching up with him in a few quick steps. Suzanne remained in the doorway, worry pinching her forehead.

"Take a long bath, Suzanne," Whit called out as he opened the car door. "Read a book. Watch *Fixer Upper.*"

Suzanne waved. "Don't do anything too exciting!"

Whit smiled ruefully and shook his head. That admonishment had never been delivered in earnest before Iris. As he started the car, he thought about the irony in fretting about a girl who had lived by herself in the woods, with absolutely jack, for three long years.

He watched Iris buckle herself in. "Ready to rock?"

"Rock?"

"Yup. It means to go, in an especially cool way."

"Yes."

She sounded as if she only half knew what he meant but wasn't interested enough to explore further. Whit could only imagine how confusing everything was to her, but it bothered him that she didn't seem to be trying that hard to assimilate. That's what he would be doing. He had joked about Iris being like a foreign exchange student, but in fact the phrase captured his view of her situation succinctly. Iris had no choice but to live in the real world, and the sooner she adjusted to it, the better for her and everyone around her. It wasn't easy, but living in your own bubble—in her case, a bubble of unspoiled nature—wasn't feasible.

Whit and Iris drove in silence out of the city limits of Charlottesville toward Hampstead Farms, passing a string of car dealerships, big-box stores, and strip malls in the process of becoming upscale shopping centers. Just when the urban development seemed to be thinning, it cropped up again. Charlottesville was expanding rapidly, meeting the demand an upscale university town with an extremely livable climate would always have. Some people saw the constant construction and infiltration of open space as a scourge in need of curbing, but Whit knew growth meant strength. The city planners were keeping hold of the reins and ensuring there was plenty of green space. People might not want to live in a forest, but they definitely wanted their views to consist of more nature than concrete.

He pulled off the main road onto a private gravel drive. Fields dotted with the first wildflowers stretched for acres on both sides, rolling gently toward the woods in the far distance. They approached a brick farmhouse. Even at a distance the weedy landscaping and cracking paint on the trim were obvious.

"That's Hampstead House. The farm has three hundred acres, with these open fields making up about a third of it." Whit pulled into a parking area beside the house where four men gathered around a truck and an SUV—the surveyors plus Gillings, a money guy who was doing his due diligence. "I've got to talk to these fellows for a few minutes; then I'll show you around."

"Okay."

If Iris were one of his kids, he wouldn't have given a thought to what she would do while she waited. Her phone would already be out. With Iris, he wasn't sure he ought to let her wander the farm on her own. Suzanne would flip out if she knew, and he couldn't risk Iris going on walkabout, not with Gillings there. "You okay just waiting here?"

"Yes."

The surveyors needed only a nod from Whit to begin work. Gillings, on the other hand, didn't seem eager to return to his office anytime soon. Whit extricated himself from the conversation as soon as he could without seeming rude and returned to Iris. She was staring out the windshield.

He opened her door. "Let me show you what I'm doing here, okay?"

They bypassed the house, behind which the surveyors had set up a transit, and followed a worn path that hugged the fence line. Whit explained the plan for this tract of land: six clusters of large, stately homes on three to five acres apiece, separated by open field, some of which would be turned into community facilities: pools, tennis courts, meeting centers, recreation facilities. He indicated the placement of the homes, twenty-four in all.

"That's Phase One. Hopefully we break ground this summer. Phase Two is harder to see because it's going to involve leveling some of this."

He swept his hand to indicate the dense forest in front of them. "We'll leave a good portion of it. People like to have trees around them."

Iris had been walking quickly, as she always did, but now she slowed. "If they like trees, why are you getting rid of them?"

"Because they like new houses more."

"Where are the people living now?"

"In other houses."

"Why don't they stay there?"

"Some just want a newer house, but most want a bigger one."

"Are these houses going to be bigger than yours?"

Whit laughed. "Yes, a lot bigger."

Iris shook her head. "I really don't understand." She pointed at the old house. "What about that one?"

"The farmer used to live there. He farmed all this land. But he couldn't make money anymore doing that, so he sold it to us."

"So people with houses already could have bigger ones."

"Yup."

"What about the food?"

"The food?"

"If the farm doesn't grow anything anymore, where will that food come from?"

Whit paused. He knew the answer, or at least thought he did. The food came from bigger farms farther away, in the Midwest, in California, and in other countries, like Brazil. He ran through an explanation in his head that included cutting down the Amazon rain forest to grow beef cattle that could easily be grown on the land under his feet, and decided not to go down that road. Real estate was his wheelhouse, not food politics, so he went in a different direction.

"Farming has become more efficient, so we don't need as much land as we used to." He wasn't sure that was true, but it was plausible.

From the look on Iris's face, she wasn't buying it. Not the particular argument about the disappearance of small farms, but the larger argument, the one they had been making to her since she first walked into their home. *This world is better than the one you left. You were missing out.* Whit firmly believed the argument was correct, but he got bogged down in justifying the particulars in making the case to Iris. Perhaps this was why she wasn't absorbing and accepting her new culture as readily as she might have. She would see the advantages eventually, get used to the rest, and learn to ignore the contradictions and compromises like everyone else.

Whit regarded Iris. Those big purple-blue eyes full of innocence and wisdom confused him. He was a man who did what he had to do to get where he wanted to go. She was a girl wishing only to stay in one place.

He checked his watch. "Let's keep walking."

She nodded, and they headed off across the field.

~

In the two months since Suzanne had carried Iris out of the woods, Iris had changed her mind about many things. Not everything her parents had led her to believe was true, not completely. She admitted she liked having enough to eat every day and appreciated the luxury of indoor plumbing, especially hot running water. She liked clean clothing and a warm bed, and felt guilty about it. In her head, the voices of her parents were becoming quieter, muted by the new reality in which Iris found herself. Honestly, she couldn't see what was so wrong with it. Maybe being soft wasn't bad by itself—conveniences weren't evil—but only because the price of those conveniences was invisible, or hidden, or just not that interesting to most people.

Much of what Iris saw around her—the houses, the cars, the clothes, the thousands of kinds of foods in the supermarket—went far beyond basic convenience and comfort and left her bewildered. She wanted to know how it was justified, how the price exacted on the natural world was reckoned against the extra comfort gained, but didn't know how to ask. And if she did, as she had just done with Whit, she didn't seem to get anywhere. The deeper she explored the new world into which she had been plunged, the more she felt her parents were right and the more she wished she could retreat into the woods and never emerge again, even if it meant no more hot showers.

"Breaking ground," Whit had called it, with pride in his voice. He was proud and he was eager, but in his eagerness Iris thought he was skipping over a lot. She'd heard him talk to Suzanne about money, and his voice had an insistent quality when he did, like the buzzing of a bee deep inside a flower, gloating in the abundance. How much money Whit required was something Iris could not even guess at. She might ask him one day, when she understood more, if she was around.

Iris lifted her eyes from the shin-high grass around her to the tall trees beyond, now in full leaf, shimmering in the breeze. The tulip trees were covered with yellow and orange blossoms the size of teacups held open to the sky. Birds darted from branch to branch, eager in their preparations for new life. The air smelled tangy and Iris felt the urge to run. The muscles in her legs were bound tight with unused energy, but she knew if she took off, Whit would follow her. Suzanne would find out and be upset again. It might be worth it. Whit and Suzanne's lack of understanding of her was not her fault. In those woods she might find a moment of freedom, a small quiet space away from the terrible calculations of what people would destroy for something that, as far as she could tell, did not necessarily make them happier. In those woods she might breathe easily and deeply, and remember who she was.

In those woods she might find Ash.

Whit interrupted her thoughts. "Iris, if you could, would you really go back into the woods? Would you really do that?" He had read her mind. Or maybe it was a question he'd been carrying for a while.

She looked at him out of the corner of her eye. The wind had ruffled his hair and the sun had brought color to his cheeks. He had a friendly, pleasant way about him when he stopped pushing so hard. Iris felt sorry for him then, for everything he believed he needed to chase from here to there, as if the world were laid out before him flat, with a finish line at the end and prizes for the first to cross it. Whit didn't seem that soft to her. He was stretched out thin and brittle. He and Suzanne both.

"Yes, I would go back. But what I guess I'd like to know is, why wouldn't you?"

He smiled. "I don't think I'd last very long."

"You wouldn't have to be alone. You could have help, other people. I did, for most of the time."

Whit studied her a moment, then pointed behind them to the old house where they'd left the car. "We should get going."

They cut across the field, the breeze now at their backs. A pair of meadowlarks swooped past, dipping into the grass and out again with stuttering wing beats.

By summer this ground would be broken, and Whit would have more money.

What would happen to her?

That night Iris couldn't sleep. She tried to empty her mind, but images and sensations kept pushing back in: Brynn sprawled on the bed in her underwear, the silkiness of the fur coat, Suzanne's face, horrified and impossibly sad, Brynn's touch and her promises, Whit's grasping for money, for more and more, the innocent land marked for destruction. Iris's room was quiet, but her thoughts roiled like the bottom of a waterfall.

Soft air, more summer than spring, floated in through the open window. The moon was already high, casting blue shadows that made the familiar objects in the room take on wondrous qualities. She shouldn't go out, she knew she shouldn't, but she couldn't stay. She would come back—at least she planned to—but tonight she had to break out into the moonlight.

She climbed out of bed and dressed in yesterday's clothes. She removed her jackknife from the top drawer of her dresser and slipped out of her room and down the stairs, her sneakers in her hand. She bypassed the front door and went straight through the kitchen to the back door. It didn't creak and was more private, plus Suzanne had hidden a key under a plant pot for when Iris slept in the hammock. Once outside, Iris put on her shoes and went through the side gate and onto the sidewalk, keeping to the shadows as much as she could.

The town slept. Iris knew vaguely where she was from being driven around, but her internal map was incomplete. It didn't matter. She followed her senses, sniffing the air and judging the height of the trees and the shape of the land from the moon shadows. She moved away from the center of town, through the university—a very large school where Iris had overheard Suzanne tell Brynn she should never go late at night. Iris guessed that whatever dangers Suzanne meant weren't ones that would bother Iris. She was just passing through and doubted anyone could catch her anyway.

She approached a large road and crouched behind a concrete barrier until the few cars had disappeared. She crossed the road and two smaller ones, the smell of trees, a great stand of trees ahead, pulling her along, reeling her in. Near the house, the streetlights had been close together. Now, wherever she was, there were hardly any. Iris broke into a run, letting her feet find their own rhythm. Running into the night, into the slipstream of the moon.

She climbed over a wooden rail fence and found herself in the woods. The moon struggled to reach the ground here, and she picked her way carefully.

"Ash? You here?"

She moved deeper into the woods. The trees knit a solid blanket above her. In her own woods, in her home, she'd be out on a warm, soft, moonlit night like this and just lie down and go to sleep. She wanted to do that so badly, she could feel the earth pulling at her, gravity times a thousand. She yawned.

"Ash," she said, impatient now. "Why don't you just come here? I'm tired."

She listened, not with her ears, but with her heart, the way she always had. The leaf-thick ground and the rough trunks gave up nothing. These woods were strangely empty. At home she would've felt the company of animals curled in their lairs, birds hunched on their roosts with beaks tucked under their wings. She would've expected a pair of yellow eyes to appear: a raccoon or a skunk. Not here. She thought maybe she'd lost her knowledge, and the forest was hiding from her.

Even Ash. Where was he? She'd been away too long, she guessed. Her chest tightened.

"Ash! Stop fooling around!"

Her voice surprised her, too fierce for the night.

Iris walked slowly, touching her fingertips to the low bushes and the slick young saplings as she passed.

A sour smell, a bad smell, made her pause. In the dark, she swiveled to her right. Something was there. Not Ash, she was dead sure about that. Her pulse sped up and she told herself not to be a fool. Probably a deer, lying down. Maybe it was hurt and afraid. It was that sort of smell.

Iris tensed, ready to run. She reached into her pocket, pulled out the knife.

"Looking for someone, girlie?" A man's voice, grating, like stone against stone, maybe thirty feet away. Rustling, then a soft sound, a blanket being thrown off. "Don't know anyone named Ash, but I'll bet I'm as good."

Footfalls. He was coming toward her.

Iris sprang away, darting between the trees, a shadow in the shadows, twigs snapping under her feet. She reached the fence, vaulted over, and paused, willing the thunder of her heart to die down so she could hear.

Nothing. Only the hum of a car driving along the road a good distance behind her.

She turned and ran, out into the reassuring moonlight and into the darkness again.

She should not have come. Ash was lost to her.

Her heart sank, weakening her knees. She choked back her tears and kept on because she didn't know what else to do.

She found her way to the university and to the right street, bathed in yellow light, and to the house. She stood before it, the windows dark upstairs and down. Here was home.

And yet she was lost.

CHAPTER 26

Suzanne retrieved two plates from the cupboard and placed them on the counter along with forks and knives. Behind her, Mia was unpacking the lunch she had brought for the two of them. Mia had called last night to announce she was coming over today. "I need to escape the office, plus I haven't seen you in forever." Suzanne hid her surprise; Mia rarely abandoned her law office for any reason short of catastrophe. Work *was* her escape. Suzanne could only surmise that Whit had said something to Malcolm, who had assigned Mia the task of finding out what the hell was wrong with Suzanne. Did her outburst at her parents' house really warrant this?

Mia piled kale-and-radicchio salad onto the plates and balanced a rectangle of focaccia on each. She stepped back so Suzanne could see. "Enough for you?"

"Plenty, thanks."

"Should I save some for Iris?"

"She ate already."

"And you got rid of her how?"

Suzanne sighed. "It's not hard these days. She retreats to her room whenever Brynn's not around."

Mia gave her a long look.

Suzanne wanted out from under it. "So where shall we sit?"

Mia first surveyed the kitchen counter, covered with papers, a laptop, and several botany texts and other books for Iris, then the breakfast table, where Suzanne had dumped the tower of mail she had brought in from the foyer but had not yet sorted through. Mia picked up the plates. "How about the dining room?"

Suzanne nodded and led the way. "As long as you don't expect me to break out the crystal." She pulled placemats and cloth napkins from the sideboard. *See? I can still be civilized, even without advance notice.*

Mia returned to the kitchen, filled two glasses with water, and sat across from Suzanne. "I'll dispense with the small talk. Whit's worried about you. And given what he told Malcolm, so am I."

"You're staging an intervention."

Mia frowned. "I'm worried about my best friend, so I'm having lunch with her."

A sarcasm-free statement from Mia was so rare, Suzanne began to worry, too. What had Whit said? That she'd overreacted to a playful stunt of Brynn's? She became annoyed at the thought of the whispering behind her back, not that Whit hadn't expressed his concerns directly as well. "Not the woman I married," she recalled him saying that night. It had stung but she couldn't argue. The woman he had married was dutiful to a fault, and docile. Whit and she had stated dating when Suzanne was living at home because she couldn't hold down a job. Her anxiety was debilitating and she had trouble focusing. Antianxiety meds smoothed over the cracks, but the cracks were still there. Suzanne felt she might have a panic attack, collapse, at any moment. Whit calmed her, got her away from her parents, but now it occurred to her she might have simply traded one cage for another.

Mia began to eat. Between bites, she said, casually, "So what's going on?"

Suzanne held her fork but didn't touch her salad. Whit had asked her to account for her behavior. Tinsley had called to admonish her—and suggest yet again she return Iris, with the receipt and in the original packaging. Brynn had stopped talking to Suzanne, and Iris was taking all her cues from Brynn. And Reid? Suzanne would have expected him to understand her frustration and disillusionment, but the last few days he seemed to be avoiding her. No one had asked her the open question Mia had.

"I feel like I've failed Iris. She hasn't even been here a month and I've already lost her."

"Lost her? How?"

"To Brynn." She realized how petty and competitive that sounded. "I don't have a problem with them being friends—obviously, that would be wonderful—but I question Brynn's motives."

Mia was unfazed. "We both know Brynn is a force to be reckoned with." She took a bite of focaccia. "But what is the girl doing exactly?"

Suzanne shrugged. "That's it. I don't know. I don't think I have for quite a while. It's like she's on the other side of a piece of glass, only it's not actually transparent. Brynn controls what I see."

"She's fifteen. They all want to get away with murder—or at least mayhem."

"I know. But somehow it feels more corrupt than it should."

Mia stopped chewing. "*Corrupt* is a strong word."

"My feelings are running pretty strong. Isn't that why you're here?"

"I suppose that's correct."

Suzanne sipped her water. She still hadn't touched her food. Her stomach was sour.

"Mia, don't you sometimes wonder what it is we're doing?"

"Meaning?"

Her mind was filled with myriad thoughts, charged with emotion that sent them spinning at unpredictable angles. She willed them into alignment. "Perhaps you don't wonder what you're doing because you've held on to your career with both hands. But for the rest of us, for all the mothers who spend every waking moment striving to perfect their children's lives, don't you wonder what it serves?"

Mia smiled. "The little darlings. It serves our darling children. And make no mistake, just because I outsource a lot of tasks, I'm doing the same thing, in practice."

Suzanne nodded, although she wasn't convinced it was, in fact, the same. Throwing money at a problem wasn't equivalent to throwing your life at it. Funny how she had just called child rearing "a problem." Suzanne pushed that thought aside and pressed on. "Of course it's for the kids. But is it good for them? And I'm not sure I'm even allowed to pose this question, but what about us, the parents? Is it good for us?"

Her friend studied her. Suzanne had the full attention of an adult, and it felt like sunlight.

Mia said, "This is what you've been thinking about?"

"Yes."

"It's subversive, to be sure."

"Don't joke."

"I am, but not really." Mia paused, reflecting. Her lawyerly mind was working, running through theories, scenarios. "So first. I agree it's crazy. All the stuff, all the attention, all the details that don't make a damn bit of difference, like stressing over what shade of blue the high-tech team jersey ought to be. They can't play in Fruit of the Loom T-shirts?"

Suzanne leaned toward her. "Right. It's not exactly a revelation because everyone talks about it. Everyone is aware of it and complains about it, or at least most people do. But no one takes their own misgivings seriously. That's what gets me. Everyone agrees that it's crazy, but no one changes anything. They just laugh it off and get in line."

"Because everyone we know lives and parents this way. It's the water we swim in."

"It's the Kool-Aid we drink. Iris helped me see that."

"Iris says this?"

"Not directly. But I've spent weeks explaining this world to her: why we buy things, why we need so many choices, why we try to get so much money, why we never sit still, why we throw so much away. I hear myself explain all this—or try to—and I can't believe how ridiculous I sound." Suzanne swallowed hard. She took a breath and spread her arms out wide. "I can't believe this is me."

Mia met her gaze. "Where is Whit in all this?"

"Nowhere." Suzanne was surprised by how firm her tone was. "Whit is nowhere."

A hush settled over the room, stretching across a long moment.

Mia spoke, her voice low. "After Zane disappeared from our lives, we thought we'd maxed out on the bad luck, if that's what it was."

Suzanne said, "You tried everything. You know you both did."

"Sure. Twice. And Alex was proof. Great kid, everyone said so. Solid. Except it's never that simple. Alex was the counterweight. He had to make up for Zane, and because Zane took all our attention and then Meryl started acting up, we never saw it. Poor kid." Mia picked up her glass, setting off a tremor across the water's surface. Her voice dropped to a whisper. "The pills Alex took? I told everyone we didn't know where he'd gotten them. He didn't say anything about it. No one pressed him. Why would they? Everyone was too glad he was alive. Besides, you can get pills anywhere, right? Xanax. Codeine. Ativan."

Suzanne held her breath. A crack had opened in the veneer that separated her from her own most honest self. She blinked back tears and reached for Mia's hand.

"Thing was, they were mine. They were all mine."

Suzanne said, "Tell me."

Mia straightened her shoulders and tucked a loose strand of hair behind her ear. "You know how I joke about my father."

Suzanne nodded. "Cy the Cyborg." She couldn't help but smile a little at that.

"Exactly. I joke about him. I joke about everything." Her face became grim. "My father's not funny. I didn't realize until Zane, but they are the same, Suzanne. The same."

Suzanne tried to picture Mia's father, details about him. Nothing specific emerged, only a persistent feeling of unease in his presence, which she'd always ignored.

"Zane got it from me, through me. I should've seen. I should've known and not have been blindsided. And now Alex is suffering because I couldn't figure out what to do. I've ruined both my sons."

Mia's distress was so vivid and unexpected, Suzanne faltered. "You haven't."

"Haven't I?" Mia wiped her eyes with her napkin. "Isn't this what you've been saying? We agonize over every decision, every damn detail, and we still get it wrong. We lose them, Suzanne. No matter what, we ruin them and we lose them."

Suzanne went to her friend and held her. She knew she should make an effort to dissuade Mia, but she couldn't think of what to say.

CHAPTER 27

Reid carried the last of the card tables to the storage room and hiked up the slope to the Birdwood Grill to meet his grandfather, as he had promised. He wasn't looking forward to it. He had nothing in common with Anson Royce and had already wasted an entire day helping out with a golf fund-raiser. At least the cause was legit—an Alzheimer's foundation. But he didn't understand why all these people had to go to the trouble of organizing a golf scramble, chewing up the time of club personnel and volunteers, when they could have simply written a check. Like they couldn't let go of their money without having an event to draw attention to how generous they were.

He rounded the clubhouse and made his way to the restaurant patio. His grandfather sat at a large table with several other members. Reid had helped draw up the teams and recognized two of the women as part of Anson's foursome. Reid didn't know the others, but why would he? He wasn't exactly a regular at the club.

Anson spotted him and waved him over. "Have a seat. Everyone, this is my grandson, Reid."

Reid dragged a chair over from another table, shook hands with the man nearest to him, and nodded to the others.

Anson handed Reid a menu and signaled to a waiter. "Take a look, but the burger's what you want."

Reid ordered French fries and a lemonade.

Soon after the food arrived, two men dressed in tennis gear approached the group. Reid recognized the older guy as his father's new business partner, Robert Shipstead, who had been over to their house a couple of times. The younger guy had to be his son, given their identical Brooks Brothers, don't-touch-my-hair look. They had tennis shoes on at the moment, but Reid would bet a limb they wore their Sperrys without socks.

Anson introduced Robert and his son ("Robby"—what else?) to each person at the table, unlike the blanket introduction Reid had been honored with. Robert moved around the table for a prime spot next to Anson, but Robby, to Reid's surprise, pulled up a seat next to him.

Robby eyed his plate. "Mind if I snag a few fries? I'm starved."

Reid nudged his plate toward him. "Help yourself."

"Thanks, bro."

Bro? Reid had to stop himself from laughing out loud. Truth was, the rate at which Robby the Bro was wolfing down his fries wasn't funny at all.

The waiter came over and asked Robby if he wanted anything.

"Nah." He finished off the last of the fries and licked the salt off his fingers. "I'm good."

Reid couldn't wait to leave but needed a ride from his grandfather, or his dad, who was playing tennis. No choice but to hang here.

Robby leaned back in his chair and fished his phone out of his pocket. "Want to see something?"

Reid shrugged.

Robby's thumbs worked the screen until he found what he was looking for. He tipped the phone so Reid could see.

"Check out this piece."

A girl, naked except for a white bra and matching underwear, was sprawled on a bed. She had very long legs. Her face wasn't visible, but some of her straight blonde hair was hanging over one shoulder.

Reid wasn't sure how the bro expected him to respond. He went with the most innocuous thought that popped into his head.

"Is that your girlfriend?"

"Nah. Just a haul from Tinder. Hey, want to come to a party Saturday?" He tapped Reid on the shoulder with a loose fist. "You should totally come."

"Where is it?" He had no interest in going but couldn't see how to get out of talking with this guy.

"Near campus. On Wertland."

Reid nodded. Everyone knew the party street. He drained his lemonade and scanned the patio for the waiter, thinking he'd order another one, and maybe some more fries. His dad might be a while.

He turned to Robby, who still had his phone out. "What time is it?" He caught a glimpse of the photo of the girl again. Something about it bugged him.

"Four twenty-five."

"Can I see that again?"

"The girl? Sure." Robby handed over the phone.

Reid scrutinized the photo, concentrating on the bed, not the girl. The corner of what looked like a dark gray blanket was under one of her legs. Under her right arm was a pillow with a design on it. He enlarged the photo with his fingers.

"Getting a better look, huh?" Robby said. "Can't say I blame you."

He could see the design now: a red horse with only the front half visible. The horse's body was decorated. He'd seen the pillow before somewhere.

Oh my God, Grammy! I just love the horses!

Robby's father got up. "Come on, son. We're expected at home."

Robby took the phone from Reid. "See you Saturday?"

Reid's mind was buzzing. He answered reflexively. "Yeah, maybe."

Robby wagged the phone in the air as he rose to join his father. "She'll be there!"

What were the odds? How many pillows like that could there be? He pictured Grammy showing them his mother's room last year after a family dinner—Fourth of July, maybe? Grammy had transformed it from teenager's room from a magazine to an adult's room from a magazine. He hadn't cared about seeing it, but his mother had pulled him along. Brynn, on the other hand, had gone apeshit over it.

I just love the horses!

What were the odds?

Brynn. His little sister.

A wave of nausea came over him. He pushed back his chair, muttering an excuse as he left the patio. He had to find his father and tell him about Robby. About Brynn. Robert was his father's partner, so his father could talk to the dad, let him know what his arrogant creep of a son was getting up to with a fifteen-year-old. As Reid followed the concrete path between the fairways to the tennis center, he tried not to think about what might have already gone on. Robby hadn't bragged about it, so maybe nothing yet. The photo was bad enough.

He found his father playing singles on Court 4, on the far side of Court 3, which was also occupied. Reid took a seat on a bench, watching impatiently. He thought about calling his mother, but the way she'd flipped out the other night made him reluctant to pile anything else on her plate. Plus, she didn't have a relationship with Robby's father. Reid was sure that telling his father was the right move.

The match ended. Reid hadn't been keeping track, but judging from his father's light step off the court, he had won.

His father noticed him and came over, wiping his face on the towel hanging around his neck. "How'd it go? I was on my way to the Grill."

"Fine. It was fine." Reid realized he should have thought about what to say. "I need to talk to you."

"About what?"

"I met Robby, you know, Robert Shipstead's son."

"I've met him a couple times. Nice kid."

Reid pressed his lips together to stop himself from smirking. "Here's the thing. He showed me a photo of a girl on his phone." He felt his face get hot. "She was nearly naked."

His father tried to look serious but underneath he was smiling.

"No, Dad. You don't get it. It's not that he showed me this girl."

"What is it, then?"

Reid closed his eyes, remembering the photo, the pillow. A wedge of doubt pushed into his confidence. But it had to have been her. He exhaled hard. "I think it was Brynn."

"What?"

"I think it was Brynn."

His father took a step back. "You *think* it was?"

"Well, I couldn't see her face."

His father shook his head and his eyes narrowed. "If you couldn't see her face, why did you think it was her? Did Robby say?"

"No. He didn't give a name."

"Then why, Reid?"

Reid's heart made a whooshing sound in his ears. He was trying to do the right thing and his father was attacking him. "I saw the pillow. From Mom's old room? Grammy redid the room and there were these pillows with a red horse on them on the bed. And I saw part of that pillow in the photo."

His father leaned toward him, dissecting Reid's expression. "You're kidding me, right? This is a joke?"

"No!"

"A pillow?"

"Yes!"

His father turned away, walked in a circle, wiping his face on the towel again, and came to stand in front of Reid. "Let me get this straight. Robby showed you a photo of a girl who wasn't even naked, whose face you couldn't see, and because you think you saw part of a pillow that looked something like one your grandmother put in your mother's room, you want me to go to Robert and tell him his son should stay away from Brynn?"

Reid opened his mouth but nothing came out. He was too confused. And furious.

His father wasn't finished. "I know exactly how you feel about my work, Reid. How you find real estate ventures and capitalism in general to be corrupt or dishonorable or whatever. It disappoints me and, frankly, it hurts." He licked his lips, gathering himself. "But the game you're playing here is going too far. You're too smart not to realize what's at stake if I go around accusing my business partner's son of running around with my fifteen-year-old based on your shaky deductions."

"Dad . . ." Reid's voice was quavering. He cleared his throat. "Dad, I wasn't trying—"

"I'll ask Brynn about it."

"She'll just deny it. She sent the photo."

His father's face hardened. "She did not send the photo, Reid. It's ludicrous. But I will ask her if she knows Robert's son, see what she says."

Reid started to make the argument again, from the beginning, but his father held up his hand.

"Enough. And don't even think of sharing this crazy story with your mother. She's got enough on her mind." He waited for Reid to promise.

Reid wasn't intending to tell his mother, not after his father's reaction, but he wasn't about to give him that.

His father went on anyway. "I'm grabbing my bag and having a drink at the Grill, like we planned." He jogged over to collect his tennis bag and began walking toward the clubhouse.

As Reid followed his father, his clenched fists gradually loosened, disappointment taking over from anger. He thought about what he had said about Brynn sending the photo, and it occurred to him for the first time that it wasn't a selfie. Someone had taken it. One of Brynn's friends? A boy? Maybe he didn't know his sister at all.

Wait. The shot was taken at his grandparents'. Why would Brynn's friends be there?

Who, then? Iris? The thought made him nauseous. Iris was pure. Or at least she had been until Brynn had taken her over. Reid wondered if he shouldn't protect Iris, do a better job of being a big brother to her. It had never been a role Brynn had allowed him to play. She'd always been in charge of herself, and if she needed anyone, she went to their father. But Iris was different, and she had been comfortable with Reid in the beginning.

Reid watched his father drinking a beer with his friends. Looking out for Brynn hadn't worked out so well. Why would looking out for Iris go any better? Let his parents deal with it. This wasn't his fucking rodeo.

He dug in his pocket for his phone and texted Alex.

REID: Up for a party at UVA Saturday?

ALEX: You pledging?

REID: Cutting loose. Way loose.

CHAPTER 28

Suzanne hung up with her mother and stormed upstairs to find Brynn. Her daughter's door was closed, and Suzanne took a moment to calm down before knocking.

"Who is it?"

The person who gave birth to you, who held you when you were sick, who could not imagine a more hopeful sight than your innocent face, and who now wonders how estrogen and oxytocin could make such a fool out of an intelligent woman. "It's Mom."

"Oh. Come in."

Suzanne opened the door and stepped inside. Brynn was sprawled on her bed on her stomach with a textbook and a highlighter. She pulled out her earbuds.

"What's up?"

"Your grandmother just informed me that you asked her to arrange for a limo to drive you and your friends around on Saturday night."

"Uh-huh."

"You didn't think to run that by us?"

She swished her hair to one side and twisted it between her fingers. "I did mention it to you a while ago."

"We talked about transportation for the prom, yes. And I said we'd be happy to drive."

"Which is why I asked Grammy Tinsley. She thought the limo was a great idea."

"It wasn't her place to arrange it."

Brynn tipped her head sweetly. "That's between you and Grammy, isn't it?"

"I'm still your mother." Suzanne sighed inwardly. She didn't want to fight with Brynn about prom. Suzanne had intended to finalize the arrangements with Brynn and had forgotten. Brynn was wrong to have gone behind her back, but Suzanne probably would've agreed to the limo if they had discussed it again. She crossed the room and perched on her daughter's bed. Brynn sat up and tucked her legs under her.

"Look," Suzanne said, "Your father and I just want you to be safe."

Brynn stared at her, lids drooping, jaw slack in an archetypal pose of boredom.

Suzanne tried a different tack. "Okay, say the limo takes you and Sam and your other friends from here, after pictures, straight to prom. What then?"

"After prom, it takes us back here, so I can change."

"Really?"

"Mom? The dress?"

Suzanne thought there were simpler ways to protect an expensive dress—such as putting it in a bag—but wasn't going to argue Brynn out of stopping by the house. Suzanne and Whit would be able to see if everyone had managed to stay intact and sober for the first few hours. "Okay, so you change—all your friends change, I guess—then the limo takes you to Lisa's for the party."

"Maybe Lisa's. We're still checking."

"Brynn, the prom is Saturday. What's to check?"

"Maybe Kendall's instead."

"Let's nail it down." Brynn blinked slowly, as close to assent as Suzanne would get. "And you're staying there all night." It wasn't a question.

Her daughter exhaled, exasperated. "You can call her parents, okay? You can even come over and do a full inspection. I'm sure they'd appreciate that."

"Brynn . . ."

She held a mechanical pencil between her index finger and thumb and wiggled it, tapping a rapid rhythm on her book. "Sure. I get it. It's like your job to suck the fun out of my life."

Suzanne let this go. It was such a standard teenage complaint, she couldn't take it personally.

Brynn went on. "Do you know some parents rented rooms at the Omni for their kids? For the whole night?"

Suzanne shook her head in disbelief.

"It's true. So instead of getting on my case about a stupid limo, maybe you should be thanking me for not asking Grammy Tinsley for that." Brynn raised her eyebrows. "Because she totally would've."

"Maybe that's true, Brynn. And if I'm getting on your case about anything, it's because I'm looking out for you." She leaned over and kissed Brynn's forehead. "Because I love you."

Brynn didn't say anything, but at least she didn't smirk.

～

The following day was Monday, and Suzanne had never been more relieved for the weekend to be over. The conversation with Brynn had left her nerves frayed, and she still didn't feel comfortable with the plans around prom. It was possible, she supposed, that no parent ever did. She ought to have been delighted that Reid had decided not to attend, but her son had returned from the club fund-raiser in a sullen mood, brushing off her inquiries about the cause. Not surprisingly, Whit didn't have any insight into Reid's state of mind, only confirming that their son had done everything the organizers of the event had asked of him.

Whit's take on Tinsley's limo order was predictable; he could see nothing to object to.

If she was honest, Suzanne would have to admit she had been happy to see all three of them disappear down the walk that morning.

While Suzanne cleaned up the dishes from breakfast and last night's dinner, Iris worked on her math problems in the dining room. Suzanne had enrolled her in the Kumon program, and the self-paced approach was a perfect fit. By the end of the summer, Iris would probably be ready to take high school algebra, a remarkable achievement considering the girl had been homeschooled only in basic arithmetic. No doubt she was bright and blessed with an orderly mind, but it did make Suzanne wonder what purpose all that classroom time truly served, especially in a trade-off with the freedom and self-reliance Iris had enjoyed for most of her life.

Having restored some semblance of order to the kitchen, Suzanne considered the remaining disarray on the breakfast table, on the dining table, and in the laundry room, wondering which area to attack first. Her phone buzzed on the counter beside her. She thought about ignoring it, certain it had to be someone from Boosters complaining about her lack of direction, or Tinsley demanding help with yet another fundraiser, or a class mom asking her to chip in for a bake sale, a carpool, or an appreciation lunch for the vastly underappreciated, but knew whoever it was would be as persistent as she had once been and call back. To her surprise, the phone screen read Detective DeCelle. She accepted the call and headed through the pantry into the living room, closing the door behind her. She and the detective exchanged greetings.

"I tried to reach your husband but couldn't get through."

"He's in meetings all morning."

"I figured. Ms. Blakemore, I'm calling because we've got a lead on Iris's family."

Suzanne lowered herself onto the couch. "Go on."

"We sent the father's sketch and the approximate date he went missing to all the jurisdictions in central and southern Virginia. Got a lot of leads that didn't pan out for one reason or another. But yesterday an officer in Salem—that's near Roanoke—thought the sketch looked familiar, someone he helped put away."

"Prison?"

"Yes, ma'am. He did three years for assault with a deadly weapon, plus resisting arrest. Served his parole. The date of the felony was close to when the girl said her father disappeared."

"Jim Smith?"

"I can't give you a name until we know more."

"Is he a veteran?"

"No confirmation on that yet."

Suzanne's mind was spinning. If Iris's father was alive, what would happen to her? Would she go off to live with him, just like that? What about his criminal record?

The detective continued. "Here's the thing. We had the police down there follow up on his last known address. The guy who lives there said he never saw him after his parole was over."

"So where is he?"

"Who knows? The uniforms mentioned to the friend that this guy might have family looking for him, in case he knew where to find him and just wasn't saying. It might bring him out." He didn't sound convinced.

"Do you think he's Iris's father?"

"It fits. Plus the friend? Name's Henry, but he goes by Buck. Then again, so do a lot of fellows down there."

Detective DeCelle said he'd let her know when they had more information and suggested she hold off on telling Iris anything.

"A guy like that, with a record, a loner. Hard to tell which way he's going to fall."

Suzanne agreed.

215

She closed the call. Her limbs were numb. The news was so unexpected. Iris had insisted her father was dead, and Suzanne had believed her. Or had she simply wished it were true? Suzanne wanted a chance with Iris, to help her fit into this world for which she was so ill prepared. It wasn't turning out the way she had hoped. She had expected Iris to soak up all the comforts and pleasures of the civilized world Suzanne introduced her to. Instead Iris was holding back, picking and choosing what she allowed to affect her, what she permitted to alter her. Suzanne didn't have the power she'd thought she would. And, more, she was learning that Iris was probably wise to not accept this new world with open arms. Iris's parents had been more right than wrong. The water Suzanne and everyone around her were immersed in, that they all kept swimming in, was a toxic soup. Suzanne had known this for a very long time. When she left for college, she had rejected her parents' false existence, their loveless marriage, but she had faltered. She had not been strong enough and had allowed herself to be swept up, carried along, despite what she knew. She had been leading a false life, one that Iris saw through easily. The girl wanted to return to the woods, to a hard, simple existence, and Suzanne could not blame her.

Whether or not Iris's father appeared, whether or not he wanted his daughter, Suzanne vowed to do the right thing by Iris, to protect what was pristine and free in her. It wasn't the same as parenting her, at least not by any standard Suzanne was aware of, but she would do her best. For far too long she had been floating along in a sea of compromise, dammed up by walls of fear. If Iris could maintain her integrity in the face of overwhelming odds, so could she.

Suzanne rose from the couch and went to see Iris, who was still at work. The girl needed a break; they both did. She gently placed a hand on Iris's shoulder.

"Iris?"

The girl looked up from her notebook. "Yes?"

"Are you up for an hour's drive?"

"I think so."

"Let's go to a botanical garden."

Iris considered. "Aren't all gardens botanical?"

Suzanne laughed. "Bring a jacket; looks like rain."

~

The drive was long and flat. The closer they got to Richmond, the less Iris liked what she saw out the window. So many roads, buildings, huge trucks. It was quiet inside the car, but imagining the noise and the smells made her anxious. She was about to ask Suzanne if they could turn around and go home when they drove through an area that was just houses with trees scattered in between. Soon it was green all around. Suzanne turned left through a gate.

"The Lewis Ginter Botanical Garden. I haven't been here for ages, not since a field trip with Reid's eighth-grade class."

A gigantic building, like a palace made of ice, loomed ahead.

"That's the conservatory. We can go there first."

Suzanne parked and led Iris into the Palm House at the entrance of the conservatory. Iris had read about cycads and palms in Suzanne's books, but that wasn't the same as standing beside them, examining their texture, experiencing their solemn pride. They moved through to another room, where the air was as thick and moist as on a mid-August day. Suzanne showed Iris the orchid collection and explained about the different types: the showy cattleyas with their ruffles and frills; the oncidiums with their dainty little flowers, looking just like their nickname, "dancing ladies"; and the dendrobiums and phalaenopsis, with a dozen or more intricately painted blossoms on each graceful arching stem, almost too beautiful to look at. Iris peppered Suzanne with questions about how the orchids grew and lived.

Suzanne pointed to a pair of blooms, each as large as her palm. The petals were the color of lilacs, with throats of deeper purple and yellow.

"This one, a cattleya, has an amazing scent, but only at night because it's pollinated by moths."

Iris imagined sleeping outside with orchids hanging from the trees above, waiting for the nighttime scent and the arrival of the moths, wings silver and ghostly in moonlight. If only she could enter the world of her imagining, or her past.

They moved on to the dry part of the conservatory, where cacti and other desert plants grew. Iris knew a little about them from her books and a National Geographic show about the Sonoran Desert, but she found the idea of life with little water disturbing. If she had to live without a stream or a river, she, too, would become hard and thorny. She followed Suzanne out of the conservatory and toward the Woodland Walk. On the way, they passed through gardens that reminded Iris of those planted around houses: neat groups of plants and trees arranged around paths, benches, fountains, and small ponds. Iris saw signs for the Healing Garden and asked to see it. One part was for meditation, although no one was sitting still the way Reid had demonstrated for her. The other part of the Healing Garden was a circle of plants around a grassy area. In the middle was a huge mortar and pestle on a stand.

"My mother used one like that." Her voice caught in her throat. To regain her control, she concentrated on a sign by a stocky tree whose gray bark was covered with knobby thorns.

Suzanne came close to her; their shoulders touched. "Prickly ash."

"Good name."

"Says its bark can be used to treat toothache."

Iris had a bad toothache when she was about seven, before Daddy left. Mama had mixed up something for it, boiled leaves and roots for a tea, put a compress on her cheek. Mama hadn't minded when Iris clung to the pink bear with the rainbow tummy patch Daddy had given her, even though Mama had a fight with him about it. Iris didn't understand most of what they said except that Mama thought the bear was bad. Daddy said it was just a stuffed bear, and it seemed to Iris he was right because she wanted very badly to keep it. Every time Daddy brought things home for Iris and Ash that Mama said didn't belong, they had a fight, but he kept doing it anyway.

Iris had no idea what herbs and roots Mama had used to ease her toothache, and it saddened her. It was like forgetting Mama's face, or the smell of her hair. She could only just recall those, and now she doubted herself. She had a hole in her mind where Mama used to be, and another for Daddy. And they used to be just about everywhere.

Lost in her thoughts, Iris walked the rest of the circle, not bothering to look at the plants. Suzanne followed her without a word.

They crossed two bridges and reached Woodland Walk. All the right trees and bushes and flowers were there—not just the Virginia ones that Iris recognized, but also ones that came from other similar places. But Woodland Walk had no wildness in it. Nothing struggled for life or was joyful in living it. It was like a TV show of the woods. Nothing surprising would ever happen there the way it did in real woods, all the time, if you knew how to watch. Ash would not show his face in Woodland Walk.

Iris lagged behind Suzanne, wishing herself away from here, this mockery of the place she loved more than anything else, the only home she had ever had and the only one she'd ever wanted. She'd rather be inside the ice palace with the cacti. It was more honest.

Suzanne called her name. Iris caught up. Suzanne pointed at the base of an old oak. "I'm wondering if you've seen that plant. The one about a foot high with the five leaflets."

Iris hadn't seen it for a very long time, but she'd spent too much time with it not to remember. "I used to help my mother dig it up."

"Really?" Suzanne seemed surprised.

"We had a big patch. We dug it up in the fall."

"And you sold it?"

"Some. My father took a sack with him."

Suzanne was frowning. "You never mentioned ginseng."

"I hadn't thought about it. It was a long time ago."

Suzanne stared at her as if Iris had a whole bunch of secrets wadded up in her brain. Maybe she did. Sometimes it was hard to know what to say and what to leave out. When it came to her life in the woods with Ash, with Mama and Daddy, most of the memories were so hard to find and so hard to hold on to they seemed like secrets to her, too.

Iris pictured herself squatting next to her mother, carefully brushing the dirt from the twisted root of the plant, still attached to the vivid green stem and the cluster of red berries in the center.

"Sang. Mama called it sang."

Suzanne put her arms around Iris, then, and Iris didn't pull away. Her tears came without her permission, hot and fast. Iris let Suzanne hold her, let her stroke her hair.

She let Suzanne rock her a little, in those fake woods.

CHAPTER 29

Brynn had maybe a half hour to get Iris ready for photos. It would've been simpler to have let Iris come along to the salon with her for an updo and makeup, but that was out of the question. Iris wasn't the starved rat she had been when she first showed up, but she still wasn't normal. She was a stick and moved too fast all the time. And something in her eyes was sketchy, like she knew a lot more than she let on. For tonight, Brynn needed her to look better than someone you'd find living beneath an underpass. Iris had to look, well, hot, or at least lukewarm.

"The color is super pretty on you, Iris."

Iris glanced down at the dress like she'd forgotten what she had on. Brynn's dress from sixth grade was too long on Iris, but the lilac color did bring out her eyes. And it was stretchy and hugged Iris's so-called curves. Brynn's mother was not going to approve, but by the time she saw it would be too late.

Brynn wielded the flat iron like a magic wand, setting loose curls in Iris's hair.

"Lift your chin and close your eyes." The girl did as she was told. Brynn applied eyeliner (navy, not black this time, and not all the way around, lol), mascara, blush, and pale lip gloss. "Ta-da!"

Iris studied herself in the vanity mirror, turning first one way then the other.

"I hope you're not going to scowl like that in the photos."

Iris pouted, lowered her chin, and widened her eyes. A perfect duck face.

Brynn laughed. "You're learning, Iris."

Iris smiled, genuinely this time.

Brynn heard high voices from downstairs. Her friends were arriving. Not all of them would fit in the limo, but they wanted to take pictures together while their makeup and hair were fresh. Plus Brynn's house, with the white columns, wide porch, and huge flowering bushes, had the best scenery. Some of the boys would already have smoked weed, not caring if it showed, but all the girls would wait until after the photos. What was the point otherwise? Brynn had to pace herself anyway. She didn't want to be trashed before she got to Robby's party. When she'd seen him a few days ago, they'd hooked up—not all the way, but enough that she knew he wanted her. Seriously wanted her. So she'd get loose at Kendall's but wait to get way live with him.

Iris got up, teetering on her heels.

"One sec." Brynn went to her desk and opened the top drawer. "I got you something." She handed Iris a phone.

"I have a phone."

"But you can actually call on this one, and text." She winked at Iris. "And take photos."

Iris turned on the phone. The screensaver was a rainbow.

"Iris was the rainbow goddess, right?"

"Yes, the messenger for Zeus. That's what my mother told me." Iris held the phone by the edges, like it was delicate. "Thanks, Brynn."

"No problem. I put my number in there for you. Just don't let my mom know, okay? She treats you like a baby." Brynn put her arm around Iris's shoulders and guided her to face the full-length mirror. "Wait until the boys see you, Iris. Wait until Sam sees you."

Iris blushed.

"Just wait. We'll have so much fun." Every teenager deserved to have fun, live on the edge a little. Even Iris.

~

The house was filled with people, and there were more outside on the porch and spreading over the lawn. Iris had thought it would only be a few of Brynn's friends, but parents were there, too, and brothers and sisters and even some grandparents, including Suzanne's parents. Worse than the crowd, though, was the look on Suzanne's face when Iris came downstairs. Her mouth opened, but she didn't say anything. She bit her lip, and her eyes were so sad, Iris had to look away. Suzanne went outside and pulled Brynn from her circle of friends, and although Iris couldn't hear the conversation, she could tell Suzanne was angry from the way she grabbed Brynn's arm. Whit took Suzanne away. Iris was confused. All the other girls had dressed up. Why shouldn't she?

Iris stood beside Sam for one photo. He was even more attractive in person than on the computer. His smile made her stomach feel the way it did after riding in the car for too long.

"We finally meet!"

He slipped his arm across her bare shoulder, which felt terrible and delicious at the same time. She had to stop herself from wriggling away.

Suzanne went inside to get Reid, then asked Iris to be in a few photos with the whole family. Brynn said something in private to Whit. He handed a phone to Iris and asked her to take the photos, and she understood Brynn didn't want Iris included. It didn't matter, though, because Reid left before they'd finished.

Iris, overwhelmed by the noise and activity, retreated to her room and settled in with her coloring books.

A bird whistle came from under her pillow where she'd hidden the phone Brynn had given her.

BRYNN: I'm leaving now. Back later. Wait up for me?

Iris typed slowly, using her index fingers, worried about making a mistake. When she was done, she couldn't find the send button. The blue arrow?

IRIS: I will. Have fun. Send me photos.

BRYNN: (yellow cartoon face blowing a heart)

Iris smiled. She searched the screen for where the pictures might be. Maybe her phone didn't have them. Finally she found them.

IRIS: (yellow cartoon face blowing a heart; rainbow icon)

She went back to coloring for a while, checking the phone every few minutes for texts from Brynn. She felt guilty about having a secret phone, but it seemed everyone in the family had secrets. Brynn sent secret photos to Robby, Suzanne had asked Iris not to mention what had happened to her in the woods, and Reid had told Suzanne he was going to be at Alex's tonight, but Iris had heard him talking on the phone about a party. Iris came to the conclusion that keeping secrets and telling lies was the only way people could manage their complicated lives. It took too much time to explain your choices, so you just did whatever you wanted and fixed the problems later, or ignored them, as Brynn had done by dressing up Iris.

Iris had drifted off when Brynn texted her that they were coming back. Iris checked her clock: almost eleven p.m. She slipped her penknife and phone into the small bag Brynn had loaned her and waited until she saw the lights of the limo in the driveway before going downstairs. Suzanne and Whit were watching TV and drinking wine. They both looked tired—and surprised to see her.

"We thought you'd gone to bed," Whit said.

"I'm waiting for Brynn."

Whit smiled, but Suzanne just sipped her wine. A moment later, headlights swept the wall of the entry. Brynn rushed through the front door, holding her shoes by the straps, her friends in a small herd behind her, each carrying a bag of some sort. They ran up the stairs.

"Be right back!" Brynn shouted.

Iris hung by the living room doorway, wondering where the boys were. Maybe they didn't change their clothes.

Reid came in from the kitchen, half a sandwich in his hand. "Hey, Iris." He was looking at her dress. She crossed her arms in front of her body. Reid spoke to Suzanne and Whit. "I'm going to Alex's now."

Suzanne said, "Text us if you decide to go anywhere, okay?"

"Sure thing."

"Or if you need a ride somewhere," Whit said. "It's never too late to call."

Reid let out a grunt and bit into his sandwich.

A stampede of feet on the stairs. The girls, led by Brynn, rushed past Iris into the living room.

"How was the dance?" Suzanne asked.

"Great!" Brynn was acting like a squirrel. "Daddy, can Iris ride in the limo with us? Just for a bit?"

Suzanne frowned. "I don't think that's a good idea."

"It's a lousy idea," Reid said.

Brynn swung her hair. "Who asked you?"

Whit looked past the other girls at Iris. "Do you want to, Iris?"

Reid stepped over to where Suzanne was sitting. "Mom, this is so wrong."

Whit ignored him. "Iris, do you want to ride in the limo?"

She looked from Suzanne to Reid to Brynn to Whit. Everyone was staring at her. "Yes."

Whit turned to Suzanne. "Let her go for a half hour. No big deal."

Iris wondered if Brynn felt the way she did at this moment when her parents didn't agree about what was right for her. Iris was thrilled that Whit was sticking up for her and excited that she might be able to go. But Suzanne's reaction worried her. If it was no big deal, then why didn't Suzanne just agree? Brynn was always saying her mother tried to suck the fun out of everything. Maybe that's what this was. At first

Brynn's anger with Suzanne had confused Iris. Now Iris understood something about what Brynn felt.

"Please, Suzanne?" Iris drew out the "please" the way Brynn did.

Suzanne sighed.

"Jesus, Mom," Reid said.

It had worked.

Whit came out and spoke to the driver. Iris climbed inside. It was darker than she'd thought it would be, but her eyes adjusted quickly. The boys were there but not in their dress clothes.

Sam was in the back seat, the one facing forward. "Hey, Iris. Sit next to me. Riding sideways can made you sick."

His eyes were glassy and bloodshot. Iris squeezed in next to him, and the rest of the girls found seats, talking all at once. The limo started to move.

Brynn was in the middle of the long seat, taking photos with her friends. She pointed the phone at Iris and Sam.

"So cute, you guys!" She took the photo. "Iris, sit in Sam's lap." The other kids hooted, sounding like coyotes.

"Come on, Iris." Sam opened his arms.

Iris hesitated.

One of Brynn's friends jumped into the lap of the boy next to her. "It's a limo tradition, see?"

Sam put his arm around her, lifting her under her arms. She tugged down the hem of her dress.

"You don't weigh anything," Sam said, settling Iris on his lap.

"She's a spinner!" another boy shouted, and everyone laughed.

Sam felt so warm underneath her, and his breath was hot across her forehead. She didn't know what to do with her arms. Brynn and some of the others took photos.

Iris remembered to smile.

~

The limo dropped her off. Suzanne was waiting on the porch, hugging her sweater around her even though it was a warm night. "You okay?"

"I'm fine." In truth, she was more than fine. She was excited because of Sam. She also had another secret and wanted to get away from Suzanne before she figured it out. "And I'm really tired, so good night."

"Good night, Iris." Suzanne kissed her on the forehead. "I'm glad you had a nice time."

In her room, Iris changed into the shorts and T-shirt she slept in, in case someone checked on her. She'd wait an hour, she decided, before she went to the party, longer if she heard anyone downstairs. Brynn had said it would last a long time and had shown her where it would be on a map on Iris's phone. "Text me when you get there and we'll get you in." Iris knew "we" meant Sam.

He'd said he'd be waiting for her.

CHAPTER 30

Fucking Alex. Reid had to hand it to him, the guy scored the best weed. Reid couldn't feel his face. Luckily, they'd waited to smoke it until they got close to Wertland Street, where the party was; otherwise they probably wouldn't have found it. They'd walked from Alex's house, which was maybe a mile and a half, and had crossed into campus and hunkered down in the shadow of a huge tree, out of sight of campus police.

"One more for the road?" Alex offered him the joint, burned down to a nub.

Reid held up his hand. "I'm good."

"Want something else?" Alex dug into his shirt pockets, fumbling.

"What you got?"

"Usual shit."

"I thought you were done with all that. Considering the Zoloft."

"Well, Mommy, I was, but then some asshole texts me about wanting to cut loose."

Reid held out his hand. "Excellent point."

Alex dropped something into his palm.

"What is it?"

"How the hell do I know? I can't see a damn thing." He opened a water bottle, tossed a pill in his mouth, and took a long drink. "But it might be E, so drink up. Safety first."

They ducked out from under the tree, crossed Main Street, and wound through the collection of shops and restaurants known as the Corner. Robby's house was near the end of Wertland, on the T intersection. On this warm night—Reid hadn't bothered with a jacket—the windows at the front were shut, probably trying to keep most of the noise inside so the cops wouldn't have an excuse to shut it down. A handful of people were hanging out on the porch, and a few more sat on folding chairs on the lawn, looking like they were waiting for a parade. A couple of the guys gave them looks, but Reid followed three girls inside, catching the door for them.

"Thanks," one of them tossed over her shoulder, her dark ponytail swinging like a horse's tail. She made for the back of the house, where the music was coming from, before Reid could tell if she was pretty.

More kids were milling around in the narrow hall. No one seemed to care who came in.

Reid moved into the doorway of what turned out to be the kitchen. Whatever he and Alex had taken under that tree started climbing up the back of his legs and into his armpits, like tingling knife points digging in. He checked behind him for Alex, who was practically on top of him. From the look on his face, that shit had hit him, too.

"Different," Alex said. "Go with it."

Reid slipped farther into the kitchen, the slicing, zinging feeling moving across his chest and up into his balls. There was a heat to it now. His heart was beating too fast. Alex was ahead of him, making a path through the swarm of bodies. The smell of beer and Axe and lemons (some girl's perfume?) reminded Reid of furniture polish, and that bugged him. Alex found the keg. The room pulsed, matching Reid's heartbeat. An acid taste invaded the base of his throat.

"Get me a beer."

"I'm on it." Alex passed him a Solo cup.

The predictability of the red Solo cup filled with beer annoyed Reid. In fact, everything here annoyed him: the faux-edgy music, the girls with their heels and backless shirts, long hair spilling everywhere, the guys with their monogrammed button-downs or, worse, athletic gear, signaling life was a game and they were always ready to hit the field. Why had he and Alex bothered to come? What had they expected? Conversations about existentialism with short-haired multiply pierced girls whose motto was that life sucked? Not here. Life never sucked here, not as long as the keg held out.

Reid found an empty spot on the wall to lean against and drank his beer. Alex was grinning and nodded at everyone who walked by and made small talk with a girl in jeans and a muscle tee with Tweety on it. Maybe Alex had taken different stuff than Reid had. He drained his beer. The sharp tingling was easing off. His heart was still racing, but he didn't care.

Alex leaned toward his ear. "Flip cup out back. Come on."

They followed the girl outside. Reid scanned around for Robby. The guys all looked like Robby, in one way or another. The backyard was lit up with Japanese lanterns and Christmas lights. Each little light had a prism hovering around it. Pretty. The girl, Kiley or Kailey, led Alex into position at the table with a row of beer-filled cups lining each side. He was laughing, swaying, touching the table to ground himself. Through the screen of the weird sensations inside him, it occurred to Reid that he shouldn't have taken random pills with his friend. But he couldn't hang on to it; it was only a thought and it didn't last. Reid moved away from the game, past a picnic table. Two girls and a guy were dancing on top of it to the shitty music, kicking off half-empty cups. The crowd egged them on, and the girls started rubbing themselves up and down the guy, who was having trouble staying upright. The girls kissed.

Reid's temples ached and his mouth felt stuffed with newspaper. He started to go back inside for another beer—anything to improve his mood—when he spotted a couple making out against the brick wall, shadowed by a tree. The guy had his hands on her butt and she was grinding into him; that much he could see. The couple broke off kissing. Reid kept walking, embarrassed, but a second later looked over his shoulder and caught sight of the girl's face. Brynn.

Holy shit.

Seeing him, she froze, unbelieving, or maybe so lit she wasn't sure what she was seeing. The guy stepped back, out of the shadow. Robby, of course.

Perfect. Just perfect.

Reid jogged the three steps to the back door, swung it open. It smashed against the side of the house.

"Hey!" someone said.

"Fuck you!" Reid barged inside, his head swollen with fury.

He was almost to the front door when he remembered Alex. "Shit." He pushed his way to the backyard and found Alex waiting his turn at the drinking game. He didn't look so hot. "We have to go."

"Now?"

Reid fought the urge to look over to where Brynn had been. "Right now."

Alex let himself be dragged inside. A bunch of people blocked the front door, arms around each other, singing something incomprehensible. Reid pushed his way around them, impatience and disgust frothing inside him. That stinging in his groin was back, and his heart was thumping. If only these douchebags would move out of his way. On the wall by the door was the control panel for the alarm system. He flipped it open. Three buttons on the side marked with a red flame, a green cross, and a blue shield.

He hit the red one.

The siren went off. The throng in the hall loosened. He pushed through, opened the door, and thrust Alex ahead of him. "Run!"

His friend took off down the street, away from the Corner. Reid sprinted after him.

～

Iris crouched with her back against the wall and her hands clamped over her ears. She'd been there for a while, since Brynn had gone outside with Robby. Iris had wanted to follow but knew she shouldn't. Brynn wouldn't want her.

Just like Sam.

He'd been there when she got to the house, standing on the porch smoking something with Brynn and two of her friends. Iris would've liked to have stayed out there, but they herded her inside.

Sam had his hands on her shoulders. "Come on, Iris."

Sam gave her beer in a red cup. She was thirsty—being nervous made her thirsty—so she drank some and felt light-headed right away. The others were drinking one cup after another. Sam was behind her and moved his hand onto her hip. The room tilted and an ache washed through her lower belly. Brynn was watching her, grinning, and snapping photo after photo.

"Show us your drink, Iris!"

Sam pulled her closer. It felt so good and, at the same time, so wrong. His hand moved over her breast. She gasped. Brynn took a photo.

"Sammy boy!" one of Brynn's friends shouted.

Iris wriggled away. Her hands were shaking and her beer spilled.

"Watch out!" Brynn shouted, jumping back.

Iris spoke into Brynn's ear. "Those photos are private, right? Like yours?"

"Sure." Brynn winked at her. "Sure they are."

Sam disappeared into the crowd with the others. Robby took Brynn outside.

Iris slunk along the walls like a mouse. She found a spot against the wall, covered her ears, and closed her eyes. That was where she stayed.

There was too much going on. The music was too loud, and people were shouting and laughing, touching each other, kissing and grabbing. A sick, nasty feeling swirled inside her, a new feeling and one she never wanted to have again. She wanted to leave but couldn't figure out how to do it without going through the crowd, touching all those people, or them touching her. If she just sat there, it would be over eventually. It couldn't go on forever, could it?

A wailing, screaming noise startled her. She opened her eyes. Everyone was looking around, wondering what to do.

Iris stood, hands still over her ears, took a deep breath, and headed into the crowd, slipping through the small spaces between people who were making for the front door. It was open; people were spilling out. She reached the porch. The fresh air hit her face.

She crossed the lawn, picking her way around overturned chairs, beer bottles, and red cups, and crossed the street, to where it was quieter and darker. She hurried, keeping to the shadows, and pulled the knife from her purse, holding it at her side.

Iris could not go back to the Blakemores', not now. She desperately needed somewhere familiar, somewhere safe. She'd made a mistake trusting Brynn. She'd been foolish in thinking Brynn was letting her into her life, accepting her, helping her become someone she had never in a million years expected to be. For a short time, Iris had thought she could fit in, and she had wanted to become the teenager everyone expected her to be. She'd even imagined Sam was attracted to her, but it was only a game. She didn't understand its purpose and she didn't want to. There was nothing to learn except this: she didn't belong.

When she reached the area with stores and restaurants, Iris crossed the main road and entered the campus. She knew the layout from walks with Suzanne and from her own nighttime excursions. As late as it was, a few people were around, including what she guessed were some sort of police, but it was simple to avoid them. She slipped along the shadows.

Ducking between parked cars, she crossed a narrow, empty road and found the place she was looking for. She jumped the low stone wall and zigzagged between row after row of upright slabs and towers of stones. A nearby streetlight cast a dim light as far as the center of the cemetery. She moved into the dark, drawn by scent to an evergreen, an unfamiliar species, and lay down beneath it on her back.

She had no one. Ash would never come here. He might never come again, knowing how fully she had abandoned him, how she had sold her soul (and his) to this barren world in exchange for exactly nothing. Iris listened to the never-ending traffic noises, the whirring of machines whose purpose she did not know, the barking of a chained dog, the insistent piercing whine of a siren in the distance. She listened: passive, uncaring, lifeless.

CHAPTER 31

Suzanne awoke on the living room couch. A black-and-white movie was playing on the television. The sound was off. She pushed herself to a sitting position and checked her phone for the time—3:35—then checked her texts. Nothing unread. She had texted Brynn around one a.m., and her daughter had replied that she and her friends were playing Apples to Apples. The text had seemed lucid enough. Suzanne had texted her again an hour later and gotten no response. She had considered contacting Kendall's mother but didn't want to second-guess the woman who had done plenty by hosting the party and who had promised to check on the kids. The boys were due to go home before two. Suzanne surmised that Brynn hadn't responded because she was occupied with her friends—or fast asleep.

Reid eschewed check-in texts, citing their pointlessness. Mia had called just after eleven to say the pizza she'd ordered for the boys had disappeared from the kitchen counter, prima facie evidence that they were alive and well. Suzanne had giggled at the phrase *prima facie*. After she had hung up with Mia, Whit had gone to bed, but Suzanne had stayed, saying she wasn't tired yet. And then she'd fallen asleep.

Now she carried the empty wineglasses into the kitchen and drank a glass of water. A car stopped on the road in front of the house. The bushes along the sidewalk partially obscured her view, but she heard a door shut, and when a flashlight swept over the car, she saw emergency lights on the roof. She dropped the glass in the sink, where it shattered, and ran to the front of the house. Torn between going to the door and running upstairs for Whit, Suzanne stood paralyzed in the entry.

"Whit!" She scrambled halfway up the stairs. "Whit!" A light came on in the upstairs hall. Suzanne rushed to the door and opened it. Two figures were on the walkway, cast in shadow by the streetlight. Suzanne flipped on the porch lights. A female police officer was half carrying Brynn toward the house. Suzanne ran toward them. Brynn's face was slack, her eyes unfocused. Her hair was matted, and one sleeve of her shirt was torn, the bra strap hanging off her shoulder.

"Brynn!" Suzanne grasped her daughter by the arm to help support her. The sour smell of beer and vomit coming from Brynn's hair and clothing told Suzanne what was wrong. She spoke to the officer as they hoisted Brynn up the steps. "Where did you find her?"

"Let's just get her inside; then we can talk."

Whit appeared at the door in pajama bottoms and a T-shirt. "What's going on?"

"She's drunk," Suzanne said.

"Here, let me take her." He slipped his arm around Brynn's waist.

In the light of the entry, Suzanne noticed Brynn's jeans were unzipped. "No."

Whit followed Suzanne's gaze. "Jesus."

"I'd get some towels," the officer said to Suzanne. "She made a mess of my cruiser."

Suzanne hurried to the kitchen, grabbed a roll of paper towels and two water bottles from the pantry, and returned to the living room. Brynn was propped up on the couch, her head lolling on Whit's shoulder.

The policewoman pulled a phone and a paisley ID case from her pocket and placed them on the coffee table. "At least she was carrying ID. You be surprised at how many don't."

"What should we give her?" Whit asked. "What if she took something else, like pills?"

Suzanne's throat locked tight. That hadn't occurred to her.

The officer said, "The Breathalyzer result was high enough to account for her state. Otherwise I'd have taken her straight to the hospital." Her tone was matter-of-fact. She looked at Suzanne. "You might not remember, but I met you at the benefit last fall. The one for Matt Schuster. I'm Pat Nguyen."

Suzanne nodded, although she couldn't remember the woman or anything else at the moment.

Officer Nguyen pointed to a chair. "Mind if I sit down? It's been a long night."

Suzanne said, "Please. Can I get you coffee or anything?" Her voice sounded odd, like she was acting a part and doing it badly.

"I'm fine, thanks." The officer sat. "First off, where did you think your daughter was tonight?"

Suzanne said, "At a friend's house. It's prom night and the parents agreed to host. The mom said she would supervise."

Officer Nguyen raised an eyebrow. "We got a call about an hour ago about a fire alarm at a house on Wertland. A party was under way, mostly college kids but also a few younger ones." She nodded at Brynn. "Your daughter was on the front lawn."

Suzanne pictured it. Drunken kids running from the building, stepping over her daughter, passed out on the lawn, half-undressed. Suzanne glanced at Whit. His face was ashen.

"The ID says she's fifteen, is that correct?"

"Yes." Whit cleared his throat. "Was she, was she dressed?"

"She was pretty much as she is now. Her pants weren't off, just unzipped."

Suzanne wiped her face, surprised to find it wet. "Whose house was it? How do we find out who was there?"

"We talked briefly to three students who lived there. All over twenty-one, and we didn't see anything other than a lot of alcohol. They all said they didn't know your daughter."

Whit's eyes flashed with anger. "They would say that, wouldn't they? Right after dumping her on the lawn?"

The officer nodded. She pointed at Brynn's phone. "You might find some answers in there, if she won't talk." She put her hands on her knees and stood. "I'm going to have to charge her. Public intoxication and underage drinking." Whit began to protest. The officer held up her hand. "Rules are rules."

They thanked Officer Nguyen for bringing their daughter home and showed her out. Whit roused Brynn enough for her to drink a bottle of water; then they brought her upstairs. Suzanne cleaned Brynn up as best she could, took off the soiled clothes, and managed to get her into a fresh shirt. Suzanne sat on the edge of the bed and stroked her daughter's hair from her face, wondering what had motivated the girl to do this. Suzanne couldn't accept that this was normal teenage behavior; if it was, she would insist on recalibration of the word *normal*. Why had Brynn taken such risks? All the things Brynn had wanted—limos and designer dresses and staged photos—had not been enough. How had her daughter ended up this way, and how had Suzanne been oblivious?

Brynn's phone was downstairs, and Suzanne wasn't certain she could bear to explore what it might contain. Not tonight.

She kissed her daughter's forehead and left the room. In the hallway she heard Whit climbing the stairs and met him at their bedroom door.

He pulled her into his arms and held her tight. "It'll be all right."

Suzanne's thoughts went to Reid. She wished she could talk to him, but he would be asleep. She let go of Whit. "I'm just going to check on Iris."

"All right."

She went to Iris's door and opened it slowly so it wouldn't creak. The room faced the backyard and was dark. Suzanne stepped over to the bed, straining to make out the girl's sleeping form.

"Iris?" she whispered.

Suzanne touched the covers where Iris's shoulder should have been and felt only bedding. She reached for the switch on the bedside lamp and pressed it on.

The bed was empty.

Suzanne ran from the room. She checked for the girl in Reid's room and returned to the hall. "Whit!" Without waiting for an answer, she flicked on the lights and flew down the stairwell. She hurried through the dining room, the kitchen, the living room, back to the entry, hoping Iris was curled up in a chair somewhere. Whit rushed down the stairs. "What now?"

"Iris is gone! She's gone!"

"Jesus! What the hell is going on? Did you check outside?"

"No. I didn't think of it. Can you?"

He took off toward the kitchen and she followed. He opened the back door, threw on the security lights, and crossed the patio. Suzanne waited in the doorway while he made a circuit of the yard, moving in and out of the shadows.

Whit jogged across the patio, spread his hands, and told her what she already knew. "She's not there."

"Oh God." Why would Iris have left the house? Suzanne knew instantly it had to do with prom, with Brynn.

She went to the living room, snatched Brynn's phone from the table, and unlocked the screen.

Whit appeared at her side. "What are you doing?"

"Looking for photos." Suzanne fixed her attention on the screen. Her trembling fingers refused to obey her. She opened the photo folder and accidentally closed it. "Shit!" She took a seat, dropped the phone in her lap, and wrung her hands to stop the shaking. She tried again, moved to the right folder, and scrolled through the most recent shots, ones taken at the house, in the limo, at the prom itself. Nothing more recent.

Of course. Snapchat. Photos evaporating in a virtual cloud.

She returned to the home screen, clicked on the message icon.

Whit sat beside her. "Suzanne."

"Wait. There's another folder." She pressed it open. "Oh my God, Whit. Look."

She showed him the photo of Iris in the lilac dress, sitting on Sam's lap. "That's in the limo, Whit." He winced. Suzanne swiped to the next photo. Iris and Sam again. Iris holding a cup, Sam's hand on Iris's breast. The expression on Iris's face betrayed confusion and fear through an awkward smile.

"Is that Kendall's house?" Whit said.

"I think it's the party." Suzanne's throat closed. She clicked back to the home screen and opened the message folder. IRIS. KENDALL. SAM. ROBBY. She touched the first thread. "These messages. These are to Iris."

"How? Her phone doesn't work."

"Not the one we gave her." Suzanne tapped the phone symbol beside Iris's name and put the phone to her ear. Whit stared at her, concern etched on his face. She turned away. Brynn. Iris. The limo. The party.

Three rings. Four. Five.

"Hello?"

"Iris." Her throat clogged with tears. "Iris, it's Suzanne."

"I know." Her voice was faint.

"Where are you?"

"Under a tree."

Whit touched her arm. Suzanne nodded at him. "Iris, can I come get you?"

"No."

"Please, Iris. We want you safe." The skin across her palms tightened. She rubbed her free hand on her thigh and tried to think of what else to say. "We want you home."

"It's not my home. I don't want to be there."

"I know."

Iris's voice was stretched thin, close to breaking. "I don't belong there."

Suzanne winced and pressed her fist into the hot, painful ball below her rib cage. "I know you don't. I understand." As she said it, Suzanne realized it was truer than she'd previously known. She understood because she felt it, too. "Let me bring you back and we'll figure it out." She reached inside herself for the conviction she knew Iris needed. "Iris, I promise. We'll find a way to make you happy again."

A long pause. "Okay."

Suzanne smiled. "Okay. Thank you." She gave Whit a thumbs-up. "So where should I pick you up?"

"I'll walk."

"It's dark."

"I don't care."

"See you soon." Suzanne closed the call and put down the phone.

Whit got up before she could say anything. "I'll turn on the porch lights."

Suzanne leaned back against the cushions, disgust with herself for failing Iris mixing with relief that the girl was safe. Dread pricked below her skin. She rubbed her temples and stared at the phone on the table.

Who the hell was Robby?

CHAPTER 32

Whit managed a couple of hours of sleep after Iris came home but awoke at nine, bleary and lethargic. He texted his tennis partner to cancel their scheduled match and holed up in the living room with the Sunday paper. When Brynn finally crawled downstairs around eleven, she took the route to the kitchen through the dining room, avoiding him. Fine. Whit was in no mood to lecture her on the rules she had broken and the lousy judgment she had exercised. He had left water and two Advil on her nightstand before he had gone to bed, and that was all he could offer, at least for now. Suzanne seemed to be taking the same approach. Since he hadn't seen her downstairs all morning, Iris, he assumed, was asleep in her room. She had come home with twigs in her hair but, unlike Brynn, hadn't shown any signs of intoxication.

Whit was drifting off on the couch when the front door opened.

"Reid?"

His son ambled in, pale and serious, his hair wet from showering. "Hey."

"Did you come straight from Alex's?"

"Yeah, why?"

He checked his watch. "It's noon."

"So?" Even for Reid, his tone was hostile.

"So were you guys out last night? Because you didn't text us."

His son looked straight through him and headed for the kitchen.

"Reid!" Whit tossed the paper onto the coffee table. He listened for an answer, or at least a conversation between Reid and Brynn, but all he heard were cabinets opening and closing and someone rummaging through the refrigerator. Frustration mushroomed in his chest. Since Iris had moved in, his home had become utterly chaotic, and it was unacceptable. Suzanne had given up on keeping things running smoothly, and Brynn was acting out, no doubt in response to the disruption and having to vie for her mother's attention. This wasn't the way to raise teenagers.

Suzanne was coming downstairs. Once they'd had a chance to talk with Brynn and set her straight, he'd take the time to sit down with Suzanne and address the real problem head-on—Iris. Headstrong girls like Brynn would always push the envelope and risk getting into trouble. That's how they discovered their strength and gained confidence. Naturally, he didn't want her to get hurt, and she'd been patently stupid last night, but he would not break her spirit. Brynn had always needed a lot of attention, and having to compete with Iris for it was not bringing out the best in her.

"Is Reid back?" Suzanne had changed into dark jeans and a white button-down shirt and had pulled her hair into a ponytail. This, he recognized, was her armor. If she looked tidy and put-together, she might feel that way.

"He's in the kitchen with Brynn."

She marched by him. He had no choice but to follow.

Brynn was slumped at the breakfast table with a glass of water and a plain bagel. Her skin was the color of marble and her eyes were closed. Reid was eating Raisin Bran at the counter. They looked like strangers at a late-night diner in a bad neighborhood.

Suzanne approached Brynn. "We have a lot to talk about. Did you take the Advil?" Brynn nodded, almost imperceptibly. Suzanne walked around the counter to face Reid. "You all right?"

He spooned cereal into his mouth and didn't look up. "I'm fine."

"Good. I'm glad." Suzanne ran water over a sponge and wiped the counter, the crease over her left eye deepening. "Brynn got into some trouble last night."

Reid nodded. Whit wasn't certain what the nod meant, but the lack of a verbal response was irritating.

"And Iris," Suzanne said.

Reid looked up, his spoon suspended in the air. "Is she okay?"

"I think so."

He nodded again and went back to eating.

Something about the boy's posture, his attitude, sent a creeping sensation across Whit's neck. He ran a hand through his hair and busied himself getting a glass of orange juice from the fridge, trying to dispel the feeling that he was missing something.

Suzanne rinsed out the coffeepot and the sink, wiped the counter again.

Whit said to her, "Maybe you and I should conference about this first, huh?"

"Maybe." She seemed to be considering it, then abruptly turned to Brynn. "Who's Robby?"

"Huh?" Brynn's voice was gravelly.

"Who's Robby?"

"Can we talk about this later? My head hurts."

Reid peered over his shoulder at his sister. She studied her bagel.

"Robby who?" Whit offered it cautiously. The room seemed filled with water, sloshing one way, then the other. He felt seasick or like he was the one with a hangover.

Suzanne said, "Last night Brynn texted someone named Robby."

Reid laid both forearms on the counter and addressed Whit. "Come on, Dad. You know. Robby." He drew out the name. "Robby. Commonly short for Robert."

Whit placed the carton of orange juice in the door of the fridge. He did it slowly, not eager to turn around. *Robby. Robert.* Suzanne would be standing behind him, looking worried and exhausted and, now, puzzled. Reid would be smirking. Whit exchanged the position of the orange juice and the milk, then shut the door and took a sip of juice as casually as he could.

"You remember, Dad. At the club. I told you I met Robby. Son of Robert." He snapped the *t* sound. Whit couldn't figure out why the sound bugged him so much, but it did.

"I remember you mentioning him."

"Do you remember me mentioning a photo he showed me? Do you remember who I said it was?"

"Well, sure." Right away, Whit regretted the admission.

Suzanne tilted her head and eyed him, like a robin examining a worm it was about to spear. "What's this?"

Brynn let out a huge sigh. "Can we not do this now? My head?"

Reid spoke to his mother. "*This* is something Dad didn't want me to bother you with. At the club, at that fund-raiser, Robby Shipstead—I think we all know who we're talking about now—showed me a photo on his phone. It was a girl, blonde hair, mostly undressed. Her face wasn't in the picture."

"Right." Whit organized his thoughts. Reid was saying this all wrong, confusing everything. "Suzanne, Reid recognized a pillow. Part of a pillow." He waited for her to say it was ridiculous.

She was stone faced. "A pillow."

"Yes. I should've said he *thought* he recognized part of a pillow."

Reid said, "With a red horse on it exactly like the one in your old room."

"There must be a million—" Whit began.

"A million, Dad? Seriously?"

Suzanne's eyes were trained on her son. "With a white background? A red horse with designs on it?"

Reid nodded.

"Wait." Brynn straightened a little, holding on to the edge of the table. "Let me get this straight. Robby showed you a photo of *me*?"

The color drained from Suzanne's face. Whit moved toward her, but the look she gave him stopped him dead.

Reid twisted toward his sister. "Your buddy Robby didn't know who I was, obviously. He probably showed it to everyone."

"Shut up. Just shut up." Brynn slumped in her chair, her tangled hair covering most of her face.

Whit detached himself from his wife's glare and took a step toward Brynn. "I can't believe you would send someone a photo like that."

Reid said, "Why not, Dad? Why can't you believe it? I told you, after all. And you said you'd talk to her."

Suzanne's voice was low and calm. "And did you, Whit?"

He looked around at his son and his wife, their faces angry, disappointed, accusing. He avoided Brynn, whose sickly pallor was its own commentary. "Before she left for prom, I told her to be careful, so, yes, I did talk to her." Suzanne's expression hardened. "I didn't talk about the photo, about the part of the pillow, okay? Because it was absurd! It was too damn absurd!"

The room fell silent except for the sound of Whit panting in furious impotence.

"Brynn." Suzanne's voice faltered for the first time. "The party was at Robby's, is that right?"

"Yeah."

"He invited you?"

"Yeah."

"Who else was there?"

"What do you mean?"

"Any of your friends?"

Brynn sighed and dropped her head onto her arms. "Sam. Ophelia. Lisa." She uncrossed one arm and pointed at Reid.

Whit scowled at his son. "You didn't tell us."

"Yeah, well, there's a lot of that going around."

"You saw your fifteen-year-old sister at a college party and you didn't do anything?"

Reid scraped his stool back and stood up. "I'm not going to be the fall guy, okay? You can't make this about me." He started to leave and turned in the doorway. "And who says I didn't do anything? Why do you always assume the worst? No one forced Brynn to go. No one forced her to get drunk and climb all over that guy." He spun away.

"Reid!" His son walked off. "Christ!" Whit swiped at the air in front of him. "Suzanne, did you know about this?"

She was crushing the sponge in her hand, and her mouth was a grim line. "About Reid? No." She paused, opened her mouth and closed it again, appearing to change her mind about what direction to take. She went to the breakfast table and sat across from Brynn. "Do you know where the police found you?"

Brynn lifted her head an inch.

"On the lawn." Suzanne's voice thickened. "Someone, Robby probably, dumped you on the front lawn."

Brynn sat up and pulled her sleeves over her hands. She blinked hard and rubbed her eyes.

"Brynn, are you remembering something?"

Their daughter scanned the room. "Where's Iris?"

"Upstairs."

"Is she all right?"

Suzanne leaned closer, her voice trembling. "Do you honestly care, Brynn? Do you?"

Their daughter lowered her lids, exhaled loudly, and dropped her head again.

Whit waited a moment for Brynn to answer or for Suzanne to repeat her question or pursue a different line of questioning. The silence grew too large for him to bear, but he couldn't leave. That would only make things worse, if that was possible.

~

Suzanne gave up on Brynn, who was too hungover to be communicative, and retreated upstairs. She curled up in a chair in her bedroom facing the window. A light drizzle shrouded the view, muting the vibrant green of the newly leafed trees. Her limbs sank, heavy with weariness, so heavy she was numb. She would've crawled into bed were it not for the anxious, heated energy coursing through her. She could not relax. Sleep, as desperately as she needed it, was out of the question. She was far too furious to sleep.

She waited for Whit to come in. When she'd left the kitchen he had stayed with Brynn, and cowardice was keeping him there. The longer she waited, the hotter her anger grew, as if she were an incinerator and the thoughts and feelings she could access by simply sitting still were a kind of fuel. She thought about asking Whit to come upstairs so she could say what she had to say, but when she imagined herself at the top of the stairs, calling to him, she knew she would scream his name and keep screaming it. In the bedroom, at least, the door could be closed. She might contain her fury.

Suzanne rose and paced the room, lifting logical thoughts, rational plans from out of the overheated slurry in her mind, considering what she was going to do. Her life had become intolerable. It might, indeed, have been intolerable for a very long time, but she was only now acknowledging the fact. The timeline, the road that had brought her here, didn't matter. What was important was to change course. In her mind the image of a glacier arose, a mile-thick slab of ice sliding inch by inch across the earth, transforming what had been cold but alive into something hopeless, crushed, and frozen solid. She had been overtaken and crushed by a glacier.

The door opened and Whit entered. Suzanne stopped pacing and returned to the chair, where she would be more controlled and have something to hold on to.

Whit lifted his hands. "Before you say anything, Reid did not get the story straight, the one about the photo. You know how he is."

"No. Tell me."

"He's idealistic and he's stubborn. Once he sees something a certain way, he never reevaluates."

"And what, exactly, was he supposed to see differently?"

He stepped closer, sensing a chance to explain his position. "What that photo seemed like to me, last Sunday, a week ago. Not now, obviously. Not with hindsight." He spread his hands in innocence. "You didn't see his attitude when he told me about it at the club. He'd spent the day doing something he didn't want to do, and it seemed to me he was taking an opportunity to rile me."

Suzanne clenched her teeth and measured her words. "It was about you? Your son tells you about a photo he saw that he thinks is Brynn, and your first thought is that he's doing it to score points."

"At the time, yes. That photo could've been anyone, Suzanne. It could've been anyone."

"Then it could've been Brynn."

Whit jammed his hands into his pockets. His cheeks flushed and he turned away.

Suzanne went on. "And you told Reid you would talk to Brynn. If you had actually talked to her about the photo, she might at the very least have had second thoughts, knowing this guy was showing her photo around." Suzanne stood, unable to control her agitation. "But there was more to it than that, wasn't there, Whit? It wasn't, in the end, about Reid or Brynn, was it?"

He'd had his back to her and now turned halfway around. "What are you talking about?" But he knew, he knew exactly what she would say. His shoulders were hunched, ready to absorb the blow.

She felt not a drop of pity for him. "The reason you didn't believe Reid or talk to Brynn had nothing to do with the credibility of what Reid said. It had to do with Robby, and with his father." She circled around him so he had no choice but to face her. "You knew if I found out, I'd insist on talking to Robby and his parents, and that wasn't something you could handle. Instead of protecting your daughter, Whit, you chose to protect your precious deal!"

Whit straightened his shoulders. "That's not how it was. That's not it at all."

"Isn't it? Then why haven't you called Robert and told him what his son did? Why is it that the only person you're angry with is Reid?"

He blinked slowly and let out a long breath. "I didn't mean to endanger Brynn. You've got to believe that." He paused, waiting for her assent.

Suzanne let him hang there. Wasn't failing to act to protect someone the same as endangering them?

"I know I should've listened to Reid. At the time, what he was saying seemed so far-fetched. I wish to God I had listened, but it seemed so crazy."

"Crazy or inconvenient?"

"Suzanne. I know you're mad—with good reason—but you can't lay the whole mess at my feet."

"I'm not. I take blame for what happened to Iris. I should have been stronger. I should have stuck to my gut feeling that getting in a limo with Brynn and her friends was not going to end well. I blame myself for that." Suzanne crossed to the bed and sat. Now that she had vented her anger, sadness welled in her chest. Her nose stung. She rubbed her eyes and smoothed her hair.

Whit dropped his voice. "Don't blame yourself. I'm the one who let Iris decide." He moved closer. "Maybe we made the wrong decision taking Iris on."

Suzanne jerked up her head. "What?"

"Maybe we're not as good at being parents as we thought. What happened last night pretty much proves the point. And Iris has been a huge strain on us, you especially."

"You're blaming Iris?"

"No." He took a step back, two. "I feel for her, I really do."

Suzanne looked at Whit a long moment. Did he mean what he said? Had he always been so self-serving? She didn't know anymore. She'd lost her ability to judge, if she had ever possessed it. Perhaps she been too busy—always busy!—to see Whit and the rest of her perfectly constructed life clearly. She had chosen to march on, iPhone in hand, through the blizzard of duties, tasks, and obligations that she'd believed until this very moment had been mandated by her choice to bind herself to this man.

Suzanne got up, went to the closet, and pulled a small duffel bag from the shelf.

Whit followed her and pointed at the bag. "What are you doing?"

She dropped the bag on the floor, pulled a few items from a dresser drawer, and stuffed them in the bag. She added a pair of pants, a couple of shirts, a fleece jacket, sneakers, and the toiletry case from her gym bag and zipped the duffel closed.

"Suzanne!"

She pushed past him with the bag, grabbed her laptop from the table next to the chair, stowed it in her computer case, and gathered both bags.

Whit stood in front of her. "Where are you going?"

"Away."

"For how long?"

"I don't know, Whit. Long enough to think. Hopefully long enough for you to talk to Reid and Brynn without me in the way or running defense or enabling you or whatever it is that's been going on for a very long time."

He placed a hand on her arm. "Please don't go. Please."

She shook her head. "You want to blame Iris because it's easy. It's misguided, Whit. You ought to be thanking her for showing us who we truly are."

"What are you talking about?"

"I hope you figure it out. I really do." Suzanne moved past him, stuck the computer bag under her arm, opened the door, and turned to him. "Unless you object, I'm taking the Navigator." His face was a canvas of pain, resentment, and confusion. Suzanne's perennial response to her husband's distress was to restore order so he could find peace again, or at least launch himself forward, always forward. Now she resisted the impulse to smooth his path so he could move through this difficult terrain. Her path mattered, too. She didn't know what it looked like or where to find it, but nevertheless, at this moment, hers mattered more.

"And Iris," Suzanne said as she left. "I'm taking Iris, too."

She crossed the hall into Iris's room and stood over the bed. The girl was curled on her side, hands pressed together under her cheek, knees drawn up. Her hair had fallen across her face. Suzanne fought the urge to brush it away and instead smoothed the cover over the girl's shoulder.

Suzanne had promised Iris that she would find a way to make her happy again. She intended to keep that promise. Somehow, at this moment, it seemed to be one she'd be able to keep, and perhaps the only one worth honoring.

CHAPTER 33

Iris buckled her seat belt and glanced out the car window at the house, wondering if she might not see it again, and surprised to discover an ache of sadness take hold in her chest. She had already asked Suzanne where they were going—twice—and hadn't gotten an answer, so there was no point in asking again. The reason for leaving was clearer to her. She'd heard most of the argument floating up from the kitchen and all of the discussion between Whit and Suzanne in their bedroom. She hadn't been spying, but she had come to realize her hearing was more sensitive than other people's.

Suzanne started the car, and they began to roll down the driveway. Reid stood on the porch, his hands laced behind his head and his elbows sticking out, as if his head had gotten too heavy for his neck. Iris couldn't see his face clearly, but everything was there in the way he stood, rocking a little from one foot to the other. He was sad and worried and probably afraid. Iris remembered how it felt to know she was about to lose her mother. It was like falling in a dream: the sickening dread of hitting the ground seemed to last forever and was worse than the crash could ever be.

They turned onto the street and drove through town, quiet on a Sunday afternoon. They passed the school and kept heading south. The day was gray and it was spitting with rain, and the gloominess mixed in Iris's stomach with the unsettling feeling of leaving without knowing where she was headed. That, too, felt familiar. Years ago she had left the cabin on a morning like this, except it was late summer, and had struck out into the woods, knowing she had to leave but not knowing how far or in what direction she would go. North, as it happened, on that day.

The rain came down harder and Suzanne flicked on the wipers.

"I'm sorry," Iris said.

"For what?"

"For going to the party."

"I understand why you went, but thank you."

"I thought it would be fun."

"That's pretty normal, wanting to have fun."

Iris thought of Sam grabbing her, and of how Brynn kept drinking more and more—how everyone did—until they didn't know what they were doing.

"I'm not sure the point of the party was to have fun."

Suzanne looked at her a moment, then returned her attention to the road. "No?"

"When we got there, people were already bumping into each other, falling down. It seemed like the point was to find what happened after fun."

Suzanne didn't say anything.

"Anyway, I'm sorry I went and I'm sorry I didn't come straight back."

Iris could feel Suzanne thinking past what Iris had said. Iris looked out the window. The houses were farther apart now.

Suzanne broke the silence. "How about we drive up to the parkway?"

"Isn't that where you found me?"

"Yes, it is."

"What are we going to do there?"

Suzanne stopped at a traffic light. "Drive. I think I'd just like to drive."

Iris was still thinking about what Suzanne meant and was a little concerned about what they were doing, but she'd hardly had time to mull it over before signs for the Blue Ridge Parkway appeared. Two turns later they were driving toward the spine of the mountains. The rain eased and the wind picked up, pulling the clouds into pieces and scattering them across the sky. A few cars passed by but mostly the road was empty. The tires hissed on the wet road. Iris opened the window a crack, and the smell of damp vegetation and moist, wormy dirt filled her nostrils. At first she strained to see into the woods, to catch a glimpse as they sped by and extract a clear, still picture of what the woods were like in that spot, what might be growing or blossoming or creeping along. It was impossible, though, and left her dizzy. So she leaned back in the seat and took in what she could easily see and wondered if they would just drive forever. Without a home, it was hard for Iris to imagine where she belonged, and she had the feeling Suzanne felt much the same.

They pulled off and parked in a small cleared area with a picnic table. Suzanne turned off the engine and hung on to the steering wheel, staring ahead. The rain had almost stopped.

"What are you looking for?"

"I don't know." Suzanne pointed to a set of stone steps leading up to a level area, hidden by trees. "That's an old railroad. That's where I found you."

"I don't remember it at all."

"You were so sick." She twisted to face Iris and smiled for the first time today. "I'm so glad I found you. And not just because you needed help."

"Then why?"

Her brown eyes filled with tears. "Because I need help, too."

Iris waited for an explanation. She couldn't think of how she could help Suzanne, especially since she didn't know what was wrong, at least not in detail. Suzanne was unhappy with her family and her life, but that wasn't the sort of problem Iris had any experience with. Iris wanted to help Suzanne, she really did, but she had no idea how.

"Iris, you told the police that after your mother died, someone came to the cabin, and that's when you left."

"Yes."

"I'm just guessing about why you couldn't stay after that. It wasn't your place anymore." Suzanne spread her hands, helpless. "That's how I feel, too."

"And I'm the stranger that showed up?"

"In a way." She shifted in the seat, lining up her thoughts. "I'll bet that cabin wasn't home after your mother wasn't there anymore."

Iris hadn't realized it, but it was true. She dropped her gaze to her lap, remembering the emptiness of the cabin, the hollow space, too quiet, too still. Iris had been waiting for a reason to leave the cabin behind, even knowing how hard it would be to survive without its shelter. When the strangers had shown up—two men with backpacks—Iris stayed hidden until they'd left, then collected her belongings and fled. In escaping the contained emptiness of the cabin into the vast emptiness of the wilderness, Iris threw off the last tether to the parents who had created her. She was reborn without love or grace, and did what she could to survive only because she could not do otherwise. She was purely animal. Suzanne might have understood why Iris had left her home, but she could not possibly understand what Iris had become afterward. Sitting in the Navigator, Iris herself was so altered from the wild, solitary girl she had been that she feared losing the thread of her essential self yet again. How many times could she be reborn?

Suzanne spoke, her voice thick. She was crying. "Sometimes it takes a stranger to show you what should be obvious, how far you've drifted from who you want to be, from what's right for you, your true place."

Iris tried to swallow but her throat was pinched tight. She peered into the woods and was stunned to discover she didn't ache to leap from the car, run up the stone steps, and fling herself into the world of green waiting there for her. Only the possibility of finding Ash again made her yearn to leave the car. Only that. Knowing she had, without intention, become connected to some part of this noisy, crazy, busy, unnatural place frightened her.

Suzanne wiped her eyes and took Iris's hand. "Let's walk for a bit, okay?"

They followed the curve of the railroad tracks, dappled here and there by light breaking from between the clouds. From the top of a young tulip poplar, a Carolina wren lifted its beak to the sky and released its song, a cascade of liquid trills. A pair of squirrels gave chase across the tracks and scrambled up the trunk of a black oak, disappearing into its boughs. Iris smelled water ahead, and in a few moments the crowd of trees parted to reveal a hill marked by a series of moss-covered limestone ledges over which water trickled, glistening. Iris noticed a cluster of bloodred flowers tucked beside a fallen log. She knelt to inspect them. Each plant bore three heart-shaped leaves above which three red elongated petals were evenly arranged. Three olive sepals, edged in red, poked out of the spaces between the petals.

Suzanne knelt beside Iris and fingered one of the delicate petals. "Red trillium."

Iris nodded. "Wake-robin. I like the pink ones, too."

"What pink ones?"

"They're like this, but the leaves are narrower, like a finger, and the flower is pale pink, almost white."

Suzanne seemed shocked. "Do you remember where you saw them?"

Iris stood and brushed off her knees, confused about why Suzanne would care about this particular flower. "Sure. Only one place, but they'd come up every year."

Suzanne's sadness was gone, replaced with a sense of energy in her limbs and an eager spark in her eyes. "Was it near your house?"

"Pretty near."

Suzanne walked a few steps off, then came back again. She was intent, like a robin cocking its head, tense, listening for what was below-ground. "I think I know where we need to go."

"You want to go to the cabin?"

"Yes."

Annoyance rose inside her. She'd been over this with the police more than once. "I don't know where it is. I can't just walk off into these woods and find my way back there!"

"Maybe you don't know exactly where it is, Iris," Suzanne said, pointing at the flower at their feet, "but I think you know enough."

Iris didn't know what Suzanne meant and didn't want to ask. She wanted to see her house again more than anything but also feared it. If Ash was anywhere, if she could ever find him again, he'd be there. If he wasn't, she wouldn't have a thing left in this world that belonged to her.

Iris turned in a circle, scanning the rocks, the water, the trees, ferns, and flowers, fixing the spot in her mind. It was her portal, through which she had exited her beloved woods. Was it a one-way door, like the narrow chute of a cave, or could she truly go back?

CHAPTER 34

Suzanne and Iris retraced their path along the railroad tracks, returned to the car, and rejoined the parkway, heading south again. A half hour later Suzanne turned right, descending from the parkway via Route 60 through the desolate city of Buena Vista into larger, more affluent Lexington. Home to two colleges, Lexington offered an array of choices for lodging and, Suzanne hoped, resources beyond the internet she might need to find a remote cabin. Although Iris might have been more comfortable in a bed-and-breakfast on the outskirts, Suzanne selected a hotel in the center of town for anonymity. She didn't want to have to explain their trip or make excuses for Iris's manners to a well-meaning but overly friendly host.

While they ate takeout burgers in their room, Suzanne explained to Iris how they might locate the cabin. Iris listened intently until exhaustion consumed her, falling asleep before eight o'clock. Suzanne lay awake on the other bed, worrying about what she had done in abandoning her family at its lowest point. Guilt, so familiar as to be comforting, washed over her. She imagined waking Iris, shepherding her to the car, returning to Charlottesville, walking up the front steps to her house. What then? What would make a difference in the direction in which their lives were heading? Suzanne remained firm in her belief—no, her conviction—that her life had become unbearable. As the hub of the family, if she did not change, no one else would. She had left because she could not stay. But she had also left because no one else could change without her action. Whit would have no choice but to deal with the fallout from Brynn's (and Reid's) deceit and dangerous behavior. He would not be able to wave his hands and make excuses for Brynn, and he would be forced to find a way to bridge the yawning chasm between himself and Reid. That was her hope. That was her prayer.

But, if she was honest with herself, the main reason she'd left was that she was too angry to stay. She was angry with the actions and inactions of Whit and her children and with the perfidy of her parents, and, more than anything else, angry with herself for going along with everything: the materialism, the shunting of responsibility, the shallowness, the lack of compassion. She was angry with herself for not being her best self, for hiding behind the injuries of her past, pointing to her scars, licking them as if they were wounds, saying again and again, *I can't.*

She turned toward the outline of Iris's sleeping form. A sixteen-year-old girl who didn't weigh ninety pounds had more tenacity and resolve than Suzanne had ever possessed, and Iris was losing it, piece by piece, on Suzanne's watch. Suzanne didn't know how to make Iris whole again, but she would try. And with Iris's help, Suzanne would find a place where she might regain her own strength, her self-determination, and her integrity.

Somewhere in those blue-green mountains, dissolved now in the ink of the night sky, was a cabin, a house, a home. She could not picture it. Instead, in her mind's eye, she saw a stand of acacia along a dry riverbed, yawning blue sky above, pulled taut to the edges of the earth, and underneath the delicate weave of branches, the fleshy pink lobes of a plant, thrust into sunlight, emerging from its hidden underground lair. Suzanne saw Tennyson, in his faded, oversize Carl's Jr. T-shirt, grinning, pleased for her. She felt anew the euphoria of discovery, potential spreading out all around her, ripples across the savanna, the probability that this, like most scientific beginnings, would come to nothing, but nevertheless harboring the slender hope of *something.* Suzanne felt that surge, and more, because she had been, at that moment, a woman with a passion and a woman in love. She cherished the world and a man cherished her. Together, that had been everything.

On her hotel bed, Suzanne closed her eyes and allowed the residue of remembered happiness fool her into sleep.

~

The next morning, Suzanne and Iris went out in search of breakfast and decided on the Blue Phoenix Cafe. Iris waited at a corner table beside a window while Suzanne ordered multigrain pancakes and fruit for both of them and a large coffee for herself. She sipped her coffee until her name was called, picked up the plates, and joined Iris. Halfway through her meal, Suzanne turned on her phone for the first time since they had left Charlottesville. She had asked Whit not to inundate her with texts. He had agreed and said he would pass the request on to the kids. There were two messages: one from Brynn, an emoji of a heart breaking, and one from Tinsley saying, "Call me. It's an emergency." Suzanne knew that if it were a true emergency she'd have heard from Whit, but since she hadn't spoken to her mother about what had happened during prom night, much less why she had left, she decided it might be better to talk to Tinsley directly, lest her mother implode. Tinsley was guaranteed to pass on everything to Whit, saving Suzanne a reawakening of her anger with him and, she acknowledged, allowing her to sidestep her guilt.

"Iris, I'm going outside to make a call. Just for a minute." She pointed through the window. Iris nodded and kept eating. "If you're still hungry, have mine, too."

Suzanne paced the sidewalk and dialed her mother, who picked up immediately.

"What sort of a stunt is this, Suzanne? Do you have any idea what you've done?"

"Hello, Mother. Yes, I'm fine, thanks. Iris, too."

"This is no time for wisecracks."

"This is no time to shout at me. If you can't be civil, I'm going to go." Suzanne said this without rancor. Maybe this was why she had decided to return her mother's call. For the first time since before she had left for college, Suzanne felt impervious to her mother's judgment and interference.

Tinsley sucked in a sharp breath. "When will you be back?"

"I don't know."

"I have to tell you that Whit is simply devastated." She paused, and when Suzanne said nothing, continued. "You shouldn't do this to him, Suzanne. He worships you."

And there it was, her mother's ideal. To be the center of a man's life. Not to be his entire life (or he wouldn't be a real man), but to preside over his heart, to be in sole command of his yearnings, guardian and mistress of the tender underbelly of a strong, successful man. This ideal had eluded Tinsley, and it infuriated her that her daughter held the holy grail and was blithely threatening to crush it. Suzanne made a habit of ignoring Tinsley's efforts to twist Suzanne's desires to match her own, but the time for tacit resistance had, she realized, passed. "I don't want him to worship me, Mother. I want to be understood."

Tinsley laughed, a mocking bray. "Don't be a fool. You have a marriage, not a support group." Her tone became even, honed. "Whit is a rare bird: a loyal man. And because he's also a proud man, he works hard for you and the children. How can you throw that away?"

"I'm not throwing—"

Her mother interrupted, breathless. "Let me tell you something no one else will. You won't always be beautiful, Suzanne. Men won't always run after you."

"That's not a news flash. And it's not a problem. I'm not hung up on appearances."

"You ought to be! Think how this looks. It's a scandal. You've abandoned your family."

"Mother, you need to stop. This is not your business."

"Not my business? My granddaughter has been suspended from school for a week. The poor girl!"

"School policy."

"We've asked to speak to the principal. Your father's on the board, as you know."

"She should take her punishment and be thankful nothing worse happened. Don't intervene. Please."

"Of course we'll intervene! You may have given up on everyone who loves you, but your father and I continue to support you and your family in every way we possibly can."

Suzanne took a deep breath. The breadth and depth of her mother's false assumptions, misplaced energy, and outright lies were staggering. Suzanne stacked the arguments up in her mind, straightened the edges, and prepared to take her mother's illogic and self-aggrandizing nonsense to pieces. But what would be the point? Tinsley was nothing if not consistent. Suzanne had gotten one thing right over the years: she had not wasted energy in attempting to change her mother.

"Mother, I'm going now." Suzanne lowered the phone from her ear. Tinsley's protest was unintelligible.

Suzanne ended the call and turned to watch Iris inside the café. The girl ate fruit with her fingers and gazed out the window at the sky. Suzanne wished she were as detached from other people as Iris plainly was. Suzanne knew she should be sad that the girl had no family and was wary of people, but at the moment Iris's autonomy seemed like the greatest gift imaginable. To be free of the needs and expectations of others; to enjoy self-determination; to take a course of action—or even a single step—without weighing the impact on those around her. To be selfish.

She wasn't sure if she knew how to begin, unless she already had.

CHAPTER 35

Brynn was on her sixth episode of *Cake Wars* and was about to lose her mind. She'd already binge-watched the entire first season of *The Crown* and started on *Orange Is the New Black* but couldn't handle it. Prison was too gross and depressing. Being suspended was too gross and depressing. Her friends hardly even talked to her. Ophelia's parents had taken her phone away, and the rest of them were "busy with school stuff." Since when? Brynn was royally pissed at her mother for telling the school that she got caught drinking. Sure, all the kids in sports—and their parents—had to sign a pledge to report alcohol and drug use, but only her mom was lame enough to actually do it. "Integrity," said the mom who ran away from her family.

Brynn was flipping through old shows, ones not normally on her radar, when her father came home. It was only three o'clock, so clearly he thought she might be spending the afternoon doing shots and starring in her own porn video. It was a thought. At least she'd get some exercise. If she kept vegging out on the couch and snacking all day, she'd be covered in puppy fat before her suspension was over. They wouldn't even let her swim with the team.

Her father walked in, looking frazzled. "Hey."

"Hi. Can we go to the Melting Pot for dinner? I'm feeling fondue."

"Sure. I mean no." He scraped his hand through his hair. "You're not supposed to be enjoying yourself."

She gave him a sweet smile. "If I promise to be miserable, can we?"

He frowned. This wasn't going well. "Have you heard from your mother?"

"No." Her mother had been gone almost two whole days and had sent two texts, both saying she was fine. As if Brynn had asked. Her mother wasn't the one who'd been abandoned. Thank God no one at school knew she'd run away. And she had taken Iris, which should've made Brynn happy but didn't. She'd actually been feeling pretty shitty about getting Iris mixed up in Promgate. If Iris were around, Brynn could've told her that.

Her father plunked himself into a chair. "Brynn, I'd really like to know what went on at that party. In fact, I'd like to know exactly how you met Robby and how it all happened."

He sounded like he'd been thinking carefully about how to put this. It was totally a script. And his face said he hoped she wouldn't tell him anything too disturbing.

"Don't worry about it, Daddy."

"I do worry about it, sweetheart. You know I do."

Brynn had been fiddling with the remote. She set it aside. "What do you worry about?"

"You." He bent forward, elbows on his knees. "I worry about you. About what you do, about what might happen to you. And Reid, too, of course."

His expression was eager, like he was determined for her to see how much he meant what he said. She wondered if he did. Maybe she doubted him because she'd been home alone with too much time for thinking. Did her father really worry about her? Right now, his forehead was scrunched up, and he looked like he'd pulled an all-nighter. He was jiggling his legs up and down, which meant he was nervous. Maybe he was just upset about what had happened. What dad wouldn't feel that way about his darling daughter passed out on a lawn and getting hauled home by the police? That shitshow was history, though. Too late to worry about that. Worry was for the future, for the stuff you could maybe do something about.

Brynn had been working through this all day while the shows rolled and hundred-calorie packs of cookies became litter on the couch. Now that her father had confirmed what she suspected—that he was mostly full of crap—she was seriously annoyed.

"You didn't talk to Robby's father, did you?" She wasn't sure she wanted him to. She'd rather the incident be erased from everyone's mind. It was embarrassing, for starters. She would feel differently, maybe, if Robby had texted her, gotten in touch with her at all, after the party. But he hadn't. No way was she texting him; she wouldn't grovel. If she'd really been played and thrown out like the trash, then she'd prefer the whole mess be dropped.

"Not yet," her dad said. "I'm not sure how to approach Robert." He was looking at her like she might know. That pissed her off.

"How about: 'Your son is a dick'?"

Her father half smiled, uneasy. "I'm not sure what that achieves."

He was protecting his deal. Why else? Ruthless, but not so anyone would notice. But now that she had noticed it, she couldn't unnotice it. Her father liked to believe that he worried about her. He liked to tell himself that he was doing the right thing, but like pretty much everyone Brynn knew, he was actually doing what was easiest, what got him closer to what he wanted most, and it made her sad to realize that what he wanted most didn't have to do with her. He didn't see it, but she could, because she was the same. And because of that, she couldn't let him see how angry she was. Instead she pushed the anger down, like dunking a hot frying pan into a sink of water. One sizzle and then nothing.

She shrugged. "Yeah, he probably knows Robby's a dick. Maybe he's proud of what a dick his kid is."

"It's possible. I don't like Robert much." Her father leaned back in his chair, slumping down.

Brynn felt a wave of sympathy for her dad for having to deal with people he didn't like while he chased after money. But she was irritated, too. Wasn't she supposed to come first? She thought of her mom, absolutely furious that her dad hadn't stopped the whole Robby thing from happening. On prom night, she had blown right through all her mother's defenses. Her mother was lame—but she did worry and nag and insist on checking in. Pathetic flailing done with good intention ought to count for something, right?

A steel band tightened across Brynn's chest. Both her parents had failed her for their own stupid reasons. And her mother had made everything worse by leaving. How could she just leave?

Brynn struggled to hold back her tears. She should be rejoicing that her ridiculous mother was out of the way and hated herself for caring that she wasn't here to talk to. To hold her.

Her father said, "You okay, pumpkin?"

"Sure." She dug deep and gave him a big smile, looking him in the eye. And there, below his concern for her, Brynn spied his self-pity. Somehow all this—his asshole business partner, Robby the dick who lured his little girl to the party, Reid the son who ratted him out, his wife who walked out—was all about him. Sure, her father worried about Brynn, about his kids, about all of them, but only when it was convenient, when he had time, when it was easy, when it was too late. Even now, after Robby was finished with her, had thrown her away, made a fool of her, even now her father wouldn't stand up for her because it was too fucking hard.

Brynn's anger lit up inside her. She swung her feet to the floor and crushed the tears on her face with her knuckles. She stood.

"Call him."

Her dad sat up. "Call who?"

"Robert."

"I don't think that will help."

"It won't help you."

He frowned, confused. "Brynn, sit down. Let's talk."

She clenched her fists at her sides to stop herself from attacking him. "Call him! Tell him his son is a dangerous asshole! Tell him his son would've raped me if the fire alarm hadn't gone off!"

Her dad jumped up and took her by the shoulders.

Brynn threw him off. "Don't touch me!"

He held his hands up. "Okay, take it easy. I just don't see the point of talking to Robert."

"The point, Dad? The point is for you to stand up for me!" Her head was about to explode, so she stomped off toward the front door and back again. Brynn stood in front of her father, hanging on to the shreds of her self-control. Pain leaked from her; anger held it in. Her father watched with a lost expression that made her even more furious. Her throat squeezed shut and her voice came out as a thin scream. "Don't you care?"

"Brynn." He lifted his arms to hold her. She pulled back. She didn't need one of his pathetic hugs. "I said don't touch me!"

Brynn spun away and flew from the room. She ran half stumbling up the stairs, blinded by her tears, and locked herself in her bedroom. She flung open her closet door and yanked a bag off the shelf. She couldn't stay in this house with him one more second. She just couldn't.

CHAPTER 36

Suzanne held the door for Iris as they entered the Rockbridge County Library. They passed the circulation desk, magazine racks, and book displays, and found seats side by side at an empty table. Suzanne started her laptop and opened Google Earth in map view. She dropped a pin at the Yankee Horse Ridge parking area.

"Okay, Iris. This is where I found you. The first thing we need to know for sure is that you came from the south."

Iris bent closer. Suzanne zoomed out, then in again, switching to satellite view to show Iris an overview of the terrain.

Iris pointed to Highway 64, running east to west at the north end of the parkway between Yankee Horse Ridge and the city of Charlottesville. "I know that road now. I didn't cross that."

"Right. I just want to be absolutely sure."

Suzanne zoomed out until most of Virginia was on the screen, then positioned the pin at Lexington, where they were now, roughly halfway between the north and south state borders, and near the western edge. Suzanne pointed to Roanoke, a city forty miles south of Lexington and the same distance from the North Carolina border. "This city has a hundred thousand people in it. Obviously, you didn't go through it. But is there any way you could've gone past it?"

Iris ran her finger over the maze of roads north of Roanoke. "I would've turned around before I got anywhere near that."

"Okay." Suzanne checked the legend. "From Roanoke to where I found you is about sixty miles, as the crow flies." She studied the map. "The width of the forested part varies from about seven and twenty miles across."

"That's big."

"Big enough to disappear in, apparently." She smiled at Iris, disguising the sense of futility growing inside her. She returned her attention to the screen and pointed out the east–west roads that cut across the mountains north of Roanoke. There were four, but the parkway itself didn't obey a north–south vector. It snaked around. "Iris, can you say for sure how many times you crossed a road, a paved one?"

Sun was pouring through a clerestory window. Iris stared at the beam of light cutting across the room, sparkling with dust motes. "Not more than six times. Four times anyway."

"That's great. And you told the detective you mostly went north, right?"

"Yes. I'm not sure why. I guess I hoped the woods would keep on going."

Suzanne looked at the map again. "If you never crossed a road when you backtracked, then you must have started at least four road crossings below where I found you. If you never crossed the parkway either—if you stayed west of it, where most of the forest is—then you started down here." She indicated the area east of Buchanan. "But if you doubled back more or crossed the parkway, you might have started as far north as near Route 60, where we turned off to come here."

Iris said, "I don't remember exactly."

"It's fine. We've narrowed it down a lot."

Suzanne questioned Iris about mountaintop views and showed her images from the higher peaks. One, Sharp Top, was somewhat familiar to Iris.

"It would've been not too long after I left. Later, I didn't have the energy to climb hills for no reason." The girl went quiet, probably recollecting the misery she had endured.

Suzanne waited for an elderly couple to pass behind them, then turned to Iris, who was still lost in thought. "I want to find your cabin for my own sake. But I have the feeling it's going to be important for you, too." Iris didn't say anything. "Is there something wrong? Something you want to tell me?"

Iris hesitated, then tilted her head at the computer. "What about the river?"

"The river?"

"There was a huge river. I forgot until now. I had to cross it on a bridge. I waited until dark."

Suzanne clicked the Google Earth screen to show a map instead of satellite imagery. Her attention was drawn to a thick blue line, wriggling northeasterly above Roanoke, bending south and east at Glasgow, then wending through the Blue Ridge Mountains. The James River, an unmistakable landmark. Suzanne smiled at Iris. "You crossed it once, right?"

"Yes. I'm sure."

"Going north."

"Going north."

"About how long after you left?"

She thought for a moment. "The leaves were gone, I remember that much, so not more than a few months."

Suzanne strove to control her excitement. They had narrowed down the area by two-thirds. She clicked back to satellite view and studied the forested land, deeply crinkled and creased where the mountains dominated. There had to be more clues. "What about the streams near your house?"

"What do you mean?"

Suzanne touched the screen, tracing a fold between hills. "This one would flow north, I think, toward the James near where you crossed." She traced another. "But this one would flow the other way, because of the mountains." Iris nodded. Suzanne pulled a piece of paper from her computer bag and handed Iris a pen. "Can you draw the streams you remember near your house and show me which way they flowed?"

While Iris worked, Suzanne searched for the database on endangered species. Plant populations weren't mapped on the small scale they needed to find the cabin, but she was hoping information about habitat might restrict their search.

Iris finished drawing. Suzanne compared the sketch of the watershed around Iris's cabin with Google Earth images, turning the paper this way and that. It was no use because neither the satellite nor the map view showed the minor waterways. "Maybe we can get a detailed map, a topo map, in town later. For now, let's talk plants." She knew that endangered and threatened plant populations were usually listed by county and hoped that information might help. She typed "Virginia trillium" into the search bar and quickly found the flower related to the red trillium they had seen at the railroad tracks.

"Looks just like I remember," Iris said softly.

"Virginia least trillium." She explained about endangered and threatened species. The trillium was endangered in North Carolina but not in Virginia, so the county-by-county listings Suzanne had hoped for were not available. She made notes about the flower's habitat, then opened a tab for the US Fish and Wildlife Service. Together they went through the list of Virginia's threatened or endangered plants, more than a dozen. Iris pointed to a daisylike flower with drooping pink petals.

"I've seen that one. Mama used ones like it for keeping us healthy, especially in the winter. Echinacea, she called it, but she didn't harvest this one. Too special, she said."

"Smooth coneflower," Suzanne said. "Federally endangered." She clicked open the list of counties where the flower was known to exist and compared it to a county map. "It hasn't been seen in any of the counties north of Route 60, the road we drove down yesterday, and only on the west side of Bedford and Amherst Counties."

"So what does that mean?"

"Nothing for certain. The flower could be growing where it hasn't been noticed." Suzanne closed the laptop. "Let's get that topo, hopefully narrow it down some more."

"Then what?"

"Exploring."

~

Iris sat in the car, holding a list of three places: two that had rivers and streams closely matching her sketch and one that was a partial match. Who knew how accurate her memory was, especially for distances? They'd left midmorning and now had almost arrived at the first one. The easiest, Suzanne had said last night, because it was the only one they could get to through public land—the Jefferson National Forest. The idea that one of these places held her home made Iris's stomach churn. She'd never been so excited and so afraid at the same time.

Suzanne used her phone to find the way until she lost reception and asked Iris to guide her using the map. Suzanne had circled the closest access point. Road signs for Cave Mountain Lake appeared, and they turned onto a narrow dirt road running alongside a stream. Iris suspected the area they were looking for was too close to popular hiking trails to be the right place but didn't say anything. She could be wrong. Disappearing was easy if no one was looking for you.

They parked in a tiny lot and gathered their stuff. Suzanne had insisted on buying all sorts of clothing and gear in Lexington—enough for a monthlong trip, the way Iris saw it. But her boots were comfortable and the backpack was a big improvement on the old one, which had belonged to her father. Suzanne and Iris didn't plan to stay out overnight, but Suzanne wanted to be prepared. For this first stop, though, they left the sleeping bags, tarp, and stove in the car since their destination was only four or five miles away and they could follow a trail for most of it.

Suzanne hoisted her pack and clipped the belt. "Ready?"

"Yes."

At first Iris led, but she kept having to wait for Suzanne and decided to let her set the pace. A half hour in, a young couple passed them going the other way, smiling and saying hello. Iris and Suzanne continued for another hour and a half, climbing steadily through a world of green. The trail wound around to the west, ringing a big mountain, then angled to its steeper north side. Here the trees were narrower, leaning close to strain toward the sky, today a featureless gray mat. There was not a breath of wind. Birds trilled out overhead—phoebes, wrens, a lone oriole—and squirrels skittered across the ground and gave chase up tree trunks. Spring was offering up its promise of bounty. Out of habit, Iris scanned the forest floor as she walked, searching among last year's decaying leaves and the emerging ephemerals for mushrooms. It felt like morel time.

Suzanne stopped in the trail and consulted the map. "I think we turn left off the trail pretty soon." She pointed into the woods. "One of your streams should be over there."

Iris considered the terrain. "How far?"

"Maybe a half mile? Or a little farther?" Suzanne looked uneasily into the densely packed woods. "You want to go first?"

Iris slid past Suzanne and continued up the path until she found a gap in the undergrowth. She checked to make sure Suzanne was close behind and picked her way among the trees, holding aside branches for Suzanne. They were traversing the slope now, heading toward a notch between two distant hills, which made sense to Iris if they were trying to get to a stream. But she paid less attention to the geography and her memory of the map than she did to her innate expectation of what lay ahead. Landscapes, varied as they were, were logical and predictable: the types of trees, the plants blooming at her feet, the way the sunlight fell, the eddies in which dawn's moisture might be trapped. Iris read all that and more. She wasn't surprised when a patch of bluebells appeared, or when they walked past a deer yard, grasses folded flat beneath a pair of red cedars. She just nodded and moved on.

In a short while, Iris heard the stream she already knew was there. Suzanne would insist on seeing it, to be sure, so Iris led her for another ten minutes to its edge.

Suzanne looked at the stream, two steps across, burbling gently. She said, "Does this look familiar?"

"No."

"Are you sure?"

Iris sighed. There was no way to explain. It'd be like getting a fish to teach you to swim. "I'm sure."

Suzanne nodded, and Iris was grateful not to have to say more.

They returned to the car, drove to Buchanan, the nearest town, and checked into a hotel made from a railcar. After they'd been outdoors most of the day, the low-ceilinged room felt too small. Iris waited at a picnic table on the lawn behind the railcar while Suzanne went across the street to get dinner.

Suzanne unwrapped the sandwiches, handed Iris hers, and checked her cell phone. "I can't get reception."

"Who were you going to call?"

"No one." Suzanne put the phone in her pocket as if she could tuck her whole family away in there. It seemed like she could, at least for now. "Are you disappointed about today?"

"Not really."

"Don't you want to find your house?"

Iris stopped chewing, the bread suddenly dry in her mouth. She took a sip from her water bottle. "I don't know. It was your idea to look for it."

"And you don't want to?"

"I don't think I ever spent a lot of time thinking about wanting things I can't have. If I ever did before, I've stopped now."

"But we might find it."

"I don't want my house. I left it, remember? I left it and never went back. I left it empty."

Suzanne put a hand on Iris's arm. "We don't have to search anymore, Iris, not if you don't want to."

Iris shrugged. "I don't know what I want right now."

Suzanne nodded and went back to eating.

In the yard next door, two boys kicked a ball back and forth, the bigger one yelling at the smaller one to stop using his hands to steady the ball. On a wire above their heads, a mockingbird eyed them for a few moments before launching into song, repeating each call several times: cardinal, wren, titmouse, jay, bluebird, red-tailed hawk, and back to the cardinal, but a different song. Iris wondered whether, if the mockingbird learned too many other songs, it might forget what sort of bird it was.

That night, Iris lay awake long after Suzanne had fallen asleep in the other bed. The hotel was quiet compared with Charlottesville. Even the mockingbird had found a roost and gone quiet. Iris pictured the drawing she'd made of the strands of water around the cabin and tried to conjure up different places in the drawing. The cabin porch with the oak bench; the clearing straight out front; the little bend in the stream where she washed her face in the mornings, took a drink; the patch of sang on the north side of Turkey Hill—what she and Ash called it anyway. Each place she thought of, she dwelled on, concentrating, focusing. She reached into the dark edges of each memory, seeing if she might rake another detail into the light. What was beside the bench? How many steps could she take in that clearing? Were there brambles at the edge? Did Ash sink a fishhook into his shin at that spot in the stream or farther up?

The questions kept coming, and the images spun and swirled like dried leaves kicked up by a stiff autumn wind. Where were the faces, her family? She searched her memory, riffling through the scenes, catching only glimpses of what she wanted most to see: the flash of bare feet disappearing ahead of her into the brush, a head with long brown hair turning away, a figure appearing in the doorway of the cabin and dissolving into the shadows. She pursued the running child, the woman beside her, the person in the doorway, but they all had retreated and disappeared.

Iris pulled the cold, scratchy bedcover up to her chin. The unnatural sound it made and the greenish-yellow light leaking in from around the curtains reminded her of where she was, of where she was not. And doubt crept up over the end of the bed and settled alongside her legs, heavy and wet. Iris feared that these memories, frail as they were, were not memories at all but inventions, wishes for what she used to have and nightmares of what she had lost. What did she know, really know, to be true? Where was everyone?

Maybe this was why she wasn't sure about finding the cabin. Maybe it was like the detective said: there wasn't much to go on and nothing to confirm what she thought was true. She hadn't told anyone about Ash, who had been more real to her than any oak bench on a porch in a clearing somewhere in the woods. Iris hadn't wanted to look too closely at why she kept Ash a secret. She just wanted to keep him that way. Maybe there was no bench, no porch, no cabin. Maybe Mama hadn't fallen down a hole. Maybe Iris was truly lost, far more lost than she ever could have imagined, living inside a vanished world of her own making.

Maybe the real secret was she had invented everything. Maybe there was no Ash. Maybe there never had been.

CHAPTER 37

The dirt road kept with the river for a long time before heading toward the rising sun blinking through the trees. Iris shielded her eyes with her hand. They hadn't passed a house for about a mile, but someone had to live out here. There wouldn't be a road otherwise.

Suzanne drained her coffee and placed it in the holder between the seats. "Should be soon." She searched the left side of the road, maybe hoping for a turnout.

They crossed a narrow wooden bridge and bounced out of a deep rut on the far side. The road swept right. The woods had been hugging the roadside, but now they fell away, revealing a large field, flat and empty. At the far end were a two-story brick house, a dilapidated barn, and a couple of smaller buildings, all shaded by huge walnuts and maples. Beside the barn stood a tower, almost as high as the house, with thin legs and a wheel on top.

A strange feeling settled over Iris. "I think I've been here before."

Suzanne slowed the car. "You recognize the house?"

She shook her head. "The tower. Whatever that is."

"It's a windmill," Suzanne said. "Did you live here?"

"I don't know." Iris recalled her thoughts from the night before, the idea that her memories weren't the solid things she had believed them to be.

Suzanne pulled the car off the road onto a level patch of field. "Maybe you lived here before you moved into the woods."

Iris looked at the windmill again, and at the house and the barn, waiting for a detail to spring out at her. None did. "Maybe."

Suzanne consulted the map and pointed ahead to where the woods rose gently out of the field. "We'll start somewhere there, okay?"

Iris pointed to a sign on a tree. POSTED. NO HUNTING, FISHING, OR TRESPASSING. "What about that?"

Suzanne folded the map and opened the door. "Ignore it."

They put on their backpacks, locked the car, and skirted the edge of the woods, searching for a path. Iris glanced over her shoulder several times, getting a different view of the house and the windmill, wondering why it felt so familiar yet failed to conjure any specific memory. Suzanne looked behind her, too, as if she expected someone to appear out of nowhere. A pair of crows swooped in and landed on the roof without circling first, a clear indication no one was around. From where she stood, Iris sensed the emptiness. The place was like a skeleton with no blood or flesh or soul inside.

They couldn't find an obvious path, so Iris chose a deer trail pointing in the general direction of the location on the map. The topo map wasn't detailed—one inch covered one mile of reality—but it didn't matter. These mountains were rugged. Even with a better map they couldn't just walk straight from one place to another. The woods were so dense it could seem like dusk in the middle of the day, and what seemed like an easy path could stop dead at the bottom of the sheer cliff. Iris followed her instincts, and the deer.

As they walked, Suzanne asked her about the windmill again. Iris answered by hiking faster. She didn't want to talk. She felt a tug in the center of her chest, and in the center of her forehead, too, a soft pull, a yearning. Iris let herself be led, but she was also under her own guidance, mindful of her surroundings: the contours, the appearance and disappearance of certain plants and trees, the sighing of a breeze in the crowns at the top of the tall, straight trunks. As she breathed in, she tasted the changing scents and touched the leaves and branches as she passed, feeling her way.

"Iris!" Far below, Suzanne had stopped to lean on a cedar. She took a drink of water and caught up to Iris. Suzanne was breathing hard as she pulled the topo map out of the side pocket of her pants. "Don't you want to check this?"

Iris shook her head.

Suzanne looked around. It was only trees and shrubs and flowers and sky to her. "Do you recognize this?"

Iris wasn't sure how to answer. If she said yes, Suzanne would ask more questions. But denying what she felt would be a lie.

She shrugged and walked on.

Deer trails appeared and disappeared. Iris chose the ones leading mostly west toward the larger mountain she intuited lay beyond her view. They crossed a small stream, but the sounds it made spoke an unfamiliar story, and Iris did not turn to hike alongside it. At the top of the hill, the trees were spaced farther apart. Crowded between them were blackberry bushes, white with blossoms. The sun had climbed with them and showered the understory with light. Iris paused.

Suzanne offered her water. While Iris drank, Suzanne was silent. Perhaps she sensed what Iris now felt with certainty and dread. Her woods—her home—were near. Iris passed the bottle to Suzanne, avoiding her gaze, and set off again, more slowly now, not for Suzanne, but for herself.

Iris picked her way across the hilltop and down the gentle western slope into a shallow crease between this hill and the one to the south, then continued along the next rise, tracing the contour of the large mountain she had been heading toward all morning. Suzanne kept pace with her. The birds had quieted in their midday roosts. Suzanne and Iris's footfalls in the damp mulch and the occasional frantic rustling of a squirrel were the only sounds. They skirted a tangle of downed tree limbs overgrown with brambles. On the far side stood an enormous boulder and, beyond, a lightly forested area filled with dappled light and blanketed in delicate white flowers.

Iris stopped.

Suzanne came up beside her. "Look at that." She crouched and lifted the petals of a flower with two fingers. "Least trillium. The one you talked about, Iris."

Iris nodded. She adjusted the backpack on her shoulders and wiped her mouth with the back of her hand, trying to account for the sliding sensation in her belly. She scanned the area. There, near the boulder, was a wooden sign, half-hidden by the flowers that had grown up around it. She approached the sign, placing her feet with care among the flowers, and squatted in front of it.

"What is it?" Suzanne said.

The sign was two feet square and made of hickory, the streaky grain running horizontally. A name had been carved in the wood. Iris held her breath and touched the grooves of the letters.

Ash.

The edges of her vision darkened and she blinked hard. She ran her fingers down the board, pushing aside the flowers.

Numbers. Dates.

April 1, 2002–July 27, 2011

Iris placed her hands on the ground to steady herself. Her heart beat loudly in her ears. Her lungs squeezed and she winced in pain.

July 2011? Six years ago. When Daddy left.

She pictured him, his face hard and broken, going out the door, stepping off the porch with long strides. Sweat stains down the back of his shirt. Thin, bare legs dangling from his right side. Ash.

Iris ran after them, shouting, crying.

Mama caught her, scooped her up, and held her, the way Daddy was holding Ash. Wouldn't let her go no matter how she tried to wrestle her way out of Mama's grip.

Daddy passing the wood pile, the sang patch, disappearing down the hill. Gone.

April fools, Ash. April fools.

A hand on her shoulder.

Suzanne talking. Questions.

Iris closed her eyes and opened them again.

Ash.

She jumped up, threw off Suzanne.

Ran straight through those white flowers and into the woods.

CHAPTER 38

In the grove of trillium, Suzanne stood facing the woods into which Iris had disappeared. The sound of the girl's steps receded, fading into silence. Suzanne crossed to the edge of the grove, as if to follow Iris, but hesitated, peering between the trees, over the shrubs, to where the growth became a seemingly impenetrable mass. It was, she knew, no different from what she had been hiking through all morning, and yet now that Iris had gone, the woods had taken on a different aspect, as if they were not three-dimensional but a solid green curtain. Iris had found the parting and slipped through.

Suzanne was alone.

Her shirt was soaked under her backpack. All at once her skin chilled. She stared again into the woods, wishing she had pursued Iris right away when she had a chance of keeping up. The girl could be anywhere now.

Suzanne spun in the direction from which they had come, looking past the boulder to discern the path, such as it was. She started in that direction, imagining the Navigator waiting patiently by the road. She imagined sitting behind the wheel. She took a deep breath in and it caught in her chest. Her heart was beating too quickly. She closed her eyes and took several more deep breaths, willing her lungs and her heart to obey her, willing the signals of panic cascading from somewhere in her brain to stop. Her faithless nervous system was a toddler on the verge of a tantrum. She opened her eyes and took inventory of what she might do to forestall an attack.

Look, she said to herself. *I am surrounded by flowers.*

She knelt and focused her attention on a trillium, the dark green of the leaves, the blush of pink on its petals. Three petals, three sepals, three leaves. The petals wavy at the edges. The leaves slightly veined and without stalks. She examined one, then another and another. Her heart slowed.

Not daring yet to stand, she moved in a crouch to the carved wooden sign, the marker. She examined the grain of the boards, the intricate notches, the stakes nailed to the back and driven into the ground. She ran her fingers over the lettering, marshaling her senses to hold tight the reins of her emotions.

Ash.

A boy or a girl? The child had died at nine during the same year that, according to Iris, her father had left the cabin and never returned. But that was nearly six years ago. The sign could not be that old. Who had been here? And how much of what Iris had told them had been true?

Suzanne's mouth was parched. Slowly she came to her feet, lowered the backpack to the ground, and removed the water bottle from the side pocket. She drank, keeping her eyes on the marker, on the flowers, on her steady, even breathing. She put the water away and turned in a slow circle.

She was alone.

A finger of dread crept up her spine. Suzanne reached into her pocket for the drawing Iris had made. The cabin had to be nearby. They had been heading in the same direction for at least two hours, so it was reasonable to stay on that course. If the map was right, Suzanne would encounter the first stream pictured on the map and, shortly after that, the cabin. She could attempt to go after Iris, but it would be a false move. Iris didn't need her, not out here. The girl's backpack contained food, water, and extra clothing; she had survived for years on much less. And Suzanne had no doubt Iris could find the cabin on her own, if she chose.

Suzanne retrieved her phone from the pack and checked the screen. No service. She stowed it, hoisted the pack onto her shoulders, clipped the hip belt, and crossed to where they had emerged from the woods. It was mostly downhill to the car. She was confident she could find the way and be safe in her car in less than three hours. From there she could return to Buchanan and call Whit. Or the police. But what would she say? That she had almost found the cabin? Did she really want them to know? And what would she say about Ash's marker?

In truth, she didn't want to talk to anyone, not about what she'd found, not about Iris and her cabin and her family, and not, most of all, about why she had left. She wouldn't know the answer to that until she stopped looking over her shoulder at her past and understood what was in front of her.

Suzanne stepped from the grove of flowers into the woods. As she walked, she absorbed everything around her with the same intensity she had applied to examining the trillium, inviting this spectacle of life surrounding her to guide her onto Iris's map, both the one in Suzanne's pocket and the one in Iris's heart.

~

The stream appeared sooner than she had expected, its gentle gurgling a welcome sound. She followed it upstream for a few hundred yards until she found a ginseng patch, probably the one Iris had included in the drawing. Suzanne was sure she was close now, and her excitement grew larger than her lingering anxiety about being on her own. Her stomach growled—she hadn't eaten since breakfast—but she didn't want to stop to eat. She noticed an overgrown trail at the end of the ginseng patch, pushed the arching branches of brambles aside, and pressed on. After a short while, she descended to a smaller stream, not more than a rivulet, and followed it upstream, as the drawing indicated. The hillside she had been skirting on her right flattened, and the terrain opened, revealing a clearing. Across from where she stood was a cabin of weathered wood, darkened by weather, smoke, and time. The porch was narrow, and a stovepipe poked through the debris-covered roof. She could hear water running beyond the cabin. Other than an outbuilding tucked off to one side, there was little to suggest a family had lived here. She had expected buckets, stools, rusted implements, crude toys, a laundry line, perhaps. Suzanne approached with caution, and, as she neared, it seemed the cabin had not so much been placed on the land as grown up from it, as if the lumber from which it had been constructed had reverted, in its nature, to tree.

A small shed with a moon carved in the door was half-hidden in a cluster of red cedars to the right of the cabin. The outhouse, Suzanne surmised. She reached the porch and watched for movement behind the small windows on either side of the door, but was fairly certain no one was there. Her chest constricted and her palms became sweaty. She had been able to quell her panic until now, but her control was slipping. Maybe inside the cabin she would feel less exposed, less alone. She fumbled with the hip belt of her pack, unclasped it, and shed the pack. She went to the door and knocked. The sound rang through the clearing. She waited a moment and knocked again, louder, and, when no one came, lifted the latch and stepped inside.

"Hello?"

The dust disturbed by the swinging door clouded the air before settling again. Suzanne slowly swung the door open wide and advanced to the middle of the room. Centered on the wall to her right was a fireplace made of stone. A few pots and a skillet stood on the hearth, and an iron arm with a hook at the end hovered over dusty, charred logs. A long table with benches occupied one side of the fireplace, and a tall chest, a set of shelves, and a stack of plastic storage containers filled the remaining space. The chest was fashioned of wood like that of Ash's marker. On the opposite side of the room, two rocking chairs and a table holding a kerosene lamp were arranged by the window. A set of bunk beds occupied the rest of the wall. Suzanne crossed to the back of the room and lifted aside a curtain covering the doorway of another room, just large enough to contain a full-size bed covered with a faded quilt. A porthole offered a peek at the back of the house.

Suzanne returned to the main room. The scene out the front door was peaceful: a gently sloping field, dotted with yarrow, buttercup, daisies, and a blue flower she couldn't identity from this distance, giving way to a row of upright tree trunks surrounded by blossoming berry bushes. Birds called in the distance. The air was windless and as warm as a spring day should be. Suzanne stood at the threshold, knowing she could walk into the clearing and not succumb to a panic attack. Here, where the cabin belonged to the land and where the people who had lived there belonged as well, inside was much the same as outside, and being alone was as natural and right as breathing, as flowing water, as sunlight. She would not hide from herself while alone in a gentle wilderness.

She brought her pack inside, carried it to the table. The rose-patterned tablecloth was stained and sprinkled with mouse droppings. She folded it back to expose the bare wood and unpacked her lunch. The sight of food reminded her of how hungry she was. She checked her phone. Two fourteen and no service.

As she ate, she kept an eye on the doorway, hopeful of seeing Iris, and examined the cabin again. Even as she picked out more detail—a basket of knitting tucked under a chair, a fiddle leaning against the wall, heavy coats hanging behind the front door—she was struck by how little the family of three, or four, had owned. Undoubtedly there was storage under the beds and perhaps outside, but she guessed their possessions could nevertheless fit inside the Navigator. And it had been enough.

Suzanne finished the packet of trail mix, rose from the bench, and went to the shelves beside the tall chest. She scanned the spines of the twenty or so books—all practical volumes of one sort or another. If the children had had storybooks, they were elsewhere. Suzanne doubted it, though, as Iris didn't seem to have had any contact with worlds of myth or magic. Above the books were jars and containers of assorted sizes. Most were labeled: *Adam's flannel, burdock, blue cohosh, echinacea, stitchwort, sumac.* A mortar and pestle and a small set of scales rested on one shelf, and another mortar and pestle, the size of a soup tureen, sat on the floor. Iris's mother had been an herbalist and this was her apothecary. Suzanne lifted a few of the jars, inspecting the contents. Under a large, empty container, she discovered a stack of three notebooks, black hardcover and simply bound. Suzanne carried them to the table and opened the topmost, labeled A TO H.

There was no inscription inside the cover. The entries began with the first pair of pages. ADDER'S MOUTH was written in capitals across the top of the left-hand page. The handwriting was small, neat, and upright. Under the plant name was a brief description (an orchid with a single glossy leaf and numerous small green flowers on a single stalk) and its habitat (open upland woods), along with a simple line drawing executed by a confident hand. The rest of the page listed various preparations and uses. Suzanne flipped through several pages. Each plant had been granted at least one page; some, such as agrimony and arnica, had several. Suzanne noticed annotations in a different, more fluid hand, but not Iris's, and guessed the writing belonged to Iris's mother, while the original entries were likely the work of someone older, perhaps Iris's grandmother. Suzanne turned page after page, fascinated by the wealth of information. Although Appalachian herbalism was not her specialty, she was surprised by how many of the plants she was unfamiliar with. Even the uses of those she knew were broader than she'd realized. The entries were observations, not established fact, but as she read she tempered her natural skepticism with an open mind. Plants were more complex than most people would credit, except those who revered and depended on them.

Something skittered across the roof, startling her. She went to the door, pointlessly searching the clearing for Iris. The shadows were lengthening. Only the tops of the trees now caught the sun. Suzanne was more concerned about Iris's state of mind than about her safety, but could do nothing other than wait for her. It was the logical place to meet, and Suzanne had no doubt that Iris knew precisely where the cabin lay.

Suzanne returned inside and considered where she would sleep. The beds, the floor, every surface was covered in dust and rodent droppings. Who knew what else was lurking in the corners, behind the furnishings? Snakes could have found their way between the chinks in the walls. No, she would sleep on the porch. A broom leaned against the fireplace. Suzanne retrieved it and caught sight of a piece of paper under the bench, where a shadow had kept it hidden. She picked it up and shook off the dust. The letter was dated September 20, 2016. The handwriting was different from those in the notebooks, angled and uneven. Suzanne skipped to the signature. LOVE ALWAYS, JIM. Iris's father. He had been here last year. Suzanne read the letter from the beginning.

Dear Mary,
I don't expect you'll ever see this. I've been coming up when I could and knew you hadn't been here for a while. Now that I've been here solid since June, I know you and Iris aren't coming back.

I wanted to tell you to your face what happened to our son and how everything came apart after he died. I'm sorry it took me so long to come back. I'm to blame for that, no one else. I've failed all of you.

I put up a marker for Ash where the white wake-robin grows. It was all I could think to do.

I've waited for you, for you and Iris, but there's no use in waiting anymore. I miss you both so much but if I ever did deserve to have you, I don't anymore.

Love always, Jim

The last lines were crooked, trailing to the edge of the page, the handwriting weak, as if Jim were fading, already on his way out the door and away from these woods. Suzanne read the note again, then lowered the paper to her side. The more she learned about Iris and her family, the less she understood. Suzanne glanced around the cabin, imagining the family there. Iris lying on the bottom bunk, probably. Ash would have insisted on the top bunk and, knowing Iris, she would have relinquished it. Suzanne imagined a boy, smiling and energetic, dangling his legs from the top bunk. He would be wise like Iris. How could you grow up here without wisdom? Maybe that was romantic idealism; Ash could have been stubborn and foolish, but Suzanne doubted it. Her heart fell as she realized the loss Iris must be feeling now, having been presented with unmistakable evidence of her brother's death. Suzanne was perplexed as to why Iris would not have mentioned him. If Iris had believed he was alive, then why wouldn't she want to find him, and if she had known he was dead, why the shock? It made no sense. The boy was as big a mystery now as before Suzanne knew he existed.

Suzanne turned toward the table and the hearth, picturing the mother, Mary, sorting through the herbs in her collecting basket, or making a fire to cook dinner on a winter night. Suzanne didn't have a clear picture of Mary, and wondered why she had never asked Iris more about her. Suzanne had told herself she didn't want to pry, was wary of spooking the girl, but the truth was more complicated. Suzanne could more easily replace a mother she knew little of. She could manage that.

And Jim. Iris had been so certain her father was dead, and yet he had been here last summer. Suzanne considered that she ought to have told Iris about Detective DeCelle's lead on Jim Smith, despite the promise Suzanne had made. It might have given Iris hope. And if they had been able to find him, he could have delivered the news about Ash himself, instead of Iris stumbling upon a marker in the forest. Whit had lobbied for a more intensive investigation, which, Suzanne now understood, might have been in Iris's best interests.

The cabin had become confining, even with the door wide open. Suzanne left the letter on the table and walked outside. How strange it was to be completely alone, not even tethered to her family—or to anyone—by the umbilicus of her phone. She felt odd, unmasked, but there was no one there to see her. If she had a mirror, she could hold it up to her face and perhaps see a change. But that wasn't right. *We are not meant to see ourselves so clearly; nor are we meant to be eternally reflected in others. It is far better, and undoubtedly the natural order of things,* Suzanne thought, *to be not only blind to ourselves, but oblivious.* She watched the sky leak blue from the edges, paling in anticipation of night. Above, swallows traced arcs, wings outstretched, diving, twisting, slicing, in obedience to nature and oblivious to it. Suzanne's wonder became understanding: *We can temper the compulsion to see ourselves. We can opt to reject the boundary, the shell behind which we operate our lives, separate from the world, the world of dirt and leaf and sky in which we evolved, the true place that holds our essential nature. We can step out from behind the glass, and live.*

This, Suzanne realized, was the life Iris yearned to return to, the only life in which she would find happiness. Suzanne had not done everything she could for Iris because of her own need to prove herself as a mother and to explore the possibility of solitude Iris knew so well and so easily. Suzanne could not keep Iris captive to Suzanne's own failures or even hitch Iris to dreams that were not of her own making. That was, after all, what Whit had done to her, Suzanne: given her a safe place to hide, but not one in which to grow. She had remained underground, in the darkness, a *Hydnora* waiting for the rain. Whit had kept her there out of ambition, out of sympathy, and, ultimately, out of love. And she had allowed it. She had embraced the cool dark, telling herself she did not have the strength to break the surface.

Suzanne stepped off the porch and into the long grass. Behind the house, the ground sloped toward a narrow stream. How many times had Iris crouched there to drink, to fill a jug for her mother, to splash water on her face on a sweltering summer's day? Suzanne decided to return to the stream later to clean up, but while she had the light she turned back, tracing the edge of the clearing. She listened to the birds call to each other in the approaching dusk and studied the cabin now and then as it blended more completely into the surroundings, her presence unnoticed.

She arrived where she had first entered the clearing and stood for a moment, listening for Iris's footsteps, but hearing only the scratching of a bird or a squirrel in the leaf litter. She walked on and there, just ahead, was a patch of blue a dozen feet wide, a carpet of diminutive irises, no more than six inches tall, but with large blooms. Suzanne knelt before them. The petals had white and yellow markings outlined with darker blue. The color was really as much purple as blue, the color of Iris's eyes. Suzanne swallowed against the lump in her throat. Iris's mother must have treasured this flower to have named her daughter after it. And this patch, so close to the cabin, would have been sacred. Suzanne pictured Iris as a toddler, her chubby little fingers touching the delicate petals as her mother told her the story of her name. Suzanne bent forward, curving her body around the ache that swelled inside her as she remembered Brynn as a small child, her dimpled fists, the sweet smell of her skin, her perfect pink mouth, her open, honest, trusting gaze. Her daughter was lost to her now, and the pain of it was so great Suzanne did not know if she would make the same choices again. She hadn't known how much of herself she had subverted for the sake of her children, her marriage, how much of herself she had left underground. She had thought of herself as in control, protected, too busy to be vulnerable, but in truth she had been buried up to her neck.

She had given herself away. If she wanted herself back, there had to be pieces of her, sacred and proprietary, that no one else could ever have.

CHAPTER 39

Reid walked home from school practically dragging his feet. He had hoped to go to Alex's, but his friend had a therapy appointment, and Reid couldn't exactly tag along to that. Since his mother had left with Iris, Reid had avoided being home. He didn't want to see his father, afraid of exploding and telling him exactly what he thought. Not that his father didn't get the picture. But so far they'd dodged a big confrontation. The only thing they talked about was whether his mom had called or texted. She had sent Reid exactly one text. She had bailed.

He busied himself with speculation about what his mom could possibly be doing. Watching movies in a hotel room with Iris didn't sound right. Maybe she was looking for a new place to live. He hadn't wanted to ask his dad about that. Reid pulled out his phone and texted his mom.

REID: I miss you.

He frowned and hit delete.

REID: When are you coming back?

That was incredibly whiny, or aggressive, depending. He deleted it.

REID: Hope you're okay.

He searched the emojis for one that expressed how it felt to have your mother leave. He considered the sad face. He was definitely sad. He was also angry. And worried. And absolutely sick of parents, adults in general. That was a lot of emojis for one text. He sighed, hit send, and put his phone in his pocket.

Reid found himself on his street, nearly home. Eventually a tortoise gets where it's going; wasn't there a Buddhist story about that? Maybe he'd skip homework tonight (rebel!), do a long meditation session, and read something escapist, like *A Game of Thrones*. Talk about messed-up families.

Brynn had been suspended and had no choice but to stay home, so Reid wasn't surprised to find the door unlocked. He expected to find her watching TV, but the house was quiet. She was probably sulking in her room. He hadn't spoken a word to her since the morning after the party. What was there to say?

He left his backpack at the bottom of the stairs and headed for the kitchen, taking the living room route in case his dad had left the paper there. Instead of the paper, he found his dad, sitting on the couch with his elbows on his knees, rocking back and forth. He couldn't read his father's face.

"Hey, Reid." His dad didn't look up, just rubbed his hands together like he had something sticky on his palms.

"Hey."

Reid waited, figuring his dad would explain what was going on, why he was home in the middle of the afternoon. Instead his father's shoulders trembled, then collapsed. He covered his face with his hands and started twitching. Reid was confused for a second, but when his father sniffed, Reid realized he was crying.

Reid stuffed his hands in his pockets. "Dad? Are you okay?"

He shook his head and sobbed for real this time, his shoulders jerking up and down. Reid didn't know what to do, what to do physically or with the massive block of resentment and anger that was crushing him. But he wasn't such an asshole that he would walk away and get something to eat while his father sat there crying, so he just stood there.

After what seemed like an eternity, his father wiped his eyes with his hands, lifted his head, and ran his hands through his hair. He looked at Reid's knees at first, then stole a glance at his face. He was embarrassed, and scared.

Reid realized something might have happened to his mom. He took a seat across from his father. "Dad. Tell me what's wrong."

"It's Brynn." His face twisted up. "She's gone."

Reid hadn't even thought about Brynn. "Gone? Gone where?"

"To your grandparents'. She's with Tinsley."

"Jesus, Dad! Is that all?" Reid had been expecting something tragic, not news that his sister was being pampered by Grammy in her mansion.

His father seemed shocked by his response, like it really was tragic. "Yes. That's it." He pursed his lips. "No. Of course not just that." He lowered his head like he was moving something heavy around in his mind and couldn't look at anything other than his hands while he worked on it. "It's Brynn. It's your mother." He glanced at Reid. "It's you." His face crumpled and he began to cry again.

Reid was about to ask what he meant, but of course he already knew. His dad had fucked up. "It's okay, Dad." It wasn't, but Reid didn't know how to handle the crying.

His father pulled himself together a little, wiping his nose and adjusting his shoulders. His eyes were bloodshot. He looked old and desperate. "I don't know what to do, Reid. I don't know how to fix what's broken. I'm not even sure how it all happened. I thought I was doing the right thing, the right thing for me, sure, but for the family, too. I thought I was making something big, something that was for all of us. That was the idea."

"I know, Dad." Reid hadn't quite seen it this way before. His father was trying to do the right thing, like he said. Problem was, he was gunning so hard he'd blown right past all the other stuff—the harder stuff, the tricky stuff.

His father's expression was intense now. "Do you know? Do you really? Because I thought you of all people didn't get me." He had his edge back, and the tears weren't even dry on his cheeks. Figured.

"Oh, I get you, Dad. I get you." Reid hesitated, unsure of how much to say. He felt the anger flare in his gut. Fuck it. "You're successful. You bring home the money. And you're proud of it." His dad flinched. Pride was a double-edged sword. "But there's everything you are not seeing, all the stuff that passes you by, that you wave away because you have your eye on the real prize and the rest is fluff."

"You guys aren't fluff to me. Don't say that."

"You're pretty damn oblivious."

"Well, I'm busy. I work a lot. I can't pay attention to everything."

Reid leaned closer. "Do you really think it's okay to tell your kids you were too busy getting money to give a damn about them?"

"Now, Reid. Don't be like that."

"Be like what? Like what?" He threw his arms out wide. "How should I be, Dad? You know, right? You know exactly what I should want and what choices I ought to make and which friends I should have, right? Right?"

His father put his hands up in defense. "Hey, whatever I was doing, it was for you."

Reid jumped to his feet. "That is such bullshit! So I could be a success, huh? Not just any success, but your idea of success. You want me to be you." Reid spit out the words, filling the word *you* with all the disgust and betrayal he felt.

His father had been watching him. Now he looked away and became very still. A long moment passed before he turned to Reid, looked him in the eye, and nodded.

"You're right. I wanted you to be me." A simple admission delivered in a boardroom tone.

Reid felt his face burning. "I'm not a deal, Dad. I'm not something you can take credit for."

"I know."

"Do you?" Reid's throat clogged. He was losing control and fought to get it back. "It's not like I'm a failure. I'm good at things. I care about stuff."

His father's bluster dissolved; his eyes filled with tears. "I know you do. You're a good kid, Reid." His voice cracked and he cleared his throat. "I'm paying attention now. I really am."

Reid nodded and wiped his nose. A wave of exhaustion came over him.

His father stood and grabbed him by the shoulders and pulled him into a hug. Reid didn't resist. It was awkward—he couldn't remember the last time his father had held him—but that didn't mean it wasn't good. His father was holding him and Reid was holding his father, who was half crying, half laughing in relief, or in regret. Probably both. Reid knew because he was doing the same, for the same reasons.

CHAPTER 40

Iris ran blindly through the woods, her mind spinning. Ash was gone, truly gone. A hill rose before her and she dug in to climb it, pressing hard, pushing away branches in her path. Her vision blurred. She rubbed her forearm across her face and swallowed hard, her throat raw. She crested the hill and careened down to a stream, splashed across and became entangled in a stand of willows on the bank. Iris thrashed her arms and screamed in frustration until the branches released her. She sprinted away. Stout twigs broke against her shins. Brambles caught her clothing and backpack. Her exhausted panting became hiccups. Unable to catch her breath, she was forced to stop.

She lowered herself onto a downed log and waited for her lungs to stop burning. She looked around, took in the terrain, the light, the trees. She knew where she was. After she had discovered the patch of wake-robin, she would not be able to run away from the familiar. A comfort as a child but now a curse. Ash was everywhere and nowhere. She could never outrun her longing for him.

After several moments she rose and continued on, walking now, because there was no reason to run. Her skin prickled as if layers had been rubbed off. Her stomach was sour. Iris walked, eyes to the ground, her thumbs looped into the straps of the pack. She wandered, but here, in these particular woods, she could never be lost, not even when she most wanted to be.

~

Hours later, Iris sat leaning against a tree on a mountainside above the cabin. Her eyes were sore from crying and her legs ached. She had zipped herself inside her sleeping bag up to her waist. It wasn't cold, but she'd gotten used to being comfortable in the last couple of months. Maybe she had gone soft, but she hadn't forgotten how much it meant to feel the rough bark against her back, to taste the spring water she'd filled her bottle with, to have night falling down all around her like a heavy snowstorm, flakes of black instead of white. It didn't feel good—she was too sad for that—but it felt right, especially now.

Ash was dead. He'd been dead a long time, but not to her. She'd kept him going inside her, her memories of him so plentiful and strong and sharp they didn't seem like memories at all. That was the best she could figure. She had needed him that much. He'd been her family when Mama wouldn't talk, and company when she was all alone. He'd been there, when she could find him, in the frightening and confusing time after Suzanne pulled her out of the woods. *If I had died then*, Iris thought, *I'd never have had to lose Ash.* It wasn't the sort of thing someone could choose, though. She was the one here, the one left behind. She could sit against this tree, long into the night, with an ache pulling along the whole length of her. She'd done it before, three years ago, at the edge of the hole.

The forest became quiet, a thick quiet like a sleeping bear with no worries and no conscience. Iris did not feel tired. Her thoughts drifted from the windmill beside the old house to the blanket of white wake-robin, and to the familiar streams she'd crossed several times that day, always expecting to hear Ash laughing or see him darting away, teasing. Her memories encircled her. In the end she slept.

Dawn came for her quietly. Clouds covered the sun, and the birds were tentative despite the urgency of the season. Iris sat up, untangled herself from the sleeping bag, and stood. She couldn't spend another day, every day, wandering through the woods. It wouldn't make her happy as it once had done. Nothing would. She had to move on and find out what was next. Suzanne would be waiting for her, she was certain about that, either in the car or at the cabin.

Iris drank the last of her water, packed up her belongings, and set off. It felt good to have somewhere to go, to have someone waiting. It didn't fix the hole in her heart, but it was all she had.

~

The cabin looked different from what she remembered, smaller and less solid somehow, like she might be able to put her hand straight through the log walls. Iris spotted Suzanne on the porch step, facing the other way, and hadn't realized how much she had wanted Suzanne to be here. She couldn't cope with venturing inside on her own. Suzanne would help Iris stay attached to what was, instead of what had been.

Iris was halfway across the field before Suzanne saw her, got to her feet, and hurried to meet her. Iris started crying as soon as Suzanne put her hands on Iris's cheeks. Her mother had often done the same. Mama was everywhere here, like Ash was scattered through the woods.

"Are you all right?" Suzanne asked.

Iris nodded and more tears spilled. She glanced toward the seep where the irises grew, to see if they were blooming. Suzanne followed her gaze and must have understood, because she pulled Iris close.

"There's something inside you need to see."

Iris loosened herself from Suzanne's arms so she could see her face. "Is it bad?"

"I don't think so."

Iris followed Suzanne to the porch and left her pack there. The door was open. Suzanne stepped aside so Iris could go in first, but Iris shook her head. She wanted to be shown. Suzanne went in and Iris stepped in after her and looked around. So much dust and dirt. Mama would have been furious.

Suzanne went to the table and brought her a piece of paper. "A note from your father. From the summer before last."

Iris accepted the paper, her eyes on Suzanne's face. "What do you mean?"

"From your father. He was here."

The letter shook in Iris's hand. She tried to read it, but the words wouldn't stay still. She drew a deep breath, started at the top, and read it through. Her mouth went dry. Daddy had been here. He might not be dead. Iris touched her fingers to the writing as if it were linked to her father's hand. She spoke, her eyes fixed on the letter. "Why didn't he come back sooner? Why didn't he?"

"I don't know."

Iris looked up. Something in Suzanne's voice made Iris think maybe Suzanne knew more than she admitted. "My father said it was his fault. What does that mean?"

"I guess he didn't want to write out the explanation. He didn't expect anyone to even read it." Suzanne pointed to the bench. "Do you want to sit down, Iris? Have you eaten anything?"

Iris took a seat and read the letter again, hoping to find more words this time. "I didn't even think about who made that marker."

"You were too upset." Suzanne sat on the opposite bench and leaned across the table. "Iris, who was Ash? Was he your brother?"

Sadness rolled over Iris. "Yes." She closed her eyes to stop the tears from coming. A flood of images streamed before her like a TV show on fast forward. Ash burning with fever. Iris in the upper bunk because he was too weak to climb up top. Mama making compresses, mixing up medicines she gave to Ash drop by drop. Daddy going in and out of the cabin a hundred times, working outside on something, then coming in again, pacing. Iris stayed out of the way, but always where she could see Ash, on the top bunk, or on the porch looking through the window.

It was the middle of summer, as sweet a time of year as they ever had, but as long as the days were and as gentle as the weather was, the days and nights were black and damp. Finally, after a night when no one slept and Ash lay white faced and quiet, too quiet, Daddy packed a few things and scooped Ash into his arms. Iris followed them out the door, would've followed them all the way to where they were going if Mama hadn't stopped her.

Suzanne's voice was a whisper. "Tell me, Iris."

"Ash, he got sick." She wiped her nose with her sleeve. "Mama's medicines didn't work. Daddy took him away."

"And you thought Ash was still alive?"

Iris covered her face with her hands. She couldn't explain it, how Ash had been with her, how she had carried him inside her like she carried these woods: the smooth river stones under her feet, the trill of a wood thrush, the smell of rain in April. It had felt as real as anything she could taste or touch.

Suzanne said, "I'm so sorry, Iris. I can't imagine how you feel." She paused for a long while. "But it's good news about your father, right? I can help you find him."

The letter was in front of her. Iris fingered the corner of it. It was good news, wasn't it? Daddy was alive, more than likely. But Iris wasn't sure how to feel. It was like she had been given her father in exchange for Ash. If it was a bargain, it wasn't necessarily one she wanted, not without knowing where Daddy had been and why he thought he'd failed all of them. Iris knew she had to find the answers, had to find her father, but there was no telling what she would do once she did.

Suzanne told her they could stay at the cabin for the night, or for as long as Iris wished, but she didn't want to stay. Sadness and regret clung to the walls and beams and windows like spiderwebs, and Iris didn't know how to clear them out or see past them. For the first time, she missed her room at the Blakemores', where her life might have begun the day she walked inside. She didn't exactly want to go back there;

she simply wanted to be somewhere, anywhere she didn't have to be reminded of what she no longer had. Of course, that place didn't exist. Iris didn't wonder that her mind had stoked the memory of her brother into existence and snuffed out the reason for her father's leaving. She only wished she could find a way to keep lying to herself.

"Let's go back." Iris got up from the table, folded the letter, and slipped it into her pocket.

"Okay." Suzanne sounded unsure, and Iris realized Suzanne didn't know where they were going any more than she did. "I think we need to tell the police about the letter."

Iris nodded.

"Is there anything you want to take with you?" Suzanne said.

Iris scanned the room. Nearly two years ago, after the intruders had left, she had done the same thing, deciding what she could and could not live without. The answer was the same now. She shrugged. "No."

Suzanne went over to the shelves where Mama kept her stores and pointed to the notebooks. "What about these?"

"If you want them."

"Are you sure?"

"They're no use here."

Suzanne took them down and placed her palm on top. She stood quiet as a heron stalking a fish. A breeze shifted the air through the open door, a cloud-scattering breeze. A beam of sunlight splashed onto the rug under Suzanne's feet, the faded pattern of ivy vines brightening to green again. A smile tugged at the corner of Suzanne's face, and Iris marveled at how in that moment Suzanne resembled Mama, even though, feature for feature, they shared little. When Iris first met Suzanne, she had thought the same.

Suzanne smiled at Iris. "Have you ever had a dream where you find something you've wanted for a long time, something perfect and special? And you know you're going to wake up and it will be gone, but you hang on to it with all your might, just hoping that when you open your eyes, it will right there, in your hand?"

Iris nodded. She couldn't actually remember a dream like that, but she understood what Suzanne was trying to say.

"Well," Suzanne said, holding up the notebooks. "It worked."

CHAPTER 41

Suzanne wriggled out of the straps of her backpack and leaned it against the Navigator. Iris followed suit. Suzanne fished the keys out of the top compartment, opened the hatch, and tossed the packs inside. As she closed the hatch and came around the side of the car, she studied the brick farmhouse. No signs of life whatsoever, only a few rusted-out vehicles between the house and the barn, obligatory in this part of the state.

"Iris? Let's take a quick look at the house."

"Okay."

The girl had been subdued since they'd left the cabin—hardly surprising given the jolts she had received. Iris didn't seem to care where they went.

Suzanne strode up the short drive and noted the house numbers peeling off the dented mailbox. Lilac bushes in dire need of pruning lined the drive, and honeysuckle had climbed to the porch roof and engulfed half of the porch railing. Along the front walk, a dozen peonies were covered in round, full buds, ready to burst.

"How old is the house?" Iris asked.

"Not sure. Mid to late eighteen hundreds?" It was a simple, boxy Federal-style house with a chimney at either end. Suzanne guessed that the porch, adorned with fussy fretwork, had been added later. She scanned the roof. Original tin, corroded along the seams, but intact.

She didn't know much about old houses except that a leaky roof could spell disaster. She rounded the corner of the house and Iris followed. A large addition had been attached to the back. She had seen uglier ones. Behind the house was a large field sloping down to a pond framed by woods on the far edge. Beyond, hills gave way to mountains. A pair of hawks soared above the field, spiraling upward as if tethered to each other. Suzanne felt an odd brightness inside her. It took a moment for it to register as hope.

She turned to Iris. "Any of this seem familiar?"

"The windmill does, like I said." Iris gestured broadly. "I don't know about the rest. It's just a house."

"Maybe. But I think it's lovely."

They strolled the property for a while longer. Iris announced she was hungry, so they returned to the car and drove the twisty route back to Buchanan. At the Good Times Cafe, they both ordered bacon cheeseburgers and fries. Anticipating how many missed calls and texts would be waiting, Suzanne had put off turning on her phone until after she and Iris had finished eating and were walking back to the car. Across the street was a small park with a playground and a gazebo.

"Do you mind if we go over there while I check my messages?"

Suzanne led the way to a picnic table and turned on her phone, bracing herself. Thirty-one texts and eleven missed calls. Guilt inched along her spine. She scrolled through the calls first. Half were not from family, Boosters business and the like. Why they hadn't simply given up on her was anyone's guess. She was relieved to find no calls from Whit or the kids in the last day or so, suggesting nothing catastrophic had happened.

A reminder appeared on the screen. Reid's SAT tutor appointment was at three on Wednesday, today. Suzanne touched the text icon and began forwarding the information to him before she realized what she was doing. Her first contact with him in three days shouldn't be a reminder. She would talk to him when she knew what to say, and if he missed the appointment, so what?

She scanned the list of texts. A few from Whit and Reid, more from Brynn. One from Tinsley. Reading their names on her phone screen was so utterly banal and yet, now, it was anything but. Whatever they were telling her or asking her for was just an invitation to get immersed again in the entanglements from which she had run. She recognized she couldn't hide forever, but even after three days she felt so much more grounded, more like someone she wanted to be and could respect. It wasn't a sea change. She hadn't had an epiphany. She had found some space, quiet, and solitude—and hadn't come unglued. It was a start, and she wasn't at all sure she was ready to give it up.

Two young mothers were pushing their toddlers in the swings. Suzanne couldn't hear their conversation, but the tone was relaxed and casual. One of the children, a girl, giggled. She sounded exactly as Brynn had. Suzanne felt a tug in her stomach, a longing, but recognized it for what it was: a reflexive reaction. Of course she loved her daughter, and her son. Of course she wanted the best for them. But she also wanted something for herself, something significant. In the meantime, they had their father, her parents, and each other. They would survive.

She shifted her attention to Iris, who was watching the swing set, too. Her posture was a sculpture of despair, and she had dark circles under her eyes.

"Iris? I'm thinking we could go back to Lexington, maybe stay there a night or two, visit the library again."

"Aren't you going to call the police about my father?"

"Yes."

"When?"

"Do you want me to do it now?"

Iris shook her head. "There's no hurry."

"I know you have mixed feelings about him." Suzanne reached for her hand. "That might not change once you know more."

"That's what I'm worried about." Her voice had an angry edge.

"But you can't know how you're going to feel until you know what happened."

The girl's eyes filled with tears. "He was alive while I was alone in the woods. That's what happened."

Suzanne pulled her close. What Iris said was true, but what Suzanne didn't say was that parents have less control than they think, that what they try to do for their children is sometimes not enough, not nearly. Whatever Iris's father's reasons turned out to be, Suzanne wouldn't judge him yet. Sometimes leaving was the best solution, even if the main result was realizing you could come back.

They passed the forty-five-minute drive to Lexington in silence and checked into the same hotel they had stayed in Sunday night. They showered and changed, then spent the rest of the afternoon at the library. Suzanne spent most of her time on the computer while Iris perused the stacks. She seemed more relaxed among the books, probably because she could satisfy her curiosity without social pressure. The next morning Suzanne suggested a walk along the Maury because rain was predicted for the afternoon, when they would return to the library. Suzanne kept her phone off the entire time and resisted the temptation to check her email. It was a hard habit to break. She repeatedly pulled her phone out of her bag only to stuff it back in again.

Suzanne awoke Friday morning to the sound of rain hammering the hotel's metal roof. Iris lay awake in the other bed, looking out at the water-filled sky. The girl turned to her, waiting for Suzanne to shape her day.

"Good morning, Iris."

"Are we going to the library again?"

"Not today." She hadn't realized until she spoke that she had made a decision. "Today we're going home."

"Okay." Iris swung her legs over the side of the bed. "Is it okay if I take a shower?"

"Go ahead."

Suzanne picked up her phone from the bedside table. Seven thirty. She folded the pillow behind her head, swept over to the messaging screen, and opened Whit's thread.

Monday, the day after she had left: Please come back. We can talk. And later: When are you coming home?

Tuesday: This is ridiculous, Suzanne. And, later: Dishwasher says it needs rinse aid. Does it really? We're out. Ten minutes later: Rinse aid not mission critical. At midnight: I miss you, Suze.

Wednesday: Thought you should know Brynn went to your mother's.

Her mother's? Why on earth would Brynn do that? Suzanne had imagined Whit would use the time without her interference to talk honestly with both kids about the events leading up to prom night, and the night itself, including his own culpability. She had hoped he would mete out some discipline, shoulder some of the parental burden instead of making excuses. What had happened to make Brynn flee? Or had Whit insisted she go? Whit and Brynn were so close; Suzanne had been counting on that bond when she left. She had been more concerned about Reid.

She called Brynn.

"Mom! Where are you?"

Suzanne had expected an accusatory tone, or perhaps a pleading one. Instead, Brynn sounded desperate and vulnerable. "Not far. In Lexington. I'm—"

Brynn burst out sobbing. "Are you coming home? Please come home."

"Oh, Brynn." Her daughter's pleas made her heart ache. "Yes, I'm coming home. This morning." Lately, if Brynn had a tearful outburst, she would slide into anger with astonishing speed whether the problem she'd been upset about had been solved or not. It was as if she was furious she had let her guard down and needed to punish someone for it. Suzanne braced herself.

"Really? Today?" No anger whatsoever, more like a first grader getting news of a trip to Disneyland.

Relieved, Suzanne suppressed a laugh. "Yes. Where are you? I had a text from Daddy saying you were at Grammy's."

Her daughter began crying again. "I couldn't stay with Daddy. He was just so wrong about everything. So wrong. I had to leave, so I went to Grammy's."

"Should I pick you up there?"

"Oh my God, please. Grammy says I can't stay. And I can't go to Lisa's house because her mom thinks I'm a juvenile delinquent." Her words poured out. She'd been waiting for someone to tell. "I was about to be homeless."

Suzanne's first instinct was to mark that statement as ludicrous. But she refrained. "I'll be there before ten. We can talk about everything then."

"Okay, Mom. That's great. Ten is great." She paused, sniffing back tears. "I'm really sorry, Mom. I'm really, really sorry."

"I know, sweetheart. Me, too. We'll talk about it soon."

"I don't want you to hang up. You'll disappear again."

"I won't disappear. I promise."

"Okay. Okay, good."

"See you before ten."

"You sure before ten?"

"Yes. If there's a problem, I'll call."

"Okay. Is Iris coming?"

Suzanne hadn't expected this. "Yes. We're coming together."

"Okay. That's awesome."

"Bye for now."

"Bye." She was crying again. "I love you."

"I love you, too."

Suzanne ended the call and wiped her eyes with a corner of the sheet. It was hard to hear Brynn so anguished, despite all the anger her daughter had directed her way. Suzanne worried, as she had so many times previously, that her own dissatisfaction had silently poisoned her relationship with her daughter, sowing doubt where there ought to have been confidence, fostering insecurity where there ought to have been strength. She had been a shitty role model.

Suzanne heard the shower turn off. Iris would be out soon. Suzanne gathered her resolve and called Whit. He picked up immediately.

"Hey!" Cheer or false cheer, she couldn't tell.

"Hi. Are you all right?"

"I hope so. I mean, now that you've called. Wait. Why are you calling?" He babbled when he was nervous. This touched her more than if he had cried.

"To let you know we're coming back this morning, right after we pick Brynn up from my mother's."

"That's great. It really is. You talked to Brynn?"

"Yes."

A pause on the line. "About that. I could've handled things better and—"

"Let's talk about it later, okay?"

"Sure. Fine. I can't be home until two or so. I could try to move things around if you want."

"It's okay." Better, even. She had trouble envisaging being greeted by Whit at the door. "We found Iris's cabin."

"Seriously?"

"Yes. And there was a note from her father the police should know about."

"So he was there? Recently?"

"I'll tell you everything, Whit. For now can you just call the detective?"

"Sure." His tone was flat. He didn't like being kept in the dark, but Suzanne didn't want to relate the whole story over the phone.

"One more thing, and then I need to get ready so Brynn's not waiting."

"What is it?"

"Can you look up a house, a property for me? Ninety-Eight Turkey Hill Road. In Buchanan."

He repeated the address. "What's there?"

"Please just find out whatever you can. I'd really appreciate it."

"You got it."

"Thanks. I'll see you later." She winced at the sound of her voice, too breezy. In person they might be less awkward, but she wasn't counting on it. She hoped Whit would accept what she had been thinking about, her next steps, as he would put it, but she couldn't count on that either. Suzanne couldn't remember the last time she'd decided anything without her husband weighing in and felt as though she were trying out for a role for which she would never be chosen.

"I've missed you," Whit said.

Her voice faltered. "See you soon."

～

The housekeeper answered the door, cleaning caddy in hand, even though Tinsley was only steps away in the parlor, reading a magazine on the sofa with her back to a rain-streaked window. Iris had elected to stay in the car. Suzanne said she'd only be a minute.

Tinsley closed the magazine and waited for Suzanne to come to her. "Thank goodness you've come to your senses at last."

"Hello, Mother."

Tinsley snaked her head to look past Suzanne. "Clara? Clara!"

The housekeeper appeared in the doorway. "Yes, ma'am."

"She probably heard the door, but would you tell my granddaughter her mother is here." She spit out the word *mother* as if it were a bitter lemon pip from a drink of iced tea and turned her focus to Suzanne. "Brynn will undoubtedly tell you that as much as we love her company, your father and I simply could not allow her to stay."

"I don't even know exactly why she's here, but why make her leave?"

Tinsley blinked once slowly and sighed. "I don't have time to look after a teenager, Suzanne. That should be obvious." She glanced toward the hall and lowered her voice. "Especially not one with a rap sheet."

"Really, Mother? A rap sheet? I'm not going to argue that Brynn didn't make mistakes, but you and I both know that's not why you won't let her stay."

Her mother raised her eyebrows, politely curious. "Do tell."

"You might enjoy doting on Brynn, but you don't like being a mother. You never have."

Tinsley adjusted the diamond pendant at her throat. "At least I never ran out on you."

"True." Her mother looked up, uncomfortable with the admission. Suzanne reached for the most sincere thing she could say, and said it without vengefulness. "You needed me too much."

Tinsley sighed. "Perhaps."

Brynn came into the room. She wore sweats, an old T-shirt, and no makeup. Suzanne was alarmed at how drawn her daughter's face appeared. Brynn dropped her bag and threw her arms around her mother, hugging harder than she had in a very long time.

"Can we go?"

Suzanne planted a kiss on her daughter's cheek. "Sure." She addressed Tinsley. "Thanks for letting Brynn stay, Mother. Do you and Dad have time tomorrow? There's something I want to talk with you about."

"I'll see you on Sunday for brunch. We can talk then."

"Sunday?"

Tinsley looked heavenward. "Mother's Day brunch, Suzanne. At the club per usual."

Suzanne had completely forgotten. She pictured her family around a table, surrounded by her parents' friends and their families, everyone dressed smartly, the mothers sipping Bellinis while the children squirmed and the fathers itched to be released onto the golf course. She could feel Brynn staring at her, waiting for her to confirm that life would continue as it always had.

"The club might be too much for Iris, and for me, to be honest. Let's do it at our house. I'll take care of everything."

Tinsley opened her magazine and recrossed her legs at the ankle. "If we must."

Suzanne had expected more resistance. "Thanks, Mother. I'd still like to talk tomorrow, though."

She raised her head, acknowledging her curiosity. "It'll have to be first thing. We're extremely busy. Nine sharp."

"Nine sharp it is."

CHAPTER 42

Whit drummed his fingers on the steering wheel as he neared home. He thought he knew his wife but had not been able to get much from her phone call, other than news. She sounded calm enough, but he had no clue where he stood with her. They had to talk—he accepted that—but what he most wanted was to skip over the talking and return to what they'd had before. It wasn't mature, it wasn't even rational, but it was what he wanted.

When he saw the Navigator in the drive, he let out the breath he'd been holding. He left his car, strode to the house, and let himself in. He didn't call out. He closed the door softly and listened, his throat tight. Low voices came from the kitchen. Suzanne and Brynn. He stood still, squeezing the handle of his briefcase and half closing his eyes, indulging himself in the fantasy that this was just a day like countless others in which he returned to his house, to his children, to his beautiful wife, whom he cherished and who loved him back. Unable to make the fantasy last, Whit placed his briefcase by the entry table, ran his hands through his hair, and headed to the kitchen.

Suzanne, Brynn, and Iris sat at the breakfast table surrounded by deli-wrapped sandwiches, chip packets, and drinks.

"Hey, everyone."

"Hi," Suzanne said.

He looked away, not quite ready. Iris had her back to him. She twisted around and smiled, a bit tentatively. The girl looked exhausted and sad.

"Hi, Daddy." Brynn's tone was noncommittal, her glance skittish as she returned her attention to her sandwich.

Whit walked over and stood between his wife and his daughter. His hands moved toward them, one to each shoulder, but he hesitated, unsure, and stuck them instead into his pockets. Suzanne had been watching him, and it took him a moment to put a finger on what was unsettling about her look. He'd seen it before, in high school, maybe the winter of junior year. During lunch break he'd been searching for his friends, who weren't at their usual hangouts. He was circling back toward the quad and came upon a group of girls sitting on a concrete wall, swinging their legs, huddled shoulder to shoulder to stay warm. The nearest was Suzanne, whom he barely knew. She wore a jacket with a fur-trimmed hood and fixed him with those intense brown eyes. There wasn't anything friendly about it, or unfriendly, for that matter. Framed by fur, her face was that of a cat. Not a house cat, but a big one, like a mountain lion. She was stunning, but a significant portion of her beauty was quiet courage, giving her a sense of power. He had turned away from her then, intimidated, and when he encountered her years later at Mia and Malcolm's reception and again at her parents' house, that expression wasn't in evidence. If she resembled a mountain lion then, it was one on the far side of a moat in a zoo.

Confronted with a version of his wife he hadn't married, Whit didn't know what to do or say.

Suzanne said, "Did you speak with Detective DeCelle?"

"I left him a message." He came around the table, settled into the seat between Iris and Brynn, and helped himself to some of Brynn's potato chips with more casualness than he felt. "So where did you go? What happened?"

Suzanne said, "The cabin is east of Buchanan, just north of Roanoke. I think it's on private property." She went on to explain how she and Iris used river geography and plant habitats to find it.

"Clever," Whit said. "Is that why you were gone so long?"

"You know it isn't." Suzanne's tone was matter-of-fact. She described the cabin itself and mentioned the note Iris's father had left.

"What did it say?" Whit asked.

Beside him, Iris pulled back from the table, coiling in on herself.

Suzanne noticed, too. "Iris, I'm so sorry. If you don't want to listen, you can leave."

Brynn said, "Why are you upset, Iris? Isn't it good news your father had been there? I mean, you didn't expect that, right?"

Iris kept her eyes on Suzanne as she spoke. "We're going to try to find him." Everyone watched as she fought to keep from crying. She was so slight and intense and strong, and here she was holding herself together with baling twine. For the first time, Whit felt intense respect, even reverence, for Iris. She folded the paper around her sandwich. "I'm going to my room, okay?"

Suzanne nodded and the girl fled the room.

Whit turned to Suzanne. "What happened up there?"

She cast her eyes to the ceiling, as if consulting with Iris before continuing. "Near the cabin, we found a marker. Iris's father made it for his son, Ash, Iris's brother, who died in 2011. Iris didn't know he had died, at least I don't think she did."

"What do you mean?" Brynn said.

Whit was confused, too. Either you know someone is dead or you don't, but he kept quiet.

"She'd blocked out the memory, I think. While we were at the cabin, it came back. Iris remembered her brother became very ill six years ago, and their father carried him away, presumably to a hospital. The note her father left said he took responsibility for what happened to Ash, which had to mean his death."

"Jesus," Whit said.

Brynn pushed her chair back, startling both Whit and Suzanne. "I'm going up to see Iris."

Whit put out a hand. "Maybe she wants to be alone."

Brynn was halfway out of the room.

"Let her go," Suzanne said. "Let her go."

Whit leaned back in the chair and let out a long breath. "What a mess, huh?"

"Iris's family, you mean?"

"Yeah. The cabin, the brother dying, the father going back." Something occurred to him. "Any idea how long he was there?"

"June to September. It said in the letter."

"Wow, that's a long time to wait."

Suzanne took a long sip of her iced tea, then stared out the window over his shoulder. "Is it? It was his home, remember."

Whit imagined a man in a small dark cabin deep in the wilderness, waiting for his family to return, judging each day whether the wait had been long enough.

"Maybe not," he said.

~

Brynn climbed the stairs and turned along the hallway, her mind swarming with thoughts. She'd been so relieved to see her mom, more relieved than she should have been, considering it had only been a few days. It felt more like they'd been apart a lot longer, and, in the ways that mattered, they had. But it wasn't as if Brynn had suddenly decided her mom was her BFF—Brynn totally expected to be pissed off with her mom any moment now—but somehow things had changed. Her mom leaving had shaken up the whole family and left them spaced differently. Probably they wouldn't stay that way, but no matter what, things would never be the same. Maybe it wasn't because her mom had run away. Maybe it was what happened at prom. Maybe, she thought as she reached Iris's room, it had all started with Iris.

She knocked lightly on Iris's door, then went in without waiting for an answer. Iris was sitting on the floor with her back against the bed and her knees pulled to her chest. She looked weird, like always, and also incredibly sad.

Brynn sat on the edge of the bed. "Hey, Iris. I wanted you to know I'm sorry about the party, about the whole thing with Sam." She paused, waiting for Iris to say it was okay, then figured she had to go further. "It wasn't very nice of me."

Iris gave her a quick look and went back to staring at the floor. "It doesn't matter."

Brynn ran her fingers through the ends of her hair. That wasn't exactly the response she'd expected. Having had so little practice, she wasn't very good at apologies. She did honestly feel bad about it. Iris hadn't done anything to deserve it other than moving in with them. Brynn rubbed her itchy eyes. Getting suspended, her mom running away, her dad being a wimp—it all added up to mega-stress, and she hadn't been sleeping.

She scooted up to the head of the bed and lay down. "I'm so tired, Iris. Aren't you?"

"Yes."

Brynn patted the spot beside her. Iris twisted around and looked at her with bloodshot eyes.

"It's okay," Brynn said. "I won't bite."

Iris climbed onto the bed and lay down facing the other way. Her hair looked like squirrels had been chasing each other through it. Brynn began untangling it with her fingers. She yawned and Iris did, too.

"One day, Iris, when you feel up to it, you'll have to tell me about your brother." As Brynn smoothed Iris's hair, the girl nodded. "I'd like to hear about him. One thing I already know, though, is that he couldn't possibly have been as big a freak as mine."

Brynn couldn't see, but she would've bet Iris had smiled, if only a little.

CHAPTER 43

During midmorning break at school, Reid got a text from his dad saying his mom and Iris were on their way home. Isn't that great? his dad wrote.

"Fantastic," Reid muttered.

Alex was sitting next to him, eating a banana, and overheard. "Your blowup doll back from the shop?"

Normally he'd give some smart-ass retort, but nothing was normal anymore. "My mom's coming home."

"That's good, right?"

Reid nodded and slid the message up and down on the screen with his thumb. If it was good news, then why did he feel so pissed off? He'd been annoyed and off-kilter since his mom left, getting more wound up as each day went by, wound up so tight he couldn't meditate, which made him stress out more. He was mad at his mom for leaving and at his dad for being the idiot who could've avoided the dumpster fire with Brynn and Robby. Sure, he felt sorry for his dad when he was crying his eyes out. Who wouldn't? But Reid didn't see how things were going to get better unless his parents got real.

What were the chances of that?

Reid couldn't decide how to respond to his father's text, so he didn't. He got up, tossed the wrapper from his energy bar into the trash, and called to Alex over his shoulder as he headed off. "See you later, okay?" Alex would think about following him to ask what was wrong, but would decide against it, which was one of the reasons Alex was his best friend.

After school, Reid walked home at twice his usual pace, trying to burn off some anger, and practically ran up the walkway to the front door. He pushed it open and went straight upstairs even though he was hungry. If his mother wanted to talk to him, she could find him. He closed himself in his room, tossed his backpack on the floor, and spread-eagled on the bed. What now? It was Friday, so no need to think about homework. He didn't feel like reading, knowing he wouldn't be able to concentrate. He should have gone to Alex's and avoided the whole situation. His neck was stiff, and a headache was starting at his temples. What he needed to do was relax. He jumped up and riffled through the pile of clothes on the floor of the closet, remembering Whitney had given him a joint yesterday and he'd stashed it in his sweatshirt. Whitney. The girl definitely wanted to hook up. If things weren't such a mess, he'd be up for that, but not now. Girls never made anything simpler.

A knock on the door. "Reid? It's Mom."

Like he might have forgotten her voice. "Yeah."

"Can I come in?"

He found the joint and pocketed it. "Yeah."

She walked in and moved toward him like she wanted to hug him, but he had his hands crammed in his pockets, so she just stood there and smiled. "How are you doing?"

He shrugged.

She perched on the bed and started to tell him everything she and Iris had found out, as if he had been throwing questions at her. He was curious about Iris's family and her house, so he let his mother talk.

"Detective DeCelle is coming by this evening. He should be able to give us an idea of how hard it will be find Iris's father."

Reid finally spoke. "And she wants to find him?"

His mother frowned. "Well, I'm not sure she knows. She's pretty devastated."

"He did disappear for six years, then came back to say he'd messed up everything."

She looked at him more closely. "Are you sure you're all right, Reid? You seem—"

"Pissed off?"

She pressed her lips together and sighed. "I'm sorry I had to go away."

"Well, you didn't have to. You chose to."

"It felt like 'had to' to me."

"And it felt like 'See ya sometime, maybe never' to me."

She got up and came toward him, looking like she might cry.

He backed away, pulled out his desk chair, and sat backward on it facing her. "I talked with Dad while you were gone. He gets that he should've listened to me about Brynn. He admits he wasn't doing his job."

"So why didn't you come to me?"

"He asked me not to. You were flipping out over Brynn's Beauty and the Beast stunt, remember?"

"Yes, but—"

"But nothing, Mom! You let things slide almost as much as Dad does. You're just like Alex's parents. They don't care what he does as long as he's not a sociopath like his brother. Like that's a valid goal. He takes a bunch of pills and their answer is more pills and a therapist. *They* don't do anything different. They never even asked him why he did it."

"I don't see what all that has to do with you. Or with me."

"I know you don't." He took a deep breath, wondering if he shouldn't just stop talking. Too late for that, he concluded. "Look, Dad thinks I'm a loser, or at least he doesn't hide how disappointed he is that I'm not, I don't know, more like Brynn." His mother started to disagree but he kept going. "But you make it worse. You try to run interference, but while you're doing it, you're secretly agreeing with him, wishing I'd be different to make things easier for you." His mother's eyes widened, but she didn't say anything. "What kind of message is that?"

"The wrong one."

"I mean, you basically ignore the way Brynn acts because standing up to her is too hard. She bites, I get it. But then because I'm not aggressive like she is, you and Dad just roll right over me, or right past me." Frustrated, he gripped the back of the chair and rocked it hard, feeling it loosen from the seat. "I'm not saying it right."

"You're saying it fine."

He had expected her to launch a defense, but she didn't. He'd thought there was something different about her when she first came in, and now he thought he knew what it was. There was confidence in her posture. Sadness, too, but with some swagger.

He remembered something he'd thought of on the way home. "Mom, think of it like this. If we lived in Portland, I'd be the most normal kid in school and Brynn would be the freak."

She smiled and broke into a long, loose laugh. She reached out her hand. He took it and smiled, feeling for the first time in as long as he could remember that his mom really did understand after all, and that whatever had stopped her from expressing it before probably had nothing to do with him.

CHAPTER 44

Whit carried two glasses of malbec into the bedroom and set them on the bedside table. Almost nine o'clock and Detective DeCelle had just left. Suzanne was changing in the closet behind the half-closed door, and all three kids were watching a movie in the living room. Whit sat on the chaise and took off his shoes. What he really wanted to do was drink a glass of wine, make love to his wife, and sleep with his arm around her the entire night. But that was fantasy. Whit didn't know what Suzanne's return meant, since they hadn't had time alone to talk. He was afraid of that conversation and would do almost anything to avoid it, anything short of losing her.

And that seemed to be precisely where they were.

Wasn't it only a couple of weeks ago that he felt certain everything was coming together for him? What, really, had changed? Not him. Suzanne, then. His wife had changed.

He picked up one of the glasses and took a long sip. Suzanne emerged from the closet wearing gray pajamas and a thin darker-gray robe. He stood and passed her the wine.

"Cheers," she said.

"To finding Iris's father."

She nodded and drank her wine. "Seems likely they'll find him soon. I hope that turns out to be a positive for Iris."

"Even just knowing what happened will help, don't you think?"

"I do."

They stood two feet apart with their glasses of wine, stalled in conversation. If he weren't shoeless and she weren't in pajamas, they could've been strangers at a reception, failing at small talk. But there was nothing small about the anxiety circulating like poison through Whit's body. He was too afraid to ask Suzanne point-blank if their marriage was failing or had already failed. He reached for another topic. If they kept talking, they would stay married.

"You gave the detective the same address you gave me over the phone," he said. "I guess I assumed when you asked me to look into it, you were doing it to help find Iris's father." Suzanne moved away and sat on the chaise, concentrating on her glass. "But you didn't give him the report I printed for you."

"You can email it to him. I should've said that."

"But what did you want it for?"

She pushed her hair away from her face and held his gaze. "I have an idea about something I want to do."

"What sort of something?"

"A project. A rather large one." She smiled.

"And this project, does it involve me?"

The crease above her left eyebrow appeared. "No. Well, that's up to you. Let me tell you about it."

The floor seemed to drop away. *Keep talking. She wants to talk.* "Great. How about I get the rest of the wine?" He left the room before she could answer, desperate for a moment to regroup. A project? Clearly not one of her charities, not in this context, the context of "something I want to do." Whit descended the stairs, turning away from the sounds of the television, the presence of his children. He navigated through the near darkness of the dining room, feeling disembodied, like he was trailing a little behind himself, part of him insanely curious about what Suzanne had in store and another part wanting only to return to their normal life.

The light was on over the cooktop. The half-dark kitchen soothed him slightly. This was their home. He could not articulate exactly what that meant, but he was certain nothing had ever meant more to him.

He retrieved the wine bottle and returned upstairs. Suzanne sat on the chaise holding a stack of notebooks. Whit placed the bottle on the nightstand, picked up his wineglass, and took a seat on the bed.

"Okay," he said. "What's this project?"

She showed him the notebooks, which had belonged to Iris's mother and to Iris's grandmother before that. The pages were filled with information about plants and their uses. Suzanne explained that most of the plants were local to Virginia, but some were found only in mountainous areas farther south and west, suggesting Iris's mother was from the Smoky Mountains or the Ozarks.

"But that's not the most interesting part," Suzanne said. "At least not for me."

Whit nodded, eager for her to get to the point and yet dreading it.

"While I was at the cabin alone, I realized what I had in my hands." She weighed the notebooks in her palms. "Not what Iris's mother or grandmother discovered per se, but what might be discovered using these observations and others like them."

"Wait," Whit said. "You were at the cabin alone?"

"Yes. I got there first and stayed there by myself for one night."

Whit stared at her, stunned.

"I was fine, Whit." She smiled to reassure him. "Totally fine."

"How?"

She shrugged. "I was determined to find the cabin, I guess. And to be there for Iris, to help her discover her family's truth." She looked down at the notebooks. "And in the process, I think I've discovered, or rediscovered, mine."

Whit had no idea what she was talking about, but her face was so animated, so full of intent, he swallowed his questions. "Okay. Tell me."

"You probably saw that the property has a house, the barn, a couple of other buildings, plus the cabin, and two hundred and fifty acres, mostly wooded." He nodded. "I want to buy it."

"Why? For what?"

"A center for the study of medicinal uses for local plants. Not a quaint museum for amateur herbalists, but a place for scientists to work, for students to learn, for the public to appreciate the complexity of what is growing in their backyards." She held up one of the notebooks. "There's so much knowledge in here, but it's just the beginning."

Whit tried to digest what his wife was saying, both the ideas she was presenting and the fact that she was having them. Meanwhile, Suzanne kept talking.

"I've done some research, just preliminary, but I think I want the focus to be the development of new antibiotics. Remember when Iris had that MRSA infection? Very soon, too soon, we're going to be defenseless against dangerous bacteria. The drugs doctors have aren't working anymore, and we're running out of ideas for new ways to fight them." She leaned toward him, her eyes bright. "Plants can help. Because they can't move, they have to defend themselves right where they are against all sorts of attacks, including bacteria."

"But aren't people already doing this?"

"A few. It's pretty new. People are waking up to the antibiotic problem now, but no one has the answer."

Suzanne looked at him expectantly.

Whit took a deep breath and took a sip of wine. He didn't know where to begin. This was all so crazy. Their kids—Brynn, mostly—had gotten into trouble, and he hadn't handled it very well, so Suzanne had gotten angry and taken off. Now she was back with a plan to save the world from deadly bacteria, and somewhere in there, he was pretty sure his marriage was hanging in the balance.

"Look, Suzanne. I know you got upset about what happened on prom night, and I take the blame for not seeing it coming. I've admitted that, not just to you, but to Reid and Brynn."

She frowned. "But not enough to talk to Robert."

"I didn't see the point. I still don't."

She exhaled sharply and pulled back from him. "I was telling you about my project."

"I know. But why now? You can't just cut and run from our life because you came up with this idea."

Suzanne raised her eyebrows. It wasn't an expression he was used to seeing on her and it unsettled him. "I'm not cutting and running, Whit. But you are right, absolutely, that I haven't yet figured out what it might mean for our life together. I honestly haven't." Her face softened. "I do know that I can't go on like before. I was a very organized, efficient zombie. That's over. I have to do something I care about."

"What about us? What about the kids? What are we supposed to do while you're collecting plants in the forest?"

Suzanne sipped her wine, regarding him patiently over the rim of the glass. "I guess we'll have to figure it out."

"Figure it out? What does that mean?" His voice was shrill but he couldn't help it.

"I can't know everything right now, Whit."

"Do you love me? Do you know that?"

He wanted her to smile, a big smile that made her eyes shine. He wanted her to tip her head sideways a little when she did it.

Instead she simply said, "Yes."

Whit realized he had asked the wrong question. She loved him because she wasn't the sort of person for whom love was a game. Suzanne's love was solid. But Whit not only loved Suzanne, he adored her. He cherished her. Suzanne's love for him might be exactly the sort of love that could persist, unaltered, in the transition from marriage to separation to divorce. She could love him that way forever. This wasn't news. It was simply news he'd never wanted to hear. As long as Suzanne was at home, tending to their lives, the nuances of his love and her love hardly mattered. Now they did. It dawned on Whit that the woman sitting across from him, as familiar as she seemed, was quite possibly someone he did not know well at all. He wondered if he loved that woman as much. And now that she wasn't driven by fear, would she still need him?

"What are you thinking?" Suzanne asked.

Whit got up and refilled their glasses to give himself something to do.

"It's a lot to take in."

She nodded. No rush.

Whit said, "I wonder if you blame me."

"For what?"

"For helping make you a zombie." She smiled a little but said nothing. "I mean, you've always been, what, *philosophical*, looking at us from the outside. I discouraged that sort of talk, relationship philosophy. Hell, I didn't even know what you meant most of the time. If that was you waving the signal flag of your dissatisfaction, then I'm guilty of ignoring it, or worse."

She reached for his hand. "Maybe you didn't understand me for a reason, Whit. Maybe we want different things."

His heart surged painfully. "Don't say that."

"Even if it's true?"

He wanted to say yes, because it would hurt too much otherwise. He closed his eyes and pressed his lips together.

Suzanne squeezed his hand. "This is what we have to figure out."

He nodded but kept his eyes shut, waiting for the pain to subside.

$\sim$

The next morning, Suzanne stopped at the nursery on her way to see her parents and purchased a Mother's Day present, a striking architectural display of grasses and succulents presented in a rectangular planter, vaguely Moroccan in design. The echeveria, with their rosette shape and pink-to-lavender-to-blue leaves, reminded Suzanne of her mother: smooth and stunning, with a sharp spike at the tip of each leaf.

Tinsley answered the door, and Suzanne showed her the planter, which she had left at the foot of the steps.

"Happy Mother's Day, a bit early." She kissed Tinsley on the cheek. "I figured it would be easier for you not to have to lug it from my house."

Tinsley peered at the display and smiled. "Thoughtful on both counts. Thank you."

She ushered Suzanne inside, clicking along the travertine floor with energy and purpose, rattling off her commitments for the day. Suzanne registered none of them. Her father was waiting in the living room, reading the *Wall Street Journal*. He folded it and set it aside.

"Good morning, Suzanne. Welcome back from your travels." His tone was neutral, but his point hit home nevertheless.

"Thanks." She sat in a white leather wingback. Her mother settled herself on the couch next to Anson. "I know you're both busy, so I'll get right to the point."

Suzanne outlined her plans. To appeal to her father's entrepreneurial interests, she emphasized the uniqueness of the project and the potential for scientific discovery. For her mother, Suzanne described her plans to restore the old brick farmhouse and to create a teaching garden.

"Three brothers inherited the land. The eldest was living there when Iris's parents first came—he probably knew them somehow—but he died several years ago. According to the Realtor who knows the family, the surviving brothers have been thinking of selling but are attached to the place. She thought my project might be just the thing to encourage them to sell."

"Especially if the price is right," Anson said.

"Sure."

"And that's why you're here," Tinsley said.

"Yes."

"Really, Suzanne. I'm surprised at you. This, this project, will take you away from your husband, from your children. And you expect us to fund it?"

Suzanne had anticipated this response. "Whit and I are putting up some of the money, but it's not enough. And I'm asking for an advance on my inheritance. I know it's not mine to ask for, but doesn't it make sense to use the money to do something positive, something important?" Her father bristled. She appealed to him directly. "I know it's invested now and that you've worked hard to make it grow. I'm just hoping I can make something grow, too, in my own way." Her father met her gaze, considering.

Tinsley jumped in. "But what about Whit and the children? And your work at the school and your other responsibilities?"

"Reid and Brynn are nearly grown. I'm not abandoning them. The property is only an hour and a half away. I'm carving out a life for myself, something I care about."

"That's selfish."

"Maybe. But maybe it's not a terrible thing for my children to see that a woman can do more than serve the family." Tinsley's eyebrows shot up. "I've done that, and now I'd like to try something different." What she wanted to say was that she felt her family had been misguided and, indeed, broken, for many years, but sharing that with Tinsley would be pointless. Her mother expected families to be broken, and Suzanne had come to believe her mother was invested in Suzanne's staying that way.

Anson said, "Well, I don't see anything wrong with the idea on the face of it. God knows we've wasted money on worse ideas."

Tinsley began to protest.

"Mother," Suzanne said, "I'd be happy for your help."

"I'm not keen on forests."

"I meant with the house, for starters."

Her mother glanced at her husband with a mixture of resignation and annoyance.

Anson pressed his hands against his knees and stood. "Draw up a proposal, Suzanne. With numbers. Then we'll talk again." He extended his hand.

Suzanne rose and shook it. In that moment she caught something of what had transpired, or failed to, between Whit and Reid. She understood what it meant to have been granted approval by a successful man to whom you belonged, whether you admired the man or not, whether the bargain struck was mutually agreeable or only a truce.

CHAPTER 45

The first time Iris went to see her father, he was standing by the window of the visiting room, looking outside as if he expected her to fly by the glass. Detective DeCelle had tracked him down to a drug abuse treatment center in Durham, North Carolina, about three hours away from the brick house in Buchanan. The outline of his story came to Iris through Suzanne, who heard it from the detective. Nearly two years ago, after Iris's father had written the note and left the cabin, he'd given up caring what happened to him. He got tangled up with some hard types and started taking drugs, painkillers, mostly, although the kind of pain he had wasn't physical. No one knew how he ended up in North Carolina, least of all him. The detective had discovered a quilt in the cabin with "M. Colton" sewn in one corner—Iris's mother's maiden name—and a search for James Colton had led to Iris's father, James Smith, who had given the false name at the treatment center, afraid of being arrested again.

Iris hadn't wanted to be the one to tell her father about how Mama had died, so Detective DeCelle took care of it and told her father what had happened to Iris, too. Her side of the story was all filled in before she made the trip to see him, giving him plenty of time to think how to explain himself, if he could.

Iris entered the visiting room, and Suzanne hovered behind. Iris's father's clothes hung loosely on him—she remembered him big and strong—but it was his face that alarmed her the most. He looked old and so tired she wondered how he managed to stay standing. She stopped as soon as she saw him, her feet rooted into the floor. He turned as if someone had tapped him on the shoulder and noticed her. His face changed, going soft all at once, like someone had let the air out of him; then he smiled, his blue eyes shining. He stretched out his arms.

Iris could feel Suzanne behind her and almost turned back. It would've been easy. But the man was her daddy, and there was nothing she could do except step forward, like walking on black ice, and let him hold her. There was nothing else she could've done. Once he had his arms around her, she remembered how she loved him. It welled up in her and spread out from her chest so fast she couldn't breathe.

They sat at a little table. Suzanne, too, all three of them wiping their eyes. He asked if Iris wanted to know the story. She said she did. He told her about carrying Ash down off the mountain and hitching a ride into Roanoke, to the hospital. They had taken Ash in, but asked too many questions he didn't want to answer. He told Iris that her mother would never have forgiven him if he'd revealed where they lived and ruined the life they'd made. Iris recognized this was true. Mama would never come out of the woods. She said she would rather die, and that was her solemn promise. So once Daddy was sure the nurses and doctors were taking care of Ash, he'd slipped out. But he couldn't stay away, and when he came back late that night, he told a nurse he was Ash's uncle, that the boy's father had gone missing. The nurse told him Ash had died.

Daddy said, "I ran off. I don't remember where, but I ended up at a bar." He hung his head and clasped his hands together to stop them shaking. "Some guy said the wrong thing. I don't even know what. I was blind."

Iris nodded. She already knew what had happened next from the police, but she let him talk. He'd gotten into a fight and knifed a man. When the police showed up, he fought them, too, and ended up in prison. That's why he didn't come back to the cabin. He couldn't, not for four years.

"I went to the cabin as soon as I could, but I was on probation and couldn't stay. You and your mama were gone, but I kept coming back. I almost ended it a couple times, I'm ashamed to say." He turned away from her. "When I finally got off probation, I went back up and stayed, but you were long gone by then." He reached out and took Iris's hand in his. He looked her in the eye, struggling to hold himself there against the weight of regret. "I'm sorry."

That was all he said about the past. He asked questions about Iris and Suzanne, steering away from the time Iris had spent alone in the woods. She understood his guilt was too large for him to tolerate too much of the truth at once, and it wasn't at all clear to her how much fault lay at his feet in any case.

Iris visited her father twice more during the summer. He'd have to leave the treatment center before long and find work, make some sort of life. It wasn't that different from what Iris herself had to do. They talked, sometimes about the time before Ash got sick, sometimes about afterward, easing toward a reckoning of the past the two of them might be able to bear. It wasn't something that could be hurried, Suzanne said, or something Iris was required to do at all. And yet she felt she did.

He was her daddy. She'd always loved him and couldn't find a reason to stop now. Maybe he should've taken Ash to the hospital sooner. Maybe he should've tried harder to find her. Maybe he should've been stronger.

Iris knew being strong wasn't enough, because life could weigh more than you ever imagined. You had to bend, like a branch laden with snow, arcing toward the earth. Daddy had been folded in half until he could no longer see the sky, knees forced to the ground. It seemed to Iris he deserved less weight, not more. Along with Mama, he'd given her what she treasured most: the woods, the streams, and the mountain breezes. Iris held those gifts in her heart, where there was also room for him.

CHAPTER 46

In the light-filled room that served as her office, Suzanne pored over the plans spread out on the massive oak table. Andreas Thierry, the architect, would be arriving after lunch to discuss the final revisions for the barn conversion. She'd chosen Thierry for his experience in laboratory design, but she wanted the space to be both functional and beautiful. The barn and the rest of the property were too special to turn into an industrial park, so she was making use of the existing buildings and striving to retain their character. The house would be her residence when she wasn't in Charlottesville and would eventually also have reception and meeting rooms. The barn would contain the lab, the storage facility for specimens, and a library. The garage, which at one time had been a carriage house, was destined to become a bunkhouse with its own kitchen. Once the center was established, she would consider adding other facilities, but for now the plans in front of her were sufficiently ambitious.

Rivulets of condensation streaked the glass of iced tea at her elbow. The brick walls, three courses thick, kept the house somewhat cooler than outside, but even so it was warm on this humid August day. Suzanne jotted notes on a pad, then straightened her back, tight from leaning over the drawings, and surveyed the room. Tinsley, Suzanne had to admit, had done a stellar job with this room and the other parts of the house restored thus far—two bedrooms, one bath, and the kitchen. Suzanne had asked for a minimalist approach; the last thing she wanted in her work life was clutter. Tinsley had selected natural materials—wood, sisal, linen—in natural colors, giving the rooms a feeling of having been borrowed from the landscape. In fact, Suzanne was so impressed with her mother's ability to translate Suzanne's wishes into reality that she'd encouraged Tinsley to consider interior design more seriously. Tinsley had waved away the suggestion. "We don't all need to follow you into the ranks of working mothers, my dear." And yet Suzanne sensed her mother hadn't dismissed the idea out of hand.

Suzanne checked her watch. Just past noon. She left the plans as they were and went in search of Brynn. Not finding her in the living room, Suzanne walked out the front door and along the walk that led to the barn. She paused at the sign that had been installed last week: MARY COLTON SMITH CENTER FOR MEDICINAL BOTANY. Suzanne pulled a few weeds from the flower bed at the base of the sign, then continued toward the barn. The heat of the sun seeped into her skin, and she left the path for the shade of the walnut trees. There, between the barn and the pond, was Brynn, adjusting a camera on a tripod. Suzanne stopped to watch her.

Not surprisingly, Brynn hadn't been eager to spend time at the Buchanan house, especially not before the basic renovations had been completed and the Wi-Fi installed.

"I don't do rustic," she had said.

In mid-July she twisted her ankle during a game of Frisbee with her friends, tearing tendons and requiring her to use crutches for six weeks. Brynn found sitting with her foot elevated in Charlottesville no more exciting than doing so in Buchanan, especially when Tinsley enlisted her granddaughter's help during decorating trips. One weekend, Brynn brought her friend Lisa to the center. While Suzanne made breakfast, Brynn and Lisa laughed at a pair of bluebirds being pursued by begging fledglings. They called the adults Mom and Dad and named the fledglings after their friends, dubbing in teen dialogue. After the girls finished eating, Suzanne handed them binoculars. Brynn hobbled outside and Lisa followed. To Suzanne's surprise, they spent the morning sneaking up on birds.

"Don't tell anyone we were doing this," Brynn warned Lisa when they retreated inside from the heat. "Social suicide."

Brynn tried to photograph the birds with her phone but became frustrated. Suzanne consulted with Whit, and together they chose a camera and zoom lens that they presented to Brynn on August 1, her sixteenth birthday. Since then, she had been eager to accompany Suzanne to the center, waking early to catch the birds and butterflies during the height of their activity. She had even entered one of her photos in a local contest and received an honorable mention, which seemed to legitimize her interest and render it less dorky.

Now, as Suzanne observed Brynn moving stealthily behind the camera, she understood how quiet work—observing, waiting, listening—had been a boon to Suzanne herself as a young woman, offering the chance to become immersed without the risk of being overwhelmed, and how Suzanne, unlike her daughter, had not had to suffer the crush of social media during her adolescence. Brynn still drew her energy from her friends and their cultish obsession with posing, rather than being. But her new hobby—this quiet work—might become her daughter's salvation, Suzanne believed, providing a neutral space into which to withdraw, a space without mirrors, or even glass.

Brynn turned and waved. "Lunchtime?"

"If you're ready."

Brynn collapsed the tripod with the camera still attached and carried it over to where Suzanne waited.

"Show me the photos later?" Suzanne said.

"Sure. Is Iris back?"

Iris's room was upstairs in the farmhouse next to Brynn's, but she stayed at the cabin, too. "I wouldn't expect her until tomorrow at the earliest." Suzanne's phone beeped. She pulled it from her pocket and checked the screen. "It's Dad. I'll be five minutes."

Brynn started off. "Tell him hi."

Suzanne accepted the call. "Hey. How's everything?"

"Great. Just checking to see if tomorrow's still good."

She smiled. Call it politeness or walking on eggshells—or dating. "Tomorrow's very good. I'll even cook."

"Best news yet. Reid's been trying. He's better than me by a long shot, but, you know."

"It's okay to say you miss my cooking."

"I miss your cooking."

"Thank you."

"And many other things."

"Best not to mention cleaning or laundry."

"Wouldn't dream of it. I know what probation means." He paused. "Yesterday in the car I heard that Elton John song on the radio."

"What song?"

"The karaoke one." His voice grew thick. "I took it as a sign."

About a year after they started seeing each other, they'd spent a weekend in Virginia Beach and landed in a bar. Karaoke duets were the featured entertainment. Whit had convinced Suzanne they should give it a shot.

"You know I'm not much of a singer," she said.

"Same." He grinned at her. "Let's do it anyway."

Whit chose Elton John's duet with Kiki Dee, "Don't Go Breaking My Heart." Suzanne's microphone shook in her hand as the intro played. What was she doing up here? Whit sang the opening line—badly. She missed her first line and looked at him in apology.

He held her gaze and sang the title line again. Suzanne croaked hers in response. After the first chorus, she began to relax. She forgot the audience. She forgot she couldn't sing because together they could, perhaps not beautifully, not even competently, but the joy and the promise in the song was theirs.

Remembering that night, Suzanne realized Whit had given her more than a safe place to hide. He had given her belief in them, in what would become their marriage. He wasn't afraid to love.

"Oh, Whit," she said, "I'm so glad you're coming down." She hadn't been sure at all when she launched this project how Whit would react, or how she would feel about him and their marriage. Now that she was choosing him not out of fear, but out of desire, her love for him felt genuine in a way it never had before.

"I can't wait to see what you've been up to. Sounds like it's coming along great. Did Reid tell you he was skipping this trip?"

"He texted me yesterday. He said it was his job, but I'm guessing that's mostly cover."

"I doubt it. That's not like him."

"True."

After she placed an offer on the farmhouse, Suzanne had lived at home in Charlottesville, with Whit bunking on an air mattress in his office. The atmosphere had been civil but awkward. The sale went through in June, and Suzanne announced her plans to spend the majority of the summer in Buchanan. Reid had surprised her by opting to stay with his father. "We've got stuff to figure out," he had said. Whit and Reid had taken up karate together and seemed to be getting along so much better that Suzanne was ashamed to admit she felt left out. Reid had taken a job at a nonprofit promoting climate-change awareness and was absolutely dedicated to it, as he was with everything he did, but his schedule meant Suzanne didn't seen him often. Practice for fledging, she supposed. Maybe if she invited Mia and her son Alex for the following weekend, Reid would be more likely to accept.

She said goodbye to Whit and ended the call. While she had been talking, she had wandered and now found herself on the far side of the barn and close to the margin of the woods. Surrounded by a low picket fence were the graves of Iris's mother and brother. Iris had spent more time choosing the flowers and shrubs for the site than the markers themselves, small pale granite rectangles flush with the ground, engraved only with their names and the years Mary and Ash had been born and had died. It was a beautiful spot, nestled against the protective wall of trees and overlooking the rolling fields now dotted with black-eyed Susans, ironweed, and golden aster.

Iris hadn't been sure about creating the grave site. The police had retrieved Iris's mother's remains from the cave into which she had fallen and, days later, had located Ash, who had been buried in a municipal plot in Roanoke. Suzanne had insisted on a creating a proper site for the burials. The girl had had no experience of memorials, or family tradition, or indeed of any of heritage extending behind her and stretching in front, to become part of her future and the future of the children she might have. But once Ash and Iris's mother had been laid to rest, Iris gradually came to accept the site, and to rely on it. After each visit with her father, Iris came to sit by the graves, no matter the weather, and afterward walked into the woods to stay at the cabin by herself for a time. She was there now.

Suzanne turned from the graves and the trees standing tall above them and headed back to the house. She hoped Iris would return soon, not because she worried about her, but because she missed her. Suzanne had her family, her project, her dream, all of it a work in progress, including herself. Iris was a bonus—a messenger of the gods, so the myth went. Sun breaking through clouds and illuminating a mist-filled sky was wondrous. A rainbow was a godsend.

CHAPTER 47

Iris worked her way among the blackberry bushes. It was late in the season, so she had to hunt for the few berries that were still plump and sweet. Suzanne had packed too much food for her already, but Iris could not pass up them up, because once the last berries were gone, Iris would have to acknowledge that summer was winding down. The signs of it were everywhere. The trees sighed under the weight of their limbs, and the goldenrod and asters had appeared in the meadows. Even the birds had grown quiet, carelessly leaving molted feathers behind like sleepy people shedding clothes on their way to bed, except for the blue jays, who only got noisier, and the doves, who mourned each dawn as plaintively as the last.

When the berries ran out, Iris started back to the cabin, taking the higher route. She walked through the forest and across the streams using memories that didn't benefit from her direct attention. Her mind was somewhere else, with her father, not that she could think about her family too long or too deeply. It hurt: Ash's tragedy, their mother's, both Daddy's pain and hers. Suzanne said time would ease the pain, like working through a sore muscle. Iris hoped Suzanne was right, but sometimes Daddy reminded her only of what she no longer had, and as guilty as it made her feel, she wished he had stayed lost. At least then she could attach whatever she wanted to the mystery of his disappearance, or forget him altogether. But she didn't have that option, because once he had been found, she couldn't lose him again even if she wanted to. He was locked inside her heart.

Iris had questions for her father that she kept stacked in her mind. The last time she saw him, a little more than a week ago, she had asked about her mother's family. He told her the Coltons had scratched out a living deep in the Ozarks. Iris's grandmother, her mother's mother, had died when Mary Colton was fourteen. Iris's father had never met any of them, and Iris understood from his tone that distance had nothing to do with it.

"Your mother didn't like to talk about it, but your grandfather was a hard, hard man," Iris's father told her. "When your grandmother died, he got even harder. Your mother was the youngest of six and the only girl. Too much fell on her, and it didn't seem anyone was looking out for her. She didn't say exactly what went on, but as soon as she could, she left and never went back. I met her near Asheville a few years later." He paused, shaking his head as if the memory of her were too fine to belong to him. "She was pretty and strong, just like you, but terrified of people, shied away from everyone. Everyone except me, for some reason." He smiled at Iris. She recognized this part of the story. She had always known her parents trusted and loved each other. Whatever else had happened to her family, they always had this one true, straight, incorruptible thing.

Iris's reverie dissolved as she arrived at the place where the wake-robin grew in the spring. It was just an ordinary patch of woods now, except for the giant boulder and, of course, Ash's marker. She accepted that what remained of her mother and brother was buried by the old brick house, but in her mind, Ash would always be here. Iris knelt in front of the marker and pulled at the plants crowding its edges.

"Can't stop things from growing, Ash. You just can't."

Or from changing. Her own life was a handy example. How she had fought to keep things the same, to stay in the woods, live the only life she knew, the one that had shaped her. Her cradle and her crucible.

Growing and changing. Iris had been afraid of both, and she still was, but Suzanne had shown her what courage could do, how you could alter the shape of a life without breaking it. Iris wasn't sure about who she might become, what shape she might take, but she wouldn't live her mother's life, molded by fear. Mary Colton Smith had loved these woods as she loved her family, but she had been hiding. Iris would not hide.

Suzanne wanted her to study and work at the center after she finished high school. Iris said she might. Plants and medicine were her legacy, after all, passed down to her from the grandmother she would never know. Suzanne knew Iris better than anyone, which gave Iris comfort. But Reid had been talking to her and sending her articles on meditation and global warming. The way Iris thought about it, her own mind was the smallest place to learn, make changes and make a difference, and the Earth was the biggest. Iris didn't know which intrigued her more. Maybe both, or something in between. She had time to decide. She could even change her mind. Sometimes she became swamped by the possibilities and felt she had been launched into a wide-open space and could fall forever, as in a dream. Being in the woods helped her to find her feet again.

She finished clearing the plants away and squatted on her heels with one hand on the top of the marker, listening. The wind sighed through the tops of the trees, shifting the pattern of light falling to the forest floor. A pair of dusky-blue butterflies, no bigger than her thumbnail, danced in a shifting column of light, then alighted, first one, then the other, on the damp ground, violet blue against brown, before twirling upward once more. Beyond the clearing, in the undergrowth, a bird kicked through the leaf litter. A towhee.

Iris stood and stretched her arms to the sky, her shirt sticking to her sweaty back. The heat was lying on her. She had slept on the cabin porch last night, and, if she stayed, she'd sleep there again, putting herself in the path of whatever breeze might arrive.

"See you later, Ash."

Iris rubbed a mosquito bite on the back of her neck and walked away, heading south along the curve of the hill toward the cabin. When she got there in a little while, she'd see how she felt about staying another night on her own. It might be that she'd rather just gather her things and make her way to the house. She would get there well before dark. Suzanne wouldn't be expecting her, but she'd welcome her all the same.

ACKNOWLEDGMENTS

I am indebted to my agent, Maria Carvainis, for her wisdom, expertise, dedication, and perseverance. I rely on you and you never let me down. Thanks also to everyone at the agency, especially Martha Guzman.

Thanks to my editor, Chris Werner, for his enthusiasm, clear direction, and keen insight, and to the astute Tiffany Yates Martin and her delightfully sharp red pen. To the entire team at Lake Union, thank you for transforming my manuscript into a book and planting it in the sunshine.

Thanks, too, to Claire Zion and Lily Choi for guidance and comments on an earlier version, and to Steve Crowder for advice on police policy and procedure (but any flubs are mine).

Heather Webb and Kate Moretti gave me so much: laughter, cheerleading, hand-holding, and advice of all sorts; I leaned on you both. Aimie Runyan, thank you for being my champion and my friend. Heartfelt thanks to all the Tall Poppy Writers—my sisters, my buddies, my coconspirators—and to my other author friends, Holly Robinson, Karen Lanning, and Lisa Tracy, for your patience, humor, and companionship. I'm also grateful for my faithful readers, those lovers of story whose kindnesses are too numerous to recount, and to my family—daughters Rebecca and Rachel and siblings Helga and Ricky—for listening and for caring.

I've saved the best for last. Thank you to Richard Gill, my patron of the arts, my trusted friend, my walking companion, my heart.

DISCUSSION QUESTIONS

1. Suzanne and Whit decided to bring Iris into their home. Was it the right decision for everyone in their family? For Iris?

2. "Giving too little, giving too much. Subtracting from here, adding there. Caring for your marriage, your children, your parents, your reputation, your future, and, if you could manage it, your younger, more idealistic self. This complex calculus was based on theories of love and motherhood, and equations of duty and self-worth. But Suzanne could not work out the solution." What do you think of Suzanne's thoughts here and what they say about motherhood and marriage? How does Suzanne work out this "life math"? How did her mother?

3. What strengths and knowledge did Iris gain from her unusual upbringing? What do you think of Iris's parents' decision to raise their children in the woods?

4. Suzanne's terrifying experience in the African bush had repercussions extending to the present day. Why do you think it was such a powerful, pivotal event for her? Have you had such an experience in your life?

5. Suzanne's mother, Tinsley, is needy and self-absorbed, but Suzanne allows her in her life. Is this decision, on balance, the right one? How did you feel about Whit's alignment with his in-laws? Was it a betrayal of his marriage or his right as an independent person?

6. What did you think about Ash at the beginning of the story? How did your understanding of him evolve?

7. Suzanne believes she has done everything she could for her children and yet feels like a failure as a parent. Is this the inevitable consequence of having teenagers, or are Suzanne and Whit simply poor parents?

8. How did you feel about Suzanne's decision to pursue her dreams? If she had been able to pursue that path earlier, how do you think it would have affected her life with Whit and their children?

9. Brynn and Reid are very different people, to put it mildly, but family dynamics can often cause siblings to fill disparate niches. How much of a role did their parents play in how Reid and Brynn behaved and in how they saw themselves? What do you imagine the future will hold for Brynn and Reid?

10. Iris was attached to the natural world in a way few people are in our society. Were you envious of this? Does the idea of doing without modern conveniences appeal to you in any way?

11. Did you think Suzanne and Whit would stay together? Did you want them to?

12. The story is filled with botanical imagery and themes. Can you connect these to the overall narrative, especially Suzanne's transformation? What was the significance of the name Iris and its mythological root as the name of a messenger from the gods?

13. The title of the book originates from the Melville epigraph but is connected to the story, particularly here, in Suzanne's thoughts: "We can opt to reject the boundary, the shell behind which we operate our lives, separate from the world, the world of dirt and leaf and sky in which we evolved, the true place that holds our essential nature. We can step out from behind the glass, and live." What do you think this means? Does the idea of stepping out from behind the glass and away from the mirror have particular significance for women? How might this connect to Brynn's interest in photography at the close of the story?

ABOUT THE AUTHOR

Sonja Yoerg grew up in Stowe, Vermont, where she financed her college education by waitressing at the Trapp Family Lodge. She earned a PhD in biological psychology from the University of California, Berkeley, and wrote a nonfiction book about animal intelligence, *Clever as a Fox*, before deciding it was more fun to make things up. Her previous novels are *House Broken*, *The Middle of Somewhere*, and *All the Best People*. Sonja lives with her husband in the Blue Ridge Mountains of Virginia.